T0147752

Praise for

Twelve Drummers Drumming

"An atmospheric, engaging, and well-crafted story."
—ANNE PERRY, *New York Times* bestselling author
of *Treason at Lisson Grove*

"*Twelve Drummers Drumming* is a beautifully written mystery set
in an enchanting English village. May Father Christmas
(he prefers Tom) long share his wisdom and goodness."
—CAROLYN HART, bestselling author of *Dead by Midnight*

"This perfect blend of murder and mistletoe is a brilliant launch
for C. C. Benison's new series." —*Tucson Citizen*

"Splendid . . . An intelligent and empathic protagonist and
skillful prose make this a winner."
—*Publishers Weekly* (starred review)

"C. C. Benison brings the English village mystery into a more
demanding era, crafting a story with dimension and subtlety, in
which resoundingly real characters grapple with loss and danger
and matters of immortality—without losing the whimsy, the tight
plotting, and the palpable delight in Traditional England found
in his predecessors. I look forward to the further
adventures of 'Father Christmas.'"
—LAURIE R. KING, *New York Times* bestselling author
of *God of the Hive*

"This marvelous series debut by Ellis Award winner Benison is a
satisfying, character-driven read. The author presents a full plate of
options, leaving the reader puzzling through the possible motives

"Promising . . . This English village mystery moves slowly while the many interesting characters are fleshed out, but it proceeds deftly to a grim conclusion." —*Kirkus Reviews*

"A fast-paced entertaining whodunit with a great surprising final spin." —Genre Go-Round Reviews

"Easily falls into that most loved of all mystery categories— the picturesque English village cozy." —*The Denver Post*

"Mr. Benison does an admirable job balancing humor with suspense. His village characters are well-drawn, and his vicar-sleuth sympathetic and capable." —*The Wall Street Journal*

"Who knew that a successor to Agatha Christie was living and writing in Winnipeg? *Twelve Drummers Drumming* will please the most discriminating lover of the traditional British mystery. It has a village, a vicar, atmosphere to burn and a perfectly constructed puzzle plot."
—*The Globe and Mail*

"Benison crafts a lovely story with humor, surprises and some endearing characters, as well as some truly evil baddies."
—*Calgary Herald*

"The perfect treat for suspense fans in a holiday mood."
—*BookPage*

Twelve
Drummers Drumming

Twelve Drummers Drumming

A FATHER CHRISTMAS MYSTERY

C. C. Benison

BANTAM BOOKS TRADE PAPERBACKS

NEW YORK

2012 Bantam Books Trade Paperback Edition

Copyright © 2011 by Douglas Whiteway

Excerpt from *Eleven Pipers Piping* copyright © 2012 by
Douglas Whiteway w/a C. C. Benison.

Published in the United States by Bantam Books,
an imprint of The Random House Publishing Group,
a division of Random House, Inc., New York.

BANTAM BOOKS and the rooster colophon are registered trademarks
of Random House, Inc.

Published in the United States by Delacorte Press, an imprint of
The Random House Publishing Group, a division of Random House, Inc., in 2011.

This book contains an excerpt from the forthcoming novel *Eleven Pipers Piping*
by C. C. Benison. This excerpt has been set for this edition only
and may not reflect the final content of the forthcoming edition.

Library of Congress Cataloging-in-Publication Data
Benison, C. C.
Twelve drummers drumming: a mystery / C. C. Benison.
p. cm.
ISBN 978-0-440-24646-6
eBook ISBN 978-0-440-33983-0
1. Vicars, Parochial—Fiction. 2. Widowers—Fiction. 3. Single fathers—Fiction.
4. Murder—Investigation—Fiction. 5. England—Fiction. I. Title.
PR9199.3.B37783T94 2011
813'.54—dc22   2011000924

www.bantamdell.com

Book design by Karin Batten

147028622

Cast of Characters

Inhabitants of Thornford Regis

The Reverend Tom Christmas	Vicar of the parish
Miranda Christmas	His daughter
Florence Daintrey	Retired civil servant
Venice Daintrey	Her sister-in-law
Liam Drewe	Owner of the Waterside Café and Bistro
Mitsuko Drewe	His wife, an artist
Julia Hennis	Music teacher
Dr. Alastair Hennis	Her husband
Sebastian John	Verger at St. Nicholas Church
Penella Neels	Co-owner of Thorn Barton farm
Colonel Phillip Northmore	Retired banker
Colm Parry	Organist and choirmaster at St. Nicholas Church
Celia Holmes-Parry	His wife, a psychotherapist
Declan Parry	Their son
Sybella Parry	Colm's daughter
Roger Pattimore	Owner of Pattimore's, the village shop
Enid Pattimore	His mother

Fred Pike	Village handyman and church sexton
Joyce Pike	His wife
Charlie Pike	Their son
Madrun Prowse	Vicarage housekeeper
Jago Prowse	Her brother, owner of Thorn Cross Garage
Tamara and Kerra	His daughters
Karla Skynner	Postmistress and newsagent
Tiffany Snape	Her assistant
Tilly Springett	Widow
Eric Swan	Licensee of the Church House Inn
Belinda Swan	His wife
Daniel, Lucy, Emily, and Jack	Their children
Violet Tucker	Young mother
Mark Tucker	Her husband
Ruby Tucker	Their daughter
Anne Willett	Neighbourhood Watch chair

Visitors to Thornford Regis

Colin Blessing	Detective Sergeant, Totnes CID
Derek Bliss	Detective Inspector, Totnes CID
Màiri White	Police Community Support Officer

For Gaylene Chestnut and Henrietta Wilde

Twelve
Drummers Drumming

The Vicarage

Thornford Regis TC9 6QX

26 MAY

Dear Mum,

When I sat down to write this morning's letter, I couldn't help
but think about that May Fayre 30 years ago when I moved
back to Thornford R from London, you all dressed up as always
in that red shawl Dad found that time at Newton Abbot market
and your pink brocade turban with Grannie's ruby broach stuck
in. I remembered when I was little I thought you looked like the
Queen of Persia. Everyone who's old enough in Thornford says
the May Fayre never had a more beautiful fortune-teller than
you. I still have our old ~~golf~~ goldfish bowl you would turn upside
down to make a crystal ball. It's sitting on my window ledge
right now picking up the sun which has now climbed well over
the hills. I put heliotrope and white roses from the vicarage
garden inside it. The blooms look to be glowing. So pretty, I
think. No sense putting goldfish in the bowl as Powell and
Gloria, being cats, would make a meal of them in a minute!
Funny that bowl surviving what happened that terrible day.

Perhaps, now I write this, I shouldn't stir memories of the last time you told fortunes at the May Fayre. The sudden storm that year was like nothing on earth and of course, Mum, I know you've always thought you and Venice Daintrey's husband were being punished, but really it was only chance Walter pulled the Death card from your tarot pack and then got struck dead by the same ~~lightenin~~ lightning that made you deaf. If only he had listened to you and stayed inside! Well, I really mustn't go on about that now, must I. It's so long ago. The weather report says we're to have sun all day today and as it is the new vicar's first May Fayre ~~we~~ wouldn't want anything to spoil it. I don't think there's anywhere lovelier than Thornford in May! When I pushed my head out my bedroom window earlier to take in the ~~smell~~ aroma of the late blooming lilacs, I looked down on the garden and the dew was shimmering on the grass near the border of pinks and making all these perfectly wonderful miniature rainbows. There were two larks singing a duet in the sky over the copper beeches near the millpond and the sparrows were splashing away merrily in the birdbath—that is, until they spied Powell slinking towards them. He's such a clever cat, although I do wish he wouldn't pick on the birds so. I fear Mr. Christmas may wake again to a nasty surprise in his bed as Powell and Gloria are much taken with him and like to offer him little treats. I'm not sure the feeling is ~~recep~~ shared, but Mr. Christmas does try to accommodate himself to our little country ways. So good to have a proper vicar back in the vicarage after all these months. And someone who likes my cooking! It's been very dull me preparing meals just for me. But with little Miranda we are now three! I wonder if we shall be four ever? I read somewhere once that ~~everybody knows~~ it's acknowledged ~~everywhere~~ universally that a widower in possession of a very nice cottage—or a decent stipend (sorry, I can't recall what exactly)—must be in want of a wife. We shall see with Mr. Christmas. When he was appointed and his picture went into the parish magazine, it caused a bit of a stir among certain folk in the village. But the last vicar caused a stir, too, for the same reason and look what happened to HIM! Anyway, Mum, I mustn't rattle on. Today promises to be very busy and eventful at Purton Farm. They'll start putting up the tents before very long and getting everything ready. There's one new thing this year. Japanese drummers instead of the pipe band! The drummers aren't Japanese, though. They're a dozen students of Mrs. Hennis's. It's the drums that are Japanese and a couple of them are enormous! Anyway, must go and start getting breakfast ready. Cats are well. Love to Aunt Gwen. Glorious day!

Much love,
Madrun

CHAPTER ONE

"Thinking of stealing that book, Father?"

The voice at his shoulder startled Tom Christmas. He looked down to see Fred Pike, the village's elfin handyman, smiling at him with a kind of manic glee.

"What?"

"Stealing that book?"

Tom blinked at Fred, then snatched his hand from the book. *Steal This Book* was the title. Someone named Abbie Hoffman was apparently the writer. The cover said as much.

"Despite the title's invitation, I don't think so," Tom said, running his finger between his neck and his dog collar. He put the book down next to a copy of *The Anarchist Cookbook,* which was being offered for thirty pence. In the middle distance, between two rows of stalls, a hefty lad he recognised as Colm Parry's son Declan, all got up like a Teenage Mutant Ninja Turtle, was struggling to push a large drum on a trolley across the lawn towards the stage. Another lad, similarly dressed, was pulling at the other end.

"Thou shalt not steal," warned Fred.

"Yes." Tom nodded agreeably. "I've heard that."

Grinning, Fred passed on towards the display of cider-making machinery, near the stage where the two boys were still struggling with the drum. Tom scratched his head, then turned to look at the other titles, all of them political in nature. He picked up a small volume with a red plastic slipcover. *Quotations from Mao Tse-tung.* Well-thumbed, it opened at a page that proclaimed, "Political power comes from the barrel of a gun." Gently, Tom replaced the book. The other bookstalls were a sea of used Jeffrey Archer and Barbara Cartland, but this was a stall of another colour. He thought he knew whose books these once were. But who in a village nestled in the South Devon hills could be enticed to buy them? Even at prices many pence shy of a pound?

"This is quite the collection," he said to Belinda Swan, the publican's wife, who was minding the stall. She reminded him of the Willendorf Venus, fleshy and voluptuous in a way that would have stirred a skinny hunter-gatherer, only attired in the modern way: sealed in stretch trousers and miraculously buttressed beneath a deeply scooped blouse.

"Not very Christian, are they?" she responded, picking up *Confessions of a Revolutionary* and regarding it askance. "We did wonder, but as it's for the church, we thought you wouldn't mind, Father."

"I wish you wouldn't—"

"Vicar, I mean."

"Tom is fine."

"Right. Tom it is. I'll remember this time. But with your family name, you know, sometimes we can't—"

"Help it," he said, finishing her thought. It was a bane of his existence. Once, as a teenager, he'd gone to a fancy-dress party kitted out as Father Christmas, all white cotton-candy beard and hair and itchy red wool, and the honorific—or gibe—clung to him ever after. At the vicar factory at Cambridge he was Father Christmas. As curate in south London he was Father Christmas. In his ministry in Bristol he was Father Christmas. This though he wasn't High

Church. The mercy was his late wife hadn't been named Mary. His adoptive mother had been, but she had wisely retained her maiden name.

Belinda picked up the *Quotations*. "I think Ned was the last person in the world who still cared what whatsisnamehere, Mao Tse-tung, thought about anything."

"What about a billion Chinese?"

"Oh, do you think? I thought the Chinese had rather gone off all this rigmarole." She opened the book at random and read aloud: "'We must always use our brains and think everything over carefully.'" Her well-plucked eyebrows went up a notch. "Hard to argue with that. Maybe I should have my kids read this instead of Harry Potter."

"I take it these books are all Ned's."

"Yes, his daughter said to take the lot. 'Take them, I don't want to look at them,' she said. 'You can burn them,' she said. Well, book burning didn't seem very nice, so—"

"I'll buy that one then." Tom reached into his pocket and pulled out a pound coin.

"Are you sure?"

"To remember Ned, then."

"But you never met him."

"Not in the corruptible flesh, no."

"Of course," Belinda said, taking the coin and counting out seventy-five pence change. "That's how you came to us, isn't it? In a roundabout way. Fancy old Red Ned having a Christian burial. I expect he's still spinning."

By chance—or perhaps by design, though arguing the latter was a bit teleological—Tom and his daughter Miranda had been visiting Thornford Regis the week of Ned Skynner's funeral, staying with his wife's sister Julia and her husband Alastair. A music teacher at a Hamlyn Ferrers Grammar School outside Paignton, Julia filled in occasionally as organist at St. Nicholas Church and had been called upon to do so for Ned's funeral that day in early April just over a year ago. Julia had looked at him askance when he'd volunteered to accompany her to the ceremony.

"The expression 'busman's holiday' comes to mind," she'd said with a smile, though her eyes telegraphed a deeper concern for him, unnecessarily attending a morbid rite for a complete stranger, five months after his wife's homicide. But Tom was just as happy not to be left with his brother-in-law Alastair, whose disapproval seemed to fall on him like fine rain whenever circumstance threw the two of them together. Besides, funerals, intermittent or in clusters, were part measure of a priest's life; his professionalism demanded he suspend his own grief to ease the grief of others, and he had done so: Twelve days after Lisbeth's funeral at the synagogue in St. John's Wood Road in London, he had taken a funeral at St. Dunstan's, for a child, no less, and had managed—somehow, just barely—to keep his own heart from breaking.

And, if he had been looking for another reason to accompany Julia, a more frivolous one, he had it: He had not seen the interior of St. Nicholas Church, the grey weather-beaten Norman tower he had glimpsed the day before as he'd driven down into the village. There had been only one impediment. He couldn't very well take his nine-year-old daughter, to—of all things—a funeral, not so soon after her mother's death. But Alastair, who had taken the day off from his medical duties, volunteered to abandon plans for his own round of golf and take Miranda to Abbey Park in Torquay to play crazy golf. Tom hadn't been sure if Alastair wanted to avoid his company or Julia's. Good manners prevailed before guests, but no central heating could thaw the icy atmosphere between husband and wife that week.

What he would never have known is that he would wind up taking the funeral. The incumbent vicar, the Reverend Peter Kinsey, who had had the living for a mere eighteen months, had failed to appear. Everything else had been at the ready. Ned, at his daughter's insistence, had been delivered to the lych-gate in a less-than-proletarian mahogany box with brass handles. Julia was at the organ gently working her way through "Ave Verum," "Love Divine, All Loves Excelling," and "Morning Has Broken." There was a lovely display of lilies, forsythia, and iris, with daffodils in separate vases. And there was a decent turnout, Tom later learned, not least because many of the old villagers were amused to see Ned, who had spent four decades declaring religion to be the opiate of the masses from his seat in the pub, getting a send-off from one of the opiate manufacturer's franchise operations.

Impatience had turned to puzzlement, then to consternation when, after about twenty minutes, the vicar didn't appear. A call round to the vicarage produced no vicar; nor did it produce the vicar's housekeeper, Madrun Prowse, who had gone to visit her deaf mother in Cornwall. The Reverend Mr. Kinsey wasn't at the pub, where the wake was to take place, nor was he at any of the other public places in the village. His mobile was switched off, too. One or two villagers thought someone might have called one or two female parishioners on the off chance, but they kept that to themselves out of respect for Ned's big send-off. Finally, someone realised that Kinsey's Audi was missing. It was a Tuesday. Vicar's day off was Monday. Perhaps he'd gone away for the day and got waylaid somewhere.

Though he might have phoned, someone groused.

It was a chilly April afternoon and the temperamental heating system in the church—adequate, Tom was to later learn, for a fifty-minute Sunday service—was less so for a congregation that had been waiting ninety minutes for the show to begin. The verger might have taken the service, but he was down with flu. The funeral director was able, but Karla Skynner, Ned's daughter and a church-warden, determined to sanitise her father's history in a blaze of Christian piety and learning there was a vicar in the house, beseeched—well, it was more "commanded"—Tom to step in. To Julia's horror he did—though dressed in corduroy trousers and a battered Barbour, he didn't feel he would quite fill the contours of the role. Never mind. The vestments were hanging in the vestry, including a purple chasuble. He acquitted himself well enough. He mounted the pulpit and intoned the familiar words: *I am the resurrection and the life.* As he did so, in this little country church, with its freshly lime-washed walls, its slightly crooked aisle, and its aromas of wood polish, old books, and gently disintegrating woolen kneelers, he felt unaccountably at peace, in a way he had not since that awful autumn day when he had found Lisbeth lying in a pool of blood in the south porch of St. Dunstan's. It was as though he had come home. As he looked past the faces of the mourners in the front pews to the shifts of light streaming through the Victorian stained glass, he found himself almost brimming with gratitude for the unexpected gift of this moment.

The Reverend Peter Kinsey never did show. In fact, the vicar seemed to have vanished from the face of the earth. Consternation had turned to outright worry three days later when Jago Prowse pointed out that the vicar couldn't have left the village in his car, because he, Jago, was servicing the very car at Thorn Cross Garage and was having trouble with a very tricky fuel injection system. After that it was police, press, and endless speculation. As the village attempted to recover from this unsettling situation, retired clergy were called upon to fill in for Sunday services. The archdeacon helped, too, as did the rural dean. Even the bishop came down from Exeter to preach a wise sermon. But after two months of intermittent police investigation, Peter Kinsey's reappearance was declared unlikely. There was, officially, a vacancy in the parish.

But a week's rest, contemplation, and solitary walks in Devon had helped soften the metaphysical rage that had scorched Tom's soul in the wake of Lisbeth's death and decided him for change. He needed a safe place for his daughter, and he needed a rest from the turmoil of inner-city team ministry. As soon as he'd returned with Miranda to Bristol, he sent his CV to the bishop of Exeter, asking to be considered for any vacancy. There was a vacancy, as it turned out—in Thornford Regis—and, in due course Tom was appointed to the living of Thornford Regis. In the magisterial terms of the Church of England, the interview and inspection process was extraordinarily speedy. But a traumatised flock needed a new shepherd. Tom packed up Miranda's and his things, bade sad farewell to his colleagues at St. Dunstan's, and made the journey to Thornford Regis for the buttercup-strewn life in a West Country village described by the *Times* travel supplement as "sleepy" and by the *AA Guide to Country Towns and Villages of England* as "really a very pretty place."

On this May morning, nine months later, that very prettiness was splayed out before him and made him smile. His eyes descended from the counterpane fields glimpsed beyond the last of the cottages on Thorn Hill, down past clusters of rooftops and chimneystacks to Purton Farm, a community field, which, he thought, looked a little like the set of *The Prisoner,* only with a coconut shy at the centre and none of those disagreeable balloons. As he pocketed Mao's book of quotations and wished Belinda Swan good luck with her sales, Tom surveyed the newly erected white-elephant stall, the hot dog stand, the beer tent, the tea tent, the tombola and the face-painting, the petting zoo where toddlers were cooing over fat rabbits, the politically incorrect Punch-and-Judy where Punch was still beating his wife and child with a stick, and the inflatable slide down which he could see his daughter careening, and, farther off, the open-air stage onto which the two teenage boys had successfully trollied the outsized drum.

It was a *tsukeshime-daiko,* a long, heavy, rope-tensioned drum, part of the repertoire of Japanese taiko drums which that weekend had set the old Victorian village hall to throbbing and lent the so-called "sleepy" village an ominous ambience—rather, Tom declared, like some old Ealing Studios idea of vexed Zulus revving up for disputatious acts. The natives are restless, he had thought, passing the hall on his way out of the village to one of the country trails where he could have a walk and a think free of the distractions of the vicarage. And they *were* restless, in a way. Having taiko drummers debut their talents at the May Fayre in lieu of the traditional pipe band had not been wholly welcomed. Even though the Reverend

Mr. Kinsey had been absent more than a year, his legacy of innovation, admired by some, loathed by many, still sparked little eruptions of novelty in the village.

At Tom's first Parochial Church Council meeting, taiko entertainment at the May Fayre reignited a few simmering tempers—notably that of ancient church treasurer Colonel Northmore, who had suffered through a Japanese prisoner-of-war camp in the Second World War and had no truck with anything Japanese. But twelve teenagers from the village and outlying area, schooled by Julia, had taken to taiko drumming like bees to blossoms and were eager to show off their skills. "Better than what they might get up to," warned Tom, who knew from his ministry in Bristol what bored youth were capable of. Colonel Northmore had cast him a rheumy eye, but was silenced.

Tom thought about his church council and its personalities as he passed the white-elephant stall attended by Joyce Pike, the village handyman's wife, caretaker of the village hall, and skivvy to a handful of Thornfordites.

"'Morning, Father," she said with the kind of smile that looked like it had been hard practised. Tom replied in kind, then stopped. There was a curious object among the obsessively tidy array of unloved gewgaws on the table. A shaft of sunlight latched on to a smooth white surface overlaid with what, to an undiscerning eye at first glance, would look like a web of black lines.

His heart leapt.

It was an exact match to his curate's egg, the one that Lisbeth had given him when he'd been appointed to his first curacy at Kennington Park. Lisbeth had had it made specially. He didn't think there was another one like it in the world. It so neatly encapsulated Lisbeth's sense of humour and wry views of the Church, and he loved it more than any gift she had given him—other than Miranda, of course. He'd been grieved when the egg somehow got lost in the move between Bristol and Thornford. He had even phoned the re-

movals company to see if they had found an egg on the lorry somewhere. They'd thought he was having them on.

"This is astonishing," he said to Mrs. Pike as he lifted the porce-
lain egg and examined it. Yes, there it was: George du Maurier's
1895 *Punch* cartoon of a hapless curate taking breakfast at the
bishop's house. *"I'm afraid you've got a bad egg, Mr. Jones,"* the bishop
is saying. *"Oh, no, my Lord,"* responds the nervous curate, desperate
not to make offence, *"I assure you that parts of it are quite excellent."*

Life was a curate's egg—a mixture of good and bad, but more
than that, Lisbeth had pointed out: The excellent parts compensate
enough for the bad parts that complaining about it just isn't on. Her
words—he could hear her voice, her saying it—sounded forcefully
in his head in the dull, dark weeks following her inexplicable, seem-
ingly random death. He'd clung to them, and to the egg. And now,
as her voice again reverberated in his memory, a sharp pang of loss
seared him. He took a moment, then looked to Mrs. Pike. "Do you
know I used to have one just like this?"

He half expected a response, but Mrs. Pike continued to smile at
him in her faintly robotic way.

There was even a little stand for it, he noted on the table. Just
like his.

"How much is it?"

"Oh, Father, why don't you just have it." She had a girlish voice,
at odds with her age and her anxious bearing.

"I couldn't do that . . ."

"Well." Joyce hesitated. "Five pounds, then."

"I'll give you twenty," Tom responded brightly, reaching again
into his pocket. "I'm that chuffed. I never thought I'd find another
one like it in my life."

Joyce received two ten-pound notes in silence. Tom studied her
a moment as she placed the money in an open cashbox. Thin-faced,
sombre-eyed, devoid of makeup, apparently oblivious to hairstyle (it
was a sort of grey mop-end), she had the look of a woman either

long suffering or long depressed. Her son, Charlie, was in his new confirmation class—a very sharp, if somewhat gauche, lad. Tom could hardly believe sometimes that Fred and Joyce, late in life, had spawned this bright fish.

"You'll want a carrier bag for that," Joyce said, offering him a used but neatly folded plastic Sainsbury's version that she pulled from a box on a chair beside her.

"Yes, thanks." Tom reached for the bag and carefully slipped the egg and its stand into it. It was then that he felt an arm slide into his open elbow.

"*B*onjour, Papa."

"*Bonjour, ma petite pamplemousse,*" Tom replied, regarding his daughter with a burst of pure pleasure. Miranda, who had been very attached to their French au pair, Ghislaine Poirier, when they had lived in Bristol, was reading Nancy Drew novels in *la belle langue,* only the heroine was called "Alice Roy" because the French, apparently, were unable to pronounce "Nancy" or, possibly, "Drew." Tom's French, indifferently learned at school, ran largely to half-remembered bits out of Whitmarsh's awful textbooks and phrases picked up busking through Europe when he was younger.

"Have you met Mrs. Pike? Her husband fixed our washer."

"Hello," Miranda responded brightly, peeking around his jacket. Then she looked up at him. "What did you buy?"

"You'll never guess." He nodded good-bye to Mrs. Pike. "It's a china egg. Just like the one your mum gave me. The one that I lost. Do you remember me trying to find it when we first moved into the vicarage?"

"Yes," she replied, slipping her arm from his and taking the carrier bag. She reached inside and half pulled the egg out. She studied it a moment, then asked: "Did you buy it at Mrs. Pike's stall?"

"Yes." Tom brushed a loose strand of hair off her forehead.

Miranda glanced behind her, then tugged her father forwards. "Daddy," she began in a whisper, "this isn't just like the one you lost."

"But—"

"It *is* the one you lost."

"What?"

Miranda smiled as though in possession of the biggest secret in the world. "Mr. Pike is a kleptomaniac."

"That's a big word for—"

"Emily told me," Miranda interrupted excitedly, full of the power of knowledge. "Mr. Pike takes things when he's on the job— he can't help himself—and every year Mrs. Pike sells them back to their owners at the white-elephant stall." Her smile grew wider. "Isn't it funny? No one seems to mind, Emily says . . . except if he takes your television remote."

"And the money goes to the church." Tom resisted the urge to look back at Joyce Pike and the white-elephant stall. Funny indeed, he thought, ruing spending twenty pounds on something that was already his. "What if the owner needs it back desperately?"

"I don't know."

"Does he ever take anything that's worth a lot of money?"

"Emily didn't say." Miranda frowned in thought as she handed him back the Sainsbury's bag.

"Well, never mind. I've got my curate's egg back and that's the important thing. Where is Emily, by the way?"

"Gone to help her sister get ready."

"Ah," Tom responded, glancing towards the pole that had been set up in the centre of Purton Farm. Its ribbons fluttered in the breeze off the river. "Well, maybe you'll be queen of the May some year soon, like Lucy Swan."

"I hope not. It's *feudal*."

"Does Emily think that?"

"No, I do. I think Emily wants to be queen of the May someday."

Tom was relieved to hear Miranda wasn't shy of her own views. Since coming to Thornford Regis, she had fallen in quickly with the swarming brood of sociable Swans, who seemed to absorb one more into their family activity with barely a notice. It had been two months of breathless "Emily says" and "Emily thinks" from Miranda. It was almost like watching someone fall in love, he thought, not without a pang for his own situation: young (relatively), widowed, alone, lonely at times (even with a child), so much missing Lisbeth, who had vanished from his side so abruptly, too soon. Before his wife's death, he had sometimes suspected Miranda disliked being a child and detested not being able to take care of herself—traits that seemed to serve her well (and Tom, who could barely manage his own grief) in the weeks and months after Lisbeth was killed. He was relieved to see her embrace childhood (or at least his idea of childhood) in league with the Swans, although he couldn't resist fretting at times that in a few years it would all be over. She would be a teenager, all the sweetness drained away.

"Shall we have ice cream?" he suggested, deciding this was not the day to brood on such things, motioning towards the stall that Liam Drewe, the owner of the Waterside Café, had set up.

"Have you seen the quilts Mrs. Drewe has hung in the village hall?" Miranda asked, skipping ahead. "They're brilliant. I even think you're in one, Papa."

"How could I be in a quilt?" Tom rummaged in his pocket for coins.

"Then you haven't seen them. Let's go look at them."

"Well—"

"They're memory quilts," Miranda rushed on. "Mrs. Drewe takes pictures, then scans them onto . . . cotton, I think, then makes the quilt. We took one of the brochures." She rooted in her own pocket. "Oh, I must have given it to Emily." Her face fell. "Anyway, the quilts are all of the village. There's the school and the hall and the church . . ." Miranda rattled off a half dozen of the village's land-marks. ". . . And, in one, it looks like you coming out of the pub."

Startled, Tom said, "Really?"

"It must have been when we visited here last year. You're with Aunt Julia. You're just coming through the pub doors."

"We must have been leaving Red Ned's wake. How odd. I don't remember—" And then he did. When he and Julia left the pub, a trim Japanese woman was photographing the exterior. He had barely registered it at the time, assuming she was a tourist who had strayed from the pack that Japanese tourists seemed to travel in. Now he realised: Of course, the woman was Mitsuko Drewe, Liam's wife.

Well, he thought, as they joined the short queue at Liam Drewe's stall, immortalised in fabric! Ought he to be gratified?

Liam Drewe was suffering the indecisiveness of Enid Pattimore, whose son owned the village shop. His lips were pinched and his eyelids had descended to tight crescents, as if he were silently com-pelling Enid to choose between vanilla, chocolate, and strawberry. He noted Tom, more than a head's height behind the tiny, bent fig-ure, and forced a quick acknowledging smile. "C'mon, love," he ad-dressed the old woman with barely concealed impatience, "vicar's waiting."

"Oh, dear, I'm awfully sorry," Enid murmured, twisting her neck to take in Tom's presence. "I think, oh, perhaps strawberry would do. . . ."

"Wise—"

"No! Chocolate. Yes, definitely chocolate."

"You're sure?"

"Yes."

"Wise choice." Liam jammed his scoop into the tub of ice cream like a man thrusting a spade into hard ground. On his first visit to the Waterside over a year ago, Tom had noted the letters A C A B tattooed between the knuckle and first joint of each finger on Liam's left hand when he'd taken Tom's money at the till. He knew what the letters stood for. The fingers of one man in his Kennington parish were similarly rendered. His parishioner had been in The Scrubs for armed robbery and had been leading a pious life since. He told Tom they were prison tattoos.

That cool April day a year ago, Liam had been wearing long sleeves. Now, on this warm May day, he was wearing a black sleeveless T-shirt. Tom couldn't help staring at the carapace of tattoos— an Eden of vines and flowers and fish and birds that coiled up the sinewy forearms, along the meaty biceps, to disappear under the dark cloth, portending who knew what along his chest or down his back: mammals and man, perhaps, Adam and Eve, the creation story traced in ink on skin? Likely not. His Christian mind was at play. But it wasn't the imagery that set his mind to wondering. It was putting up with all those bloody awful needles. He must have been lingering too long in his reverie, because only Miranda's decisive response—"strawberry"—alerted him to his new place at the front of the queue.

"Vicar?" He heard Liam say.

"Um . . ."

Liam narrowed his eyes again.

"Is there anything besides vanilla, chocolate, and strawberry?"

"Are you trying to be funny?"

"Bad day?"

When Julia had filled Tom in on the village's dramatis personae, "short-fused" had been her description for Liam Drewe. Verbal explosions in the Waterside kitchen, etc. "He's not the ideal *mein host* when he's mein hosting," Julia had continued, "but luckily he has a very capable wife, who does some of the serving duties. That is, when she's not running her little gallery or working on her own art or running the art classes at the village hall or trying to manage the usual tugs-of-war on the flower rota."

"My wife's had to go to Wales, and Sybella was supposed to be minding this stall," Liam snapped, responding to Tom's observation. "But she seems to have bloody gone missing."

"Chocolate," Tom said humbly, watching the arm once again dive into the iced confection. He recalled that he had never seen Liam in church. He had seen Mitsuko only intermittently, though she was indeed on the flower rota. As for the missing Sybella Parry, he had never expected to see a pew contain her. The girl left the impression, with her whiff of the Goth, that the dark arts were her cup of tea, but he had—to his surprise—in the last month. She came with her father and stepmother and didn't look like she'd been dragged.

Tom took both cornets of ice cream from Liam, handed one to Miranda, and passed over a five-pound note. Liam tucked it into the pocket of his apron, but proffered no change. Tom should have received a pound coin in return, but he didn't press the point: It was for charity, after all. But in the parting glance Liam cast him, Tom detected, just for the time it takes to split a second, a flash of the purest, blackest hatred.

Taken aback, he hustled Miranda away, pondering probable cause, but could find none, other than simply being despised for the uniform and what it represented. When Liam had taken the five pounds, Tom had noted again the acronym inked into his fingers. A C A B meant Always Carry A Bible—if the bearer was trying to make a good impression. That's what the man in his Kennington parish had told him. What it really meant, he had said, was All Coppers Are Bastards. But what flitted through Tom's mind now was this, improbable though it seemed: Liam had a special, private animosity. All coppers aren't bastards.

All Clergy Are Bastards.

CHAPTER THREE

"See!" Miranda gestured towards the quilt.

Tom watched his daughter's finger, sticky with ice cream, nearly graze the soft fabric rectangle hanging from a rod in the larger of the village hall's two public spaces. "Mind you don't get anything on that," he warned. But his attention was caught by the novelty before him.

Miranda shifted her attention to the fingers of her right hand and began licking them rather than the cornet in her left. "That *is* you and Aunt Julia," she added for emphasis.

There was no mistaking it. Even with the lights off and the narrow east windows affording little illumination, the detail was remarkable. About eight feet by six feet, the quilt was large enough for a bed of decent size. The border was a patchwork of tawny golds and muted greens, like Devon's countryside seen from the air, but the centre pane was the most arresting: It was an exterior view of the heart of Thornford Regis social life—the Church House Inn, with its white-daubed walls, black-lacquered window frames, and the tubs of spring blooms like sentries along the steps.

Coming through the door, as Miranda had said, was a figure

Tom recognised instantly as his sister-in-law, wearing her dark trench coat, her head bent slightly down, her hand reaching to her neck as if to tighten her scarf. Just behind her, holding the door open, exposing the golden glow of the pub's interior, was his own good self, which was now staring at his own good self in the village hall. He had been looking right into Mitsuko's camera, without being cognisant that he was doing so, or paying any attention to the person behind the camera. Clearly, something had been on his mind that day over thirteen months ago, but what?

He recalled his satisfaction at being able to salvage an awkward situation at the church; he recalled the welcoming conversation of those who attended the wake and the good cheer of Eric Swan, the pub licensee who set just the right tone, keeping the mourners focused on amusing tales of Ned Skynner, the village's Conservative parish clerk until a stroke brought out a Marxist rash, and not worrying about the missing Mr. Kinsey. He recalled the crackling fire in a fireplace large enough for a man to stand in, the moulded beams, the brasses, the scarred trestle tables, but most of all he remembered being with Julia, who so reminded him of Lisbeth that he had to keep his eyes from resting on her too often.

Physically, they wouldn't have been immediately taken for sisters—Lisbeth with her high cheekbones, long, dark hair, and calm, green-flecked eyes; Julia with her more attenuated features, lighter hair cut short, and caution in her brown eyes—but there were gestures: the way Julia held her glass of white wine with her arms folded across her chest, the tilt of her head when she was absorbed in what others were saying—that evoked Lisbeth in similar social situations, so much so that Tom almost felt Lisbeth like a friendly spirit in the room.

He had been glad that day to see Julia so animated. Perhaps the wine had helped her, or the company, or being away from Alastair. The household he and Miranda arrived at fairly crackled with tension, Julia dull-eyed, but doing her best to entertain her niece, Alastair grim and taciturn, agreeable and animated only when he engaged with Miranda, the little girl who had lost her mother.

Suddenly he remembered what he had been thinking when he had exited the pub, and why he saw, and yet did not see, Mitsuko taking his picture: He had resolved at that moment, as he stepped into the quiet lane, that he didn't want Miranda to grow up in a busy street in a neighbourhood where her mother had been killed for reasons yet to be determined, and that a rural parish—any rural parish—might offer calm and safety and a new start for both father and daughter.

Now he glanced around the spotlessly clean large hall, which was unpeopled but for him and Miranda. Past the connecting corridor, muffled sounds emanated from the small hall on the west side of the building. He recognised Julia's voice, rising above the tide of adolescent voices: the members of Twelve Drummers Drumming, which she had organised at her school. There was the occasional thud of wood against taut leather, followed by a raised and slightly exasperated voice—no doubt Julia admonishing her charges to *please* refrain from drumming until they were on stage.

"You know," he said to Miranda as he moved to the next quilt, featuring some preschool children in messy art activity in the Old School Room, "I'm not sure we're supposed to be here. No one else is."

"We're not, I don't think."

"Miranda!"

"The opening is on Thursday. I think that's what the brochure said."

"Then how did you and Emily—?"

"The same way we did, Daddy. The door was unlocked." She pointed to the small vestibule, which connected the large hall to the outdoors. There were two entrances on the south face of the village hall. One led directly to the large hall on the east side, where they were now. The other led to a short corridor, off which was the entrance to the hall on the west side, with its self-contained kitchen and bar. Between large and small halls was a corridor with storage for chairs and trestles on one side and—more vitally—toilets on the other.

"We didn't want to use those yucky port-a-loos," Miranda continued.

"But there's a sign pointing to the other entrance for anyone wanting to use the hall loos."

"I know. But Emily—"

"I can imagine." Emily was a little minx, is what she was. "I guess no harm done if we have a little preview, though I do wonder why Mrs. Drewe installed her work so many days in advance of her opening."

"Remember Mr. Drewe said she had to go to Wales?"

"Yes, of course." Tom looked over to the door leading to the connecting corridor. "And I suppose that's unlocked, too?" he asked Miranda.

She nodded. She was slowly spinning in a circle, thoughtfully nibbling at the nub of her cornet, while running her eyes over the marshallings of hanging fabric.

"Let's just slip through and pretend we were in the toilets. If I look at any more of these quilts, I won't be able to express the appropriate delight and surprise when I'm at the opening." If I'm at the opening, he thought; he couldn't recall getting an invitation, at least a written one. Or were such village events by word-of-mouth?

"Miranda? Did you hear me?"

"Daddy, there's one missing."

"You mean since you and Emily were here?"

"No." She frowned. "I don't think so." She pointed to a quiltless area near the east wall. "Shouldn't there be one there?"

Tom's glance travelled the length of his daughter's arm. "Possibly," he said, a little impatiently. In truth, there did seem to be an odd gap in the grove of quilts. If the intent was to display the entire collection down each side of the three walls of the large hall, why leave a space in that particular spot? Or, perhaps, the asymmetry was an artistic notion. He peered through the shadows at the wall's surface for the telltale sign, the exhibition label, but then noted that no labels accompanied any of the artworks. Perhaps each was sufficiently self-explanatory.

"Likely Mrs. Drewe didn't quite finish putting all the quilts up," he suggested to Miranda.

"Non, regarde, Papa." She pointed again, this time to the rod near the top of the wall, below the cornice, feebly illuminated by a drizzle of light from the window behind it. It appeared to match the contrivances for holding the other quilts in the room.

"It might be there to hold other things," he said, pushing at the door to the connecting corridor, peering through to the door opposite, to the hall. He turned to look at Miranda, who was now on her haunches rooting around on the floor by the skirting board. "Is there something else?"

"Non, Papa."

"Then why don't you nip into the ladies' and wash those hands of yours? I'm just going to poke my head in and see how your aunt Julia is coping with her drummers."

Julia appeared to be coping quite well. Her back to him, she was adjusting the headband of one of the drummers—Daniel Swan, he presumed, from a shock of red hair that hovered by Julia's upraised arm. All the Swan children had their father's red hair. Other than Daniel, of the twelve drummers only Declan Parry and Charlie Pike remained in the hall, each dressed in a brightly coloured sleeveless overcoat, each jabbing at the other with a drumstick thick enough, but not long enough, to be a light sword. He smiled watching their antics, vaguely recalling his Star Wars period and his own wooly energy at that age.

Julia had discovered taiko more or less by chance, in Exeter one Saturday morning after services at the synagogue. Someone had stuck a leaflet on her windscreen announcing a performance of a junior taiko group in Belmont Park that afternoon. Curiosity piqued, she'd gone to the park. It struck her, she later told Tom, that these great primal instruments would be just the thing to capture the interest of some of her adolescent students, particularly the rest-less boys. She had taken courses and persuaded the headmaster at her school to let her form a taiko group as an after-school activity, which included fashioning the smaller drums from plastic draining piping. The centerpieces of the ensemble, the costly wooden drums—the *tsukeshime-daiko* and the *o-daiko,* the big fat drum—she persuaded Declan's father to donate.

"Is there anything I can do?" Tom said, stepping further into the hall.

"Oh, Tom, hello." Julia turned her head, startled out of her con-centration on Daniel's headband. "Really, Daniel, however did you get this so knotted! Tom, you can stop those two from bashing away at each other. Declan! Charlie! Put down the *bachi*! This is not the way of taiko, now, is it?"

The appeal to whatever spiritual underpinnings lay beneath the Japanese art—Tom would have to find out—seemed to have an ef-fect. Grinning, the two boys slowed their swordplay and finally stopped when Tom gave each a meaningful glance. The collar still had a residual power, he found, more so than simple age or routine maleness, traits which no longer commanded much deference.

"Tom, I thought you'd be out there with your flock," Julia said with a laugh, finishing with Daniel, who made a move towards the door. "You don't need to go look at yourself in the mirror, Daniel," she called after him. "You look fine."

Daniel turned back with a pout. Of the three boys, he was clearly the best looking. Tom sensed that he knew it, too.

"Miranda persuaded me to look in on Mitsuko's artwork," Tom told his sister-in-law.

"Yes, I couldn't help looking in, too. The quilts are truly wonder-ful, aren't they?"

"There'll be no surprises at the opening at this rate."

Julia dropped her voice. "I know. Joyce is usually so meticulous, but when I was down here before nine, before the setup crew arrived,

I found the outside door unlocked and the inside door to the large hall wide open. I didn't even need to use my key."

"Isn't this place alarmed?"

"Yes, but half the village knows the code. It hasn't been changed in years. Anyway, Joyce swears she locked the hall after our rehearsal yesterday. We were the last people here." She glanced over at Charlie to confirm that he wasn't overhearing her talk about his mother. "I thought the notion was to keep the large hall closed off until Thursday. Mitsuko booked it from today through to the end of next week. Perhaps someone should put up a Keep Out sign."

The sound of a chair scraping along a floor came from the back of the room. "You might see to Colonel Northmore," Julia told him. "He's in the kitchen with Bumble and your Madrun."

"Is something the matter?"

Julia shrugged. "I think Madrun just brought him in for a cup of tea."

"But there's a tea tent outside."

"I know. Perhaps he wants to get away from the drumming—though he'll have to plug his ears for that. Or perhaps he just wants to glower at me again for suggesting taiko drumming at the May Fayre in the first place. I would never have mentioned the idea to Peter . . . to Mr. Kinsey—"

"I didn't know you had actually done a performance at last year's Fayre."

"No, we didn't. We weren't really ready as a group. And with Peter . . . disappearing . . . the Fayre last year was rather low-key." She looked away. "Anyway, the notion seemed to stick. Colm was keen on the idea. Still . . . I didn't think it would upset the colonel so."

"It's not his to say yea or nay."

"Are we being insensitive, though? I know it's ridiculous to have this discussion now—"

"You mustn't trouble yourself, Julia."

"I do understand his position. I really do, but . . ."

She left the rest unsaid. Time had marched on. Two generations had matured since the Second World War; memory of the hostilities weakened with each dying veteran. For Tom and Julia, and for Declan, Charlie, and Daniel, too, the war lived only in books and films, on the whole a period of romance and virtue. Colonel Northmore had not had a good war. He had spent three years in a Japanese prison camp, and if the horrific memories had been softened by time's passage, the bitterness and resentment had not—at least privately.

"He's become a bit frail in the last year," Julia continued in a low voice. "When Alastair and I first arrived in Thornford five years ago, you wouldn't have known he was in his eighties, even then." She gestured to the *o-daiko* drum stationed against the wall and raised her voice: "Declan, you and Charlie need to shift that drum."

As Tom made his way to the back of the small hall, he could hear the boys grunting with effort as they pulled the heavy drum away from the wall on its trolley. He could also hear Madrun remonstrating with the colonel about something, though he couldn't tell what the subject was. Then the air was fractured by a kind of amplified whine, the sort that adolescents produce when the universe is proving to be a great disappointment. "Miss," one of them groaned—Daniel, perhaps; Tom had noted his voice earlier breaking out of its boyhood timbre—"come look."

Tom turned to look, too. He saw Julia move to the other side of the drum and watched the muscles in her face suddenly shift.

"Bloody hell!" She looked his way. "Tom," she called, "come and look at this. Someone has gone and slashed the drum. Whatever possesses people to do things like this?"

"Maybe it split by itself," Charlie—he was identifiable by his unbroken voice—piped up, his pimply face registering a troubled expression. "It was too tight, like."

"Charlie, don't be ridiculous." Julia's voice was sharp with exasperation. "Look at it."

"What's the matter?" It was Miranda, on the other side of the drum.

"There's a tear in the drum," Tom replied.

"'Tear' is being kind," Julia responded tartly.

Tom, Julia, and the three boys stared at the instrument in help-less dismay. Miranda joined them. Yes, "tear" wasn't the word. The word was "slash," or, rather, two slashes, neatly and crisply executed, one vertical, the other horizontal, forming a perfect Greek cruci-form, with flaps of drum skin, released from tension, curled out-wards from the new central opening. Whoever had cut the membrane had done it swiftly with a good sharp instrument. Then, as he had at St. Dunstan's in Bristol, when he journeyed across the dimly lit nave towards the porch of the south door on the lookout for his curiously delayed wife and noted hymnbooks pitched onto the stone floor, Tom felt a twinge of unease. At St. Dunstan's, he had quickened his pace, flung open the door to the porch, and gasped at the walls defiled by graffiti, stark even in the half-light of a Novem-ber afternoon. He had stood almost in awe at the violence of the act, though that, unlike this vandalised drum, had less the mark of method. He felt stirrings of anger now as he had then, furiously picking up the hymnbooks before stumbling across the body of his wife and having his world crash around him. He must have made some involuntary movement, for Julia glanced at him sharply, and meaningfully, as though she could sense what was flashing in his brain.

"Tom—" she began gently.

But Colonel Northmore was beside them, walking stick in one hand, and Bumble, his Jack Russell, on a lead, in the other, Madrun flying behind, mug of tea in hand, the light glinting off the cat's-eye spectacles she wore in fashion and out. "Disgraceful!" the colonel barked, then coughed, as though speaking cost him some effort. "Can't imagine how that would happen."

Julia opened her mouth as if to retort, but turned her head away instead. Tom saw an accusatory look sharpen her eye like a needle. He moved to comfort her, but in doing so caught, just for a moment, the desertion of a devilish twitch to the colonel's stone face, the end of a smile so fleeting, so uncharacteristic, he had to remind himself that it had been there. But at that moment he also caught the whiff of something else, a subtle, pheromonal presence in the hall's un-ventilated air. It reminded him of moments in his ministry; it was a familiar, though never welcome, scent, not one characteristic of vil-lage halls in rural England. And when he smelled it, repulsion con-tended with pity. Only in one instance—that fateful afternoon at St. Dunstan's—did pity sweep every other emotion aside.

"Hey, there's something in there," Daniel shouted, pointing. Though fourteen and gangly, he was nearly as tall as Tom.

Yes, there was something in there, but what? Tom's anxiety grew as he moved to block Daniel from advancing nearer the drum. He glanced at Charlie, whose pocked face had gone as white as a new starched surplice.

The breach in the drum skin was almost at eye level for Tom. He arched himself forwards, pushed one of the leathery flaps aside, and peered in. The interior was grey shadow, and in that shadow lay an-other—darker, more substantial. As his eyes adjusted to the thin light the membrane permitted, he could make out the contours of a figure supine in the basin of the drum, knees bent slightly to one side as if seeking comfort in the tiny space. A woman, he recognised instantly. The feet, opposite him, at the drum's far end, were small and pointed in winklepicker boots. One arm rested awkwardly across the stomach like a pale stick. The face, turned in sympathy with the legs, was pushed forwards by the curve of the drum and partly obscured by a disarray of dark hair. But glinting along the scallop of one exposed ear was a row of small silver loops. His heart crashed. He stretched to seek purchase along the drum and looked into the figure's face. There, along the ridge of her left eyebrow, were two more tiny silver hoops. That confirmed it.

"It's Sybella," he said in a half whisper, turning to his expectant audience, glancing at his daughter. "She's asleep."

He was a priest in Christ's church. He didn't like to tell a lie.

⬧

*I*t took but a second for Declan to surge towards the drum. "You lazy cow!" he shouted. "Get out of there now!"

"Leave her be," Tom warned over Bumble's excited barking, grabbing Declan's arm before he could advance any further.

But Declan proved difficult to restrain. "Sybella, you stupid bitch, get out of my drum! Get out! *Get out!* I'll *kill* you, you stupid cunt."

That was it. "Charlie! Daniel! Take Declan outside." Tom gestured towards the two boys, who appeared nonplussed by their friend's fury. "Mrs. Prowse, would you mind taking Miranda out? Colonel . . . ?"

But Colonel Northmore, who had been glaring at Declan with disgust, turned and began to move away, tugging at Bumble's lead.

"Julia, stay with me a moment." Tom grunted as he passed off the flailing and strangely powerful teenager to Charlie and Daniel. The two boys took Declan by the arms and half pushed, half dragged their friend towards the door, but he proved too strong for them, thrusting them aside, sending one of them, Daniel, stumbling backwards across the floor. Daniel crashed into the colonel. The old man seemed to totter for a second as he attempted to maintain his footing, and then went tumbling to the tiles with a sickening cracking noise, echoed by the clatter of his walking stick as it rolled across the floor and succeeded by a noisy protest from Bumble.

"Colonel!" Julia cried, moving to bend over the crumpled figure. Oblivious, Declan struggled back towards the drum, dragging Charlie with him like a limpet. But before Tom could reengage in restraining the flailing youth, Charlie, with renewed vigor, twisted Declan around; with a look of determination and a kind of glee, he drove his fist into his friend's stomach. Declan's face blazed with shock. He jackknifed backwards, his mouth an oval as if he were about to spew; then he, too, hit the floor. The dog stopped barking in that instant, as if he, too, were astonished. The merciful silence was interrupted by a massed chorus of tiny bells, then a quizzical voice:

"Daniel? What the hell are you doing? What's going on here?"

It was Eric Swan standing in the open door that Madrun and Miranda had just vacated. He pushed his Tudor bonnet back on his brow, stirring the plaited ribbons. The bells on his shin pads continued their mad tinkling.

Tom gave a passing thought to the scene: one elderly gentleman being licked by his terrier and two Ninja Turtle youths flat on the floor, a third huffing with exertion and kneading his fist, and two adults challenged as effective referees. The intrusion of a man dressed as a morris dancer just made the awful turn of events seem that much more inconceivable.

"Colonel," Julia said gently, kneeling to the floor, resting one hand under his head, and readjusting his regimental tie, which had flipped around his neck, "that was a very nasty crack. I don't expect you're able to get up, are you?"

Northmore appeared to think about it for a moment, then a shudder of pain travelled across his craggy features. "I'm sorry, my dear." He winced. "I don't think I can. My legs . . ." He winced again.

With her other hand, Julia pulled her mobile from her trouser pocket. As she flipped it open and pressed a button, she glanced towards the *o-daiko* drum and addressed Tom. "I don't know how she can sleep through all of this."

"I hope she's in a coma," Declan moaned, clutching his stomach.

"Alastair, where are you? Good, then you can get here quickly. You're needed at the village hall," Julia spoke urgently into the phone. "Alastair, it's an emergency. Don't give me an argument. Yes, I said it was an *emergency*. Of course I mean medical. Of course I'll phone for an ambulance." She snapped the phone shut. "He's in his car," she said to Tom, who noted a flicker of fury in her expression. He wondered if she'd called her husband unnecessarily simply to be punishing.

"Eric," she said to the Church House Inn's proprietor, who, receiving no reply to his query, was eyeballing the hall's taiko paraphernalia, "would you fetch a couple of cushions from the bar? I think you'll find they're just tied to the seats. We'd better call an ambulance," she added to Tom as Eric jingled his way to the kitchen. "Torbay Hospital would be best." Northmore had closed his eyes. His lips were drawn tightly and his face, normally slightly flushed, had turned the shade of candle wax.

We'll be getting more than an ambulance before long was Tom's anguished thought, as Eric handed two plush crimson seat cushions to Julia. Impatient to clear the hall, he said:

"Eric, perhaps if you take the boys and Bumble outside." He turned to the remaining supine figure. "Declan? Do you think you're well enough to get off the floor?"

Declan groaned with measured theatricality. "I suppose so," he muttered petulantly, glaring at Charlie.

"What about our performance?" Charlie and Daniel wailed as one.

Julia adjusted the pillows under the colonel's head. "We'll see. We can do Chido-setsu and Yuki Jizoh. And for the finale, we might be able to do Heart Beat. Let us deal with things here first."

"Our lot can go on first, if you like," Eric volunteered, taking Bumble's lead and shepherding the boys towards the door. "Now that I've found my morris stick," he added, glancing meaningfully at Daniel, holding up a solid-looking wooden stave of about eighteen inches.

"Perhaps someone should wake Sybella." Julia rose and looked down at the colonel. She flipped her phone open once again. "I almost don't blame Declan. What does the girl think she's playing at? Destroying the drum skin and crawling in to sleep it off. I thought she was reformed."

"How are you feeling, Colonel?" Tom bent down on one knee, while Julia spoke with emergency services.

"I'm sure I'll be fine." Northmore opened his eyes—his irises were iron grey—and looked directly into Tom's. "I've been through worse, padre."

"I expect you have, Colonel." Tom smiled and rose. "I just need a word with Julia," he continued, drawing his sister-in-law aside when she'd finished her call. "Dr. Hennis should be here shortly," he promised the injured man. "And an ambulance."

"I'm furious with Sybella," Julia remarked when they'd moved away a distance. "I've a mind to bring in the police and . . ." Something in Tom's expression stopped her. "What? Tom, what is it?"

"Julia," he began in a low voice, "I'm going to tell you something. It's going to be very upsetting, but I'm going to need your help."

"Now you're frightening me."

He took a deep breath. There was no good way to cushion it. "Sybella isn't asleep."

Julia frowned. "Stoned, then? What do you mean?"

"Sybella is dead."

CHAPTER FIVE

"Dead, you say?"

The colonel's croak intruded into Tom's consciousness. Julia's saucer eyes, searching his own, were holding him transfixed.

"We were referring to—" Tom managed to begin, but Julia's fingers were pressing into his arm, her lips opening, as if to emit a scream. "We were referring to—" he began again, possessed by an impulse to silence her with an embrace.

"Yes, I know. To the girl. Got fixed up with a very good hearing aid some years ago."

"But how . . . ?" Julia groaned, her hand still locked to his arm, her eyes now turned to the *o-daiko* drum.

"I don't know."

"You must be strong, my dear." The colonel addressed Julia. They both turned to the recumbent figure. The simple instruction of a man who had suffered war in its cruelest strain seemed magically to lessen their dread. Tom felt Julia's fingers slip from his sleeve. He pulled his mobile from his pocket.

"Police?" the old man asked.

"Yes, Colonel, I'm just on it now."

"Màiri White is likely outside somewhere." Julia, her face pale, made to dash for the door.

"We'll need more than the village bobby, Julia. Stay with me. Let's not alarm everyone."

"Of course, you're right. Oh, my God. Poor Colm," Julia murmured. "And Celia . . . this is going to be dreadful, dreadful for them."

"Listen, best I go find them." They would be among the May Fayre revellers. "You stay here, Julia. Colonel," Tom addressed the figure on the floor as he listened to the phone ring, "I'm sure Dr. Hennis will fix you up so you'll be right as rain."

"Pleased to be of service," the colonel said, closing his eyes.

"I don't understand—"

"Diversion, my boy. I shall be a diversion."

After alerting the local constabulary, Tom exited the village hall in search of Colm Parry, whom he half expected to be loitering about the stage in preparation for his contribution to the day's festivities, a reprise of his eighties hit "Bank Holiday," only without the bubblegum synth-pop backup. Tom had been quite looking forward to the moment when the entire village—minus one or two old poops—gleefully joined in at the chorus. But a brisk walk through the multitudes while trying not to appear anxious gleaned him nothing, so Tom circled back to the hall and reached again for his mobile.

"Right behind you, mate," Colm said into his phone, giving Tom a gorgonzola grin when he spun around. "Declan said our Sybella's been giving you bother."

As always since he'd arrived in Thornford, Tom couldn't help staring for just a split second at Colm Parry and thinking how strange it was to have as his organist and choirmaster a man he'd seen on *Top of the Pops* when he'd been a teenager, who'd stood just behind Sting in the recording of "Do They Know It's Christmas

Time." In those days, Colm had been as girlishly pretty as Simon Lebon or George Michael, and you could still see a hint of the cheekbone between the jowls and puffy eyes. A quarter century had brought three stone and a paunch, but Colm still had all his hair, if it was his hair, still spikey, with blond highlights, in a way that denoted a kind of engaging immaturity.

"Father?" Colm was among those amused by Tom's surname, or at least pretended to be. "Father?"

Something in Tom's face must have sent notice, because Colm's grin slipped its moorings. "Sybella? She's all right, isn't she? My son was on about her kipping in the big drum. Which explains why she didn't come home last—"

"Colm," Tom cut him off, thinking that nothing prepares you for this, not the training in pastoral theology, not counselling or psychology nor the practice of a decade. "Colm," he repeated, "Sybella isn't asleep. I am very sorry to have to tell you this, but . . . we've found her dead."

Colm's smile collapsed. A drowned look seeped into his blue eyes as he stared at Tom. "We?" he intoned.

"Julia Hennis and I."

"Oh, God. How? Where? You mean, in the *drum*?" His stare grew incredulous as Tom nodded, then his face crumpled. He turned his back to the crowd and brought a hand to his eyes. Over his shoulder Tom glimpsed Miranda skipping towards him, Madrun in tow. He gave his housekeeper a quick warning shake of the head.

"Oh, God, how am I going tell Oona?" Colm whispered, following Tom blindly through the doors to the small hall. "I thought she'd be safe down here. I was the one who said she'd be safe . . ."

The atmosphere in the hall seemed claustrophobic now, the air simmered by the afternoon sun beating on the roof. "Colm, I'm so sorry." Julia blinked back tears as Colm stumbled towards the drum.

"Are you sure?" he whispered, bewildered eyes fixed on the instrument.

Tom glanced at Julia. "I'm sure," he replied. "Would you like to—?"

Colm stretched a hand towards the instrument, then quickly withdrew it. "No . . . no. I don't want to see her this way." He stared vacantly around the hall, at the walls with their old pictures hung awry, at the stack of folded wooden chairs, at the table with its few unclaimed *bachi*. "What was she playing at? How could this . . . ?"

Happen? Tom's mind filled in the word.

Colm's expression sharpened. "She's not been . . . interfered with? She's not been . . . beaten?"

"Colm, she looks like she's resting."

He seemed relieved. "Then what was she playing at?" he said again. "Why would she be *here*?"

"She didn't say to you she'd be at the village hall?"

"No. She was working at the café yesterday. I don't know until when. She didn't come home last night, but I wasn't overly worried. I can't police her, and she's been good as gold. It was Bank Holiday, so I thought she'd probably gone to Torquay after her shift to stay with some mates. I just bought her that Vespa, now she's got her licence back. . . . She texts or phones if she's going to be away overnight. That's the arrangement. I'd thought she'd forgotten— that's all. Oh, Jesus."

"Liam told me earlier he'd expected her to help him at his stall today." Tom moved to switch on the rank of ceiling fans.

"Oh." Colm's voice broke. "Oh, God, then how long has my daughter been lying here?"

"We don't know." Julia looked to Tom, as if for confirmation. "I came down here quite early this morning, but the hall was already open."

"But she's a young woman," Colm pleaded. "Young women just don't . . . *die*."

"People say the girl has a drugs problem." Northmore observed.

"What? No! Who'd say such a thing?"

"Colonel, you really should conserve your energy." Julia's tone turned sharp.

Colm looked wildly about him. "What is going on here?"

"Colonel Northmore's had a fall," Tom explained, guessing that Colm's mind was about to make a wrongheaded connection. "It's nothing to do with . . . with what's happened to Sybella."

Colm's face was sudden thunder. "Colonel, Sybella had a drugs problem. *Had*. She's been good as gold, I said. I should know. I'm her father."

The glance Julia flicked Tom was full of sorrow, but an intelligence passed between teacher and pastor: *Parents can be oblivious to their children's failings. They can be the last to find out.*

Catching the glance, Colm responded heatedly, "I've been down this road myself, you know."

They did know. Colm's career in pop music had been brief and when it went pear-shaped he crashed, with the predictable spectacle of drink, drugs, and infidelity recorded faithfully in the tabloids. He credited his second wife, a self-styled "rock psychologist," with saving his sanity.

"I can read the signs. Just because she wears all that black gear—"

"You're right, Colm," Julia interrupted, dabbing at her eyes. "I'm terribly sorry. I don't think anyone here means to suggest . . ."

Her voice trailed off. Tom realised he remained unconvinced. It was the drum. A vicious person might deface the instrument. But surely only a chemically paralytic one would delight in the novelty of crawling inside, oblivious to the possibility of passing out and being discovered later. Then a new thought entered his mind unbidden: suicide. Had Sybella taken her own life? And if so, why in such a bizarre and showy fashion?

But this new thought was interrupted by a new presence in the room. He'd expected it to be Alastair, in golf togs, but it wasn't. It was his verger, Sebastian John, and he was as pale as the whitewashed wall of any cottage in the village.

The Vicarage

Thornford Regis TC9 6QX

27 MAY

Dear Mum,

The most terrible thing happened at the fete yesterday! It was
just like that day 30 years ago, only without the ~~lighten~~
lightning. Colm Parry's daughter was found dead in the v. hall!
I've told you before she was an odd sort of girl, or maybe
different is the word. That probably comes from having lived
most of her life in London with her mother and her mother's
many boyfriends. I expect you've read about Oona Blanc before
in the papers. I would have said it was a good thing Colm
finally got to have Sybella live here in Thornford, but
considering what's happened, I'm not sure now. Awful to think
the poor girl might have been safer in London! As it happens, I
was in the v. hall when her body was found—inside one of those
big Japanese drums that I told you about yesterday! I was with
Colonel Northmore who wanted to have a quiet cup of tea in the
v. hall. I think he was secretly pleased that the drum was

damaged, awful to say. Of course, he hates anything Japanese, as
well you know. When I took him to the Waterside for lunch the
other week, he wouldn't go in because Liam Drewe had
advertised sushi on his signboard! He won't stomach rice. Never
has. Not since being in that prison camp where all they got to eat
was a bit of maggotty rice. And, of course, he's never said a civil
word to Mrs. Drewe. I've pointed out to him that she was born
in England, but he just gets that stubborn look of his. Poor Colm.
I feel wretched for him. He doted on Sybella and she was coming
along, I think, although she would look at you in the road
sometimes like she knew your darkest secret. I would think to
myself—but I don't have a darkest secret! Do I? Maybe you
know of one, Mum. Colm would do good to dote on his son.
Declan's such a great lump of a boy. He must be 10 stone and he's
only 13. Sybella ~~is~~ was beautiful like her mother, although you
~~have~~ had to look past all the black dyed hair and the piercings to
see it. I wonder if we shall see Oona at the funeral? I expect we
will. She could hardly not attend her daughter's funeral, though I
wonder what condition she'll be in. You still see her in the
papers, of course, but it's all drugs, not fashion modelling
anymore. Like mother, like daughter, I suppose. (Not like you
and me, of course!) And with Oona here, there'll probably be
press nosing about. Little Miranda was in the hall, too, when all
this took place and Mr. Christmas had me take her out quickly.
Poor child, she's only just lost her mother, after all. I know you've
wondered how I would take to having a child here at the
vicarage. Mr. James-Douglas had his nephews visit from time to
time, of course, but you could hardly call those young men
children, though, frankly, Miranda could have given them a
lesson in manners and deportment. I said to Mr. Christmas just
the other day, after Miranda had a little outburst after being
reminded about her bedtime, I don't know if I can be a mother to
her, and he said, don't, be a grandmother, which made me

wonder how old he thinks I am, but it was a bit of a relief, I suppose. Anyway, Miranda's good as cream most of the time. She's very independent, though I wish at times she wouldn't speak French. The rest of the May Fayre went off without ~~a h~~ any other ~~bitch~~ tragedy. I didn't mind the Japanese drumming in the end. Very loud but quite something! Of course they were one drum short, but they decided to "go on with the show" anyway. Apparently Colm insisted. It was very good of him in the circumstances. I've had my doubts about Mr. Christmas, but he comported himself well, I thought. An ambulance came for Phillip, and that caused a bit of fuss. I forgot to tell you Phillip broke his hip in the hall. What a day! Anyway ~~he~~ Mr. Christmas got the police to go into the hall through the fire exit, so most people couldn't see them and get upset. And he was very good with Colm, I thought. Poor man. He looked quite stunned. I did notice Mr. Christmas looking at Julia Hennis in an odd way when we were in the v. hall. She's his sister-in-law. I may have mentioned that before. Henry VIII married his brother's wife. Would marrying your wife's sister be the same thing? Of course, there wouldn't be a Church of England, if Henry hadn't gone off his first wife! But then that was about children and heirs and so forth, wasn't it. Shame the Hennises haven't tried again to have a kiddie. King Henry reminds me that I've got to a part in Dad's history of Thornford about the Romans, though I might leave a blank page as some archaeologists have started a dig outside the village and I might be able to add to Dad's writings. Mr. Christmas thinks I should get a computer, but I don't really want to type out Dad's handwriting all over again. Mr. Christmas suggested a scanner. I know Mrs. Drewe has one and maybe I will borrow it. But I'll worry about that later. You probably don't know what a scanner is, do you, Mum? Anyway, must dash. Mr. C. will be back from Morning Prayer and wanting his breakfast. The cats are both well. Mr. C. muttered something about getting a dog the other day, but I don't think

Powell and Gloria would take to a dog. Love to Aunt Gwen.
~~*Glorious day!*~~ *Hope you have a good day.*

Much love,
Madrun

P.S. I remembered to ask Dr. Hennis about your new arthritis
pills, but he said that as you weren't his patient it was none of
his business. He was quite rude about it!

*A*s the purest joy seized his heart, Tom grasped for an instant—and, really, for the first time—the sensations of Lazarus's sisters as they beheld their adored and freshly animated brother: the astonishment, the thankfulness, the unquestioning, unalloyed happiness. For what greater gift could God bestow than the return of a loved one from the shadow of death? Lisbeth was alive. *She was alive!* It had all been a horrible mistake. Oh, there would be time to settle later with the authorities—the police, the doctors, the undertakers—for their foolish imperceptions. How could they not have seen that she had been merely asleep, breathing shallowly, the victim of some wicked spell? How fortunate that she had awoken! *Tap tap tap. Tap tap tap.* It had been the insistent, persistent tapping that had torn him from his place of grief and sent him flying to her coffin to spring the lid. She had looked up at him dreamily, guiltily, as if caught napping when she should have been at her surgery, but yielding easily, laughing, to his eager embrace, greedily matching his barrage of kisses, as if it had been the first time they had made love. And then, just as he bent further to lift her from her confinement, darkness dropped like doom upon the earth. Lisbeth was vanished from his arms. *Tap tap tap.* The sounds came again, only this time muffled. The air, sickly warm and redolent of dust, grew close and he gasped, struggling for the breath of life against an alien presence now pressing along his face. He sensed, but could not see, his arms flailing and thrashing as he spun downwards, downwards into an abyss.

And then, just as there had been darkness, now there was light. A bit of it, at least, peeking through soft hairs that grazed his eyelashes. Tom widened his eyes and stared dully past the blurry boundary towards the bedroom wall, which was flushed with morning's first sun. He freed one hand from under the covers and pushed Powell—or possibly Gloria; he still couldn't tell the difference—away from his face. He breathed in sharply, then jerked his head up to see the cat regarding him with a kind of diabolical fixedness. *Go away, spawn of Satan,* Tom ordered the cat telepathically, hoping the creature's peanut brain would pick up the signal. Apparently, it did not. Powell—it was Powell; a quick glance at his vulgar backside confirmed the feline's sex—climbed his chest and circled it. Tom dropped his head back and began absently stroking the nesting cat, grateful that no dead bird had been deposited this time on the duvet. The tapping noise coming from the ceiling—Madrun writing her daily letter to her deaf mother on some confounded ancient typewriter—had a peculiar resonance. The dream! He had been dreaming of Lisbeth once again, dreaming that she was alive. He groaned, and wiped sleep and tears from his eyes. Only Mary and Martha had been vouchsafed the return of a loved one from the grave, if you were inclined to literal interpretation of scripture.

He allowed the tapping overhead to lull him, savouring the few sweet moments before the urgencies of living would triumph over the pleasures of a fluffy duvet and a warm cat. In such moments, when he was actually in it, he was glad he hadn't made the effort to get rid of the bed, as he had intended. It was only when he was out of it, in his dressing gown or passing through on some small errand,

and happened to glimpse it, that its sheer buggery grandiosity violated his sense of priestly propriety. Elaborately carved, heavily
draped and canopied, it was a bed a Stuart monarch might disport
in. Or die in, if he could keep his head attached to his neck. How
Giles James-Douglas had got the thing into the vicarage in the first
place was a wonder, but getting it out, Tom realised after a few enquiries, would have exacted the patience of several folks, notably
Mrs. Prowse, who had an evolving relationship with novelty. The
drab (by comparison) bed he'd bought with Lisbeth went into one of
the vicarage's four other bedrooms, which, along with the three
bathrooms, a drawing room, a breakfast room, a dining room, a boot
room, a conservatory, and a cat flap, constituted a home rather more
grand than the one they'd had in Bristol. He sometimes felt that it
was obscene that he should be living in such comparative splendour;
that he should be letting out rooms to refugees or homeless. The
square footage was better suited to vicars in ages past who had wives,
half a dozen children, and a servant or two. Not to a man, one child,
and a housekeeper.

Giles James-Douglas had had a sizeable private income. While
the Church had been busy for decades cashing in on rural property
prices and selling off the rambling vicarages and rectories built in
the eighteenth and nineteenth centuries, leaving its clergy in brisk,
modern little houses, in Thornford Regis, the vicarage had been
passed over by the angel of downsizing. James-Douglas had bought
the vicarage outright from the Church. In his will he had returned
it to the Church so long as it remained the residence of the incumbent vicar, leaving sufficient monies to maintain the extra upkeep
for so large a residence, and so long as it remained the residence
of one Madrun Prowse, housekeeper, upon whom he had—it was
rumoured—lavished a generous bequest.

It was probably one of the more unusual property arrangements
in the Church of England, but the consequence was nothing if not
agreeable. James-Douglas had been a dab hand at interior decoration and he hadn't been averse to creature comforts of the latest in-

novation, including installing, in his final year, a shower in the en suite with remarkable capabilities. Too busy and too pinched in the pocketbook to give much thought to their four walls, Tom and Lisbeth had lived for years in a hodgepodge of family discards and Habitat knockoffs. When he went to do a recce of the vicarage at Thornford, Tom decided it was hardly worth integrating very much of their old tat into the splendour, even if it meant feeling faintly like they were living in an upmarket bed-and-breakfast. At least, he thought, glancing drowsily over at his newfound curate's egg next to the clock on the side table, there were the things of sentimental value.

The rhythmic tapping continued from above. Whatever did Madrun find to write to her mother *about* every day? Village life seemed rather inconsequential, he thought, and then smiled, glad it was so. He let his eyelids drift downwards. So good to have found the curate's egg at the fête . . .

The egg!

Only the cat kept him from sitting bolt upright. Instead, he stared unseeing into the golden moonscape of Powell's cold eyes, reliving—again!—the aftermath of discovering Sybella in the vandalised drum. He remembered his own surge of dread as he jerked his head back from the drum's slashed membrane, forced to quickly gather his wits, as he had been forced to gather his wits when he had stumbled upon Lisbeth's body. The panoply of the county's emergency services making its way to Thornford's village hall the day before had had a horrible familiarity. Now, as he sank back against the pillow, he found himself praying that this tragedy would have an unextraordinary cause and a swift resolution. He recognised his prayer as selfish and shameful, unattached to Colm's profound loss, but the thought of his life, and his daughter's, being haunted by another unresolved death, and so soon, and so near, felt almost unbearable.

"Anything worth noting, Mrs. Prowse?" asked Tom as lightly as he could muster, hoping to keep the breakfast conversation off the previous day's events. He and Miranda were seated at the centrepiece of the Aga-warmed kitchen, a lovely old scarred oak table. Madrun was standing by the sink, newspaper in hand.

"*The Duchess of Gloucester, Patron, St. Peter's Trust for Kidney, Bladder and Prostate Research, attended a private view of 'Firm Favourites: Highlights and Recent Acquisitions from the Fleming Collection' at the Fleming Collection, 13 Berkeley Street, London W1,*" Madrun recited from the Court Circular in *The Daily Telegraph*, adjusting her glasses, which hung from a chain around her neck. She frowned a little.

"What's a 'prostate'?" Miranda piped up, slipping a piece of ham to Powell—or, possibly, Gloria—who was circling the legs of the Windsor chairs with a kind of mad lust.

Madrun peeked over the top of the paper.

"It's a tiny little organ, sort of around where the kidney and bladder are," Tom replied, sinking his fork into a slice of quiche, a dish he thought much too rich for breakfast.

"Oh. What does it do?"

"Not much." Tom reflected how true this was in his case, since Lisbeth's death. "It's like . . . an appendix. Sort of excess to requirements."

"Will it burst? Emily's appendix burst last year and she had to go to hospital."

"Prostates never burst. It's not something you will ever, ever have to worry about."

Miranda appeared to digest this information. "Is Sybella where Mummy is?" she asked abruptly, regarding him solemnly with her green-flecked eyes—her mother's eyes.

"Yes," he replied. He had been expecting questions and was surprised—and a little concerned—that none had come sooner. Had she been brooding? By the time the fête had ended late the previous afternoon, with the police sealing off the village hall, it had got about that not only had someone died inside, but that that someone was young Sybella Parry. On his instructions, Madrun had hustled Miranda back to the vicarage shortly after the Twelve Drummers Drumming had completed their performance, but somehow the knowledge that Sybella had not been merely sleeping in the drum had filtered into the child's consciousness, though she had said nothing about it at supper (the fête's welly-tossing and china-smashing events intrigued her more), and nothing as he got her ready for bed (her new Alice Roy book was her preoccupation).

"Yes, she is," he added for emphasis.

"A good place?"

"Yes."

"Do you think Mummy will like Sybella?"

"I think your mother will find Sybella great fun."

Miranda nodded sagely. "I liked her. She always said hello to Emily and me when we saw her in the road. One time she took me and Emily to see Uncle Alastair when Emily got really badly stung by a wasp."

"All the way into Torquay on her Vespa?"

"To Westways. It was a Saturday. Uncle Alastair was home."

"Oh. I see. That was nice of her."

"I liked her nails."

"Promise me you won't paint yours black."

Miranda splayed her fingers on either side of her plate. "Green?"

"Something in a pink shade, perhaps."

The exchange reminded him that Sybella's black-lacquered fingernails had been the first of her attributes that had caught his eye. Fourteen months earlier, on their first visit to Thornford—and their first visit to the Waterside Café—she had handed him menus. As he looked up from his seat, his eyes had travelled to the cascade of black hair, flat as if it had been ironed, then to the black eyes, which were lined with kohl so that they resembled burn holes in a bedsheet.

"I like your earrings," Miranda had exclaimed artlessly about the magnificent silver hoops that dangled from Sybella's lobes. Sybella had responded with an uninterpretable grunt, flipped her hair back with an actressy gesture to reveal a series of smaller hoops slinking up the cartilage, took their order, and ignored them for the next forty-five minutes. They were only tourists, after all.

A year later, a day or two after he and Miranda had moved into the vicarage, they paid a second visit to the Waterside. He was a little surprised to see Sybella still waitressing there—given the transience of such jobs and Liam Drewe's reputation as a difficult boss—but he was pleased to see restraint in her makeup and jewellery, though her ears were still a pincushion. Her face had a golden glow, as if from a week in the sun. She'd turned her attention immediately to Tom:

"I'd love it if you'd saw me in half sometime."

Having heard that one before, Tom responded, "Lengthwise or widthwise?"

"Oh, I don't know." Sybella tapped her cheek, her lacquered fingernail like a flickering beauty spot. "Let me think about it."

"Do so. And we'll think about what we're going to order." Tom had said this with a hard smile, though he was half amused. He didn't mind the flirtation—priests got their fair share of it—but he was uncertain of the provocation, the childish showing off, from someone in her late teens who, despite the cosmetic affectations and the near anorexic figure, was clearly no longer a child. Sybella's breasts, he couldn't help noticing, strained the man's white shirt that she wore as a kind of server's uniform. She caught the direction of his glance and smirked. "I'll come back when you're ready," she said, exposing her lovely pink ear once again.

Tom had felt vaguely caught out, exposed both as a mere man—poor, dumb thing with more brains in his trousers than in his head—and as a charlatan—someone who was merely posing as a priest. Yes, before he had felt the call, Tom had been a professional magician. The Great Krimboni he had been, purveyor of the illusory arts to all and sundry, particularly those who would pay. Close-up magic had been his trade, not stage illusions like bisecting attractive females or causing the Home Secretary to vanish in a puff of smoke. He still did the odd trick or two, but by and large, he'd taken to heart Saint Paul's line about childish things, putting them away, and so forth, though he wouldn't have voiced that to some of his old magician cronies who still sent him the occasional email. Clearly, Tom's priesthood held no interest for Sybella. She'd probably Googled him when news of his appointment circulated through the village. Anyone might have done so.

"Much good The Priory did that girl," Madrun sniffed, snapping the *Telegraph* shut and snapping Tom out of his reverie. Her glasses dropped from her nose and bounced against her ample bosom.

"We can't assume anything," Tom remonstrated vaguely. He wasn't sure why. Drugs, abused or mishandled in some fashion, seemed the ready explanation for Sybella's death, given her history, which two years ago had reached its crescendo on the pages of *The Sun* and the *News of the World*. High as a steeple, she'd been racing her car through Camden at four in the morning, transporting a couple of similarly addled car surfers on the hood. After the car met a streetlamp, the surfers met the pavement, and Sybella met her airbag, the court—in a foul mood, keen to make an example of the spoiled children of spoiled parents—ordered a £3,000 fine, a year's driving disqualification, and rehab at The Priory in lieu of jail. Thornford's curtain twitchers still pegged Sybella for a druggie, but Tom, who had seen his share of wasters on the streets of Bristol—and Kennington and Southwark before that—was pressed to find any recognisable sign.

"Do you think I could give the rest of my breakfast to Powell and Gloria?" Miranda whispered, regarding him hopefully.

Tom glanced at Madrun, who had bent over the dishwasher, and whispered back, "Just eat a little more."

CHAPTER SEVEN

*om was glad when Miranda suggested they reprise "Where in
the World Is the Reverend Peter Kinsey?" At the breakfast table, he
tried to keep Madrun from further speculating about Sybella's
death, going so far as to feign interest in the other announcements
in the Court Circular, but to little avail. Answering any more questions about Sybella reminded him only too vividly of telling
Miranda—the evening of the sombre, rain-filled autumn afternoon
when he'd found Lisbeth lifeless on St. Dunstan's cold stone floor—
that her mother had died.

So stunned by horror in the hour after Lisbeth's death, he had let
his daughter slip from his mind until a police constable's question
jolted him to the very circumstances of his wife's being in the church
at all: It had been a Wednesday, Ghislaine's day off. By custom, Lisbeth left her surgery early and walked Miranda back from school,
but this Wednesday she had phoned him and said she would first
nip into Toad Hall Toys, buy the Barbie doll Miranda was so craving for her birthday, then leave it with him at St. Dunstan's for safe-

keeping. "She would guess what's in the bag, darling" were among her last words to him.

Frantically, blinded by grief, he had phoned the school, but no Miranda was to be seen. He phoned home, then a neighbour's, then Ghislaine's mobile, all to recorded messages. Finally, he had peeled himself away from the tumult of police and ambulance and shocked church staff and raced through Miranda's path from school. He found her at last, mercifully, at home, little perturbed, quite competently having made herself a snack of bread and jam and settling in to watch *The Sarah Jane Adventures* on TV.

When her mother didn't appear, she explained, regarding him with a faintly guilty frown, she had made her own way home after a detour to the Cheltenham Road Library. He was so relieved, all he could do was crush her to him. And then, after a little time had passed, he steeled himself for the awful task. Then, he could speak— just barely—the language of death to his child; he had had to; there was no other way. But he could not make himself speak the language of murder; that is, until some pitiless older child's school taunting of Miranda left him little choice but to address the greater horror.

Yes, Mummy died very suddenly when she was coming to meet Daddy at the church, but police think she saw a man doing something bad and he didn't want her to tell anyone what he was doing, so he took away her life. No, he was a very sick man. No, police don't know who he is, but they're looking very hard for him. Yes, Myleene—for that was the gormless schoolmate's name—*is right, the police think it may have had something to do with drugs. No, not like Paracetamol. This sick man was using very hurtful drugs. Mummy would never have prescribed anyone such drugs.*

One unintended consequence was that Miranda remained chary of anything she thought was a drug, including the erythromycin she had been prescribed when impetigo had coursed through her classroom. "Will this hurt me?" she now always asked, examining intently any bottle of pills.

Which was why Tom wished Madrun had not mentioned The

Priory, the well-known drug and alcohol treatment centre. By doing so, she'd laid down a track. The conversation could proceed in only one direction, and it would, unless stopped.

"Oh, it must be drugs," his housekeeper said, reaching for the cafetière to pour Tom another cup, stepping around Powell and Gloria, who were slinking about on a quest for dropped food.

"Not necessarily."

"Nonsense, Mr. Christmas, it has—"

"Mrs. Prowse, shall we talk of other things?"

"I'm not a baby, you know," Miranda interjected. She was regarding them both candidly.

"Of course you're not, darling," Tom responded reflexively. "But it's not like it was with Mummy. There's no sick man in the village who hurt Sybella. Isn't that right, Mrs. Prowse?"

"Yes, of course." But Madrun had been arrested in her coffee pouring. Tom looked up and noted a strange, alert look in her eyes. He realised at that moment that he had given voice to an awful possibility that his mind had held shuttered: No youthful folly or accident or self-destruction had ended Sybella's life. Some outside agency, gone now to shadow, had brought about this destruction— an echo of his own wife's death so acutely painful that he had to catch a breath so that his coffee cup wouldn't shake and spill. He cursed himself for planting the seed of speculation in Madrun's mind—she'd be down at the post office with her letter to old Mrs. Prowse nattering with Karla Skynner and anyone else queued up for a stamp—but then realised he was probably being naïve. Half the breakfast tables in the village were probably preoccupied with similar worrying thoughts.

That's when Miranda suggested they play "Where in the World Is the Reverend Peter Kinsey?" Its genesis had been his offhand explanation to her the year before about Kinsey's no-show at Ned Skynner's funeral. He had told her that Kinsey was probably having sundowners with Lord Lucan somewhere in Africa, which Miranda didn't understand, but nevertheless embellished with a tangential suggestion about him visiting Babar in the jungle. When they were driving home to Bristol after their stay with the Hennises, they continued the game, which seemed perfectly innocent then. Though the village had been rife with speculation when they'd left, Tom assumed Kinsey would eventually reappear with some perfectly decent explanation for his absence. They weren't to know that before any great passage of time, he would be officially classified as a missing person.

"What made you think of that?" he couldn't help asking, wondering if she was reacting in some oblique childhood way to anxiety.

Miranda shrugged.

"Well, all right then," Tom responded reluctantly. "Where in the world *is* the Reverend Peter Kinsey?"

Miranda regarded the bit of ham on her fork. "*Le curé est parti en Espagne pour . . . devenir matador,*" she said, flicking a glance at Madrun, who, as usual, discomfited at the introduction of French, turned away.

"And what would Alice Roy do?"

Miranda slipped the piece of ham off her fork and let her arm drop beside her chair. *"Alice demanderait à Madame Prowse si le curé était très très . . . friand de la paella."* She giggled.

"What?" Madrun turned, responding to her name in the thicket of French. Her eyes went to Gloria's greedy jaws. "You'd best not be feeding my good ham to that cat."

Tom laughed. "Miranda imagines that the Reverend Mr. Kinsey decided to become a matador in Spain. And that a good detective like Alice Roy would ask you, Mrs. Prowse, if he was . . . fond . . . ?" Miranda nodded assent. ". . . fond of paella."

Madrun harrumphed, still eyeing the cat. "Then you also might imagine him performing in denim trousers and getting shut of red capes."

Tom was reminded that many parishioners found Peter Kinsey a divisive figure after so many years of the amiable Giles James-Douglas, who had been content to hone to traditions established many years earlier. A new broom in modern dress, Kinsey had shifted worship times to make room for a modern family service, decided to take out some pews so people could gather for coffee and a chat after services, removed pictures from the Lady chapel, and was musing about moving the altar before his disappearance. Shifted from their comfortable pews—literally, in a few cases—some church-goers felt they were being pushed a bit too far. A few welcomed the changes. However, Kinsey wasn't around long enough to have really put his mark on things, and so the fabled "demographic"—so much the concern of forward planners—hadn't changed significantly. They're like ripe fruit, the bishop, a wintry fellow, had mused to Tom between bites of sultana cake as he surveyed the flock at the re-ception in the village hall after Tom's induction service: Pretty soon they would begin to drop off the branch. The message was clear: Innovate to draw new blood into the church. But, added the bishop, giving him the gimlet eye, try not to shake the branch *too* vigorously. That message was equally clear: Don't be an overeager arborist like your predecessor. Softly, softly, Mr. Christmas.

One of Peter Kinsey's legacies was a splendid new bloodred Thorn Sherpa touring bicycle, the sort you might buy if you were thinking of cycling by way of France, Turkey, and Iran to India. It was a bit flash for a vicar, and rather expensive, but Tom, applying bicycle clips to his ankles, suspected his predecessor had merely to say "car-bon footprint" and all qualms—his and others'—would vanish. Well, it was true. A bicycle was a greener way to get about. But some used model would have done just as well, if a little village was the four corners of your cycling world. So, too, would a biro from the corner shop instead of a Mont Blanc fountain pen, or a pair of Boots sunglasses instead of Oliver Goldsmith's, both of which had been overlooked at the vicarage when Peter's effects were packed away pending resolution to his missing person's file. The archdeacon told Tom that Peter's parents, wealthy farmers in Zimbabwe, had been killed and their land seized just before his ordination, leaving Peter, their only child, with virtually nothing more than his stipend. That didn't seem to stop him from acquiring the finer things in life, Tom reflected, as he waved at Miranda, who was holding one of the cats in the sitting room window, and pedalled out into Poynton Shute, with its row of stone cottages opposite. Looking down Church Lane towards the lych-gate, he glimpsed Sebastian John, keys in hand, preparatory to opening the church for the day, and gave a passing thought to hailing him and asking after Colonel Northmore's condition. But the bike seemed to have a mind of its own and it whisked Tom onwards, past the Church House Inn and along towards Pattimore's shop and the post office.

Or perhaps he was attributing agency to the bicycle to avoid talking with his verger. Sebastian seemed to live in silences, approaching conversation as if it were a necessary, but not wholly welcome, obligation. Likewise, his expression often lacked animation, as if he had learned to rid his face of emotion, though occasionally, at church council meetings, say, when Karla Skynner was on her high horse about something, a gush of inner light would illuminate his deep-set blue eyes and a faint smile would curl the corners of his mouth, illuminating the suppressed intelligence. It was the infrequency of these emotional punctuations that made his entrance into the village hall the day before all that much more remarkable. Sebastian had burst through the doors, panting slightly, a line of perspiration against his hairline, as if he had dashed from the other end of Purton Farm. Tom had assumed his concern was for Colonel Northmore. He knew from Madrun that the colonel had interceded with Giles James-Douglas to secure Sebastian the verger's position, which suggested some sort of prior relationship between the men, though try as she might—and Madrun had tried—she couldn't get to the bottom of it. Too, Sebastian spent many hours tending the gardens at Farthings, the colonel's home near the entrance to Knighton Lane, and sometimes took his dinners there. They were almost like old priest and acolyte, Tom thought, occasionally seeing them together in one of Thornford's lanes, usually with Bumble at the end of a leash. But Sebastian, his bronzed face drained of colour, had eyes only for the *o-daiko* drum.

"Is Sybella . . . ?" he managed to utter.

They all stared at him, waiting for him to complete the question. No words came. Finally, with a regretful glance at Colm, Tom murmured:

"I'm afraid Sybella has died, Sebastian."

"Sybella," Sebastian had repeated in a wondering tone. He had looked at them, one by one, as if seeking confirmation. Finally his eyes settled on Colm. "I'm so very sorry," he said. His face shifted through sympathy to its normal, impassive mien. Though thinking about it now, as he rolled down the pavement past Pattimore's shop towards Fishers Hill and the turn towards the adjunct road that would take him to Thornridge House, Tom was possessed by the worrying notion that it had been relief, or something akin, that he'd glimpsed in those cobalt blue eyes. No one at the fayre had known that Sybella was anything but asleep in the drum. Yet somehow Sebastian had intuited the most cheerless of scenarios. It had been on the tip of his tongue to ask his verger if he had some intelligence on the tragedy, but a moan from the floor had redirected everyone's attention.

"Phillip," Sebastian had said, the surprise in his voice detectably genuine. "What has happened to you?"

"I've had a fall, my boy."

"Some of the boys were fighting and one of them knocked Colonel Northmore over," Julia corrected. "And, yes, an ambulance is coming," she added as Sebastian, kneeling by the colonel's side, looked up at her enquiringly. "I've asked Alastair to come, too . . . oh, and here he is now."

Julia and her husband exchanged cool glances, after Alastair, dressed as if he'd just blown in off the course, in a blue and green striped golf shirt and matching golf cap, had pushed through the door. Quickly, wordlessly, he bent down across from Sebastian and twisted the bill of his cap to the back of his head. "Old Course St. Andrews," Tom found himself reading. Alastair lifted Colonel

Northmore's arm, pushed the shirt cuff back with one hand, and felt along his wrist.

"Your pulse is strong," he commented.

"It's the colonel's *legs*, Alastair," Julia snapped. "He's had a fall."

"Do you mind? I'm the doctor here."

"Where's your bag?"

"It's at the club. Old Mr. Gill had a seizure of sorts in the locker room."

"What does that mean?"

"It means, Julia, that I forgot my bag in the locker room after I'd examined Gill. I'm quite capable of examining someone without it."

Alastair ordered the colonel to try moving his right leg, then his left. Northmore's features shuttered with pain as he attempted to shift the latter. "Ten," the colonel gasped when Alastair asked him the level of pain he was feeling on a scale of one to ten.

"Is something broken?" Sebastian asked.

"You're in my way. Move!"

As Sebastian shifted off his knees, Alastair moved to the colonel's right side, turned his suit jacket aside, and palpated alongside his hip with his hands. After a moment, he, too, rose.

"Well . . . ?" Julia said.

"Well what?"

"Perhaps the colonel would care to know your diagnosis?"

Alastair jerked his cap back the right way. "Colonel," he responded, readjusting his shirt over an incipient paunch, "an X ray will tell us more, of course, but I expect that you've broken your hip. I'm very sorry."

Northmore's lips formed a thin line. He said nothing.

"I'd be happy to stay with you, Colonel, in other circumstances, but I'm afraid I have another appointment. If you'll all excuse me . . ." Alastair touched his cap in a salute.

"It's Bank Holiday!" Julia protested.

Alastair gave his wife a tight smile. "Enid Pattimore craves my attention."

"Nonsense."

"I saw Enid not an hour ago at Liam Drewe's stall," Tom added, surprised. "She looked fine."

"My service paged me while I was in the car. I can show you both, if you like." Alastair reached into his pocket.

"Never mind that." Julia waved a dismissive hand as Alastair thrust his pager in her face. "There's someone else you must look at here. Something terrible has happened."

"What?"

"It's Sybella."

Alastair glanced around. "I don't understand."

Tom opened his mouth to speak, but Colm interjected. "Alastair, really, there's nothing you can do. It's not necessary to . . ." He trailed off.

"Sybella has died, Alastair," Tom explained. The words were awful to say.

Alastair blinked. "What? But . . . ?"

"Her body's in that drum."

Alastair frowned deeply. "I don't under—"

"Please, no one touch her," Colm moaned, lurching on wobbly legs to block the drum. "Please."

"Alastair, it's fine," Tom said, one eye on Colm, who looked about to collapse. "We're waiting for the police. Go and attend to Enid. We can . . . cope here."

"But how . . . ?"

"We don't know," Tom replied.

"I'm very sorry," Alastair addressed Colm. "If there's anything—"

"We'll be okay, Alastair, really." Julia lowered her eyes. "I'm sorry to have dragged you here."

"Oh." Alastair looked vaguely startled. "Well, under the circumstances . . ." He moved towards the door, then turned. "Perhaps someone ought to pick that walking stick off the floor. Before anything else happens."

Colm hailed Tom as he was walking his bike by the box topiaries that flanked the driveway between the gate and Thornridge House, a Nash-designed jewel of golden stone that glowed in the mid-morning sunshine. Startled out of his thoughts of the previous day's events, Tom veered down a curving flagstone path past deep beds of boisterous wildflowers towards the rhythmic scrape of chafing metal. Next to the slender pillar of an ancient sundial, Colm—dressed in a straw hat as wide as a sombrero and a pair of jeans so worn the blue had given way to strands of white at the knees and the pockets—was attacking a clematis vine with vigour.

"You have to keep after these buggers or they just get tangled and monstrous." He grunted and took a final swipe at a stem, sending it cascading to the pile of cuttings. Tom, who had vague knowledge of gardening gleaned from his two mothers and their passion for their back garden in Gravesend, had a notion that pruning clematis in late May wasn't the done thing, but thought better of mentioning it. In his years as priest, he had met with many varied responses to the loss of the loved one, of which a brisk workout in the garden was by no means unusual. When he was a curate, he had gone around to the home of a man who had lost his wife and found him feverishly hacking away at a crabapple tree in his back garden. And when he was in Bristol, a woman whose son had been stabbed outside their council house began painting an angel over the bloodstain on the pavement. By the time he arrived, a heavenly host was running up the front door and the neighbours were growing restive.

"It's a lot of work," Tom responded, surveying the expanse of plantings.

"Well, it keeps me off the sauce."

Tom half expected a smile to follow this remark—Colm had been famously off the sauce for years; in the pub, he drank orange juice or Perrier—but no smile came. Colm took another swipe at the plant. "That should do," he said, staring glassy-eyed at his handiwork.

"Shall we go in?" Tom asked.

"Oh . . . I doubt Celia's back from her morning ride." To Tom's faint look of surprise he added, "I forgot to mention you were coming. Celia thinks it's best if we all keep to our routines. I expect she's right. I would be feeling a bit cooped-up inside."

Tom glanced at Thornridge House through the almost imperceptible humid veil that softened its outlines. Certainly the largest coop in the village or vicinity by a long chalk, but he understood the sentiment. After Lisbeth's death, when family had descended upon him and Miranda, he had walked and walked and walked all over Bristol.

"Bring your bike. We'll go round to the pool garden. I don't think you've seen the back of the house before. We should be able to hear Celia when she comes back.

"This was a tennis court in the Northmores' day," Colm continued when they'd emerged from the east gardens into an expanse of lawn that dipped below the pergola at the south façade of the house. Cut into the middle was an oblong of untroubled water dotted with white water lilies, its stone corners softened by mauve irises. On each of the long sides was an iron bench, simple in design, but with sufficient length to seat St. Nicholas's choir, if need should ever be.

"It's beautiful, serene," Tom commented, leaning his bike against the grilled back of the nearest bench.

"Yes, I find it . . . comforting. At times like this." Colm settled on the bench and dropped the shears on the grass at his feet. Tom flicked him a worried glance.

"I don't think Phillip much approved," Colm added, removing his hat and squinting at the sunlight glistening off the water.

"Of what?"

"Of taking out the tennis court."

"I'm not surprised." Tom smiled. Edwin Northmore, Phillip's father, had sold Thornridge House for taxes in the 1950s, and though Phillip had had a successful postwar career in London as a bank director, he had not been successful enough to buy it back. Nonetheless, Phillip retained a proprietorial interest.

"He sort of harrumphed when I showed it to him. The old boy's not much for change, is he? Speaking of which, how is he?"

"I haven't heard. I'll be going up to the hospital this afternoon." Tom joined Colm on the bench. "More to the point, how are you?"

Colm raised his eyes to the sky. Tom followed his gaze. Above them a flight of swallows circled into a shimmer of white cloud. "Oh, stunned, I think," he replied after a moment. "Deeply sad." He glanced over at Tom, who could see that his eyes were rimmed with purplish shadows. "You would know, wouldn't you?"

"Yes . . . although—"

"Time heals all wounds?"

"I was hoping not to be banal." In the wake of Lisbeth's death, every platitude had been fed into his ears, usually by the well-meaning, embarrassed to be proximate to one with such a loss. He could do nothing but accept their awkward kindnesses, but he had learned this: In grief so deep, sentimentality has no home. "I was going to say that the awful agony does subside, I've found—perhaps it's a little like those half-lives we learned about in science class."

"One day the residual half will be tiny."

"Perhaps. Though I haven't got there yet."

"I doubt I shall." Colm plucked absently at one of the strands of cotton taut across his knee. "And your parents, tragically, too, I recall."

"I was only a baby. I have no recollection."

Colm gave him an assessing gaze. "Of course. I remember it, though. I think I was about eight or nine. It was a little like when Diana died. The whole nation was caught unawares for a moment. Sorry, I shouldn't go on about this."

"That's all right." Tom shrugged. The grieving often preferred to talk of other things. "For me, it's something in a press clipping, really."

He thought back to the newspaper and magazine stories Dosh—his aunt, who became his second adoptive mother—saved for him in a scrapbook, which she presented to him when his child's consciousness began to encompass the world beyond the garden gate. No, it wasn't anything remotely like the emotional gale wind following the death of the Princess of Wales, but his young parents' death in an airplane that plunged into the North Sea after takeoff from Stockholm, where his mother had won the Eurovision Song Contest, had captured the public imagination for a time. He himself had been a figure of sentimentality, the poor orphaned—*twice orphaned!*—Xmas (tabloid headlines were invariably truncated) Baby. He could recall from the scrapbook a particularly vivid picture of Dosh, her scolding face turned towards some news photographer, caught outside some shop in Gravesend. In her arms, a bundle of swaddling clothes. Him. Tom Livingston Christmas.

"I still have your mother's winning single somewhere, 'If Wishes.' It was a good tune." Colm's head began swaying as if to an inner rhythm. " 'If wishes were horses, then beggars would ride,' " he began, his voice, huskier yet sweeter in the decades since *Top of the Pops,* embracing the last note. " 'If time would turn back, I'd have you by my side . . .' " He faltered then; a beat passed. Tom opened his mouth to offer to allay the discomforting lyric, but Colm recovered, stronger: " 'All life's trials and sorrows would never abide . . .' " He smiled at Tom in invitation.

". . . 'If wishes were horses, then beggars would ride.' " Tom drew out the last words in the voice that ensured his exclusion from any respectable choir.

"Yes, that's right." Amusement crinkled the corners of Colm's eyes. "Your mother had a lovely, lyric voice. In your case, the apple seems to have fallen really quite far from the tree."

Tom laughed. "But I was the *adopted* son of Iain Christmas and Mary Carroll—"

"I'd forgotten that."

"—My natural parents probably had tin ears, as do I."

"Well, you have a fine speaking voice, Vicar."

"I expect the stage training didn't hurt."

"Eh?"

"My former life as The Great Krimboni."

"Ah, yes—the magic act. Did you get called 'Krimbo' at school?"

"I still get 'Krimbo' if I'm in certain parts of the southeast."

"I was christened 'Malcolm.' Dropped the 'Mal' as soon as I could." Colm's attention seemed to drift and they sat in silence in the soft air for a moment.

"I was thinking of a gospel choir for Sybella's funeral." Colm plucked again at the threads along his knee.

"I certainly don't mind, Colm, if that's what you wish." Tom hesitated. "I wasn't sure where you were planning to—"

"I want the funeral here and I want her to be buried in the churchyard. This is where I live. I want to be near to her—" His voice broke.

"I understand." Tom shifted his eyes to the pool, observing a tiny water boatman rippling the reflection of cedar branches in the glassy surface of the water. He waited for the moment to pass.

"And Sybella's mother?" he asked, after a time. "Is this her wish?"

"Oona can go to hell."

"Is she objecting?"

"She's being . . . hard to manage. As she has been her entire career and through our entire marriage. But I'll sort her out."

Tom gave a passing thought to the effects of a funeral of a young woman with celebrity (however faded) parents on the church and the village. He had had his own disagreeable experience with press intrusion—reporters idling on the street in front of their flat or the church in the days after Lisbeth's murder. One of them had winkled Tom's mobile number out of some unsuspecting neighbour; then they all had it. He'd thrown his phone into the Avon.

"And do you know a gospel choir that can arrive on short notice?" Tom asked.

"I do. Revelation Choir. They did some backup on my second album and were around when Sybella was a baby. Happened I went to sixth-form college with Delroy Francis, who founded the choir and is still with it. We've always stayed in touch."

"Perhaps it's just as well Colonel Northmore is in hospital."

A sly smile lit Colm's face. "No chance of quick recovery?"

Tom returned the smile but shook his head. He had another thought: "Was Sybella particularly fond of gospel music? Mightn't she have wanted something else?"

"I'm afraid neither of my children share my taste in music, but then I didn't share my parents' taste—at least at the time. Sybella seemed fond of a group called Demon Sexgang, I recall."

Tom frowned. "I don't detect a Christian attitude."

"I didn't detect a musical sensibility, but then I'm well past it. Besides, Sybella was growing out of this Goth nonsense. It was just a teenage thing. You know, being rebellious and so on and so forth just to get up your parents' nose. We all did it. We just all did it in different ways. Celia says Sybella has an Electra complex—you know, hates Mummy so she acts up—though I can't see how, since Oona seemed to *encourage* her bad behaviour. Revelation Choir and Sybella's first months are linked in my mind in a happy way, so gospel it shall be." Colm reached for his hat and rose abruptly from the bench. "Anyway, come up and see Sybella's artworks. I think they're quite good. You can leave your bike here."

"I didn't know she painted . . . or drew," Tom remarked, catching up to Colm, who was striding purposefully across the new grass.

"It's Mitsuko's doing. She'd really taken Sybella under her wing. Saw a talent there."

"It used to be the nursery," Colm told him when they'd reached the top floor by the back staircase. "See, the light's quite good. North light for drawing and painting. My music studio's across the hall. That's where I compose our anthems or scores for film or whatever comes along. I thought Declan might take an interest—you know, what with all the technical gear and such . . ."

"He evidently likes drumming," Tom remarked, noting the

broad drawing table, the shelves of art books, and the bank of large, flat drawers with sheets of drawing paper—surely a wealthy father's overindulgent response to a child's latest enthusiasm.

"I think Declan just likes bashing things, really." Colm gestured to a scattering of papers and open sketchpads on the table. "What do you think? I was looking at them last night."

Tom studied the artwork. The earliest drawings were faithful and somewhat fussy renderings of unremarkable objects—fruit, flowers—but soon the thick pencil or charcoal strokes became simpler and bolder, more confident. The subject matter shifted, too—the human face and form took primacy. He was surprised. He could make no claims to an understanding of art, but he felt he was capable of at least detecting if something was childishly amateur. This was not, and what a relief: He hadn't relished soothing a grieving father by telling him that his dead daughter's doodlings were Tate-worthy. He glanced at some more that were sellotaped to the wall and then a few that had landed atop the bank of drawers. He noted a certain recurring male figure.

"Yes," Colm said, as if reading his mind, "Sybella had taken a fancy to sketching Sebastian—but then he's here almost every day working with me in the garden, so . . ." He shrugged. "Even my wife finds opportunities to meander into the garden when Sebastian's about, though she denies it. I suppose I should hire an ugly dwarf in his place, but he's very good at what he does, and he's oddly companionable."

"Really." Tom reflected that he didn't find Sebastian *un*companionable, but the man had certainly honed circumspection to a fine degree. "Does he ever talk about himself?"

Colm shook his head. "That's what makes him companionable. We just go about our business. We talk about plants and the weather. I don't ask about his private life and he, in turn, doesn't ask me what it was like to play at Live Aid—"

"Oh," said Tom, who'd once considered asking Colm that very question.

"—and he showed no interest in Sybella, so no worries there."

Although, Tom realised, Sebastian's sudden materialisation in the village hall yesterday seemed to suggest otherwise. "Well," he said, "these drawings look very . . . assured."

"We'd been talking about an art college in the fall." Colm picked up one of the sketchbooks and began flipping through it. "Perhaps the one in Bristol that Mitsuko went to. She'd be nearer home. Here, that is. Far enough away from London and Oona and her pernicious influence, ha!" He slammed the sketchbook down on the desk. "She was beginning to put together a portfolio. And now . . ."

He left the rest unsaid and looked vacantly around the room.

"Sybella spent many hours up here. And she wasn't"—he turned to Tom, his eyes flecked with anger—"drugging, as apparently half the village thinks."

"That was only the colonel being obtuse," Tom responded, then thought guiltily of Madrun. And who else? he wondered. The darker thoughts at his breakfast table he pushed from his mind.

"Advertising people say that one voiced complaint represents hundreds," Colm said.

"What a few in the village think isn't important."

"What did you think?"

"Colm, I've only been here a short while."

"But you were in an inner-city ministry. You know how people Sybella's age behave and act when . . . oh God, I'm sorry . . . your wife. I'd forgotten that they thought drugs were the reason for—"

"Have you been told nothing about . . . how . . . or why?"

Colm shook his head and moved to one of a pair of chintz-covered armchairs by the window. "Nothing," he replied, slumping into the soft seat. "This not knowing. I can't bear it. It *wasn't* drugs. And she was healthy . . . and full of life. And she wasn't . . . you know, depressed or the like." His face crumpled. "I've lost my child." He released a groan awful to hear and covered his face with his hands. Tom sank into the chair opposite, glanced at the dottings of lambkin clouds past the window's frame, and felt his heart contract with a pity not untainted by the ache of his own loss and the horror, the absolute horror, of losing a child.

"It's all right. I'm all right." Colm abruptly lifted his hands from his face and snuffled. The light played cruelly along the fan of lines at the corners of his eyes, which were red-rimmed and drowning in salt water. He affected to smile.

"Shall we have a prayer?" Tom asked.

"Yes, please."

"Ought we to wait for your wife?"

"I know Celia comes to church, but I think in her heart she really communes with Saint Sigmund, if you know what I mean."

Tom did.

They closed their eyes.

"Thank you," Colm said, opening his eyes and leaning back into the chair when Tom had finished his prayer. The atmosphere in the room had leavened, as though a kindly spirit had come and gone. After a moment's comfortable silence, Colm took a deep breath. "Perhaps we should see if Celia's back. She should be by now."

They both rose. Tom took a final glance through the window, at the billowy contours of the South Downs, at the patchwork of emerald fields. Off to the east, through morning's soft haze, he could make out the outline of St. Nicholas's blunt tower. Then, his eyes alerted by movement, he glanced down onto the roof of a red Astra pulling up on the gravel apron in front of Thornridge House.

"When you said your wife had gone out for a ride, you meant on a horse, yes?"

"Of course," Colm responded from the doorwell.

Who's this then? Tom wondered. But he didn't have to wonder long. As soon as he saw the vehicle doors open and noted the stout thighs of the two about to exit he knew who the visitors were. A cold stone dropped onto his heart.

CHAPTER EIGHT

"Vicar, you look the worse for wear."

"I've been at the Parrys'."

"Ah." Eric whipped a bar towel around a pint glass, and then examined it in the Church House Inn's muted light. "Grim, that. I'd go round the twist if something like that happened to one of my lot. Speaking of which"—he directed his attention somewhere below the bar—"you, out of there. You're not supposed to be in here."

"I wondered what that noise was," Tom remarked, as he watched Jack Swan, Eric's youngest, glued to his Game Boy, emerge from between two barrels.

"He hasn't been without that thing since Christmas. Costing me a fortune in batteries. Jack—go out back. You'll just be underfoot in the kitchen." Eric grunted and placed the glass on an overhead rack. "I look forward to the end of half-term."

Tom watched Jack disappear through the swing doors and out, presumably, to the rear of the Church House Inn. At least with Miranda, he had only one child to worry about. But now, since leaving the Parrys', his worry had spread to all the village's young people.

"What'll it be?" Eric asked him. "Vicar's Ruin?"

"I'll manage a half."

After a well-practised pull on the pump handle, Eric deposited the frothy glass in front of Tom, then moved down the bar to serve an unfamiliar elderly couple gawping at the chalkboard for the lunch specials. Tom turned to look into the crowded saloon. Perhaps some seniors' coach tour had landed up in Thornford. He spotted Fred Pike by himself in the inglenook staring vacantly at the kippered ceiling. He was reminded of a cheerless task: to tell Fred to add grave digging to his week's schedule.

"How are Colm and Celia coping?" Eric's generous belly once more appeared in front of Tom.

"The police arrived when I was there." Tom dropped his voice, despite the ambient noise of conversation in the room. "CID. A Detective Inspector Bliss and Detective Sergeant Blessing."

"Ah."

"You don't seem surprised."

"Belinda called me on my mobile this morning when I was at the cash-and-carry. Some copper came round for my morris stick—"

"Oh . . ." Tom groaned. His worst fears were being confirmed.

"—and Belinda talked with Julia, who said they had taken away all the . . . whatever you call those taiko drumsticks."

"*Bachi*, I think."

"*Bachi.*"

"And none of the other morris sticks, then?"

"Not so I've heard. At least none of the lads has called to say. But my morris stick was the only one in the village hall, right? My fool son took it to see if it would work with the taiko drums. The sticks are very similar."

"When did Daniel take it?"

"I'm presuming for the Sunday afternoon rehearsal, but I don't know. And his mother doesn't know where he is. Probably some-where with a football." Eric frowned, picking up the bar towel and absently wiping at the ring of moisture left by Tom's glass. "What did the coppers have to say at the Parrys'?"

"They asked to speak to Colm and Celia privately, though I did hear them say they found Sybella's Vespa parked up the road a fair way. But their presence, their body language, their stony faces were enough. I said I'd stay on, if there was anything I could do—and I think Colm would have welcomed it—but Celia had me out the door and on my bike before you could say spongy crumbs."

"Charming."

"Well, I didn't want to intrude further on their grief. And I'm sure Celia feels being a psychologist gives her an edge over a priest in therapeutic matters."

Eric threw the towel over this shoulder and leaned closer to Tom. "Well, that's it then. Belinda and I have been here fifteen years, and this is the first . . ." He glanced up and down the bar as if the right expression were seated at one end or the other. ". . . instance of—I don't know what to call it?—'foul play'? Somehow I never ex-pected there to ever be one. Coming from Birmingham, as we did, we thought it would be—what's the word . . . ?"

"Idyllic?"

"Yes, that one. And it has been. Until now. Well, except for a spot of graffiti now and again and Fred over there nicking things when he's on the job, but that's normal. Yes, luv," he said to a beaky-looking woman who popped up down the counter, leaving Tom speculating on paradise lost.

"You stayed in the hall yesterday when the coppers came, didn't you?" Eric asked on his return.

Tom shuddered. "I watched Sybella being pulled from the drum. There didn't seem to be any blood or the like. I suppose the forensic examination might find something."

Eric shook his head in thought. "I hardly knew the girl, really. She could be a bit sarky down at the Waterside, those rare moments when I can get Belinda away for a quiet meal . . . actually, I'm surprised Liam kept her on so long. Or that she stayed. Most of his waitstaff leaves in tears before a week is out.

"Anyway, she didn't come in here much. And when she did, she was usually alone and had a sketchpad with her. Didn't seem to pay any mind to anyone, I don't think." He looked faintly puzzled. "Although . . ."

"What?"

Eric paused, frowned, and then said, "Sorry, I'd thought of something, but it vanished." He shrugged, then directed one of his servers with plates of food up and down her arms towards one of the tables near the window. "How could this have happened? When could it?"

"Julia mentioned that the hall doors were unlocked when she came early yesterday morning to prepare for the Twelve Drummers' performance," Tom mused. "And she said she thought she was the first in. So either Joyce Pike didn't lock up the evening before, or Joyce had been in even earlier than Julia."

"Then how had Julia expected to get in?"

"I guess she would have called on Joyce."

"But Joyce isn't the only one with a key, you know. All sorts have keys. Members of the parish council, members of the different clubs—the art group, the WI . . . Belinda has one because the Mothers' Union meets at the village hall. I expect Julia has her own key."

But Tom's thoughts had taken a different track. "When did you close the pub Sunday night?"

"The usual. Ten-thirty."

Tom's mind took a bird's-eye view of the village. In daylight anyone accessing the village hall had a decent chance of being witnessed. After sunset, with no street lighting, secrecy was better assured. The village was pitch. If you didn't have a torch, and you were unfamiliar with the roads and lanes, you had to grope your way, orienting yourself by running your hands over the stone walls that demarcated villagers' properties. Still, evening activity—particularly in the vicinity of the pub—wasn't absent. If you stepped out of the pub into Church Lane, you might look left, up Pennycross Road in the direction of the village hall. You might, in the bit of light reflected from the pub, see someone disappear into the darkness up the road, or appear out of it.

"I suppose you didn't see anything . . . unusual Sunday evening?"

Eric shook his head. "It was a Sunday evening like all Sunday evenings. Even though it was Bank Holiday, all we had in were a few of the regular punters." He glanced around the pub, as if reimagining the scene that night. "And if you're wondering if I saw anything unusual in the lane, no. I think Belinda served a couple at one of the outside tables early in the evening, but I stayed inside. After that couple had finished their supper, the outside tables were empty. Once it gets dark, people tend to come in where it's cosy. It's May. It's still a bit cool in the evenings."

"What about after closing?"

Eric shook his head again. "When we push the stragglers out the door and we're done clearing, I always step out and have a fag. But that can be near midnight. It's lovely, dead quiet. The village is peaceful and by that time the floodlights on the church have switched off, so I can see the stars." He released a sigh like a bellows and a kind of dopey grin settled on his face. "Sometimes I think it's the only moment of peace I get."

Tom smiled and waited.

"Anyway," Eric continued, "Sunday late was calm as the millpond in July. Some nights there're a few teenage yobs about. And sometimes someone is driving back into the village from some outing in Torquay or wherever. But not this Sunday."

"I suppose a postmortem might narrow timing." Tom reflected that it hadn't in Lisbeth's case. It hadn't mattered; her wound had been too fresh when he had found her body.

Eric crossed his arms over his burly chest and peered into the middle distance. "There were visitors to the village, it being Bank Holiday weekend and all, and there's folk in many of the holiday cottages. That couple who had supper here Sunday, for instance. Perhaps one of them is a murderous raving loony."

"Meaning Sybella's death was a random act by some mentally ill stranger?"

"Well . . . yes. I guess that's what I've been assuming. Some nutter got into the hall somehow and picked up whatever stick was lying about and . . ." A kind of dawning flashed in Eric's eyes. "You don't mean . . . you don't really think this was . . . deliberate, planned. What's the word?"

"'Premeditated'? I don't know. It's horrible to think it, but it's a possibility, isn't it? Did the police say anything to Belinda?"

A faint look of horror crossed Eric's features. "That means it could be someone from the village. I'm not sure what's worse. Having it be a stranger or having it be your neighbour. Whatever it is," he dropped his voice to a whisper, "once it becomes common knowledge it's murder, it's going to put the boot up this village's arse. Won't be good for trade. Everyone will stay home and lock their doors."

Tom raised a censorious eyebrow.

"That was an afterthought," Eric added hastily, snatching up his cloth again and rubbing vigorously at the counter. "Then why kill her? Sybella was just a kid, really. Maybe it was someone from outside after all—but with a motive. Someone from London? Someone in her past?"

"Nineteen-year-olds don't usually have much of a past."

"Sybella lived a little faster than most."

"But not in Thornford, according to Colm."

"Still . . . Never mind." He continued, speaking through closed teeth, "Here's Sebastian just come in. You can discuss this with him and it won't go any farther. That man could do self-possession for England. Sebastian!" Eric boomed. "The usual?"

"And a roast beef sandwich, if you can do that," Sebastian said, examining the chalkboard with the lunch specials.

"You could come have lunch at the vicarage. I'm sure Mrs. P. has enough to feed the Household Cavalry."

"That's very kind, Tom. I think I'd like to be alone."

Tom noted a copy of *Cricket World* under Sebastian's arm. The verger stood almost at attention, his other hand behind his back, as Eric shouted the food order into the kitchen. The way Sebastian carried himself made Tom wonder at times if he had been in the army, or gone to a very good prep school, or been in a monastery, or passed through some other demanding institution. He would have asked, but Sebastian gently but firmly managed to deflect enquiry. It was as if he were swaddled in one of those force fields that attend creatures in science fiction films. Simply asking who his people were had led to the rather cheerless statement—though equably relayed— that he had lost connection to his family. Probing further seemed churlish. Tom had thought at times of looking for Sebastian's CV— it had to be somewhere in the middens of paper he'd inherited from his previous incumbents—but Sebastian was such a thoroughly con- scientious verger, meticulous in his care of St. Nicholas's and its fur- nishings and relics, diligent in his liturgical duties, that there seemed to be no reason to do so, other than idle curiosity. Noting Sebastian absent his gardening kit—he was wearing jeans, true, but the white shirt was dress, not T—Tom asked:

"You haven't been up to see the colonel, by any chance, have you?"

"I've just returned."

"And how is he?"

Sebastian had heavy lips, a contrast to the subtle shadows and planes of the rest of his face, but they thinned to a line before he replied, "Not well."

"I'm paying a visit this afternoon."

Eric set down Sebastian's drink. "And I'm sending Daniel up with some grapes and a decent apology."

"He didn't deliberately push the colonel over—" Tom began.

"Nevertheless . . . !"

"I think Phillip might appreciate a visit when he gets home," Sebastian said gravely, taking a sip of his ale while Eric, grunting noncommittally, moved down the bar to serve another customer.

Sebastian turned to study the room for an empty table.

"One thing," Tom said. "We have a funeral on Friday."

"Sybella?"

Tom nodded, studied Sebastian's eyes a moment, searching for some hint of foreknowledge. "There seems to be every indication that Sybella's death was neither accident nor suicide."

Sebastian held his gaze for the time it took to absorb the implications of Tom's phrasing, then dropped his eyes. "I see," he said, then gave an odd little nod, as if bowing to the inevitability of fate, and headed to a table near the fireplace that a couple appeared to be vacating.

Was he wrong, Tom wondered, or had he seen a flicker of fear in Sebastian's eyes?

Eric broke into his thoughts. "Are you any wiser to the ways of the world than you were a few minutes ago?"

"Meaning?"

"Him. Sebastian." Eric motioned with his head.

Tom laughed and drained the last of his glass. He moved to leave, but he was arrested by the ruminative expression on Eric's face. He followed the publican's gaze into the saloon, past the departing couple, to the table where Sebastian was sitting, folding his magazine open. Then Eric snapped his fingers in the universal gesture of enlightenment. He smiled at Tom, satisfaction wreathing his plump cheeks. He said:

"I've just remembered what I'd forgot I'd remembered!"

CHAPTER NINE

"You don't happen to know how the colonel is?" Tom hailed Alastair, crossing paths with him as he exited the pay-and-display at Torbay Hospital.

"I'm told his pain's being managed." His brother-in-law replied with the air of a man who'd done a day's work and was off to the links. "He was X-rayed in emergency yesterday. The head of his right femur is broken, which should put him in line for a hip replacement, but—"

"Risky at his age—an operation like that."

"I was just about to say, Tom." Alastair raised an eyebrow. "There's going to be some wait-and-see. He does have some underlying health problems—high blood pressure, for instance. The orthopaedic consultant will monitor him for the next few days."

"And if it's thought he can't withstand surgery?"

"His bones won't knit on their own. The only other option would be for Phillip to go into some sort of care. He'd have to spend the rest of his life on a morphine drip." He paused. "For a man his age, though, Phillip is in reasonably decent shape."

"Well, you'd know. You are his GP," Tom responded, realising he had unconsciously echoed Julia's very words, which he'd overheard the day before, at the May Fayre, shortly after the Twelve Drummers Drumming had completed its performance and before word seeped out into the holiday crowd that a tragedy greater than an elderly gentleman's mishap had been visited on the village hall. Only Julia had inflected the words differently and more emphatically.

"There is nothing I can do in such a situation," Alastair had told his furious wife in a heated whisper that nevertheless managed to travel to Tom's ears. He was standing not far behind them. "What you do is call an ambulance."

"That's what I did."

"Then you didn't need to drag me from home, did you? I'd only got in the door—"

"He *is* your private patient, Alastair."

"—and I was set to watch the Spanish Open on—"

A breeze shifted the direction of their voices. Then, as Tom was reflecting on the strained state of the Hennis relationship and wondering what he might do, he heard Julia utter Sybella's name. From Alastair came a sigh of exasperation, the words of which Tom couldn't catch, then a more audible reprise of his earlier defence. "I feel terrible for Colm, Julia, but there's little I can do in such a circumstance. Doctors can't bring people back to life."

Recalling the row and its culmination in Sybella's name, Tom asked Alastair, "Were you Sybella's?"

"Sybella's what?"

"GP."

"Would that be any of your business, Tom?"

"Sorry. My mind seems to be on yesterday's misfortunes."

Alastair's mouth formed a thin line. "Well, as it happens, yes, I am—or was—her GP. Is this relevant to something?"

"No, I suppose not. Not now. Since it doesn't appear she died from natural causes."

"Indeed."

"You know?"

"Tom, where do you think postmortems are performed?"

"Then . . . ?"

"Then what?"

"How was she killed?"

"Aren't you a bit nosy for a new-model vicar? Does it matter *how* she died?" Alastair appeared aggressively amused.

"Of course it matters," Tom responded with some heat. "I expect the people in Thornford might want to know if there's some sort of deranged individual wandering about that they might wish to protect themselves from in some fashion!"

Alastair glared at him. His rather prominent ears had taken on a red tinge. "It is my understanding," he responded through strained teeth, "that Miss Parry suffered a subdural hematoma."

"In other words, someone hit her over the head."

"It would seem so."

"It's certain then."

"Are you done? May I go? I have other things to attend to this afternoon."

As Alastair turned sharply towards the staff parking lot, Tom reflected that in the dozen years he had known Alastair even a regular blokeish conversation had somehow eluded them. He had wrestled dutifully with his inability to forge some sort of bond—family ties added obligation to the task—and he had had Alastair in the back of his mind more than once when delivering a sermon on the subject of Christian love, that through God's grace we can love someone we might not particularly like, but he found that trying to *like* Alastair was at times the spiritual equivalent of having to go to the dentist. It wasn't his fault that Lisbeth had thrown Alastair over for him, Tom. How was he to blame for the manoeuverings of the female heart?

But blamed he was, though he had not consciously snatched Lisbeth from Alastair's arms. He knew almost nothing of the man until Alastair appeared at the Rose home in Golders Green one Friday evening arm in arm with Julia, which startled Lisbeth's parents—and Lisbeth, who had brought Tom for his first Shabbat. In those days, Alastair had advanced to Cambridge's reserve crew for the Oxford and Cambridge Boat Race, looked enviably fit, and radiated a sort of animal confidence that Tom could see—though was loath to admit—would be attractive to women. Seated across from them as Lisbeth's father recited Kiddush, Tom had sneaked a glance and had thought them a handsome pair, as surely as Lisbeth and Alastair must once have looked a handsome pair in the very seats. Julia had had the grace to let her composure falter when Lisbeth, not her parents, opened the door to her and Alastair (her driving up to London from Cambridge with Alastair had been an impulse), but she'd recovered quickly. Alastair, too, had exhibited similar rue. "Hello, it's me again," he'd said with a sheepish grin. But he, too, had quickly righted himself, as if he were permanently entitled to at least *one* of the beautiful Rose sisters. In those early days, yet unattuned to the wars of the Roses, Tom had thought the affection between the pair to be genuine, though he had been uncomfortably aware of Alastair's cool and critical gaze falling upon him—and Lisbeth—in unguarded moments the rest of that very awkward weekend.

An ice age grew up between the sisters beginning then. Lisbeth had viewed Julia's taking up with Alastair as little more than sibling rivalry run riot. As for Alastair, she had muttered darkly, as they drove back to Cambridge: He was doing little more than exacting a peculiar revenge. With her, with their combined income from medical practice, he would find the perfect village and raise the perfect children in luxury. He had life all figured out for them, Lisbeth had said, but she didn't want her life all figured out. She wanted, she had declared, turning to him in the car, smiling, a life more messy and unpredictable.

The ice age began to thaw only when Julia had miscarried a child some eighteen months before Lisbeth's murder. Tom's charitable view had always been that Alastair had fetched up with the prettier (by a titch) and more vivacious of the two sisters; therefore he ought to be well pleased with his choice. Indeed, now Julia was *living;* Lisbeth was not. And yet Alastair seemed to bristle with dissatisfactions unnamed, at least when Tom was in the vicinity. That cool gaze fell upon him still. Mercifully, with Miranda, however, Alastair was transfigured. No longer the prickly in-law, he became the attentive uncle, for which Tom was grateful and in which he could detect no insincerity. He pushed through the door to the colonel's hospital room and thought, not for the first time since arriving in Thornford Regis: Perhaps if I took up golf . . .

Tom studied Colonel Northmore's ancient head resting against the pillow and the loop of plastic tubing marrying his bared arm to an IV pole. He watched the clear liquid drip into the ampoule then drip into the tubing, where it glided down and disappeared beneath a white bandage fringed by purple bruising on Colonel Northmore's exposed arm. He felt a pang of pity for the old man. *"When I am old and greyheaded, O God, forsake me not":* The psalm passed through his mind.

Each drop soothed the old gentleman's pain, but each drop, morphine-laced, clouded his mind so that his speech, uncharacteristically profuse, was uncharacteristically unclear—but for the occasional lucid punctuation. It was these—a name, a sentence fragment, a shout—that would pull Tom from his prayers and return his mind again to the antiseptic room where the afternoon sun, cascading through open venetians, was beginning to spill up the bedclothes. "Lydia," he heard this time. The colonel's eyelids remained sealed. His grey lips returned to their mumblings. Lydia had been Mrs. Northmore, gone nearly a quarter century now, lost to breast cancer. Phillip had soldiered on alone; he had been a soldier. Tom empathised for their shared circumstance, widowers both, and imagined though greater age brought greater expectation of separation, greater age did not assuage the suffering. By all accounts, Phillip had been the most uxorious of men, dedicatedly so: His father Edwin, a dashing Edwardian known for his charm and eccentricity, had been not only profligate with the family fortune, so clobbered by death duties after the war that he was forced to sell Thornridge House, but recklessly profligate with his seed. If your great-grandmother had been a servant up at the Big House in the days before the Great War, rumour had it, chances are you had some Northmore blood in your veins.

"Stop that!" Colonel Northmore interrupted Tom's reverie with the sort of crispness that attended his contributions to PCC meetings. Then he added, "Catherine." Must be Cat Northmore, his daughter, an actress of minor acclaim living in America—Los Angeles, most likely. Or was it New York? Madrun had mentioned Ms. Northmore was in a TV program about dead people who seemed to get out and about and meddle in living people's lives. Or was it busybody angels? At any rate, Catherine Northmore communicated with her father infrequently. Regarding the IV drip once again, Tom wondered if—no, determined *that*—Cat ought to be telephoned, and soon. Alastair may well be too sanguine about the success of an operation on an advanced octogenarian.

Phillip seemed to settle back to mumbling and Tom began to question the utility of his presence, other than perhaps a shared, silent communion. At home, myriad tasks awaited: the weekly pew leaflet to organise, wedding couples to schedule, a youth service to plan, a contribution to the parish magazine to write, his sermon to reconsider in light of the recent shock to the village. Not to mention preparation for Sybella's funeral, which, given her parents' repute, was going to necessitate liaising with the diocesan press office and organising some crowd control. He needed to put in a call to the archdeacon and have a talk with the funeral director.

He glanced again at the slumbering figure in the bed, then reached into his jacket pocket for the little case that held his professional cards. He would leave a note for the colonel, saying he had been round to visit. Instead, unthinkingly, he pulled out Mao's *Quo-*

tations. Bugger. He'd thought the weight in his pocket had been the card case, not this tiny red-plastic-covered book. He flipped the pages idly and glanced at selected passages.

> Be resolute, fear no sacrifice, and surmount every difficulty to win victory.

Useful for an inspiring speech to Thornford Regis Football Club, he considered, though identifying the source probably wasn't on.

> To investigate a problem is, indeed, to solve it.

How true, he thought. His mind returned to the great disturbance of Thornford's pleasant rhythms wrought by Sybella's puzzling death. What had Eric remembered in the pub a few hours earlier? He had remembered that Sybella's occasional presence in the Church House Inn had coincided with Sebastian's. And what had Sybella been doing each time? She had been sketching Sebastian—this reported to Eric by an inquisitive barmaid. Hadn't Tom viewed the results at Thornridge House that morning? He was unsurprised that a young woman should find Sebastian, with his distinguished straight nose and his firm jawline, alluring. Sunday mornings, during the processional through the nave, he'd sensed more eyes lingering on his verger than on him. Sebastian kept his hair long, though usually banded back, but for services, and at other times, he released the band and let his hair fall like a flaxen curtain around his face. "He looks all Jesusy," he overheard one pew-warmer whisper as he passed; he couldn't tell if the tone was approving or disapproving.

What did surprise Tom was Sebastian's reaction to Sybella's attentions. Thursday last, Eric reported, in the middle of a slow, rainy afternoon at the pub, Sebastian, who had been seated at the window, thumped his half-filled glass on the table, sprang from his chair, pitched himself halfway across the room, and snatched the sketch-pad from Sybella's hands. Wordlessly, he'd ripped several pages from the pad, torn them into pieces, and thrown them into the fireplace. Eric had been the sole witness.

"Only time I've seen Sebastian lose his famous cool," the landlord had told Tom.

"And did Sybella lose hers?" Tom asked.

Eric snorted. "I think she fancied it. Getting the attention and all. Didn't say a word, sort of smiled, picked up her bag, and walked out." He reflected: "It's the last time I saw her, now I think of it."

A sharp report from the colonel's lips broke Tom's reverie. He glanced up to see if Phillip had awakened, but the lids remained shut; as before, only tremulous lips suggested the workings of a restless dreaming mind. *What was that word he said?* Sounded like "omoray." Moray was a type of eel . . . and a Scottish district. He and Lisbeth had driven through on a week's holiday once, early in their marriage. But O'Moray? An Irish name? Wait! There was that old Scottish folk song, *Bonnie Earl o'Moray*. He remembered his honorary father, the Reverend Canon Christopher Holdsworth, rector of St. George's in Gravesend, reciting it at some church function. *They hae slain the Earl o'Moray / And laid him on the green.*

Colonel Northmore said the word again, this time with more bite. Really, Tom decided, this was getting to be entertaining, rather like deciphering code. Might the injured man be dreaming of Màiri White, the village bobby? *Oh, Màiri!* Unlikely. A little too passionate for the old duffer, though who knew what lurked in the hearts of old men widowed lo these many years? Tom himself gave a passing thought to PCSO White, then wished he hadn't. Copper she might be; all kitted out in her stab vest, her bowler hat, and what looked like a hundredweight of police clobber—torch, radio, and such—she looked the very model of a modern police community support officer—prim, on the whole. But off-duty, in mufti, as Màiri White had been at the May Fayre, where he had glimpsed her chatting with some children at the petting zoo, she had looked quite fetching, the pale skin of her arms exposed to the sun and her chestnut hair released from bondage. She had green eyes, too—duly noted when she lent assistance to members of the constabulary at the village hall—and really it was too soon, too soon, *much* too soon to be thinking about these things. No, *acting* upon them. Thoughts could not be quelled. Especially those sorts of thoughts. What would Jesus do? Who knew? He was a single fellow. And He didn't have a child, unless you subscribed to that *Da Vinci Code* bollocks.

Okoo. The colonel again. *Okoo*. That was familiar, yet somehow out of reach. Okoo. Lots of *O*'s in front of words. O'Coo? Irish? The O'Coos of County Kerry sort of thing? Somehow, Tom thought, the colonel didn't hold much of a brief for the Irish. *Oh! Koo!*? Sounded like a West End musical doomed to excoriating reviews and heavy tourist traffic. Didn't Prince Andrew once have a girlfriend named Koo? Yes, that's right. Koo Stark. She was in a naughty film. He would have liked to see it, but he had been—what?—eleven, twelve, just on the cusp of adolescence when there was a flap about it. It was all around the time of the Falklands War, he recalled. Videos were only just coming in. Of course, even if it had been on video and even if they had owned a video machine, he would never have got it past his two mothers. Well, Kate might have turned a blind eye. She was American and the more indulgent of the pair. But Dosh was his adoptive father's sister, and took her *in loco parentis* role with a certain seriousness.

Tom blinked and gave his head a sharp shake. He had been drifting off; the room seemed to swim in warmth, as hospital rooms often did. Why was he thinking about Koo Stark?

Okoo. There it was again.

So familiar.

He rose from his chair, partly to shake off his lethargy, partly to more closely examine the colonel, whose agitation had grown in the last minutes. A mask but for the quivering lips, the colonel's face was now a convulsion of tics and twitches. His eyebrows, rigid as grey cliffs, turned to grey waves, while his deeply scalloped ears seemed

to bob beside his motionless skull. And then, as Tom stood transfixed, a keening sound ascended from somewhere below the thin
hospital blanket. It mutated into an anguished cry as it escaped his
mouth.

"Oh, no, okoosan!"

And then his eyes jerked open.

He stared at Tom unseeing, as if witnessing some private horror.
Tom returned the *Quotations* to his pocket and then placed his hand
gently on the colonel's. He could feel the dry parchment-like quality of his flesh. "Colonel," he said softly, "you've been dreaming."

Tom observed the black dot in the colonel's irises contract as he
struggled to take in the novel environment. "Padre?" the old man
said with a kind of surprise. Then he twisted his head and let wondering eyes travel up the tube from his arm to the plastic bag dangling at the end of the aluminium pole.

"Colonel, you're in Torbay Hospital." When this didn't quite
register, Tom added: "In England." Which seemed stupidly obvious,
but had an effect. A wave of relief seemed to smooth the furrows in
the old man's face. "You're home," he further embellished. Well, near
as Bethlehem is to Jerusalem. "You were dreaming."

Phillip released a deep sigh. The heavy lids of his eyes sank to
half-mast. "I was back at Omori," he said, his voice thick with
phlegm.

"Omori?"

Phillip cleared his throat. "POW camp. Near Tokyo. Awful
place."

Tom nodded, removed his hand. He knew Colonel Northmore
had suffered the deprivations of a prisoner-of-war camp and wondered if he was often haunted by dreams of those days. "I had a
parishioner once who had been in a Japanese camp. In Singapore, I
believe it was. His descriptions of their treatment were grim."

"Savages."

"Who?"

"The Japs, of course." Tom was treated to a stony glance. His former parishioner had been similarly unrepentant in his characterisation. "I can't forgive them."

"I promise you I won't preach forgiveness this afternoon, Colonel. In any case, it's something you must come to in your own time."

"Not much of that left, I'm afraid."

"Oh, you'll be right as rain soon, I'm sure."

"No need to jolly me along, padre." Colonel Northmore's voice was acid. *"If thy brother trespass against thee, rebuke him; and if he repent, forgive him,"* he murmured.

"Saint Luke."

Phillip opened one eye. "Mmph." He opened the other eye. "There's never been a proper apology, you know. Or proper compensation."

"From the Japanese, you mean."

"When the emperor came to London, I sent my campaign medals back to Buckingham Palace."

Tom frowned. He paid little attention to state visits of foreign royalty. This was more Madrun's bailiwick.

"It was in '71," the colonel added. "You wouldn't remember."

"I was probably little more than a zygote, if that."

"A what?"

"It's nothing, Colonel. Perhaps you should rest."

"Fed us rice with rat droppings in it, you know," the colonel continued, oblivious. "And they would beat us for nothing." He pulled his unencumbered right arm out from under the covers and began to weakly slice the air. "The guards would swank about wearing long heavy sticks like samurai warriors, you know, and if . . ."

"Yes?"

"He was mad, you know."

"Who?"

"A sadist. You could see it in his eyes," the colonel went on, his earlier clarity seeming to descend into a kind of agitated trance. "He took my socks, you know. Lydia knitted them for me. They were the last thing she . . . and when I took them back . . ."

"Yes?" Tom glanced at the IV drip, wondering if it was emitting more drips of morphine.

". . . I felt nothing. I didn't feel the pain, I was that furious. But I remember the sound. *Thwup . . . thwup . . . thwup*—"

"Of the stick hitting you?"

"You were there?"

"No, Colonel, I wasn't." Tom looked into the rheumy eyes. "Now, you really must rest."

"*Thwup . . . thwup . . . thwup . . .*"

Tom reached across the bed, took Phillip's arm, which was continuing to slice the air, and set it on the bed gently. The voicings fell to mutterings, then, with a sigh, the colonel closed his eyes and seemed to sink back into the bed. In truth Tom's former parishioner had told him few of the details of life in a Japanese prison camp. It's not something I can really tell civilised people about, he had said. So Tom had done a little research and had come across candid accounts—more often by Americans—of the brutality meted out: the beatings, the interrogations, the near starvation. He could only imagine that such horror haunted a man all his life, punctuated his reveries, intruded on his dreams, triggered by who-knows-what— a scent, a sound, a sight. What had triggered the colonel to relive— with drug-induced candour—a particular episode of brutality—over a sock, of all things—might be answered only in the sparking synapses of the brain.

Tom resettled in his chair, bowed his head, and silently said a prayer for Colonel Northmore's recovery. Then, raising his head, he glanced again at the resting figure. The colonel's mouth was hanging slightly ajar, emitting a faint wheeze with each shallow breath. He does look frail, Tom thought. Julia had pointed the colonel out in the street the very first day when he and Miranda visited Thornford the year before, and he had taken note of the robust figure in the brown herringbone jacket and the tattersall shirt, the Jack Russell's lead in one hand and a silver-topped malacca cane in the other. A year later, greeting the colonel as his church council treasurer, he had thought Phillip less vigorous, a little distracted, apt to go off on a tangent. Rising, he gave a passing thought to who among the villagers might be an adequate substitute for Phillip on the PCC—no one came to mind—then he reproved himself for contradicting in thought what he had sought in prayer—the colonel's full recovery.

As he turned to leave, the colonel's eyes once again flashed open. He stared at Tom accusingly. "What have you done," he barked with exceptional clarity, *"with my walking stick!"*

here wasn't much he could tell the detectives. Madrun had taken the call at the vicarage while he had been up at hospital and arranged for DI Derek Bliss and DS Colin Blessing from Totnes CID to talk with him at four-thirty, which he was more than willing to do, though—the churlish thought flitted through his brain— it compromised, as events so often did, the precious time he had carved out to make a start on his sermon. The regrettably named duo—Bliss shifted continually in his chair as though plagued by a scorching case of hemorrhoids; Blessing was cursed with an almost transfixing homeliness—plunked themselves down heavily (for they were both heavy men) on the leather armchairs opposite the crowded desk in his study and accepted the tea that Madrun provided.

The sorts of questions the detectives asked weren't entirely unfamiliar. Tom had been down this road before. In Bristol, it was he who had found his wife's body, and the happenstance of being first had brought with it a peculiar reversal, at least to a priest: The first were not last in police hermeneutics; the first were first. As Bristol

CID's automatic prime suspect in the death of Dr. Lisbeth Rose, Tom had been subject to the cold scrutiny of two detectives—both women, as it happened—who dissected his marriage to Lisbeth, their relationships, their backgrounds, their finances, with an almost forensic zeal.

Bliss and Blessing, by contrast, were almost matey. Blessing, clearly the older of the men, though junior in rank, took the lead, asking the questions and scribbling in a notebook, while Bliss twitched and occasionally barked a question. Chorea? Tourette's? Tom had wondered, realising belatedly that he was being drawn in sympathetically by their deficits, which may have been the strategy of this strange partnership: Sorry for them, one might easily blab all, simply to bring a little cheer to their blighted lives. He wanted nothing more than a speedy solution to the mystery of Sybella's death. But burned once and not entirely sympathetic to a breed that had yet to find his wife's killer or killers, his default was to hone to the line between verity and hearsay. Yes—again, they noted, having looked a little into his background—he had been the first to find the body, but—lucky old you, grinned Blessing—you weren't alone this time. Indeed not, Tom had observed, grimly, and relayed his version of the events of the May Fayre afternoon.

And then followed what Tom thought of as the inkling question—about his own movements late Sunday.

"We're obliged to ask," Blessing said, setting his cup on the edge of Tom's desk.

Tom studied the expression on his interlocutor's face, the matter-of-factness projected by the slightly twisted mouth and the steady gaze. He felt his hand slip across the smooth wood to grip the pencil he used for jotting notes. "There's no question then that this is—"

"We're treating this as a homicide, sir."

Tom's eyes travelled past Blessing, unseeingly, to the mahogany bookcase with its jumble of coloured spines and silver-framed pictures opposite. His thoughts were assaulted by a corrosive and unexpected spurt of rage: He was suffering, as he suffered in the days and weeks after Lisbeth's death, anger's powerful allure. He was angry now, blindingly angry, not only that the life of a young woman of his parish had been stolen, that her father had been left bereft, but—and he recognised his self-servingness—that the sweetness of this sweet village, this haven he had sought for his Miranda, had been horribly tainted. He shut his eyes. He would not be corrupted by anger. In Bristol, he had battled anger with prayer. Needs must again, and it was only an abrupt snapping noise, like a footfall in autumn leaves, that returned him to the presence of others in the room.

"Vicar?"

"Yes, I'm sorry. I—"

"Are you all right?"

Tom straightened in his chair. "Yes."

"Good."

Puzzled, Tom followed Blessing's downward glance and saw the pencil broken in his hand.

"I'm sorry," he said again. "I think I've been willing myself to believe that no such great evil had been visited on this village. It's the shock."

"Perfectly understandable, sir." Blessing said it perfunctorily. "Now, as to your whereabouts . . . ?"

Tom took a cleansing breath and replied that Sunday he had been nestled in the bosom of his family; otherwise he had not been inside the village hall since Wednesday last when he had addressed a meeting of the Mothers' Union.

"Do you know of any reason why anyone would wish to take Ms. Parry's life?" Bliss brushed biscuit crumbs from his tie.

"'Wish'?" Tom repeated. "You're referring to intent? To be precise, to murder?"

"Manslaughter is a possibility, but we're considering all possibilities."

"No, none at all," Tom replied numbly. Eric's story of Sebastian's pique over Sybella's sketching him in the pub flitted across his mind, but it was hearsay and it was trivial.

"You're sure?"

"Yes."

"Any idea why her body was placed in the drum?"

"None, I'm sorry to say."

"Seems a daft thing to do," Blessing speculated, needlessly wetting the tip of his pen with his tongue.

"Likely planned to remove it at a later hour," Bliss added conversationally, studying the contents of his teacup. "Perhaps he was about to be caught in the act."

Still numbed, Tom interjected slowly, "Are you supposing that someone from *Thornford* planned to kill Sybella?"

"Early days, Mr. Christmas, but it's a possibility, isn't it?" Blessing responded. "The drum suggests temporary lodgings. Very temporary. If it were some stranger happened across her, you'd think he'd just leave her body on the floor."

"It might be ritualistic," Bliss barked. "Sort of sending a message, like."

"Do you think?" Blessing addressed his partner.

"I don't know. What do you think?" Bliss turned to Tom with a smile that didn't spread to his eyes.

"I haven't a clue," Tom replied. "I very much wish I did."

"Noise haters?" Bliss suggested, shifting suddenly in his seat.

"Most people hate excessive noise, but—"

"Percussion revulsion?"

"Detective, I can hardly believe—"

"Japanophobia?"

Tom started. "Why would you think that?"

"The drum is of Japanese provenance, is it not, Mr. Christmas?" Blessing tapped his pen against his thigh.

"But Sybella had nothing to do with the drums, Japanese or not," Tom protested. "It was her father who bought the two big ones, including the whatsit—the *o-daiko* drum that Sybella was inside of."

"Ah, then maybe it was to get at Mr. Parry." Blessing said serenely.

Tom was shocked. He couldn't imagine anything in Colm's background that would lead to such an act of cruelty, and he said so. In the spotlight as a pop star, Colm had surely been well scrutinised; in private life, he had been pottering harmlessly in his garden for more than fifteen years, writing the occasional film score or tune for an advert, and generously lending his musical talents to a little country church and to the amateur theatre group. The villagers were very fond of him.

"And you've been in Thornford Regis how long, Mr. Christmas?" Bliss barked.

"About two months."

"Not very long, is it?"

Tom had to allow that it wasn't. And with that the interview ended. Rising from his chair, Blessing informed him that the parish council was permitting them use of the Old School Room on Church Walk while they carried out their enquiries. They would be in touch if they thought he could be any more help to them, which suggested to Tom that they didn't think he, townie that he was, would be. He watched them exit through the French doors into the late afternoon haze of the back garden and down the brick path with its borders of pinks and roses towards the millpond. Then he stared at his computer screen unseeingly, all thoughts of his sermon vanished from his mind.

CHAPTER ELEVEN

*T*om had had more successful confirmation classes in the past and, in part, he blamed the weather, which had grown unseasonably sultry as the afternoon wore into evening, portending that some cloud would soon take a notion to burst upon the village. In part, he blamed himself. He couldn't stop his mind from wandering over events of the past two days, sending him to realms untouched by the content in his copy of *Faith Confirmed*. And he didn't feel completely unfair blaming his three confirmands, or at least two of them, for the unholy bore the hour had been. Amber Sherwill was in his class; he knew through Madrun, who had heard it from Karla, who had overheard Mr. Sherwill say it in the post office to his wife—that if Amber completed confirmation, her reward would be an iPod. Apparently she insisted on a pink one, ghastly child, he thought uncharitably, recalling half an hour of her examining her nails, flicking her hair, and acknowledging the observations of others with an insufferable "whatever." He had finally had to tell her to switch her mobile *off*. She was only four years older than Miranda, he noted worriedly. Four years! It didn't bear thinking about.

Amber sat as far away from Charlie Pike as she could, taking the hard open-arm Queen Anne chair nearer the French doors rather than the soft, fat couch the others chose—which was a futile exercise in teenaged narcissism because Charlie paid her no mind anyway, and hadn't during the previous two classes. During those last two, however, Charlie had been engaged, asking some very searching questions about Jesus' death and resurrection. Once again, Tom had marvelled at the peculiar Pikes' clever spawn. This week, however, Charlie did nothing but fidget, stare off into the book-crowded corners of the vicarage study, and occasionally glance at him with a kind of dull misery.

Only his third confirmand, Penella Neels, was thoroughly engaged this Tuesday evening. She was one of eight women who collectively owned Thorn Barton, once the manor farm, dedicating it to organic produce and humanely raised dairy cows. Penella had taken confirmation classes at thirteen, but when the bishop arrived for the confirmation service, a bout of measles had kept her at home. Now, nearly twenty years later, she was keen to finish the job, though Tom wasn't sure why, as she did rather go on a bit about patriarchy, the Church's wretched treatment of women, and the like. He had thought earlier that perhaps a few of her seven cohorts had recruited her as an eco-feminist fifth columnist in the Church. If so, the undermining was bound to work, because he had been finding her—well, except perhaps for this lackluster evening—thoroughly charming. Much depends on delivery—as he had learned in his magician touring days as The Great Krimboni—and Penella delivered her comments with a kind of sweet earnestness, her head tilted, her blue eyes raised heavenwards like an ecstatic saint, one finger daintily buttressing her chin. She had a splendid set of bosoms, too, which her casual attire did little to conceal, behooving Tom to keep his eyes north of the buttressing finger, as any priest worth his stipend knew these days. He enjoyed sparring with her, as he had once enjoyed sparring with Lisbeth, who, not unpredictably, took a view that some of the tenets of Christianity were apt to strain credulity.

"I mean," Penella had said earlier, nibbling on one of Madrun's almond biscuits, "with the Virgin Birth, don't we have an entire religion founded on an oxymoron?"

Tom had been startled out of his reverie. His mind, which was much on Sybella, had been trailing around a conversation he had had earlier with Madrun, after Bliss and Blessing had left. "I was curious, Mrs. Prowse," he had said to his housekeeper as she was bending down in the kitchen garden, cutting asparagus stalks, "why Colonel Northmore wanted to have a cup of tea inside the village hall yesterday when there was a very good tea tent outside?"

Madrun had straightened up and blown away a strand of hair that had landed near her mouth. "The noise, he said. All the kids running about."

"But in the small hall noisy kids were in some concentration— Mrs. Hennis's Twelve Drummers Drumming group."

Madrun shook dirt from the asparagus stalks. "Actually, the colonel was looking for his walking stick. He said he'd left it in the village the day before—"

"Sunday."

"Sunday, when he'd wandered in while out walking Bumble. I expect he was interested in the setting-up for the fayre . . . or perhaps wanted to get a glimpse of Mrs. Drewe's quilts."

Tom had regarded the evening meal's vegetable accompaniment with a certain relish (with hollandaise, *please*). "Colonel Northmore doesn't need a stick or a cane to walk."

"No. It's more a . . ."

"Affectation?"

"Yes, that's the word."

"And, of course, he did find the stick. He was holding it when Daniel crashed into him."

"We found it on the floor in the kitchen." Madrun regarded him with mild surprise, then a little consternation, then shock as a certain intelligence passed between them. But at that moment Tom's mobile rang, diverting his attention. There had been no name on the screen; the number was unfamiliar; and it had a London prefix. He smelled "press" and, as he had at Bristol, after Lisbeth's murder, he wondered how they had managed to get his private number. Madrun had deciphered his frown instantly. "I didn't give it to them," she'd responded. "I know better than that. If you go inside, I think you'll find your answerphone is full. After Mr. Kinsey disappeared, the rural dean told me quite expressly not to talk to the papers."

Bugger and a dozen other swearwords, Tom had thought, striding across the lawn and into the vicarage study to listen to his phone messages, all of them reporters enquiring about the time of Sybella's funeral (they somehow knew the date even though he had determined it with Colm only that morning), which they used as an excuse to seek his views on the recent tragedy in Thornford Regis. One had addressed him as "Father Christmas" and snickered through his entire delivery. The last call had been from the diocesan communications officer, an efficient woman with a cut-glass accent, and so he had spent the time before confirmation class assembled, between bites of supper served to him on a tray unhappily by Madrun, working on a suitable press statement. He had switched his phones off for the class, but now, sitting contemplating Penella's question, he could see the light on the answerphone registering a new call.

Penella shot him a perplexed glance and even Amber was arrested from the study of her fingernails. Only the sullen Charlie remained oblivious, his elbows resting on his knees, his eyes on the floor.

"Sorry," Tom said, "my wife—my late wife—once asked the very same question about the Virgin Birth."

He noted a new, sympathetic interest in his female listeners' eyes, the "widower effect," as he thought of it. As usual, it made him uncomfortable. He hastily interjected: "She took a wry view of some Christian tenets."

"I don't think the village has seen a vicar with a wife in thirty years," Penella mused. "Not that I'm old enough to really know." She tilted her head fetchingly. "I expect it's difficult being a vicar without having a wife."

"I do have Madrun," Tom responded lamely. "She's a great help."

"But not quite the same, is it?"

"Er . . . no." He glanced at Amber, who had taken to peering at Penella with what looked like a womanly scepticism far beyond her thirteen years. She turned to Tom:

"So, like, what was your answer to this, like, you know, whatever . . ."

"Oxymoron," Tom supplied, giving a passing thought to Amber's barbaric syntax. "I believe I said something to the effect of—"

Just then Madrun bustled into the room. "Sorry to interrupt, Mr. Christmas, but Penella is wanted at the farm urgently. I answered the phone in the kitchen. Indira has gone into labour."

"Oh!" Penella leapt up. "I'd best rush. Vicar, I am sorry. I'm afraid I'll have to leave."

"We might as well end here then," Tom responded, glancing at his watch. "It's getting late. Which hospital?" he added.

"No hospital," Penella replied over her shoulder, rushing out the study door.

"Indira is a cow," Madrun explained.

"Whatever," Amber declared, rolling her eyes and snatching a biscuit off the tray. She made to dart after Penella.

"Amber, wait. Perhaps Charlie might walk you home. You know, because . . ."

The girl peered at him suspiciously, then her eyes widened. "Oh! You mean because of Sybella."

"Or I could call your father."

"Don't! I mean—" She flicked a glance at Charlie and seemed to weigh some option. "Like, my dad's coming anyway. I'll meet him up the road. I'm okay. It's not dark yet."

Fibber, Tom thought, as she snatched up her copy of *Faith Confirmed,* but argument seemed futile. He looked worriedly after the departing girl as Madrun lifted the tray and presented it to Charlie, who had remained mute during the exchange.

"Take the last one with you," she said.

Charlie picked up the biscuit and nibbled its edge with a distinct lack of enthusiasm. He seemed disinclined to follow the others, cocking his head instead towards a nearby shelf as if the spines of the books thereon were of overwhelming interest. Tom looked at Madrun, who raised a comprehending eyebrow and glided out of the study. Tom got up and closed the door. Though clergy were cautioned against being alone with teenagers, he decided he'd take a chance. The boy, sunk into the sofa's blue and white striped chintz, looked utterly miserable.

"What did you tell your wife, Mr. Christmas?" he asked, almost his first words for the past hour. "About the . . . birth."

"That if you believe in God the impossible becomes possible."

Charlie stared at him, then looked away. "Did your wife believe in God?" he mumbled.

"Yes. In her own way." Tom resumed his seat and leaned towards the hunched-over boy. "Charlie, I think something is troubling you," he said, prepared for the usual adolescent agonies. "Is there anything I can do?"

The boy's eyes met his again. His hands had begun a paroxysm of twisting. "I think . . ." he began, his voice cracking. He gulped and started again. "I think Sybella died . . . because of me." The last words came out in a rush while his eyes, still holding Tom's, filled with a kind of horror.

"I see," Tom responded slowly, praying for a little time. He had expected parental or school difficulties and would have been very much happier if they were. "Now why would you think that?"

"Because I was with her in the village hall Sunday night."

"Late?"

"Not really. Sort of around nine-thirty or ten or so."

Tom took a deep breath. "And why were the two of you in the hall at that time of the evening?"

Charlie's face flushed. "Please don't tell anyone."

"I can't promise that, Charlie."

"But you're a priest!"

"Charlie, I'll do my best to keep your confidence, but if I think the police need to be involved then I'll have to take it further."

The boy released a soft moan. "It was her idea."

"Meeting in the hall?"

Charlie nodded.

"Whatever for?"

Charlie studied his feet. New trainers, Tom noticed. "She said she would sell me some stuff . . . drugs."

"Which drugs?"

"I don't know. Just, you know . . . something."

Tom received this information with dismay. It contradicted Colm's insistence that Sybella had been staying out of trouble. And it amplified what much of the village was likely thinking was true: that Sybella had not reformed. But he was alert to Charlie's phrasing.

"You mean," he responded, "that Sybella was going around offering some sorts of drugs to you and your friends?"

Charlie continued to stare at his feet. "No," he mumbled finally. "I mean, not that I know of." He flicked a nervous glance at Tom. "I asked her."

"And she agreed, I take it."

"Yes."

Tom looked at the boy writhing in shame, vaguely recalling his own experimentations at that age. The allure. Thinking one was so sophisticated. Poor Charlie—he didn't even know *which* drug he thought he wanted. "Then what happened?"

"She didn't have any."

"On her?"

"At all."

"I don't understand."

"She didn't use any of that stuff anymore, she said. She said she only pretended to, to get up the noses of people in Thornford, and that I was a prat for even wanting to because it would fu . . . mess up my life and get me into trouble and she knew because she had been there." Charlie stopped, as if surprised at his own volubility. Then his face was suffused again with blood. His voice rose a notch. "She laughed at me. She said I had *spots*!"

Tom suppressed a smile. Not only had Charlie spots, they were Himalayan. Though his own had been nothing like Charlie's, he could recall his own mortal agonies over adolescent acne—the mirror gazing, the popping, the creams. Then a cheerless thought intruded. He recalled the fierce blow Charlie had inflicted on Declan only the day before. Then, the punch had been triggered by simple frustration and perhaps a little chivalry. How had Charlie reacted to Sybella's taunts some few hours earlier?

"What did you do?"

Something in Tom's expression must have alerted the boy, because his face blazed. "I didn't hit her! I didn't! I . . ."

"What?"

". . . I heard something. I heard someone come in the front doors. So I ran out."

"But wouldn't you have crossed paths with—"

"I went out the fire exit, by the kitchen."

"In the small hall? You were in the small hall?"

"Yes."

"And no alarm was set off?"

"It says 'fire exit,' but it's not alarmed."

"And Sybella stayed behind?"

Charlie snuffled. "I expect so."

Tom let his mind range over the possible chain of events. "Your mum locks up, yes?" Charlie nodded. "Then how did you get in? Was Sybella already inside?"

"My mum leaves all her keys—to the village hall and to the cottages she cleans—in a drawer in the hallway, so I took them. I met Sybella outside the hall. She said to meet there at ten o'clock and we'll . . . you know, inside."

Tom frowned. By ten o'clock, even in late May with the solstice less than a month away, the village was plunged into darkness. He could think of several secluded spots in and around the village that would offer haven to a would-be drug dealer: the Old Orchard, the deeper reaches of the churchyard, the trees along the millpond. Why inside the village hall? He said as much to Charlie.

"I don't know. I didn't ask. Sorry."

Tom regarded the miserable teenager. "And you have no idea who it was coming into the hall? A familiar voice? No one called out? Outside, did you see anyone? A familiar car?"

To each question, Charlie shook his head.

"Did you switch on the lights in the small hall?"

"I wasn't supposed to be there. I mean . . ." He hung his head. ". . . I didn't ask if I could take the keys . . ."

"It would have been quite dark inside."

"There was a bit of moonlight, but my mum's the caretaker so I've been in the hall lots of times."

"You know your way around."

Charlie nodded.

Outside, drops of new rain splattered against the vicarage windows, lending a cosy insularity to the room. Tom ran his finger absently around his dog collar. "Charlie," he said gently, "you're not to blame for Sybella's death, you know."

"But I was the one who was on at her about buying drugs," he wailed.

"But, as you said, it was *her* idea to meet you in the village hall." Clearly, Tom thought, Sybella had had some other reason for seeking entrance to the hall Sunday night.

But, he wondered, whatever could it be?

The Vicarage

Thornford Regis TC9 6QX

28 MAY

Dear Mum,

When I wrote yesterday and told you that young Sybella had died, it never occurred to me that she might have died by someone else's hand. But it turns out to be true! Two detectives came around yesterday afternoon and talked with Mr. Christmas and they've been talking with other people in the village, too, though not me yet. It feels very odd for this to have happened in dear old Thornford R and of course when I went down the post office yesterday to mail your letter Sybella was all everyone could talk about. No one could recall anyone being murdered in the village before. Can you? I shall have to go through Dad's history very carefully and see if there's any mention. All I could think of was the time one of the Jecks twins put an axe into the head of the other, only being drunk he hit his brother with the blunt end and his brother being so thick skulled, he lived. I think I was about 8 at the time. Anyway, at the post office no one had any good idea why anyone would really want to take poor Sybella's *life. I use the word "really" because a couple of people did mention that Sybella gave them the same feeling she gave me which I told you about yesterday—that she somehow knew something secret about you. But how could she, I said, as she hadn't lived in Thornford all that long, but it was a bit funny, Mum, since everyone started to look a bit as if they really did have a guilty secret. Karla finally said they were all being very silly and that they'd see in the end that it was some drugs thing involving someone from London or maybe Torquay, and I supported her, though I was tempted to say that Mr. Christmas is certain it isn't anything to do with drugs. He said so after his confirmation class last night—something to do with Charlie Pike who stayed behind to have a private word with the vicar, though I'm not sure what as I couldn't hear through the door, though I could tell that Charlie was very upset about something. The Neighbourhood Watch has called a special meeting tomorrow morning at the v. hall to consider all this as there is some worry that there might be someone very unsavoury in the area up to no good. But you mustn't worry. The vicarage is safe as ~~houses the grave~~ Windsor Castle and Jago is very good with his fists, as you know from when he was a lad, so I expect if anyone tries to get into his cottage, they'll wish they hadn't. Sybella's funeral is set for Friday morning and vicar's talking about getting in something called CCTV so the service can be broadcast outside on a big television as there will likely be a crush of folk since Colm knew people in the entertainment business and, of course, there's Oona Blanc, who will probably come with some great entourage. ~~Quite exciting, really, though I mustn't think about it that way.~~ Poor Colm. I do feel so badly for him. Less so for Celia, which is uncharitable of me, but I can't help it. I was at the farm shop at Thorn Barton yesterday morning getting some lovely chicken for Mr. C.'s and Miranda's supper, when Celia trotted up on her horse dressed as casual as you please—here's a death in her family and you'd think she'd stop in and console her husband*

*rather than be seen out enjoying herself, but there she was
putting in a large order for the Big House, though perhaps it's for
a grand funeral tea—just thought of that now! Anyway, I said
how sorry I was and she was very gracious, in that practised
way she has, of course, but I could tell there wasn't much love lost
on that unfortunate child. Funny, Celia believes it's drugs-
related, too, involving some nasty person from Sybella's past, and
she must know since she's a ~~psycolo~~ psychologist and probably sees
the signs. Perhaps I shouldn't have mentioned Colm's first wife to
her. Penella Neels came out from the back when we were there
and offered her condolences, too. And of course she was at
confirmation class again last night. Funny how Penella was
never interested in being confirmed when Mr. James-Douglas
was vicar, but as soon as young Mr. Kinsey and young Mr.
Christmas came into view, suddenly the Church is just the thing.
She didn't quite finish her classes with Mr. Kinsey, as he went
and disappeared, so here she is all over again. She was wearing a
very tight jumper, but if she fancies her chances then she's got
another think coming. Mr. C. is too clever for that kind of show,
and she wouldn't be a suitable mother to Miranda. Late
afternoon, I went up to hospital to visit Phillip, who wasn't in
the best shape, poor man. At least he's in a room of his own, but
then he can afford to go private. They have him drugged for
pain, so he did ramble on a bit. He seemed very fretful. I'm not
sure if he even knew I was in the room. Well, must go and start
breakfast. Holy Communion this morning, so we're off to an
early start what with everything else to do. Cats are well. Jago
told me he was going to have his Kerra apply to Liam Drewe for
a server spot at the Waterside. I said I thought it was a bit
previous what with Sybella gone and all, but you know what
Jago's like—can't bear to see the grass grow under anyone's feet. I
think Kerra will have a time. She's a sweet girl and Liam's a
terror. Sybella could stand up to him—tough as nails, she was.
That's what London can do to you, I suppose, though why the*

*daughter of Colm Parry and Oona Blanc was working as a
waitress seems peculiar. "Work therapy" Celia called it at one of
her WI talks. But all the other village girls who have worked at
the Waterside haven't lasted long. We shall see. Love to Aunt
Gwen. Hope you have a better day than we're having in TR!*

*Much love,
Madrun*

*P.S. Mr. Christmas was asking me about Phillip's walking stick
yesterday, which I thought was peculiar, until I realised he was
worried that Phillip's stick might be the thing that killed
Sybella! You see, ~~he'd~~ Phillip had forgotten it overnight in the v.
hall, so someone could have picked it up and done the deed!
Dreadful!*

*P.P.S. What has the doctor said about your leg? It's very odd that
only one would swell and not the other. Can anyone help you on
with your compression tights?*

CHAPTER TWELVE

*H*ad Sebastian left the vestry door unlocked last night? Tom wondered as his key met no resistance in the Yale lock. He pushed against the stout old oak door, the events of the past few days triggering unwelcome thoughts for what might await inside, and scrutinised the untidy room as shadow yielded to sunlight. Then, through a haze of dust motes, he saw the figure of a woman silhouetted. Small, trim, she was turned away from him, hair silvered by light from the single lancet window.

"Good morning, Vicar." The figure did not turn.

"Ah, Miss Skynner, good morning," Tom responded with a modicum of relief and a dab of apprehension, recognising the no-nonsense voice as he stepped into the vestry. "I didn't expect to find you in here."

"I'm checking the list of weddings. I wanted to see if a certain date in September was free."

"May I be of any assistance?"

"No. Thank you. I can manage." She turned, the sunlight catching the sharp eyes behind the lenses of her spectacles. Tom had the feeling, as he often had in the presence of this particular churchwarden, that she was weighing him in some balance, as she might a parcel in the village post office that she managed, and was finding him wanting—poorly sellotaped, perhaps, or incorrectly addressed.

"I understand Charlie Pike has gone to the police about this worrying business at the village hall."

Tom gave a moment's thought to the many marvellous linkings that brought a private conversation to public knowledge within twelve short hours.

"I see the village drums have been beating," he responded.

"I'm not sure 'drums' is an *apt* metaphor in this instance, given that young woman's death," Karla countered predictably, brushing a dust mote off her shoulder.

"Yes, quite. I'm sorry." Tom stepped around her to the vestry's inner corner where his cassock was hanging from a peg in an open closet. As he did so, his leg banged against the sharp edge of a framed picture sticking out between the closet and the scarred black oak vestry table.

"Christ!" he exclaimed, groping for his shin, as the picture toppled over and crashed onto the stone floor, sending a nasty crack across the covering glass.

"Mr. Christmas!"

"I was merely invoking the deity, Miss Skynner; I am a priest," Tom gasped, hopping on one foot.

"Mind how you pick that up," Karla cautioned, making no move to do so herself. "A shard may slip out onto the floor."

As he indulged himself by caressing his shin, Tom surveyed the litter of papers, the old parish registry records and magazines, the towering piles of old hymnals, the limp drapery, the jumble of cleaning supplies, the boxes of candles. He muttered: "This vestry really is a tip."

"I don't disagree, but I don't think we should be throwing things out, do you? We might have need of them."

How typically Anglican, Tom decided, bending to lift the artwork off the floor. The dust on the frame edge adhered to his fingers. "Mr. Kinsey was wont to throw things out," Karla continued. "But I was able to prevail upon his better sensibilities to at least store them in here for the time being."

"Such as this picture, I presume." Tom gingerly slid it under the vestry table. Mercifully, the glass remained secure, though it would have to be replaced if the picture was to be returned to the sanctuary. It was a reproduction print of Saint Nicholas—presumably—ministering in some fashion to three children squashed into a wooden bathing tub, a garish and syrupy Victorian portrait that he was just as happy to let remain tucked in the vestry.

"A number of pictures and other things were taken down from the Lady chapel when the church was repainted a year ago . . . well, a little more than that—before my father died." Karla slapped closed the records book she was looking in. "Mr. Kinsey preferred a simpler aesthetic, and I can't say I disagreed, really—the place was a bit of a hodgepodge. Phillip and Roger wanted everything put back up, of course. They're both rather sentimental in that regard."

"You could have put them back up, I suppose, once Peter had—"

"Having a missing vicar rather concentrates the mind elsewhere, Mr. Christmas." Karla turned to him, her mouth set thin and bloodless. Her hair was pulled so tightly into a grey bun that her face was reined to the smoothness of tautly drawn cotton. Tom wondered, not for the first time, whether she ever let her hair down. Perhaps it fell—literally and metaphorically—on her annual January holiday with Madrun in Tenerife.

"Quite," was all he could think to say. He had been made aware of the commotion that ensued. A priest leaving is one thing; a priest vanishing is very much another. He looked again at the picture. "Anyway, I expect everyone's got used to the way things are now. No one has mentioned to me the notion of restoring this"—he wanted to say "treacly thing," but didn't—"picture to the church."

"Oh, I shouldn't mind if this one went up," Karla declared, perversely. "It's been in the church for over a hundred years, I believe. I was less fond of the other two."

"What other two?" Tom asked, glancing around the melancholy little room. Perhaps some new lighting, he thought, raising his eyes to the low-raftered ceiling with its single fluorescent light.

"They were rather . . . *Romish.*" Karla reset her glasses to peer at him. "One, I believe, depicted the Immaculate Conception, which I'm sure I don't need to tell you, Vicar, is not quite the thing in the Church of England."

Tom sighed inwardly. *How these things mattered to some people.* Instead he said: "But Mr. James-Douglas was a bit High Church, was he not?"

"A bit, I suppose you could say." Karla's lips set a disapproving line. "But he was really just being kind to old Mr. Northmore."

"The colonel?"

"No, no, Vicar. *Old* Mr. Northmore. The colonel's father. I'm sure someone's told you about old Mr. Northmore's reduced circumstances in the years after the war. Mr. James-Douglas bought the paintings from old Mr. Northmore, I think, just to help him along financially. Mr. James-Douglas was a very kind man," she added and flicked him a glance to suggest that perhaps he wasn't, or at least lacked the potential to be. "Anyway, I remember the two paintings going up in the Lady chapel when I was, oh, not quite a teenager. There was a little ceremony, I seem to recall." She paused and tucked an errant hair into her bun. "But as you say, Vicar, people get used to things. After a time, no one gave them a second glance."

"Where are they now?" Tom buttoned his cassock.

"I expect they're here somewhere. They weren't anywhere near as big as the Saint Nicolas portrait."

Tom watched her glance around as he reached for his surplice, then noted a look of enlightenment cross her face.

"I'm wrong," she said, and Tom thrilled to the words: So nice to hear them from the lips of a churchwarden, particularly this one. "Mr. Kinsey sent them out for cleaning . . . or restoration. Or both."

Mildly surprised, Tom said: "Then he must have been reconsidering them for the Lady chapel."

"Possibly."

"The restorers are certainly taking their time."

"Possibly," she said again. "But then I know very little about art, Mr. Christmas."

"Nor I."

"But I do know what I like. What a good thing you bumped into that Saint Nicholas. Being as its back has been to us all these months, I'd quite forgotten about it, but now that I see it . . ." Karla sidled past him towards the door that connected to the sanctuary. " . . . I think we ought to put it up, don't you? We'll need to send it off to those restorers to fix the glass."

"And would you know who they would be?" Tom gave a passing thought to leaving the outside door to the vestry unlocked. Perhaps art thieves with poor taste might be glad of an opportunity. . . .

"I don't. There must be a record somewhere."

Tom looked at the vestry's paper middens and thought about the middens in the vicarage office. Somewhere indeed.

CHAPTER THIRTEEN

*T*he south porch of St. Nicholas Church opened to a pea shingle path that descended through a terraced lawn to vanish into a shadowy border of trees that stood sentry along the millpond. To the east and to the west, gravestones—those nearest the church lichened, worn, and as irregularly set as wobbly teeth; those in the farther corners of the churchyard straight-edged, upright, and as evenly set as dentures—were a spectral counterpoint to the surround of sunlit blue and vivacious green. Adjusting his eyes to the brilliance of the midmorning, waiting by the porch's door for his tiny flock to pass and make their way along the downward path, Tom espied Fred Pike, a spade over his shoulder, standing above—just barely, it seemed, given his height—the new gravestones at the far southwest near the churchyard's high stone wall.

It was Sebastian who kept the grass between the gravestones closely mown and maintained the grounds, but by long-standing tradition, grave-digging duties were given over to Fred, rather than the funeral director's contractor, because he seemed to relish the task. Although Tom wondered why a man of his age—or any age—would willingly shift great clumps of Devon's red soil on a warm day all by himself. Fred took great pride in his tidy excavations, though Tom considered the pride a bit misplaced. He had taken only one funeral in Thornford to date—it had been Ned Skynner's, more than a year earlier—and he'd thought when he'd glanced down into the cavity just before the coffin was lowered that he'd seen better spadework. He wasn't badly placed to adjudicate these things—who, other than priests, sextons, and funeral directors' contractors, spends much time gazing into open graves?—but he allowed that perhaps country standards were less exacting.

He had a notion to ask after Fred's son. The previous evening, he had pulled a couple of umbrellas from the hall stand and accompanied Charlie down Poynton Shute and Orchard Hill to his parents' small wisteria-wreathed cottage. His unexpected presence at their door, he was assured to know, was the spur that sent the Pikes to the police.

"Vicar?"

The ladies—and they were all ladies—stood like birds in a flock at the top of the first terrace, regarding him inquisitively.

"Coming," he shouted, turning back momentarily to push shut the south porch door, thinking as he did so of the door to the village hall, and one of the last questions he had for Charlie as they tramped down Orchard Hill the evening before: After he had escorted Sybella into the hall, had he left the front door latched or unlatched? Did he turn the key partially—which opened the door but left it locked once it closed behind—or did he turn it fully—which left the door unlocked? Charlie couldn't remember, simply couldn't remember. And Tom could only imagine that in the excitement and fear he wouldn't remember. Too bad. But if the boy left it unlatched, anyone could have wandered in. If latched, then whoever Charlie had heard come in had had a key.

And who, as Eric had mentioned, had keys to the village hall?

Far too many people, most of them unaccounted for, just as too many people, many of them unaccounted for, likely had keys to the church—a circumstance that warranted scrutiny.

He stepped down the path, his feet crunching the gravel. The only other sounds came from bees, busy among the bluebells poking through the lawn between the gravestones, and the breeze brushing through the canopy of sycamore and alder trees. Fred, he noted, had placed his spade in the shadow of a great copper beech and had begun measuring along an untrammeled patch of grass. Several of the ladies followed his glance and by the time he reached them, they were all turned solemnly towards the southwest corner as though it were Mecca.

"Poor child," someone murmured.

"So wretched for Colm."

"I can hardly believe something like this has happened in Thornford."

There was a hubbub of agreement, then a weighted pause, pierced by the call of gulls over the millpond.

"Did you hear?" Someone broke their silence. "Colm's having this black choir come for the funeral."

"Oooh, never! Really? How interesting! What do you think, Vicar?"

"Anything that gives him peace of mind," Tom replied evenly, sensing a rising tide of tittle-tattle as they resumed walking, passing down through the canopy of trees to the millpond path.

"And Oona!"

"Won't that be something!"

"She's ever so thin, you know. It's the drugs."

"Yakking up in the toilet, more like. They don't eat, of course."

"She must be well past her sell-by date as a model, surely."

"Who else do you think is coming? Do you think Cliff Richard will be here?"

"Oh, Enid, don't be silly."

"You're showing your age, Enid. Sir Cliff was big in the sixties. Colm was a star in the eighties."

"For about *two* minutes."

"Who's Cliff Richard?" asked Violet Tucker, at twenty-three by far the youngest of the party.

"Good people," Tom interrupted in his best "good people" voice. He had been casting his eyes over the millpond waters sparkling in the sunshine, half his mind on the day he and some fellow ordinands had hired a punt at the Mill Pond in Cambridge. Some smartarse standing on the Clare College Bridge had reached down and grabbed the top of his pole, tipping him into the water. Shallow as the Cam was, not being able to swim was Tom's secret shame. As the punt drifted unguided under the bridge, he had panicked. Sitting on the bordering lawn reading had been medical student Lisbeth Rose. Her senior swimming certificate and her St. John's Ambulance first-aid course had proved most useful.

"Good people," he said again. "Remember, a young woman has died."

"We're not gossiping, Vicar," Florence Daintrey boomed in the voice that commanded the WI. Added her more demure sister-in-law, Venice: "We're simply very . . . concerned."

Tom was hard-pressed to see the distinction.

"*Very* concerned," Venice repeated for emphasis. "We've been double-bolting our door the last two nights."

"Me, too," Marg Farrant piped up.

"Do you think it's someone from the village?" Enid glanced tentatively at Tom. She was overdressed for the warmth of the day in a purple anorak and mincing along the path, as though each step required consideration.

"There was blue and white tape around the hall yesterday," Marg interjected before Tom could reply. "And these people wearing transparent overalls and boots going in and out and such."

"That would be scene-of-crime officers, dear."

"I *do* watch television, Flo," Marg responded witheringly, patting the braid knotted into a crown on the top of her head.

"But do you think . . . ?" Enid began again.

"That it was someone from the village?" Florence finished her thought. "Oh, surely not. Isn't there a Gypsy caravan over at—?"

"I thought it had to do with drugs?"

"Gypsies *sell* drugs, Ven."

"This is highly speculative, ladies." Tom managed to get a warning word in.

"But if it isn't someone from—"

"Well, who, Enid?" Flo interrupted with her carrying voice. "Sybella wasn't the most charming child in the village, but who would want to hurt her so?"

In the pause Tom thought he could see little thought clouds hovering in wooly bunches over his flock's heads. They were nearing the turn where the millpond path curved to join the walkway along the quay. Early season visitors sat on wooden benches, some with children (this being half-term) nearby feeding the geese.

"Liam!" Tilly Springett blurted, speaking for the first time. Her hands flew to her mouth. She looked at Tom guiltily.

The thought clouds vanished one by one. Breath passed sharply up five female noses.

"Do you think?" Ven squeaked.

"He was in prison at Bristol." Tilly was studying Tom nervously. "Did you know he'd been to prison, Vicar?"

"It crossed my mind he might have been," Tom allowed, the provenance of the tattoos on Liam's fingers on his mind. "But that doesn't mean—"

"I remember!" Florence interrupted, oblivious. "It was for GBH. He was one of those door-supervisor people at a club in Cheltenham. He wouldn't let some lad in . . ."

"That's right," Venice picked up the thread. "Hit him over the head."

"Really?" Tom interjected.

"Can't remember with what," Marg added with new excitement, as if Tom's interest had given them leave to gossip unrestrainedly. "But it caused permanent brain damage. He was sent down for four years or something."

"Oh, dear, I'd forgotten that bit," Venice said.

"I've always wondered why Mitsuko married him?" Enid murmured.

"I know why." Violet started to giggle. "He's ever so muscle-y. You know what I mean? Sort of . . . *forceful*." She hugged her purple cardigan around her middle.

"Violet!" several exclaimed.

"Makes my Mark seem a milquetoast," Violet added, a bright silly expression enlivening her chubby cheeks.

Marg cleared her throat loudly and jerked her head warningly in Tom's direction.

"Sorry, Vicar." Violet blushed. "My Mark's lovely."

"Really!" Florence added before Tom could remind them that wearing a dog collar didn't make him a prude. "Anyway, it's not funny. He has the most wretched temper—Liam I mean. He looks *very* capable—"

"And he's awfully jealous of Mitsuko, that's for certain," Venice added.

"I remember him once glaring at Mr. Kinsey," Marg said. "If looks could kill!"

"That's right," Enid added. "Mitsuko never much came to church when Mr. James-Douglas was vicar."

"Enid!"

"Well, it's true, Flo." Enid glanced at Tom speculatively.

"And what would this have to do with Sybella Parry anyway?" Florence harrumphed.

That silenced them for the moment. Tom looked over at Tilly, who had absented herself from the chatter and was wearing a worried frown.

Violet broke the silence. "Mark and I were able to get someone to sit with Ruby so we could have a meal at the Waterside Sunday evening," she began, lowering her voice as they approached the quay. "There was an *awful* row in the kitchen."

"What about?"

"Oh, Liam's often banging on about something," Florence butted in dismissively. "You can hear him through the doors to the kitchen cursing the chip pan."

"Liam doesn't do chips, Flo," Venice corrected her sister-in-law. "Remember, Marg, your Laura, when she was visiting that time, asking for chips with her sea bass rather than herbed potatoes?"

"Yes, he did get a bit shirty, now you mention it." Marg frowned, as if at the memory. "Anyway, I really think in the end, it's more of a bark-bite thing with Liam. The bark being worse and all. Hasn't he taken one of those anger-management thingies?"

"No, Marg, this was different."

"How?"

"I don't know. It was . . ." Violet paused, then added darkly, "the tone."

The bunch of them had stopped, as if not daring to step farther if they were going to continue this conversation. They were crushed together like commuters at Euston Station platform Friday after work. Tom could see various people on the quay regarding them with mild curiosity, then abruptly turn their attention towards some disturbance, possibly, on the other side of the Waterside.

"How do you mean—*tone*?" Marg asked.

Violet appeared to think about it. "Well, it wasn't the usual back-and-forth, no-we're-*not*-having-Sunday-lunch-with-your-mum, oh-yes-we-*are*-having-Sunday-lunch-with-my-mum sort of thing. It was mostly Liam carrying on. Quite sort of . . . distressed he sounded."

"Could you hear what they were saying?"

"No, not really. I thought perhaps I heard something about money, but maybe I think that because Mark and I always argue about money. Anyway, that's what I mean by 'tone.' It was embarrassing. We tried to ignore it. We'd only sat down. There was no one else in the place but for some couple I didn't recognise. We just gave each other these gruesome looks and tried to make light of it." Violet grimaced to indicate the expression they wore. "And then Sybella popped out of the kitchen."

"Oh!" Venice exclaimed. "Liam was shouting at *Sybella*. I thought it would be—"

"No, Mitsuko had been in the kitchen, too. At about the same time Sybella appeared in the dining room, I happened to glance out the window—we were seated sort of facing west—and I could see Mitsuko walking back up Fishers Hill with that determined little walk of hers."

"Then I wonder which one he was shouting at?" Enid asked.

Violet shrugged. "Both of them?"

"How did Sybella appear?" Tom asked despite himself. Over the women's heads he could see Bliss and Blessing walking from the restaurant towards a red car parked under the trees near the quay.

"Like the cat that got the cream. She sort of rolled her eyes at us, but she looked awfully pleased with herself."

"She does—did—like to provoke," Florence commented to a murmur of assent. "I mean, her ears! They looked like pincushions! Oh, look! There's those two detectives! Did you know they're commandeered the Old School Room? I wonder if they've been interrogating—"

"Really, Flo!" her sister-in-law interrupted. "'Interrogate' is a little strong, don't you think?"

"Shall we go in?" Tom sighed, eyeing the sandwich board glinting in the sun. "We look like we're waiting for a bus. If we stand here much longer, it'll be time for lunch."

❦

"I'm afraid it's self-serve this morning, ladies . . . Vicar," Liam said gruffly, gesturing to coffee urns on a side table that he was busy wiping with a cloth. "I'm a little understaffed at the minute and I've had other . . . interruptions this morning."

He turned to glance at them. No one had moved. It seemed as if the women had stepped into the restaurant as one and chosen to remain in a huddle. They stared at Liam. Liam stared at them. Then he scowled. His brow furrowed under a kerchief wrapped around his skull.

"What?" he snapped.

"Nothing," Tom lied. Bringing up the rear he had bumped into Venice's substantial backside, then ricocheted off her slimmer sister-in-law, setting the women jostling and swaying like bowling pins trying to right themselves.

"I'm sure you're familiar with self-service." Liam continued, his voice edged with sarcasm, mistaking the source of his patrons' reaction, "It's what you'd bloody get most places."

A gasp arose.

Liam looked taken aback. "Well, pardon me for—"

"Really, Mr. Drewe!" Florence huffed. "A young woman has died!"

Where have I heard that admonishment before? Tom wondered as Liam, first quizzical then comprehending, retorted:

"You don't think I know that?" His expression struggled for contrition as he lifted used coffee cups from a nearby table. "Look, I'm sorry if I've given offence. I've been run off my feet these last days." He gave his customers an assessing gaze as they unknotted themselves and plunked proprietary handbags on various of the small tables. "If any of you ladies fancy a job . . . ?"

"Oh . . . !" Venice began.

"Don't you dare," Florence hissed. "You have a perfectly good pension."

"Never mind."

"Well, if you do, Miss Daintrey . . ." Liam's face fell as he studied Venice edging her girth between the tables. "Anyway, as I say, coffee's here. There's a French roast and decaffeinated. And there're pastries baked fresh this morning. I have pear croissants; most of the chocolate croissants have gone, I'm afraid. There're some rosemary muffins and . . . a few other things—they're in back."

"Oh, goodie," Venice clapped her hands.

"*Really,* Ven!" Florence snapped as Liam cast his cloth over his shoulder and retreated through the push doors into the kitchen.

Tilly held back as the others stirred towards the serving table, cooing over the artful baking.

"Mrs. Springett?" Tom said to the old lady who appeared glued to the flooring. "Nothing for you?"

Tilly looked up at him. She seemed to have made a decision. "Will you sit with me, Father?"

"Of course."

"Alone?"

Tom raised an eyebrow. Tilly blushed and slapped at his hand. "Now don't be silly, Father. I'm old enough to be your grandmother."

Tom smiled. "Shall I get us two coffees? You sit and I'll bring them."

"And a chocolate croissant, please, if there's one left. Mr. Drewe's baking is awfully good."

Tom was the last in the queue. As he was pouring the coffee, Liam reemerged from the kitchen, a tray of pastries in hand. As he placed it on the table, Tom noted again the tattooed letters, one on each knuckle.

A C A B.

Always Carry A Bible.

All Coppers Are Bastards.

All *something* Are Bastards.

His eyes travelled from fingers to face. Liam witnessed the inspection and glowered at him.

"They came to see me yesterday," Tom remarked.

"Who?"

"The detectives who left here earlier. Bliss and Blessing."

"Wankers," Liam muttered.

"Do they have any idea who—?"

"Yeah, me, of course."

"You mean," Tom began, taken aback, "they're about to—?"

But Liam cut him off again. "They will. Just because in the past I . . . never mind! Look, you're spilling."

"Oops." Tom looked down to see a pool of steaming liquid spread across the table surface. "Sorry."

Liam furiously snatched paper napkins from a nearby pile and pushed Tom aside.

"I'm sorry," Tom said again, snatching the cup to his lips to catch the overflow. How little it took to set the man off. Seeking a different conversational gambit, he asked, "How is Mitsuko taking it?"

"Taking what?"

"The news about Sybella."

"How would I know? She's in Wales. Her father's having an operation. I thought it better not to bother her."

"I see. And she hasn't contacted you about it?"

"About what?" Liam mopped the dark liquid with impatient strokes.

"Sybella, for heaven's sake!" Tom replied with rising asperity. "I'm sure it's been on the news!"

"Is any of this your business?" Liam snarled.

"Well," Tom began, striving for an even tone, "let's see, your wife was a very good friend to Sybella and since your wife is one of my parishioners, I'm concerned for her well-being. I'm concerned about the well-being of this whole village in this sad time. I'm concerned for yours, too, come to that."

"Yeah, right." Liam slapped the wet napkins into a nearby bin. "That's the sort of bollocks Kinsey talked."

There being no suitable response to this oblique retort, Tom ignored him and reached for some dry napkins to wipe the side of his cup. He half expected Liam to stomp back to the kitchen—the bit about his predecessor seemed like an exit line—but he remained, fussily and unnecessarily tidying the array of cutlery and china on the table. Tom flicked him a glance, which Liam met, only this time hostility seemed to do battle with uncertainty in his razor-blue eyes.

"Look, I'm sorry," he muttered as Tom crumpled the damp napkin in his hand and took a second cup to fill. "I do try, you know."

"Try . . . ?"

"To . . . you know, keep it together. But . . ."

Tom waited. For a moment, the undifferentiated clucking voices in the background seemed to switch off and he found himself silently pulled by the strange spectacle of Liam beseeching him with his eyes, as if he were desperate to convey some message. Then, just as quickly, the sensation was gone. Sound rushed back like a wave. Liam's face shuttered. He turned abruptly and stepped towards the back of the room, towards the doors that led to the kitchen. Startled and a little disturbed, Tom could only wonder what—if anything—he had been vouchsafed.

"My granddaughter took me to a restaurant once in London where all the waiters were very rude."

"But London waiters are almost always rude," Tom said to Tilly, setting the coffee on the table. His mind was still tingling from his encounter with Liam.

"No, these were *very* rude, deliberately so," Tilly responded, turning her cup round to reach the handle. "They were all student actors, I think. The Guildhall drama school was just down the road."

She gave him a quizzical frown as he moved to take the chair opposite. Then he understood: He'd forgotten something important.

"I'll just nip back for that pastry."

"'Abuze,'" he said on his return, setting down two plates each conveying a croissant. "With a zed. I remember reading about it."

"That's right. I don't think it lasted very long."

"It's an off-putting name for a restaurant."

"It was comic, in its way. I suppose my granddaughter thought it would be a treat. But I found myself rather flustered having to defend my choice of starter. The staff mocked you at every turn." She took a dainty nibble on the edge of her pastry. "But for all that, the meal was disappointing."

"Not like this," Tom added after biting into his own.

"I expect that's why everyone puts up with Liam's temper. The food here is so very good. And the prices are decent. I don't know how he manages to stay in business, with the economy being so poor."

Tom glanced at her. Beatrice—Tilly to all—was the widow of a local farmer. She had moved into the village on her husband's death some ten years earlier. He suspected she was living on investments that had gone pear-shaped and that a meal out was a rare treat.

"Is there something you wanted to talk about?" he asked gently, unsure whether she was deliberating on something or simply enjoying the nosh. "Other than the flower rota or the linen rota . . . ?"

She smiled weakly. "Father—"

"'Tom,' if you can manage it. Or 'Vicar.'"

"I'm sorry. I got so used to Father James-Douglas . . . and then Mr. Kinsey preferred to be called . . . but he wasn't with us very long . . ." She trailed off. "At any rate . . . Vicar," she lowered her voice, "I'm a bit betwixt and between."

"Yes . . ."

"I'm sorry I brought up Liam's name when we were walking by the millpond."

"I thought you might be. The look on your face—"

"Well, you see, I've been worrying about what to do. What would be the Christian thing to do?" Tilly regarded him earnestly.

She had a sweet, plump face. "Liam's been much on my mind this last day or so."

"Mmm."

"Vicar, have you read Agatha Christie's novels? Greenway, her home, is in these parts, did you know? Just over the river."

"I visited it with Julia Hennis last year and read some of her books when I was a teenager. Why?"

"In them, there's sometimes a character who has seen something extremely important, but doesn't know it's important, but somehow the murderer knows that she knows and before she can tell anyone, he . . . kills her."

"Er . . . yes," Tom responded, after a quick parsing. "So you've seen something important."

"I don't know if it's important."

"But it's important enough to talk to me about it possibly being important."

Tilly chewed her croissant thoughtfully. "Yes."

"Well, then, you're farther ahead than those unfortunate characters in Agatha Christie's novels. You recognise the dilemma and are reporting it to someone, which is a kind of insurance against anything happening to you . . . I suppose . . . unless . . ." Tom smiled slyly. "I take it as a compliment that you don't think that *I'm,* you know . . ."

Tilly gasped. Put her hand up to her cheek. "The murderer? Vicar! I would never think that!" But she regarded him askance.

"I'm sorry. I think I may have added to your worry." He put down his coffee cup. "Perhaps I should preempt you and suggest that if you think you've seen something that might help the police with their enquiries about Sybella's death—which I presume is what this is about—that you do get in touch. I'm sure PCSO White could offer some advice if you're feeling tentative. Or I'll go with you to the Old School Room . . ."

"It might be nothing. And I don't want to cause bother."

"This is about Liam, yes?"

"I know he's a trial. And I know he must have some redeeming qualities—this food for instance. But I know he had a bad history. But he's also paid his debt to society, so it seems so unfair . . . and Mitsuko's such a sweet young woman, such an asset to the village. I don't believe for a minute that she and Mr. Kinsey . . ." Tilly glanced worriedly over at the women at the other tables. "And—"

"You're rambling a bit, Mrs. Springett."

"So I am. Avoidance, I daresay."

"Well, as Jesus said, 'Spit it out.'"

"Vicar! Jesus did not say that!"

"He might have. Much went unrecorded."

"Oh, Vicar," Tilly simpered.

"Then, as the psalmist said, 'Take heart.' That would be more in keeping." He waited for Mrs. Springett to come forth, but her attention had been diverted to the Waterside's door. Tom followed her glance.

"Oh, look!" she exclaimed. "Here's Mitsuko back. My, how very *unhappy* she looks."

CHAPTER FOURTEEN

"The laptop was there, and the external hard drive just behind it." Mitsuko pointed to a Jacobean trestle table against one wall, which was covered with the detritus of an artist's life—notebooks, coloured pencils, stacks of papers—all of it untidily framing a bare rectangle of dark oak in the middle. Only a couple of thin white cables, snaking over the table's back edge and falling behind stacks of clear plastic boxes filled with threads, fibres, and paints, hinted of the missing items.

"Oh . . . oh!" she gasped, surveying the table, then spinning around to look at the rest of the room. "Oh, no! The camera, too! My little digital! Ohhh."

"Are you sure?" Tom asked. He hadn't been in Mitsuko's studio before, but he marvelled at the amount of material she packed into the small back room of the Blackbird Gallery, which, in its previous life, had been a pet salon. God knows the village had enough dogs, but the owner had overestimated the need for canine shampoo-and-sets and had absconded before the bill collector arrived. Still, Tom thought, sniffing the air discreetly, the place did smell a bit doggy, even after all these years.

"Yes," Mitsuko moaned. "The camera gear—and the case of memory cards, too—were on that shelf next to the sewing machine." She slumped onto a stool, her long black hair moving like a curtain across her shoulders to frame her delicate features. "I remember thinking when I was leaving for Bridgend, perhaps I should take the camera with me, but my father's operation wasn't really a family occasion, so I changed my mind."

"And how is your father? I neglected to ask."

Indeed, at such a smart pace had they trotted from the quay up Fishers Hill to The Square, and so imperative had their mission seemed—or at least had Mitsuko's—that small talk seemed unworthy and beside the point. Earlier, after she had stepped into the café, Mitsuko had quickly surveyed the patrons, then shot into the kitchen. Conversation had dipped when she'd first materialised in the restaurant, but it ceased altogether when the voices from the kitchen began to swell. For a few moments, everyone strained to distinguish the words, but then, as if conscience commanded, they snapped back into their midmorning chatter, only burnishing it to a fine clatter—anything to obscure the discomforting blasts coming from behind the swing doors at the kitchen end of the restaurant. When Mitsuko reappeared, her expression showing only a hint of strain, they had feigned disinterest superbly, at least until she had made her way to Tom's table and had asked if he would come back with her to the Blackbird Gallery. Then curiosity gave new life to profound silence. Tom could feel everyone's eyes on them as they left the restaurant.

"Oh, Dad's fine," she replied distractedly to his question. "His colon resection went well. That's why I was able to beg off and come home today. My mother's very dependent on my father, and she doesn't drive, so it was me taking her from Bridgend to the hospital in Cardiff, you see. But then I had the radio on early this morning and heard about . . ." She stopped, as if the words were too awful to voice. "Anyway, I had to get back. Liam would be without help, for one thing . . . and then I come in here and find my equipment missing . . . gone . . ."

"And no evidence of a break-in," Tom mused, having already examined the doorwell and, as best he could, the two high windows on either side. Nothing appeared smashed or cracked. "Odd the alarm didn't go off."

They both glanced at the little white box near the door, one of its several lights silently pulsing. Then Mitsuko's eyes drifted to the ceiling, to the floor above, which contained her and Liam's flat. She looked pensive. "The alarm was switched off when Fred was in and out to fix . . ." She blinked and flicked her hair back fretfully. "Fred . . ."

Tom frowned. "Oh, surely not."

"You know about Fred's . . . tendency?"

"I've been told." He reflected on his curate's egg, now nesting safely on his bedroom side table. "But from what I understand, Fred only takes little things—things he thinks are innocuous. That's if he's thinking at all when he goes about doing this sort of thing. So nicking your computer equipment doesn't seem to fit his . . . modus operandi. I could imagine him taking your mouse, for instance, but there it is on your table."

Mitsuko glanced past Tom's pointing finger at the white plastic casing and its unmoored tail. "I suppose you're right," she responded doubtfully.

"Why was Fred in and out?"

"Oh, the toilet in our flat suddenly cracked on Sunday afternoon. Apparently old ones can do this without notice. Sybella . . . Oh, God, Sybella!" Mitsuko faltered. "I can't wrap my head around it." She shivered, then took a shaky breath. "She was so *good* on Sunday. So levelheaded.

"She was minding the gallery while I was at the village hall installing the quilts," Mitsuko explained to Tom's quizzical glance, "when she suddenly heard this odd sort of snap above. She came in here to investigate, then noticed some water seeping down the wall."

Mitsuko gestured to the ceiling near the stairs leading to the flat, where Tom noted a grey blotch bleeding into a stain that ran down the white-painted insulation board covering the walls of the room.

"She got into the flat and had the presence of mind to put a stick under the stopcock and turn the shutoff valves, but there was a bit of a mess. At any rate, she phoned Fred, reasoning that getting a plumber on the Sunday before Bank Holiday would be impossible, then she phoned me to say what she had done, which was perfect. Fred fiddled about with the plumbing and cleaned things up and said he would fetch a new toilet for us from Paignton and install it Tuesday. Which I gather from Liam he was able to do. I haven't even had time to go up to the flat. The first thing my eyes went to when I came in was the space where my laptop used to be—"

"And the alarm?"

"On. I punched in the code, as usual, to stop it going off when I came in."

Tom thought for a moment. "So Liam had switched it back on."

"Yes, he said he did, although exactly when after Fred was finished, I'm not sure. It was likely off Monday and yesterday. Sybella had nobbled it on Sunday so Fred could go about his business."

"What about keys?"

"I told Sybella on Sunday to give Fred the extra set to the back door, which normally . . ." Mitsuko reached over from her stool and rolled a white plastic artist's taboret towards her on its casters. She pulled out one of the drawers, then another, then a third. ". . . which normally resides here," she continued, "but doesn't. Fred must still have the set."

"So Fred has had keys since Sunday."

"Now *you're* suspecting him."

"No, I'm not. Not at all. But he might have left the door ajar yesterday when he was bringing in the new toilet, and someone saw an opportunity."

Mitsuko sighed. "Perhaps. That seems about the only explanation."

"Otherwise someone would need both keys *and* code to get in without causing a disturbance, right?"

"Yes, I expect so." There was a hesitation in her tone. "Normally. If the alarm is on."

"Who has keys?"

"Well . . . I do. Liam, of course. Sybella—"

"Sybella?"

"She minds . . . minded the gallery from time to time, as I said, and sometimes she sketched here when it wasn't busy. She's really very good—" Mitsuko's expression crumpled. "Well, she was . . . I shouldn't bang on about my missing computer, should I? when this awful awful thing has happened to Sybella . . . but all my photographs, videos, graphic experiments, all my documents and accounts—years of work—all of it gone . . . it's so unfair."

Sybella's death? Or your missing equipment? Tom thought, but said nothing. His expression must have registered disapproval, for Mitsuko sagged a little on her stool. "I'm sorry. I'm being selfish."

"Understandable. You've had at least a couple of shocks this morning."

Mitsuko bit her lip. "We were putting together a portfolio so she could apply to art school for fall. Look." She pulled a few sheets of drawing paper off the worktable. "Her figurative work is superb. She's extraordinarily gifted. Was gifted, rather."

Tom glanced at the drawings. "I saw some like these at her father's yesterday."

"Here's one of you."

Tom grimaced. In the picture, he was on Kinsey's touring bicycle. His cassock, which he rarely wore outside church, flapped behind him like a raven's wings. The rendering was accurate, but the posture cartoon.

"I think I prefer the one of me on your quilt."

"Oh, you've seen it, have you?" Mitsuko clucked with annoyance. "It seems like half the village wandered through on Sunday when Sebastian and I were putting them up, and I did lock the door to the large hall afterwards. There's going to be *no* surprises at the opening tomorrow." She paused. "*If* there's an opening tomorrow. Perhaps I should put it off. It seems so frivolous in light of . . . what's happened."

Tom's inclination, born of his own tragedies, was to see village rhythms restored as swiftly as possible. "What would Sybella have wanted?"

"To defy convention," Mitsuko replied promptly. For the first time, she smiled. "But in a sort of conventional way, as people do at that age."

"You might ask her father what he thinks."

"Of course. I must call him anyway. He must be devastated."

"He is."

"You know," Mitsuko picked up a sketchbook from the table. "I don't think most people knew Sybella very well."

Tom glanced at her sharply with a mind to probe the remark, but Mitsuko drew his attention to the new page. "Look at the expression she's captured in this one. Look at the mouth—sort of defiance and vulnerability all at once—but subtly done. A very well executed self-portrait, I think, for someone so new to the game."

"For a second there, I thought this was of you. I mean, the hair, the—"

"Tom, you want your eyes examined. I may have been born in the U.K. but there's nothing British about my ancestry." She closed the sketchbook. "I'm feeling a bit shattered. Would you care for a coffee upstairs? Or had you had enough at the Waterside?"

"I never quite finished mine."

"That would be my doing. My apologies for dragging you away."

"I think I interrupted you when you were telling me who had keys to this place," Tom said, climbing the stairs behind Mitsuko. He couldn't help noticing her slight but shapely figure, encased as it was in tight black trousers and short-sleeve top.

"No one, I don't think," she replied, stopping to fit her key into the lock to the upstairs flat door. "Well," she continued, grunting a little as she pushed the door open, "Sebastian has a set . . . well, *had* a set."

"Had?"

Mitsuko held the door open while Tom passed through. "Liam and I went to Tunisia for two weeks after Christmas. Sebastian volunteered to water the fig tree and a few plants in the bedrooms and keep an eye on the place while we were away."

"Not Sybella?"

"No, she was away, too, around the same time—when the school term ended for Declan. Colm and Celia took them to . . . Cleveland, I think it was."

"Odd, I didn't think Colm or Celia had family in the north."

"No, the Cleveland in America. The one with the rock-and-roll museum."

Mitsuko moved down a short hall and turned in to a narrow kitchen that ran against the back of the building. Having never been in the Drewes', Tom was interested to see how the couple lived. His eyes took in a space that was as spare as the studio downstairs was cluttered.

"So Sebastian *had* a set of keys," he remarked, figuring the Drewes likely took most of their meals at their restaurant. He couldn't see a crumb or a used spoon.

"Yes, Liam took them back. I didn't mind Sebastian having them. You know, if there's any emergency or something. He's very capable."

"Yes," Tom agreed, mildly, sure he detected little daubs of strawberry burst along Mitsuko's cheeks. "He *is* very capable. But . . . it seems your husband has another view."

"My husband," Mitsuko responded fiercely, her face disappearing behind a stripped pine cupboard door, "has the wrong end of the stick about many things."

Tom heard a scraping of glass and tins, then Mitsuko's face, strawberry daubs in retreat, reemerged. "I hope you don't mind instant." She held up a jar of Nescafé. "I'm feeling a headache coming on and the cafetière will take too long."

"Then perhaps I should leave you be."

"No, please don't. I . . ." Mitsuko faltered. "Go into the sitting room, Tom. I'll be in soon as I get the kettle boiling."

Tom's first impression on entering the Drewes' front room was of one of those showrooms of sleek contemporary furniture. A console table, a coffee table, the shelving—all black—and the couch—an extra-long model, sheathed in black leather—suggested craftsmanship of a particular variety or imagination, since the eye was immediately shocked by a single red pillow among the four black that backed the elongated curve of the banquette. With the exception of the green canopy of a potted fig tree, it was the only spot of colour in the room. The walls were whitewashed, punctuated with framed charcoal portraits, the blinds rolled at the windows overlooking northwesterly over The Square were white canvas, and white goatskin rugs covered the stripped pine floor. The large flat-panel TV and the Bose stereo, Tom suspected, were a concession to Liam, but they were most definitely white. Carefully chosen by Mitsuko, no doubt, not to violate her crisp aesthetic. Only one thing blighted the pristine setting: Next to the television remote control on the coffee table was a midden of lager cans, most of them twisted and crushed, along with several crumpled crisp packets. There was a discernible beery fug to the room. Since he doubted Fred Pike imbibed so openly on the job—installing the Drewes' new toilet, in this case—only one person could have left this clutter. He lifted one of the cans and shook it, to see if there was a residual slosh. There was. His mind was sent back to his conversation earlier with Tilly Springett in the Waterside.

"The reason," she had whispered once Mitsuko had gone into the restaurant's kitchen and the ladies' conversation had been reignited, "that I'm at sixes and sevens is that I'm sure I saw Liam going up our road towards the village hall Sunday night. Which really," she hastened to add, as though embarrassed by the triviality of the observation, "shouldn't be something to remark on, only Liam's just not someone I ever expect to see near my cottage at that time of night. You know how busy he is. I'm told he only seems to beat a path between this café and his flat, and I'm not on the way to either—I'm the last cottage in Pennycross Road before the village hall—and I wouldn't have given it a second thought," she continued breathlessly, "but for Sybella's unfortunate . . . you know . . ." She looked at Tom pleadingly.

Tom's brows knitted. "About what time?"

"Well, let's see." Her hands fluttered over her cup. "I'd been watching a film on ITV, but couldn't quite get through it—the plot confused me, so I switched it off, oh, a little after nine-thirty, I think, and went to make a cup of cocoa, and then . . ."

"Yes?"

"Oh, dear, I wish I'd looked at a clock. Closer to ten, by the time I got to bed, I would think. You see, I was drawing curtains in the bedroom and happened to look out . . . and saw him . . . Liam, that is. Oh, how odd, I thought, but didn't think much more about it at the time."

"You're certain it was Liam."

"Well, it was the back of him, but he does have a strong build, doesn't he? And I'm quite sure I saw the tattoos."

"It's rather dark, though, by ten."

"Yes, that's true, but the lamp from the bedroom cast a little light on the road . . . before I closed the curtains, of course."

"Did he see you?"

Tilly gave him an apprehensive glance. "I don't know. This is why I feel like a character in an Agatha Christie. I don't think he saw me. He had gone past by the time I got to the window. I saw the back of him, as I said. But he might have noticed the light come on when I came into the bedroom and *think* that I—"

"Mrs. Springett, you mustn't get yourself into knots. It's most likely nothing, but—"

"—And," she interjected, leaning towards him, "*and* he was carrying something."

"I thought you saw the back of him."

"It was the way his arm—his left arm—was crooked. I'm sure he was holding something to his chest."

A weapon. The thought intruded, unbidden. Tom sought to dismiss it then, as he did now in the Drewes' sitting room, but he couldn't help the threadings of his imagination, tying a furious row Sunday evening at the Waterside to a peculiar sighting along Pennycross Road to a liquid attempt at anesthetising horror, dread, and guilt.

Or maybe, he thought, glancing over at the Drewes' huge telly, Liam had merely settled to watch *Match of the Day 2* after a brisk trot through the village and, as the Americans were wont to say, "kick back" with the wife out of the picture. He preferred this view. But to Mrs. Springett, he could no more *not* exercise the moral authority that went with his vocation than he could *not* preside at the prize-giving at school at the end of term.

"You really must," he'd said to Tilly, regretfully, "take your concerns to the police. They'll sort things out."

"Yes, I thought you might say that, Vicar," she responded, but before he could reassure her that her confidences would be kept—by both him and the police—Mitsuko had whisked him away.

Replacing the lager can with its fellows, Tom moved towards the room's only cosy feature, a Georgian fireplace surround, painted white to blend with the walls. On the mantel, under a large mirror, a collection of black-and-white photographs in matching silver frames drew his attention. Family—Mitsuko's, not Liam's, he presumed—from the Japanese cast to the faces. He reached for the last photograph, but movement reflected in the mirror alerted him to Mitsuko's presence in the room. She was carrying a black lacquered tray with two white mugs of coffee, and matching milk jug and sugar bowl.

"Is this your brother?" he asked, lifting the relevant picture from the mantel and turning. "I feel like I've seen him somewhere before."

"He's an ornithologist in America," she replied, placing the tray on the coffee table. Tom noted her lips form an irritated moue as she took in the pile of ale cans. "You might have seen his picture on the back of a book or two."

"That must explain it. Dosh—my mother—is an enthusiastic twitcher. She has a couple of his books, I think. *Birds of Eastern North America* and such."

"Her interests range afar."

"Her partner comes from Virginia. They travel there from time to time. I've been, too."

"Oh," Mitsuko responded vaguely. She transferred the coffee things to the table and stacked the cans onto the tray.

"What's your brother's name?" he asked over the metallic clatter.

"Hari Oku."

"Of course. Oku's your maiden name, then."

"Tom, I'm just going to remove these to the kitchen."

Oku, Tom pondered as Mitsuko bustled the offending detritus from the room. *Oku.* The name seemed to ring in his memory. *Oku. Oku-ku-k'joob. I am the walrus!* A childhood memory of Kate crooning Beatles songs to him slipped in and out of his consciousness. No, that wasn't it. What was it? Oh, yes, it was intermixed in the colonel's ravings at the hospital the afternoon before. Perhaps he had been hallucinating about Mitsuko, for what was logic to the hallucinating mind?

"Hari works at the Smithsonian." Mitsuko reappeared. "Akemi—my sister—works in London as a fashion buyer. And of course," she gestured towards a picture of an older couple, "those are my parents."

"Your father manages the Sony plant at Bridgend—is that correct?" Tom recalled this among the flotsam and jetsam in Julia's précis of the village folk.

"Managed. He retired last year." Mitsuko perched on the edge of the leather couch, black jeans melding with black leather. "He came from Japan to open the plant in the seventies."

"And stayed on."

"Yes . . . well, more than half his life has been here and he loves it. He's taking Welsh lessons in retirement and is involved in Welsh folk dancing—at least until this operation. I think my mother sometimes entertains the idea of moving back to Japan—she has a sister near Tokyo—but Akemi and I live relatively nearby, and Hari visits often . . ."

"You were born . . . here?" Tom took the seat with the red cushion.

"Yes. Hari's the oldest. He was born in Japan, but Akemi and I were born in Wales. So despite appearances," she drew an imaginary circle around her face, "the only Japanese I know are a few remembered words and phrases from childhood that my mother taught me. My father was quite adamant that we stick to English." She smiled ruefully. "I'm afraid I'm no use to Japanese tourists lost in London."

Tom smiled in return. "Have you visited? Japan, I mean."

"No. I . . . it was never really encouraged. Other than my mother's sister and a cousin, there's little family there. My father was an only child, you see, and . . ." She stopped and stared into her coffee.

"And . . . ?" Tom prompted, after a moment.

"Oh . . ." Mitsuko shrugged and shifted in her seat. "It's nothing, really. There's an estrangement of some nature. My father never speaks of my grandfather."

"Speaks? If your grandfather's still alive, then at least there's a chance for reconciliation, yes?"

Mitsuko's mouth formed a tight frown, then she said: "The Japanese are a long-lived people. I shall live to be a hundred, I expect." She brought the coffee to her lips at last. "Oh, that's very good." She sighed. "I needed that."

Tom lifted his cup and likewise took a sip, wondering at her oblique response, but aware that her mind had other preoccupations. The coffee was hot and certainly strong.

"Would you like me to ring the police?"

Mitsuko started. "Whatever for?"

"To report your stolen items," he replied, taken aback.

She stared at him; then her alarm vanished. "Oh! Of course, that's what you meant. Sorry. I was thinking about . . . No, Tom, thank you—I'll ring them. I have the registration number for the laptop and the other things somewhere." She looked away and sighed. "I think reporting to the police is really more a formality for our insurer. I'm sure my laptop's gone for good, poor thing. Besides, the local constabulary has more important things to worry about, doesn't it?" She turned back to him. In the blackness of her pupils, he thought he detected a new unease. "Sybella, I mean," she added.

"The CID will be busy," he agreed, trying to suppress a surge of unpleasant memories that attended his wife's homicide investigation. "Theft would probably land in some other pigeonhole."

Mitsuko lifted her legs and folded her body into the corner of the couch. "Maybe I should be grateful the laptop was stolen."

"Whatever for?"

"It's managed to distract me. On the drive back from Wales, Sybella didn't leave my thoughts. But the news reports were so sketchy—they talked about her death being treated 'as suspicious.' I kept fiddling with the dial on the radio for something more precise, but all they seemed focused on was Sybella's parentage: 'Eighties pop star's daughter dies'—that sort of thing—until I was driving into the village. Then the news said it was confirmed as homicide. I expect it's been in the papers."

Tom nodded assent.

Mitsuko leaned over and placed her cup on the coffee table. "But it didn't say *how*."

"I think the police sometimes like to keep certain details to themselves." He had hoped to keep the speculation from her ears. "It helps them in their investigations."

"Oh." Mitsuko began a rhythmic stroking of the hair framing one side of her face. She pulled a few glossy black strands forwards and examined them, the way Lisbeth had sometimes when she was tired or anxious, ostensibly looking for split ends. "But you must have an idea," she said, regarding him through the scrim of her hair. "I'm sure the whole village knows by now. They usually do."

"Well, I think people have guessed," Tom responded. "Given the kinds of questions the police have been asking." He paused. His heart sank a little. He could sense Mitsuko's apprehension and he knew the root of it. "Sybella died from a blow to the head."

The hair fell from her hands and swayed onto her breasts. She stared at him, her face parchment white.

"I'm sorry" was all he could think to say.

"Then you know."

"I'm sorry," he said again. "It is rather a small village. But that doesn't mean—"

"But that's what people are *thinking*, isn't it?" Tom thought guiltily of his little flock only an hour before on the millpond. His lack of response was acquiescence. "It was years ago. It was an accident. Liam never meant to hit that man at that club. He paid his debt." Mitsuko continued to stare at him, her face a palimpsest of fear; then she glanced away. "I know he has a dreadful temper. I know he can be irrational about"—she stopped herself suddenly—"about things. Oh, God, they'll ask us questions, won't they?"

"Who?"

"The police."

"They've already had a conversation with your husband, I'm

afraid. You and Liam were her employers. But I don't think you need worry unnecess—"

"But it was Sunday night she was killed, wasn't it?"

"I'm not sure they've pinpointed an exact time, but yes. Or early Monday morning."

"Oh, God."

"What is it?"

"I . . . it's nothing."

Tom raised both eyebrows.

"Really, Tom, I can't say."

Tom gazed unseeingly out the window towards the holiday cottage across The Square and pondered his situation. He took no pleasure in being a conduit of tittle-tattle; he despised tittle-tattle. Neither was his intent to give the Drewes an opportunity to prevaricate before the law. But he felt a need to at least forewarn them, to give them time to look into their hearts that they might not bear false witness.

"You were in the Waterside's kitchen Sunday evening, around supper time, yes?"

Mitsuko blinked. "Yes."

"But you left by the delivery door."

"Yes . . . but how . . . ?"

"I wasn't there, if you're wondering that. But there was a local couple at a table and—"

"And they heard us rowing. Oh, God," she said again, closing her eyes as if to stave off some awful truth. "Surely they didn't hear what the argument was about. Please tell me they didn't hear that."

"Mitsuko, I think simply the fact that you and Liam and Sybella were rowing in the restaurant a few hours before Sybella's death will be enough to pique police interest. I don't know what it was about. I don't want you to tell me what it was about, and it may be utterly irrelevant. But it's best if you don't try to—"

"I can't, Tom! If I tell them, they'll think—"

"Think what?"

The new and strident voice filled the room. Tom looked over the back of the couch to see Liam, his arms like tattooed hams crossed over his shirtfront.

"Think what?" Liam said again, louder this time.

"What are you doing here?" Mitsuko unfolded her lithe form and twisted to face him. "What about the lunch trade?"

"I've closed the place. What's he doing here?"

"You wouldn't come back and help me."

"I have a restaurant to run."

"Well, you're not running it now, are you?"

"I don't want you hanging about with the likes of him."

"He's my *priest*, Liam. That's all. That's all it is. That's all it *ever* was."

"Get out." Liam's eyes burned into Tom's. He jerked his thumb towards the door.

Tom suppressed an adrenaline rush of anger and glanced at Mitsuko, wondering if 5 The Square was a safe haven for a tiny woman, but her return glance betrayed no new anxiety. *Sorry,* she mouthed to him silently as he rose. Giving a passing thought to the challenge of blessing them that curse you, he manoeuvred past her legs and the coffee table, their eyes meeting again when his shins brushed her knees. He opened his mouth to apologise, but a flicker in her eyes—sharp and bright, like a match struck in a black cave—stopped his tongue. He was certain it was fear.

CHAPTER FIFTEEN

Tom switched on his computer, hoping to divorce his mind at least for a time from the mystery of Sybella's death and engage with the certainty of her young life, as well as with the terrible loss to her family and the anxiety in the community. He glanced at the entry in the lectionary for Sunday, June 1, and then set the booklet aside. This was no ordinary week and it would not be an ordinary Sunday. But he had barely begun to organise his thoughts when Miranda peeked around the door.

"Daddy, are you writing your salmon?"

"Yes, darling, the 'salmon's' not quite done, but come in and talk to me." Tom swivelled in his chair towards her. "I thought you'd gone crabbing with Emily. Wasn't Daniel to show you how?"

"Yes, he did. I caught lots, but a crab bit Emily so she went home." Miranda came beside him and slipped her arm around his neck. Tom leaned his head against hers and took in her aroma. She smelled of salt water and, oddly, bacon that had gone off. Then he remembered that crabs went mad for gamy bacon. Cats, probably, too, he thought, noting Powell and Gloria curling around her legs.

"Was Emily hurt very badly?"

"Not really. Daniel was mostly being mean to her. I think that's why she went home. He was nice to me, though. He helped me bring my bucket and net home."

"Did you give them to Mrs. Prowse?"

"She has visitors. So I left everything outside." Miranda reached to pet one of the cats that had leapt onto the desk. "Who is she talking to?"

"Two policemen, from Totnes."

"Why are they talking to Mrs. Prowse?"

"They're talking to lots of people in the village."

"About Sybella."

"Yes, darling, about Sybella."

Miranda slid onto his knee, something he realised suddenly she rarely did anymore.

"Did the policemen talk to you, Daddy?"

"Yes, they were here yesterday."

"This is like when Mummy died, isn't it?" She twisted her head and regarded him with serious eyes.

"Only a little teeny-tiny bit. But you mustn't worry. The police only want to find who hurt Sybella. It's very sad for Colm and Celia and Declan, but we're going to keep on living here in Thornford and you'll start last half of term next week and Mrs. Prowse will keep trying to stuff us with rich food, and everything will be as it should be." He rocked her on his knee.

"Will they want to speak to me?"

"Oh, I don't think so," he said lightly to the back of her head, recalling his repugnance at Bristol CID questioning her, the little girl who'd lost her mother and who had no useful information anyway.

"That's good."

"Why? Is there something you wanted to tell them?"

"No," she said slowly. He could see her wrinkle her nose. "They look scary. One of them has bumps on his face."

Tom laughed. "Now, you mustn't be unkind. People can't help the way they look sometimes."

But Miranda was no longer attentive. *"Regarde, Papa."* She pointed to the French doors, partially opened to the garden, flanked by urns of pink and purple geraniums. *"Monsieur Pike s'en vient par ici."*

Fred Pike was indeed coming their way, up the brick path through the sun-drenched lawn at a trot brisker than Tom had ever seen in the man.

"Father?" he gasped, holding one hand to his chest, leaning into the study and peering into the relative darkness. "Father . . ."

"Fred? Are you all right?" The man appeared to be having a heart attack. Tom lifted Miranda off his lap.

"Father, you must come—" An adverb died on his lips as he took a step into the study and noticed the child. His lined face strained to temper alarm as he sought to catch his breath. "Father, I think there's something you ought to see."

"What is it?"

Fred glanced again at Miranda in an agony of indecision.

"Miranda," Tom said, "why don't you go and have a wash and I'll see to Mr. Pike, okay?"

"May I come?" she asked.

"No!" Fred's tone was uncharacteristically sharp.

"No," Tom repeated more gently, rising from his chair. "Best not. I won't be long."

He followed Fred out the door and into the garden. "Whatever is it?" he asked, but received no reply as Fred picked up speed and led him at an increasing pace across the lawn, down the steps to the millpond, west along the shaded path, and then up the stone steps to the churchyard, wending between the gravestones until they reached the southwest corner, in which he had been toiling earlier that morning.

"It's that," Fred replied finally, pointing into the freshly dug grave.

Tom leaned over and peered in. Cast into shadow by the over-arching beech tree, the rectangular cavity looked nothing more than what it should be—a black void. "What am I looking for?"

"You'll see it." Fred's voice was strained.

Then he did see it. A gust of wind parting the leaves of the tree illuminated for a moment a small pale shape at one edge of the bottom of the pit. With his eyes fixed on it, he tried to make sense of the thing's contours. Frowning, growing a little impatient, he was about to ask Fred to offer up a clue, when suddenly he realised what he was looking at.

"Oh!" He straightened sharply. "It's a hand!" He felt his gorge rising. "Good God . . . how on earth . . . ?"

"It's not Ned's, Father."

"Ned's?"

"Ned Skynner. Right here." Fred pointed to the adjacent grave.

"Are you sure?"

"That coffin of his were solid."

"That's right. I remember. Karla spared no expense."

"Besides . . ."

"Besides what?"

"It's got a ring on it. Ned had no truck with such frippery. Booj-wah, he liked to say when he were in full flight down the pub. So it can't be Ned's hand."

Tom peered back into the grave. Indeed, even from six feet up, he could make out a large golden oval covering the exposed bone of the little finger of the putrefied hand. Yes, he supposed it was a little bourgeois.

"But how . . . ?"

"There were a great stone on the side nearest Ned's I had to pull out or the coffin wouldn't fit." Fred pointed to a hefty reddish-grey rock now at graveside. "I've had surprises before, but it's always been the bones of some poor old blighter. Never this."

They both gazed into the grave in silent horror. Tom thought back to Ned Skynner's funeral. He recalled thinking then that as graves went, he'd seen more proficiently dug ones, not that he got more than a glimpse before the coffin was lowered. It seemed clear from the relative freshness of the disembodied hand that a coffinless someone had been placed in the hole sometime after Fred had dug it and before Ned's casket had been lowered on top.

"Well, there's nothing for it then, is there?"

"I expect not, Father."

"Will you stay here while I fetch Bliss and Blessing?"

"Bliss and blessing, Father?"

"You'll find out soon enough."

The Vicarage

Thornford Regis TC9 6QX

29 MAY

Dear Mum,

I hope you're sitting down because you won't believe what's
happened! Now they've found the body of Mr. Kinsey who
disappeared all those months ago and it looks he's been done in,
too! Well, that's what everyone is saying. You don't go sleeping in
open graves, do you? Because that's where he was found! Do you
remember when Karla's father died last year, while I was
visiting you? Well, it looks like someone had gone and tucked Mr.
Kinsey's body into ~~his~~ Ned's grave before they planted Ned. Poor
Karla. She's disgusted because they've had to disturb her father's
coffin to get at Mr. Kinsey. Anyway, yesterday after lunch, the
two detectives from Totnes who saw Mr. Christmas on Tuesday
had only just started interviewing me in the kitchen when Mr.
Christmas interrupted and he didn't look his usual self. He'd gone
all serious and asked the detectives—Bliss and Blessing were
their names. Weren't there Blessings up around Staverton way?

I'm sure I was at the big school with a Sandra Blessing. Anyway, Mr. Christmas asked them to come with him. He was quite insistent. As they hadn't finished with me, I was going to come, too, but Mr. C. asked me to stay with Miranda, which made it seem all very mysterious somehow. At any rate, before the day was done, there were police cars and a van and the churchyard taped off so no one could enter and a team of people in white suits to dig up the body. They wouldn't let Fred do it, not that he wanted to. I forgot to say that it was Fred who found the body, as he was digging a grave for Sybella at the time. I gave him tea at the vicarage, he was that shattered! And oh my aren't we all? I probably could have given tea to half the village who came down to the church yesterday afternoon when the news got around, but most went into the pub for something stronger. I suppose you could say the good thing is that that mystery is solved, since it's been troubling folk for a long time. But the really troubling bit now is who put Mr. Kinsey in Ned's grave? And why? At least I know it wasn't me, as I was with you at the time of Ned's death and didn't get back for his funeral, which Karla hasn't quite forgiven me for, even though you were having your hip replaced. Just think—you're my alibi! Anyway, I do feel sorry for Mr. Kinsey. I know we didn't really get on, but I wouldn't wish such a sad end on him. I know some around here thought he'd got amnesia and would suddenly come to on some street in London or somewhere. Anyway, Mr. Kinsey had no family so there's no one who will grieve terribly I expect, although the village is in a state of shock. A state of more *shock, I should say, what with Sybella's death. He was an only child and he had lost his parents some years ago. Both of them killed, as it happens, but then they stayed on at their farm in* ~~Rho~~ *Zimbabwe when they should have got out. Become an awful place, according to what I hear in the news! At any rate, I always thought Mr. Kinsey had disappeared because he was about to be caught out about something. I think that's what the police thought, too, as one of them was in the vicarage for a time last year going through his diary and sorting through his post, which I told you about before. But I guess they never found anything certain. The police that is. Now that it looks to be murder it's all very different. Poor Mr. Christmas looked wretched over dinner. I'd done lovely salmon and dill fishcakes that were one of Mr. James-Douglas's favourites and Mr. C. barely touched his plate. But then he was up and down the whole time. He wouldn't leave things to the answerphone. He was on with the rural dean and the Bishop and the police and Thompson's, the funeral people, and with Sebastian and Mrs. Hennis but anyway Sybella's funeral is still set for tomorrow and I expect there'll be even more press attention now—TWO dead bodies in TWO days! I think this is what's troubling Mr. Christmas. You know the terrible thing that happened to him in his last parish, of course. I think he thought Thornford would be a nice place for him and Miranda, but look what's happened! I'm not sure how this is affecting Miranda, as she is such a bright child! I was in her room after supper picking up clothes for today's wash and she was playing with her Barbie doll who was wearing a Burberry and carrying a magnifying glass and she was pretending Barbie was a detective, only she calls her Alice instead. I was turning out the pockets of her clothes and sorting what bits and bobs should go in the bin and I pulled out this odd little yellow wooden thing shaped like a gnome's hat and she said, no, that's a clue! So perhaps she is "sublimating" as Celia Parry calls it. I went to a couple of her talks at the WI and she was on about people channeling the negative things in their lives into positive action as a kind of therapy or something like that. She does make the most ordinary things seem complex! Celia, that is. A little of Celia always goes a long way, I must say, though I suppose I shouldn't go on about her as her stepdaughter's funeral is tomorrow. Must go and start breakfast. Cats are well.*

*Jago tells me Kerra went round yesterday to the Waterside and
got the serving job. She starts today. I have my fingers crossed.
Love to Aunt Gwen. Make sure you have a good day.*

Much love,
Madrun

*P.S. Fred Pike made off with my potato peeler when he was here
yesterday. Good thing I have two!*

*P.P.S. I should go to the meeting at the v. hall later this morning
as someone important from the police is coming down from
Exeter to talk to us, but I told Mitsuko Drewe I'd make my
famous yewberry mini-tarts for the opening of her art exhibition
at the hall this evening. Life goes on, it seems! I'll tell you all
about it tomorrow.*

*P.P.P.S. I worry about you worrying about us in Thornford, but
you mustn't. Mr. Christmas says what has happened in the
village this week has happened for particular reasons that have
nothing to do with any of us at the vicarage. At any rate, I'm
sure the police will have it all sorted out before terribly long.*

"Do you know," Julia intoned, "it's said if you walk seven times backwards around this yew, you'll be granted a wish?"

Tom flicked a glance at his sister-in-law. Julia was staring intently at the enormous old tree whose circumference of gnarled, tangled branches stretched and twisted across the northwestern portion of the churchyard to the very roof of the lych-gate. It was this observation rather than a morning greeting that escaped her lips when Tom—on his way to see if Bliss and Blessing were settling well into the Old School Room—had noted her step through the lych-gate and followed her. Bluish shadows like bruises marred the skin under her eyes, and the muscles of her neck above the grey T-shirt—which looked like a hasty choice of apparel for an otherwise fastidious woman—were taut. Her hair was still damp from a shower—or some dousing—and she had that vaguely unfinished look Lisbeth would sometimes have between a wash and the application of a spot of makeup.

"Actually," he responded, feeling a sudden keen pang of yearning for his wife and her morning face, "you told me that when Miranda and I visited last year. Are you off to the Neighbourhood Watch meeting then?"

"No. We're out of milk, so I was going down to Pattimore's."

"A roundabout way to get to Pattimore's, through the church-yard, isn't it?" Tom observed.

"I fancied the walk."

Tom's puzzled gaze followed Julia's. He could find nothing compelling about the ancient tree to warrant such study. "Were you wanting a wish granted?"

"Wouldn't we all want a wish granted?" Her eyes turned to his. He was shocked to see depths of misery in them.

"Yes, of course we would." He paused. "Julia, you look—"

"I didn't sleep very well."

"I understand."

"Do you?" Her tone was sharp.

Taken aback, Tom retorted: "I didn't sleep well either, Julia. The last few days have been troubling. The fabric of this very pleasant village has been torn—and twice in one week. All of us are affected. That's why—"

"I'm sorry. You're right, Tom. I'm being selfish."

"Hold on," he backtracked. "I mean, you've a right to feel—"

"You don't have to be so bloody agreeable, you know," Julia interrupted, pushing a damp strand of her hair back over her ear. "Sorry." She looked up at him sheepishly, then gave herself a little shake as if to rid herself of some cobweb.

"Don't be. I think I know how you're feeling, so here's me being disagreeable: In the wee hours this morning, I was thinking that somewhere in Bristol the man—man, presumably—who killed my wife is walking around free. I left Bristol because I couldn't bear the thought of it. Now I'm living here in Thornford, and the same thing is happening. The police in Bristol were inept—or unlucky, I don't know—but the two detectives fannying about here fill me with no more confidence than the two in Bristol did. I want the killer or killers or whoever is creating this havoc justly run to ground. I don't want to have to uproot my child a second time!"

"I'm not sure I've heard you so angry before."

"I'm not sure I've felt quite this angry before—at least not since Lisbeth's death."

Julia regarded him sombrely. "How is my niece coping?"

Tom snatched a calming breath before replying. "If you mean, are there echoes of the days after her mother's death, then I would say she doesn't seem to be too visibly affected. I think Sybella's death has stirred some memories—Miranda crawled on my lap yesterday, which she hasn't done in a long time, after the detectives came calling. But Peter Kinsey is an abstraction as far as she's concerned. I told her we can't play 'Where in the World Is the Reverend Peter Kinsey?' anymore because he's been found, and he was in the village all along, but he died. She seemed to accept this. The details I've spared her, however."

"Perhaps children take things more in their stride than we think."

"I'm not sure. It's difficult to have a sense of oneself as a nine-year-old."

"I remember envying that Lisbeth had budding breasts when I was Miranda's age and I didn't." Julia's eyes closed. She shuddered.

"Are you cold?"

"No. It was the vision of Peter in the—"

"Try not to think about that part, Julia."

She opened her eyes, the expression in them mournful. "I'll take Miranda for a treat somewhere."

"I wish you could take her away from the village tomorrow, but—"

"But I'm filling in as organist at Sybella's funeral. I've talked with Colm about the music, by the way. That choir of his should be arriving after lunch. He's putting them up at Thornridge, and we're rehearsing here at St. Nicholas's this afternoon. Anyway, as for my favourite niece—"

"The best thing for Miranda is routine," Tom interjected. "You'll be taking her to synagogue Saturday?"

"Of course."

"Good." He regarded his sister-in-law. Lisbeth had not been particularly observant, except for certain High Holidays, spent, if possible, with the Roses in London. Faith, she thought, put people's heads in the clouds. Tom thought faith grounded you to the world. How he missed her contrariness. He'd never had a reason to think Julia didn't share her sister's sensibilities, but he was surprised—and thankful, for Miranda's sake—that she had recently connected with the synagogue in Exeter.

Julia had returned to her contemplation of the fantastically contorted yew. Abruptly she grabbed his arm. "Shall we go round the tree?"

"What? Backwards? Now?"

"Yes!" Her eyes glittered.

"But—"

"You don't have to be at the hall until ten."

"Yes, but . . . it's pagan," he concluded, groping for an excuse not to do this silly thing.

"Oh, don't be dull!"

Tom studied her for a moment as she tugged at his jacket. Her behaviour this morning had a maniacal edge. "All right, then," he finally said as she led him over the grass to the base of the tree, whose stout trunk was protected by a low rough-stone enclosure. "But be warned: I may be sleight of hand, but I'm not fleet of foot. I recall stepping on your toes dancing at your wedding."

The path around the enclosure was itself rough, worn to a red-brown hue, largely by the feet of holidaymakers to the village, and a few credulous villagers. Tom looked into the crown of branches, which twisted up to the heavens, and was reminded forcefully of something. Of course. It was of kissing Lisbeth under the yew tree in St. Oswald's churchyard, in Grasmere, in the Lakes, where they had had their brief—and long postponed—honeymoon ten years ago. How could he have forgotten? And there was something else that had happened at Grasmere. What was it? If only Lisbeth were here to remind him.

He turned to Julia. *What do you wish for?* seemed the question appropriate to the moment, and when he asked it, he was stunned by the intensity of yearning telegraphed by her eyes. Had she read his mind? Might her wish be the same impossible one as his? In the wake of Lisbeth's death, Julia had been an angel rushed to his side, and he had been enormously grateful, but in those bad days in Bristol he realised he had been witnessing her atonement for the sin of neglect for the estrangement spawned by girlhood rivalry and amplified by Alastair's shift in affections from older to younger sibling. Lisbeth had died. Rapprochement could not happen. But if Lisbeth were here now . . .

Julia didn't reply. She took his arm and together they took a first step back. Tom felt compelled to glance over his shoulder, wary that some fallen branch, protuberant stone, or errant banana peel might sabotage them, but Julia remained confidently face forwards and heels backwards.

"I remember trying to moonwalk as a kid," he said, feeling slightly foolish, grasping for levity. He glanced towards the churchyard path, which, mercifully, was devoid of witnesses. "Do you remember? Like Michael Jackson? I never got the hang of it."

But Julia remained mute, fiercely concentrated on their unnatural task. Soon Tom fell into the rhythm and began to find a strange peace in the pace with the revolving kaleidoscopic views of the churchyard through the screen of branches. Oddly, it all felt familiar, but then he'd probably walked backwards around something in Gravesend as a child, simply for the novelty. Thus lulled, he found his thoughts returning, as they had the previous evening, to the end-of-spring-term holiday he and Miranda had spent with Julia and Alastair the year before. After Peter Kinsey's exhumation that afternoon—a grisly event he hoped never to witness again—it had struck him that his predecessor had been buried—and in all likelihood died—while he and Miranda were going about their holiday in the village.

What did he recall?

They'd left Bristol after services at St. Dunstan's and after Sunday lunch, arriving in Thornford in time for a late tea and their first glimpse of the Hennis home, Westways, perched on Thorn Hill, with—as estate agents might say—excellent views of the village below. Alastair had not been home to greet them. It was an indication, Tom thought at the time, of his disenchantment with their visit. Had he been golfing? It had been early April and a cool day, so perhaps not. Or perhaps he had been on call, as he often was weekends and evenings, his pager ringing, and him popping in and out. Tom couldn't remember. What he did recall was the wood fire crackling in the grate that afternoon, Julia's groaning tea, like the ones Grannie Ex provided when Dosh and Kate took him to his grandmother's thatched cottage at Sevenoaks, and a mellowness slink up his limbs. All that was shattered when Alastair finally appeared. He'd noted a hardness come into Julia's face at the sound of the door opening to the first-floor living rooms, followed a moment later by an impatient rebuke when Alastair said he'd already eaten.

It was then he sensed the rift in the Hennis marriage. Perhaps there had been evidence earlier, but he had noted nothing the last time he had seen them together—at Lisbeth's funeral in London (where he had been blinded by grief)—nor had Julia alluded to anything when she came to Bristol soon after to comfort Miranda and help sort through Lisbeth's effects (but, again, his mind had been elsewhere).

At Westways, the evidence could be totted up in averted eyes, strained smiles, curt nods, a scrupulous courtesy trotted out only for guests, and this: Alastair was sleeping apart, in the small ground-floor suite. When the two were together in the house, a deadly calm prevailed, like the atmosphere before a vicious squall, but none came.

Away from her husband, Julia had been returned, like a maiden released from a spell, to her agreeable self. As it was her half-term holiday as well, she'd arranged a series of entertainments for them. Alastair drove daily to the Cadewell Health Centre in Torbay Hospital in Torquay, once or twice paid a home visit to one of his few private patients in the village, and played golf when he could, except for the Tuesday when Julia substituted for Colm at the organ at Red Ned's funeral and took Tom along on what would become a life-changing episode. Alastair took Miranda to crazy golf at Abbey Park, then a meal at McDonald's. Miranda returned to Westways thrilled with her uncle, and Tom had to concede Alastair's attention to Miranda was unaffected and genuine. He'd tried probing Julia a little about the state of her marriage that day. (There were not many moments when Miranda wasn't present.) He was sure aftershocks remained from the miscarriage two years earlier. But she deflected enquiry, insistent his visit be cheerful. And maybe, he thought guiltily to himself now, as he encircled the yew once again, he had been too fatigued by his own heartache to respond to the emotional state of another. He had wanted peace, and he had been finding it in Thornford.

What had they done on the Monday, on the first full day of their visit? A lazy morning walk through the village, then down to the quay, where Miranda fed the swans, then up the path by the millpond to St. Nicholas's. The church had been locked—a recent, and regretted, move in the wake of the theft of a couple of Jacobean funeral stools—so they had toured the churchyard, where Ned Skynner's freshly dug grave reminded Julia of her Tuesday duties as organist and which had stirred Tom to accompany her, to view the church interior, rather than visit Paignton Zoo. After lunch that Monday, Julia had driven him and Miranda to Totnes for the prosaic, but comforting, family task of grocery shopping at Morrisons. Monday evening had been a simple supper of linguine marinara and asparagus and artichoke salad at home with the four of them around the kitchen table, followed later by a Disney DVD—fine viewing for Miranda, but dull for adults. Tom had been almost relieved when

Alastair was paged before they'd even opened the DVD to attend to Enid Pattimore, the variety of whose medical conditions was, Julia said, legendary.

Tuesday had been Ned's funeral and the peculiar—though not at that point worrying—nonappearance of Peter Kinsey. Wednesday, Julia had given them a tour of Dartmoor, with the morning at Widecombe-in-the-Moor and lunch at Princetown. It was in this austere and lonely landscape of craggy tors and great sweeps of heather, before ominous afternoon dark clouds chased them back towards the safety of the South Hams' high hedgerows and soft downs, that "Where in the World Is the Reverend Peter Kinsey?" had its innocent beginning. But through Thursday morning (to Plymouth) and by Friday, after lunch at the Waterside (to Agatha Christie's home), as Kinsey failed to make his whereabouts known and consternation grew to anxiety, the game began to lose much of its enchantment for Thornfordians such as Julia. Saturday, he and Miranda returned to Bristol.

During the latter part of his and Miranda's visit, curiosity had grown over Kinsey's movements in the hours after his Sunday services. At the time, unfamiliar with the village dramatis personae, Tom could barely piece together the information, most of which came from an increasingly worried Julia. Later, installed as vicar of St. Nicholas's, with the village folk a panoply of familiar—or almost familiar—faces, Tom found that the pieces, burnished by time and fuelled by speculation, fell better into place: That April Sunday, with Madrun visiting her mother in Cornwall, Peter Kinsey had taken his lunch with Florence and Venice Daintrey, who had waved him off at about two-thirty. Several witnessed him walk through the village to the vicarage. Several more witnessed the vicarage windows glow as daylight died. There had been no evensong that Sunday.

Kinsey had been alive next Monday morning when Eric saw him pull his Audi into Poynton Shute and turn up Pennycross Road and out of the village. Religiously, one might say, Peter Kinsey deserted Thornford Mondays, his one true day off. Where he went, he kept, with equal religious conviction, to himself, though Marg Farrant had once spotted him coming out of a private gallery in Exeter— perhaps not a complete surprise as Kinsey had read art at Oxford— and even Julia allowed that she had once seen him lunching alone at an outdoor café in Torquay. Kinsey had not disappeared with his car, however. He had returned to Thornford late that Monday afternoon, but instead of driving into the village, he had taken the car to Jago Prowse's garage at Thorn Cross, troubled by an engine warning light flashing ominously on his dashboard. Jago had offered to drive him to the vicarage in his own car while Kinsey's was being serviced and the offer had been gratefully accepted. Jago might have been the last person to see him alive. Certainly—so far—he was the last person to *admit* to seeing Peter Kinsey alive—which, to his disgust, had made him a subject of intense police scrutiny as the disappearance finally gained the attention of authorities.

What had he and Kinsey talked about in the car, the coppers wanted to know? Not bloody much, Jago, a man given to bluntness, had responded. Or at least that was how Madrun described it to Tom much later. The weather, the price of petrol, how Jago's daughters were getting on. Small talk. Yes, the vicar seemed in good spirits, as much as Jago bothered to notice. He'd been up to Exeter, Vicar'd said. No, he didn't bloody know why. It was none of his business anyway.

A search of the car garnered little more than the usual effects of a childless and fairly fastidious man—an AA road atlas to Britain, a Devon street atlas, a good pub guide, a pair of prescription sunglasses, a tire-pressure gauge, several CDs, and a well-thumbed copy of that day's *Times*. Jago had repeated the list to Madrun, who had savoured the details, but, alas, could find nothing more meaningful in them than the police could.

The very thought of Madrun, and there she was, hoving into view along the path, no doubt having posted her daily missive to her deaf mother. "I hope you two know what you're doing," she called after them.

"We're hoping to be granted a wish," Tom called back, feeling very silly but trying hard not to sound it for Julia's sake.

"That's not all that might happen!"

"What do you mean?"

But Madrun's reply was lost as he and Julia disappeared behind the yew's trunk.

"Are you not going to the Neighbourhood Watch meeting?" Reappearing, Tom glimpsed Madrun's back.

"Can't, Mr. Christmas," she called over her shoulder. "I have pastries for this evening and your luncheon to prepare."

"I'm going to be sixteen stone before very long, if she doesn't stop this incessant cooking," he muttered to Julia. "I feel like a French goose, sometimes. Perhaps she has plans for my liver. *Foie vicar* . . . Julia?"

But his sister-in-law remained silently concentrated on their ritual. "And that 'not all that might happen' was ominous, don't you think?" he added, going over in his mind the other myths attached to yew trees. "What do you think she meant?"

Julia made no verbal response. She jabbed his ribs with her elbow.

"Yes, I see your point, or feel it, rather," Tom responded, lapsing into silence. Only two more goes around this bloody tree, he thought, letting his mind return to the Kinsey conundrum.

At first, the question had been, *Why did the priest disappear?* Madrun's view—and it had been shared by others—was that Kinsey was about to be found out about something and that whatever it was it was so devastating that career ruin and prison sentence loomed like a tor over Dartmoor.

That meant Sex or Money.

As for Sex, the youths of Thornford Regis remained unmolested—at least by the clergy—as far as anyone knew. No one believed Peter Kinsey was anything other than unrepentantly heterosexual and psychologically sound. But the question was: If he was a normally functioning heterosexual male, who might be receiving the benefits of his attentions? Was it anyone in the village? It wasn't unusual for a priest to be the object of a misplaced and inopportune infatuation. But any wise priest in an unmarried state would be a fool to have a dalliance, with, say, a married woman in his parish. Nonetheless some thought Peter Kinsey seemed unusually attentive to Mitsuko Drewe, for one. And to Violet Tucker, for another. And to Penella Neels, for a third (though she was unmarried). This Tom had learned late yesterday afternoon when he'd gone into the Church House Inn for something large and liquid after the exhumation—unthinkably unpleasant to witness—was complete. A single topic dominated conversation in the pub, packed with folk who had trotted down towards the church thanks to the bush telegraph, but been barred from the churchyard by the strength of the local constabulary.

Then there was Money. The rural dean had shared with Tom what the police had discovered and what no one in the village knew, but for Colonel Northmore, Church Council treasurer: that in a safe-deposit box at a NatWest branch in Exeter, Kinsey had kept about £90,000 in notes—mostly twenties and fifties. Safer than keeping money under one's bed, one supposed, but a poor hedge against inflation. Peter Kinsey might have been an eccentric when it came to his savings, but a little forensic accounting shed no light on how the money had arrived in the safe-box—there was no electronic paper trail of cashed cheques, for instance, and virtually no monies had been forthcoming from his late parents' estate, given that the Kinsey farm had been seized by the Zimbabwean government without compensation. Meanwhile, his monthly stipend from the church was paid by direct deposit into a bank, not in Exeter, but in Totnes.

Tom knew the potential for malfeasance. People sometimes gave him £10 or £20 to put into the collection, if he did them a small favour, and it would be easy simply to keep it. Similarly, many paid cash for weddings and funerals, and though the money was shared with the organist, the verger, or the bell ringers, a priest could merely pocket the money and never declare it to the diocese. But all the weddings and funerals and collections in Kinsey's relatively short career couldn't account for the sum in the Exeter bank's safe-box. Nor had any legacies left to the church by the parish's deceased appeared to have greased their way into the vicar's palms.

Colonel Northmore had opened his cashbook and files for examination and defended the parish's accounting. He had become treasurer in Giles James-Douglas's day and even if his own banking background hadn't made him mindful when it came to sums—which it had—he was doubly mindful when he realised the absentminded and privately wealthy James-Douglas had a vague relationship with cash. Madrun would regularly go through the priest's clothes before cleaning and pull out pound notes of uncertain provenance and give them over to the colonel for recording and safe deposit. Northmore, according to the rural dean, had been unable to find any reason for the mysterious sum in the Exeter safe-box.

Now the question was not why Peter Kinsey had disappeared, but why he had been murdered.

Perhaps it was overconfidence—getting the hang of walking backwards—or perhaps it was a noise—the sharp sudden blast of a car horn in Church Lane—or perhaps it was a combination of the two, for just as they completed their seventh circumambulation, Tom's heel stubbed a slight rise in the beaten path which sent him stumbling backwards. Alerted, Julia tried to grip his arm more firmly, but his greater weight was too much and he slipped, landing on his back.

"Oh, Tom! Are you all right?"

"I'm fine," Tom gasped. "Just give me a minute."

He looked up into Julia's concerned face, then past her towards the tree's labyrinthine crown patterned against the sky. He turned his head left, then right. "Didn't work, did it?"

Julia's body sagged a little. "No."

"This isn't the age of miracles."

"Are you sure you're not hurt?"

"I'm fine," Tom insisted. "Really. It's quite peaceful lying here. I feel . . . Wait! Now I know why this yew tree lark of yours seems familiar. It's because I've done it before. When Lisbeth and I finally got our honeymoon, in the Lakes, we visited Wordsworth's gravesite, which happens to have a yew tree. I remember kissing her under it, but I'd forgotten we'd circled the tree, too—only I walked backwards and Lisbeth walked forwards. I can't remember how many times. Probably seven. It's always seven in these things, isn't it? Anyway, I tripped over my feet then, too. It's shameful I'd forgotten that, because that's how we conceived Miranda."

"I hope you're not telling me you and my sister were having it off in a graveyard."

"Sorry, I didn't put it very well. I meant to say that Miranda was conceived while we were in Grasmere."

"Then what's the significance of you walking backwards and Lisbeth forwards?"

"It's a fertility ritual," Tom replied, struggling upright. "Which is what I expect Mrs. P. was nattering on about just now. It's said fertility is achieved for a woman if she walks forwards around the yew and for a man by walking backwards."

He was so preoccupied dusting off the back of his trousers that at first he didn't pay attention to the low keening that challenged the chirruping birds in the churchyard, but when he turned back to Julia, he was startled to see her face crumpled with misery, her mouth biting the fleshy part of her hand between thumb and forefinger in an attempt to suppress the piteous sound. But it didn't work, for as he reached out instinctively to hold her in her distress, her hand fell away and a raucous sob escaped her lips. Her face only inches from his, she stared at him despondently. But before he could ask her what in heaven's name was the matter, she turned and darted out through the lych-gate and into Church Lane, turning not towards Pattimore's but towards home.

ather than turn left into the small hall as everyone else was doing, dutifully obeying the arrow on the sign, "Neighbourhood Watch Meeting," Tom turned right to the large hall, following Mitsuko Drewe, who was carrying a lumpy padded envelope. He had some information for her. He stepped into the village hall's larger room just in time to hear Mitsuko release a sound that fell somewhere between a shriek and a gasp. *Jesus wept,* he thought, glancing back at Watch chairperson Anne Willett to see if she had heard— she had, and gave him the sort of judgmental frown he expected she'd once used when she'd been principal of Thornford Regis Primary. *Two* distressed females in one morning, he thought, with a sinking heart.

For not unlike Julia, whose sightless staring at the yew tree had augured distress, Mitsuko was looking intently at the wall. Her body, in black vest top and matching knee shorts, was rigid.

"Mitsuko?" he ventured. He hoped he would have more success with Mitsuko's unhappiness than with Julia's. He had considered chasing after her earlier, but he doubted he could be useful, and falling down had temporarily hobbled his backside, making any chasing, in the literal sense, painful.

Mitsuko kept her eyes on the wall. "There's a quilt missing." Her voice was heavy as lead.

"Then Miranda was right." Tom joined her. "She said there ought to be one there. I think I mentioned we were in here looking at your artwork on Monday afternoon," he explained when she turned a puzzled frown to him.

"So it was gone by then."

"Apparently."

"This is so unfair!" Mitsuko exploded. "I've spent a year preparing this exhibit. And it's set to travel to Dartington this summer and Exeter in the fall. And this *on top of* having my computer and camera stolen!"

"I can imagine someone being keen on one of your quilts," Tom soothed. "They're exceptional."

"They'd be welcome to *buy* one!"

"Yes, there is that."

"If it's someone from the village, they're not going to get away with it for very long—people will notice if you're hanging one of my quilts in your sitting room."

"If your missing quilt wound up covering someone's bed, then perhaps it could be kept secret."

"It's *art*! It's not intended to cover a bed."

"Of course." Tom had a notion of purchasing one for Miranda's bed, since she had been so taken with them, but apparently he was a philistine.

"It must be someone from outside the village."

"But who from outside the village would have known you were hanging these quilts last Sunday?"

Mitsuko twisted her mouth in thought. "No one," she said, after a moment. "At least that I can think of."

"Then . . . ?"

"Maybe someone at the fayre?"

"But with so many people about?"

"They're only lightly filled with batting, Tom. They do fold up."

"Still, it was gone missing by the early afternoon, when I was here with Miranda. And she had been viewing your work earlier with Emily Swan. And there was a fair bit of traffic in and out of the village hall, all day. Many of the women don't care to use the port-a-loos outside, for one thing. And," he continued, ticking off items on his fingers, "there were the Twelve Drummers Drumming kids going in and out. And there were some setup crew here after nine, adding the finishing touches. Any number may have decided to have a sneak preview of your work."

"I would have insisted this room be kept locked, as I paid to have it for a fortnight, but the same key opens all the doors in the village hall, so it would have been futile."

"You need to report this."

"The police didn't take a blind bit of notice when I phoned yesterday about my computer theft. All I was given was a report number for my insurer. And I'm sure my art will get short shrift given the events of the—"

"Unless . . ."

"What?"

"Unless someone came through on Sunday afternoon when you were installing these quilts, took a fancy, then came back later."

Mitsuko said testily, "You'd think people would be home digesting their Sunday lunches. Really, I don't know why I'm bothering to have an opening. Half the village seems to have wandered through here one day or the other."

"The opening is still on?"

"Yes, Colm's insisted." Her temper eased. "He's being very gracious."

"Can you recall who passed through on Sunday?"

Mitsuko tapped the envelope against her cheek. "Well, Sebastian was very kindly helping me. It took much more time than I'd thought it would to install these quilts. You can see," she explained, pointing, "how wires had to be hooked to those rafters to hold the doweling rods that hold up the quilts. Anyway, Fred stepped in early on—this was before the toilet crisis—with his son. Charlie was due at the Twelve Drummers rehearsal next door . . ." She paused. "Fred!"

Tom shook his head.

"No, you're right, of course. Not his thing."

"Fred does have your extra set of keys to your flat," Tom said. "Which was what I came to tell you. I asked him about it yesterday in the pub. However, he has no particular intelligence about your alarm. Sybella switched it off for him on Sunday, as you told me earlier, and it was off when he delivered the toilet on Tuesday."

"Liam says he has no memory whether it was on or off Monday. Off is my guess. Our insurer won't be pleased." Mitsuko sighed noisily. "Anyway, who else was through here Sunday afternoon? Well, there was Liam. He showed up with my mobile and a message to phone my mother. I'd left my mobile at the Waterside and he couldn't get through to me on the village hall phone because the drums were so loud no one could hear it ringing." Mitsuko paused in thought. "And Colonel Northmore walked in with Bumble—I think to register a complaint about the peace of the Lord's Day being ruined by the drums, though I don't know why—Farthings is well out of earshot, I should think. Or maybe it was to talk with Sebastian. I don't know. As I say, it was hard to hear at times. Anyway, the colonel came in here and looked around—in that disapproving way of his, of course, and then when—"

"When?"

"Oh, nothing." She looked away. "He's a silly old man."

"Is that everybody?"

"The Daintreys poked their heads in, I recall. And Alastair came in, near the end of rehearsal. He was waiting for Julia. They had some golf club do to get to. That's it, as far as I know. Of course, sometimes I was up a ladder or otherwise distracted, so someone else might have wandered in."

Tom absently ran his forefinger over the rim of his dog collar. A little shiver travelled his spine. There couldn't possibly be *two* malefactors wandering through the village hall in a single evening,

surely? He looked at Mitsuko. Her face remained stamped with irritation. Hesitating to broach a connection between the missing
quilt and Sybella's death, he said instead:

"You're not thinking of running up a replacement on your
sewing machine?"

Her glance told him she thought he was thick for asking. "I
haven't the time or the material. And, of course, all the Thornford
pictures are stored in my computer, which has also gone missing."

Tom looked over at the nearest quilt. The scene was the fore-
court of the primary school, complete with clumps of bright-
coloured children at play. In the left corner he noticed a detail that
had escaped him when he'd viewed the quilts with his daughter.
Mitsuko had incorporated into her design the date stamp the digital camera imprinted on every picture, if programmed to do so. It
was an autumn scene, and if the touch of rust on the trees hadn't
given it away, the date did: October 24 of last year.

"What is the subject of the missing quilt?" he asked her.

"I was particularly fond of that one," Mitsuko responded sulkily.
"It was lovely—a view over the churchyard towards the millpond
and the river taken in the early evening."

Tom frowned, trying to visualise it. "But how—?"

"From atop the church tower."

"Really? It's so inaccessible. How did you get up?"

"The church architect had been scrambling around one afternoon. Sebastian had been accompanying him. So I asked if I could
go up the tower after they were done. Sebastian said it was okay."

"When was this?"

Mitsuko's eyes telescoped, as if she were viewing some inner
landscape. "I . . . I can't remember. I took absolute mounds of pictures over nearly a year. Of course, you can with digital."

"You captured Julia and me coming out of the pub the day of
Ned's funeral. That was"—he stepped down the hall to the relevant
quilt and peered at the bottom left corner—"April 6. And this one
is"—he stepped to the next one, a scene at the quay—"is July 19.

And this one, a grey day, it looks, is, yes, November 13—of course, Remembrance Sunday. There's Colonel Northmore laying a wreath at the memorial in The Square. You did record rather a lot of . . . Mitsuko? Are you sure you can't remember when you took the churchyard picture? Mitsuko?"

She shuddered. "I'll try to remember, if you think it's important," she said impatiently. She put her hand into the envelope and drew out a roll of masking tape. "Look, I really must put these labels up—"

He watched Mitsuko push the tape roll up her arm, then pluck from the envelope what appeared to be a white card, about six inches by three, mounted on, and framed by, black mat board. He glanced at the pool of lettering in the middle.

"How interesting!" he exclaimed. "It's a little poem."

"A haiku."

"Three lines. Seventeen syllables. Very . . ."

"Japanese?"

"I was going to say 'unusual.'"

"It was Liam's idea."

"Really?" Tom hoped he didn't sound too incredulous.

But Mitsuko had tucked the envelope under her arm and was concentrated on ripping a piece of tape off her roll. "I thought it might be a trifle stereotyping, but I did enjoy writing haiku as a teenager, so I thought, well, why not? Of course, it might have helped if Liam had installed these as I'd asked him to. There's so little time for everything . . ."

But Tom's attention had become gripped by the envelope. He stared at it, his mind roiling.

"Are you all right?" Mitsuko flicked him a glance.

"Oh . . . just a little heartburn," he white-lied. "Mrs. P. thought I needed to fortify myself with a full English this morning, given yesterday's events."

Mitsuko grimaced, whether in response to the notion of a greasy fry-up or the reality of Peter Kinsey's disinterment was unclear.

"I was actually sort of wondering," he began lightly, "why you didn't put these cards up on Sunday."

"Well, that was my intent, of course," she responded, applying the tape to the back of the card. "But the installation took more time than I'd expected. So I said I'd have to come back in the evening, as I was going up to Bridgend in the morning, but then my mother called in a state, so . . ." She pressed the card to the wall next to the quay-scene quilt. ". . . So I left this stuff and my key to the village hall at the Waterside and asked Liam if he could please find a moment during my absence to stick these things up on the wall . . . or get Sybella to do it. And, of course, when I get back to Thornford, the envelope hasn't travelled any farther than our flat. Liam said he didn't have the time."

Tom murmured sympathetically. But his mind had sped elsewhere, to the details of Tilly Springett's conversation with him at the Waterside: Liam walking towards the village hall Sunday night, holding something to his chest—not a stick of some nature, but a padded envelope and, more important, a key. A key to the village hall. He studied the punctilious woman before him, painstakingly applying tape to the back of another card. Liam had said nothing to her about travelling farther than their flat with the envelope Sunday night. Nor did she know that Tilly Springett was a witness. Tilly had held her tongue. At least with other villagers. So far.

"You haven't had Bliss and Blessing pay you a visit, have you?" he asked.

Mitsuko pushed the second of the cards against the wall. "Not yet. Liam has," she replied, stepping back and frowning at her handiwork. "Perhaps they think I'm still in Bridgend. Why do you ask?"

"No reason, really." Tom watched her hand dive into the envelope again. "Might I have a look at the haiku you wrote for the quilt that's missing?"

Mitsuko turned. Tom was surprised at the wariness in her eyes. "Okay," she agreed after a moment. She pulled all the cards from the envelope, hugged them to her chest, and rummaged through the lot. "Funny," she said, "it doesn't seem to be here."

om paid less mind to the Neighbourhood Watch meeting than he probably ought to have. In an ordinary week, he was sure, Watch meetings probably pulled fewer than a dozen villagers from their routines. But this was an extraordinary week, and villagers seemed out in force, coalesced into a buzzing hive of worry and outrage, whose pulse he felt surround him as he perched on one of the blue plastic chairs marshalled before a table of village worthies in the small hall. Said table was for table tennis, dragged from below the stage in the large hall, unfolded, and net removed, surely because it was the only thing the Watch executive, parish council members, and police representatives could possibly crowd behind without looking like they were wallflowers at a dance. DI Bliss and DS Blessing weren't in attendance. They were, explained a detective superintendent, a smoothie dispatched from Middlemoor, Devon & Cornwall Constabulary headquarters near Exeter, engaged in the *very real day-to-day work* of the investigation, though Tom wondered if HQ either was reluctant to trot out the untelegenic duo to an audience or was somehow unhappy with their progress.

Tom's heart went out to the villagers. Many seemed wont to believe some malign force from outside the village bore the blame for shattering their tranquillity. The gathering seemed more an exercise in jollying everyone along, as much as anyone could be jollied in the circumstances. The DSI preferred nothing more than what Tom—and, he suspected, half of Thornford—already knew, which wasn't a great lot.

Instead he found his mind going walkabout: Julia's worrisome behaviour, Mitsuko's latest disappointment, funeral arrangements for Sybella, his unfinished Sunday sermon, the sadness of being in the small hall three days after finding a young girl's dead body in it—all had a brief audience with his frontal lobes. However—and he could barely explain himself to himself, other than to think that he needed some distraction from worry—he found rather more lizard-like portions of his brain to be active and engaged, and focused on the other uniformed person at the front of the hall: PCSO Màiri White.

The local police community support officer, PCSO White had stopped by on her electric bicycle as he and Miranda were moving into the vicarage two months earlier. At the time, surrounded by partially opened boxes, the detritus of a life interrupted, and one small, vivacious child, he had paid scant attention to the uniformed figure with the Scottish accent. It had been a courtesy visit and he'd observed the courtesies. Glimpsing her *sans* uniform at the May Fayre three days earlier, however, had been somewhat of a revelation. He had a notion she might be unattached, knew she lived at Pennycross St. Paul, site of the other church in his benefice, and was aware she hadn't attended any of his services.

A little earlier, after leaving Mitsuko and joining the villagers stepping into the small hall, he'd noted Màiri White and found himself wondering if she had had a partner (what brought her to Devon?). As she approached him (she was wearing her uniform, damn), he wondered what she looked like naked.

"A change from Monday, I expect, Vicar," she observed, turning to survey the room, before he could register anything in her eyes, which were the blue of . . . something poetic, he thought. Cornflowers? Lisbeth would have sniggered at a reference so impossibly wet.

"'Tom' is fine."

She turned to him, her brow crinkled slightly. A smile played at the corners of her mouth. "I'm pleased to hear it, but . . . do you commonly refer to yourself in the third person?"

Tom felt a blush creeping up his neck. "I meant, you may address me as 'Tom.'" As soon he said it, he realised he sounded a complete prat. "*May* address" indeed, he groaned inwardly as he watched her smile gather force.

"Well, then, you may address me as Màiri. Long on the *a* and a wee roll of the *r* wouldn't go amiss."

Tom tried, but failed the *r* test. Over-rolled it.

"Never mind." PCSO White lifted an eyebrow. "'PCSO White' will do in a pinch."

"'PCSO' for short?"

"But not forever, I don't think."

"PC, then? Joining the regular force?"

"Perhaps." Her smile turned enigmatic. "And you? Bishop's throne? A yen for Lambeth Palace?"

"I'm happiest in the trenches."

"Not happy trenches at the minute, are they?"

"No, they are not," Tom agreed, eyeing the villagers filing into the room. None had been in the small hall when Tom had found Sybella's body. Colonel Northmore was in hospital; Madrun was likely busy rolling pastry with Miranda helping her; Julia was managing a milkless cup of tea; and the boys were probably up Gratton Lane with a football, more likely to be the targets of Neighbourhood Watch than its advocates.

"Do you happen to have any news on Peter Kinsey's death?" he asked PCSO White.

"I understand the pathologist's report has come down, if that's what you're after."

"And . . . ?"

She looked at him, seeming to weigh something in her mind. "I should keep my gob shut, but—as he died on your patch, so to speak, and as he was a previous incumbent, and"—she lowered her voice—"as long as you keep it to yourself—"

"I will."

"—the DSI, I expect," she nodded towards a man in a smart suit by the tennis table, "may not be forthcoming just yet about cause of death—"

"Oh?"

"Still early days. Sometimes they like to keep cause close to their chests to see if they can catch out any possible suspects. Anyway, between you and me, it appears the Reverend Mr. Kinsey died from severe head trauma."

"Merciful God, another one."

"It's not an uncommon way to dispatch someone, Vicar . . . Tom."

Tom accepted the likely truth of this reluctantly. "In the wider world, I suppose. But this is a little end-of-the-road village. It's supposed to be . . . arcadian."

"You're naïve."

"I realise I'm indulging in wishful thinking."

"You know what Sherlock Holmes said of village life, don't you?"

"Something to prove your point, I'll wager. What is it?"

" '. . . *That the lowest and vilest alleys in London do not present a more dreadful record of sin than does the smiling and beautiful countryside.*' "

"I might point out that Sherlock Holmes is fictional."

"You might, but it would do you little good." Màiri studied his face. "I understand your unwillingness to disavow the"—she groped for a word, then smiled—"*wickedness* . . . of village life." The smile vanished. "I know about your wife, and I'm very sorry."

"You're well informed."

"It's my business to be so, I'm afraid."

They both noted Mitsuko enter and survey the room.

"A case in point," Màiri remarked softly.

"You mean her husband," Tom murmured, for Liam had been flickering in the corner of his mind since PCSO White had passed on the intelligence about Peter Kinsey's death. *All Clergy Are Bastards.*

"No, I meant her recent burglary. What did *you* mean?"

"Oh!" Feeling he had been caught out tittle-tattling, Tom stammered. "I just meant . . . I mean . . ."

Màiri said evenly, "Tom, I know all about Liam Drewe's conviction for GBH. But I think the whole village does, too, does it not?"

"I suppose it does." Tom groaned. "I'm beginning to discover how difficult it can be to have a private life in a place this small." He heard the rue in his own voice: He had a sudden wild notion to ask Màiri if she fancied a coffee sometime, but instantly thought better of it. If he was seen at the Waterside with her in anything but her uniform, it would be all around the houses before he'd settled the bill. And if he was seen with her in a café outside the village, it would look like he was sneaking about. And, anyway, she might rebuff him. And—good heavens!—he was having anxieties he hadn't had since he picked up the phone in his rooms at Cambridge to thank the delightful Lisbeth Rose, again, for rescuing him from the turbulent (ha!) Cam and invite her out for a meal.

"At any rate," he heard Màiri say in a low voice as Mitsuko approached them, "I doubt Mr. Drewe is the only man in Thornford to have had trouble with the law."

"Come out into the garden. We can talk there," Tom told Sebastian, pouring each of them a whisky after everyone else had been ushered out through the front door of the vicarage. The late afternoon meeting of the church council, along with two members of the local con-

stabulary, including PCSO White, had been called to sort through
some security details in advance of the next day's funeral, and had
proceeded smoothly but for the occasional brandishing of a tut-tut,
until Sebastian made the disconcerting announcement that he could
not—or, rather, would not—be present at Sybella's funeral. Several
people in Tom's sitting room had regarded Sebastian with puzzlement—though vergers weren't required at funeral services, they usually attended anyway—and looked to Tom for guidance on how to
react. Karla, about to bite into a slice of Madrun's excellent ginger-
bread cake, beat Tom to the punch.

"And why not?" she snapped as if confronted at her wicket at the
post office by a customer who refused to pay for stamps.

"My reasons are entirely private," Sebastian had replied evenly,
informing them that he had asked Dickie Horton, the verger at St.
Paul's in Pennycross, if he would fill in. Dickie, who had filled in on
occasion the thirty years he had been verger of St. Paul's, was happy
to do so. Thrilled, Tom suspected, as he'd found Dickie poring over
a copy of *Hello!* magazine in the vestry of St. Paul's the first Sunday
he'd taken services there. Still, Tom was not pleased: Dickie was adequate to the task, but apt to be unreliable, due in part to a fondness
for drink and possible interferences from the steel plate in his head.
And Sebastian had not consulted him first, before approaching
Dickie, which was surprising and out of character. Taking their cue
from Tom, however, whose only comment was, "I expect we'll have
to manage," the others quickly moved on to other matters.

"I would have to say I'm disappointed," Tom told Sebastian, taking a deep breath of the air frothy with the scent of elderflowers in
bloom. He settled into one of a set of wicker chairs under an ancient
pear tree that grew next to the side of the house, lifted his glass of
whisky to his eye, rather than his lips, and peered through the cut
crystal at refracted images of St. Nicholas's. Bright rainbows limned
the edges of the church tower, which stood black against the late afternoon sun. His ears picked up the muffled tremolo of the organ—

Julia in rehearsal—and the muted chorus of Revelation Choir, and he gave a passing thought to the spectacle the next day's funeral might be. Several of the downmarket tabloids had already seized upon Sybella's death as an excuse to revisit her mother's very public excesses. "I know you said your reasons were private, but now that the others have left, I wonder if you might share your reasons with me."

Sebastian balanced on the edge of his matching wicker. "I'm sorry, Tom. It's not my intent to upset anyone . . . or anything. But it's vital I absent myself."

"I am your priest, you know," Tom responded, lowering the glass, surprised. What could be so vital? "If there's something troubling you, you can tell me. It won't go any farther, you have my word."

"I know that."

Tom's attention was drawn to a butterfly, its wings tipped with bright orange, which had fluttered in under the pear's low-hanging branches. It hovered over Sebastian's glass.

"I'm surprised," he continued, noting Sebastian's expression soften almost imperceptibly as he watched the delicate creature fan the air, "that you wouldn't wish to help. You work with Colm in his garden nearly every day. I can only assume—"

Here, Tom caught himself, suddenly recalling another expression on Sebastian's face—the one on Monday when he'd burst into the village hall. Tom chose his next words carefully.

"I can only hope," he began again, "that you don't harbour some . . . antipathy towards Sybella . . ."

The butterfly settled on the edge of Sebastian's glass.

". . . because," Tom continued with a dash of provocation when no response was forthcoming, "I think Sybella found you not *un*interesting." He allowed a smile to play along his lips. "A sort of crush, you might say. Which might explain her presence in church the last month."

Sebastian leaned forwards and blew gently on the butterfly. They both watched it unfold its wings and flit off towards the lawn, where Powell—or, possibly, Gloria—streaked into view from a bed of hyacinths and narcissi and began pawing at the air.

"Tom, I paid her no attention. She's a child. *Was* a child."

"You paid her enough attention to tear up a drawing she was making of you."

"I see Eric's been free with information." Sebastian lifted his whisky and took a grim sip. "All right, yes, I did destroy a sketch she was doing of me in the pub. But she didn't ask my permission. I found her drawing me without my permission intrusive." He attacked the whisky again. "I expect she got me at a bad moment, that's all. I did apologise." He glared down the lawn, where the cat continued to jab mercilessly at the orange-tip. "Look, Tom, as I think you know by now, I very much value my privacy."

How much do you value it? Tom couldn't help thinking. *And to what length would you go to protect it?* Instead he grunted: "You're sort of a riddle, wrapped in a cassock, inside an enigma—to make a pig's breakfast of Churchill. You do know that, don't you? By being so circumspect about your life, you provoke the opposite—you arouse curiosity."

"I can't help that."

"I'm sure some in the village have trawled the Internet to see what they might glean."

"You, for instance?" Sebastian turned from the cat swatting at the butterfly.

"No, Sebastian. Despite your . . . guardedness, you're a welcoming and calming presence in the church. And a great help to me in many matters. If you want to keep yourself to yourself, that's perfectly fine with me. Only . . ."

"Only?"

". . . occasionally it occurs to me to ask where you went to school. Or what your father does for a living. Or where you were confirmed. That sort of thing. Such questions don't seem all that intrusive."

"And the answers aren't all that interesting," Sebastian replied evenly, then tensed. "That bloody cat! Look—it's caught that butterfly."

Tom turned to see Gloria—or, possibly, Powell—bring the insect to ground and leap upon it with feline glee.

"Too late." He watched the butterfly's orange tip disappear into the cat's greedy maw. "You should see what it brings me some mornings in bed. Tributes of mice and birds. I even had a vole last month." He noted Sebastian's pained expression. "Not fond of cats, I take it."

"No, not really. We always had dogs when I was growing up."

"Really. Where did you grow up?"

Sebastian smiled. "Somewhere in the United Kingdom."

"Well, I suppose that narrows it a bit," Tom responded dryly. He sipped his whisky. "Presuming the police asked you the same question, what did you reply? I expect Bliss and Blessing have interviewed you. You work for Sybella's father, after all."

"I gave them a more precise answer."

"And were they satisfied?"

A shadow passed over Sebastian's face. "For the time being."

Tom studied him. How long, in the face of a police investigation, could Sebastian preserve his privacy? Surely, if Sybella had had a crush on Sebastian, it couldn't have escaped the attention of other, gossipy, villagers. And surely that snippet, feeble as it was, would send the two detectives back to the verger's cottage with more questions.

"I expect Eric hasn't been as free with information as you might think," he mused.

"You mean about the incident with Sybella's drawing? I expect you're right. The police didn't ask."

"And should the police ask?"

"I shall tell them what I told you."

Tom lifted an eyebrow, but said nothing. Mightn't the detectives wonder, too, how much Sebastian valued his privacy? He took another sip of his whisky. It was an excellent single malt, left over from Giles James-Douglas's day, which made him think to ask:

"It was Phillip Northmore, was it not, who approached Giles James-Douglas about taking you on as verger?"

"Yes." Sebastian hesitated. "Phillip was a great friend of my grandfather's. They were in the same regiment in the war."

"Presumably, then, they were in the same prisoner-of-war camp."

Sebastian nodded. "Unfortunately, the experience shattered my grandfather's health and he died sooner than he ought to have. On the other hand, given what they endured, Phillip's stamina has been remarkable . . . well, until recently."

Tom waved his arm at the approaching cat. A wing jutting from its mouth fluttered helplessly. "Perhaps if Powell and Gloria weren't pitch-black . . ."

"Yes, a priest with two black cats . . ."

"It doesn't do, does it?"

"At least King Dumb—Powell and Gloria's brother—was calico."

"So I understand . . . but I heard the previous incumbent ran over him with his car."

"Peter wasn't fond of cats either."

Tom glanced at Sebastian sharply, then laughed. "You're not suggesting . . . ?"

"King Dumb was aptly named," Sebastian replied. They both watched the rest of the butterfly disappear into the cat's mouth. "Slept in traffic. Probably deaf."

Tom frowned. An oblique reply. But then he had an oblique verger. He lifted his glass and sloshed the tawny liquid absently. "So," he continued, one eye on Powell—yes, it was Powell—who made his way to the base of the tree, extended his body along the trunk, and began ferociously scratching at the bark, "it was a familial connection brought you here. I didn't know that."

Sebastian hesitated again. "No one does," he replied finally.

Tom blinked. "Well, one does now. I'm sort of surprised you've shared even this detail with me."

"I think I can trust you, Tom."

"I'm flattered. But why? I've had the living barely two months. You can't say you know me well."

"No, but I know enough. Perhaps I've become adept at watching and listening. I've watched you and listened to you. I don't think you're someone who would intentionally let someone down."

"I could go rooting through some regimental history," Tom joked, faintly embarrassed by the vote of confidence. "I know which one Phillip was attached to, and that could lead me to—"

"You could, Tom," Sebastian interrupted, "but I know you won't. And in any case," he added with a tight smile, "you would find it of little use."

"I see." He didn't really, but was grateful for the expression of trust, though he wasn't sure what engendered it. "But surely Giles knew your background. Whatever it might be," he added. Candidates for verger had to go through a Criminal Records Bureau check, for one thing.

"No. Giles was remarkably incurious. Some on the church council questioned Phillip when he introduced me as a candidate, but I gather he was able to persuade them of my merits."

"Then what about introducing you to the parish? 'Sebastian John comes to us from . . . ' oh, Ham Parma in Gloucestershire where he was under-gardener to the Marquis of Tiswas or something like that."

"I believe Giles introduced me by saying that I arrived in Thornford thanks to the grace of God."

Tom laughed. "True, perhaps, but a bit over the top."

"More than a bit. But Giles was rapidly descending into senility when I arrived. He probably wouldn't have remembered, even if he had been told."

"Surely the villagers expressed some curiosity?"

"A little. But I don't think they expected me to last very long. Giles, you see, ran through rather a few vergers later in life."

"Odd."

"Well, the villagers were fond of Giles, you see, so they turned a blind eye to his—"

"Ah, yes, that was just crossing my mind. The vergers were likely all young, possibly blond, most certainly male, very likely low on funds, and probably not from these parts."

"I'm not sure about blond, but the rest of the description fits, I believe. I don't think there was ever any scandal. Most of them grew bored with country life soon enough and returned to London. Giles was never anything but kind and decent to me." Sebastian's eyes followed Powell as he scrambled up the tree into the thicket of branches. "And anyway, he died within a few months of my arrival."

"And Peter Kinsey? What did he—"

But Sebastian's expression shifted suddenly as he continued to stare into the tree.

"What . . . ?" Tom began. Then he, too, saw. "Miranda, what are you doing up there?"

"Daddy, the branch goes right by my window!"

Tom twisted his head towards the back of the vicarage. It was true. The branch did run by Miranda's bedroom window, but it looked barely strong enough to support even a cat's weight.

"Miranda, come down. You're too high. What if you fall?"

"I won't."

"You might."

"Powell's in the way."

Tom contemplated tossing his whisky tumbler at the cat.

"I'll get him," Sebastian volunteered, standing. Powell, just within reach, howled as Sebastian peeled him off the tree.

"How long have you been up there?" Tom asked when his daughter had slipped down the branch safely to the lawn. His heart was pounding. He glanced at Sebastian, who was gripping the struggling cat. The shift in his expression had been to one of alarm and it had little modified.

"A while."

"You were very quiet."

"I was thinking." She leaned in towards Tom's chair and looked up at Sebastian shyly.

"About what?" Tom asked.

"Stuff."

Always a satisfying answer. "What stuff?"

"Madame Drewe. J'avais raison, Papa. Au hall de village, il y avait un absent . . ." She frowned and put her hand up to her mouth.

"Daddy's French has its limits, darling."

"Édredon," Sebastian supplied.

Tom raised an eyebrow. Sebastian's education evidently encapsulated more than tourist French, and the loss of the quilt—for that was what *édredon* could only mean—had already, it seemed, reached his ears. And Miranda's. The bush telegraph was in top form.

"Yes, you're right about there being a quilt missing. You're very clever. You must be my daughter." He gave her an assuring squeeze, and glanced at his verger. "Now, Daddy was having a private talk with Sebastian. You know what I mean by 'private,' don't you? It means that we've talked about things we want to keep to ourselves. You know because I'm a priest I sometimes hear confession from people, don't you? They tell me things and I must absolutely keep them to myself. It's a bit like that now. There are times when it's best to keep things you've heard or seen or know to yourself, because if you didn't, it might be very very hurtful to someone."

Miranda's mouth twisted. "But what if you think someone's done something very bad?"

"Well, that's different. Then you tell someone—me or Mrs. Prowse or your teacher or Aunt Julia." He bent so her face was nearer his. "*Is* there someone you think has done something very bad?"

Miranda glanced away, towards Sebastian, who seemed oblivious to the creature struggling in his arms. Tom followed the glance. He frowned, puzzled.

"No," she replied, but there was a shade to her tone that sent his parental radar twitching.

"You're sure?"

"Yes, Daddy." Miranda slipped from her father's grip just as the cat tore from Sebastian, shredding the fabric of his shirt along the shoulder.

"Looks like cats aren't fond of you, either," Tom observed. "I'm sure Mrs. Prowse will be happy to mend that, if you like."

But Sebastian was studying Miranda, who crouched to pet the sulky cat and straighten its madly twitching tail.

"Bon chat, bon petit chat," she cooed. *"Mais que dirais-tu de l'édredon absent de Madame Drewe?"*

"You mustn't worry about Mrs. Drewe's quilt, darling. It's probably just misplaced. It'll turn up somewhere, I'm sure."

"Oh, Daddy, don't be silly. It's been stolen."

"Oh." So hard to mollify a clever child. "Well, then," Tom sighed. "What would Alice Roy do if this was 'The Case of the Missing Quilt'?"

"Alice would look for a clue."

"Ah, a clue. What kind of clue?"

"Je ne sais pas." Miranda rose off her haunches as Powell scuttled out of her reach. *"Je devrai penser cela."*

"Well, while you're thinking about it, perhaps you should see if Mrs. Prowse would like any help preparing supper."

"She's making salmon en croute."

"Good God. Lisbeth and I could barely manage that if we had a dinner party." He watched Miranda dash after the cat then veer towards the door to his study. "You wouldn't care to join us, would you, Sebastian?"

"Very kind of you to ask, but I have something at home."

"You mustn't worry about Miranda, you know. She's good as gold. And I'll have another word with her after supper."

Sebastian nodded.

"Sit a minute. Miranda's concern about Mitsuko's artwork brings me to something I want to ask you. Do you know which piece was stolen?" he asked, as Sebastian resumed his seat.

"No, I don't. All I learned in the pub at noon was a quilt had gone missing. Why? Do you?"

"It was of a view over the churchyard towards the millpond. Do you recall it?"

Sebastian looked away from him, studying Powell's huffy march across the lush lawn. "I'm not sure. I . . . It was tricky mounting the quilts. My attention wasn't much on their content."

"It's odd anybody would take *a* quilt, to begin with. As Mitsuko pointed out to me this morning, it would soon get about the village if someone had an interesting new coverlet on their bed. And it's difficult to imagine someone coming from afar to nick a quilt. In addition, there was so little opportunity. You and she put it up Sunday afternoon. By Monday morning it was gone. I can only assume someone who was in the village hall Sunday afternoon—someone who saw it—must have taken it later."

Sebastian's expression tightened. "Do you mean me? Is that what you wanted to ask?"

Tom was taken aback. "No, actually, I wasn't thinking of you at all." He regarded Sebastian curiously. *Ought I to be?* he wanted to ask. "It's just that I can't help associating this theft with Sybella's death. It's too much of a coincidence that sometime late Sunday evening or early Monday both a murderer *and* a thief were busying themselves at the village hall."

"You mean the thief and the murderer were one and the same person."

"Precisely."

"I'm not sure I can be of much help."

"Well, as I said, the picture Mitsuko chose for the missing quilt was one of a series she took of the churchyard, with views towards the millpond and towards the village and such. There's only one vantage point from which she can do this—atop the church. It's the highest point in the village. She tells me she got the idea because the church architect had been in town one afternoon and the church tower was unlocked right to the top. She said that you let her up."

"Yes, I expect I did. It's . . . I'd sort of forgotten . . ."

"I asked her when this was, but she said she couldn't remember. Anyway, I have the quinquennial inspection report somewhere in the piles of paper in my study, and I was going to root around to find it and see what the date of the inspection was, but it seems just as easy to ask you since you're here—and since you were *there,* opening up the church and guiding the architect and the like. Was the inspection before Peter went missing, or after?"

Sebastian shifted in his chair. The wicker squeaked.

"Sebastian?"

"Before."

"Did Peter not meet with the architect?"

Sebastian hesitated. "No," he said finally. "I told the architect what he ought to look for and what problems we were having with the building."

Tom frowned, thinking it rude for a priest not to meet the church architect. He came only once every five years.

"You see," Sebastian continued, "the architect came on a Monday, and Peter always took Mondays as his day off and always went somewhere out of the village."

"I see. Then do you remember which Monday the architect arrived?"

Sebastian did. And the date he supplied set Tom's brain alight.

CHAPTER NINETEEN

"*T*hird time today."

"What?"

"I say, it's the third time today we've run into each other."

"Hardly 'run into.'" Màiri White eyed him, sipping something pale from a plastic flute glass. "The first two were scheduled events."

"That's true," Tom responded awkwardly to this blunt truth. "But somehow I didn't expect to see you here."

"Oh, aye. 'What's the plod doing at a cultural event?' you ask yourself."

"That's not it at all." Tom was dismayed "I just thought . . . I don't know what I was thinking . . . that you live over at Pennycross? That . . . ?"

That you have a husband/boyfriend/partner/four cats/three dogs/two children/and a budgerigar in a pear tree—all of which so absorb your off-hours you don't have a moment to catch a rerun of The Bill, *much less swill pinot grigio at an art opening.*

". . . That . . . that . . ." he continued stammering.

A smile plucked at the corners of Màiri's mouth. "You're an

earnest bugger, Tom Christmas. I'm no stranger to the odd art open-ing, and I think Mitsuko Drewe's a clever lass, and I like to see what she's up to, but I'm mainly here to keep my eye on you lot in this murderous village."

"Hardly mur—"

"Keep your eyeballs in your head, Vicar. No one can hear us."

It was true. The village hall's large hall had a herring-barrel qual-ity to it this Thursday evening, with folk edging and twisting around each other for advantage in art inspection and nosh acquisition, ratcheting up the volume into a range more hubbubby than mur-murry, with only the hanging quilts acting as damper. It seemed like *tout le village*—as Ghislaine might have said—had come out.

"It's a bit of a crowd, isn't it?" Màiri said.

"You're not in uniform," Tom observed, noting her light blue jumper and neat black trousers over her slender hips.

"I don't live in the bloody thing, you know. Not like you." She gestured towards his neck. "You'll asphyxiate yourself."

Tom ran his finger around his dog collar and let his tongue hang unfetchingly outside his mouth. "It's my housekeeper's cooking. I think she's fattening me up for market."

"What market?"

"I'm not sure," he replied, though the marriage market flitted through his head as an implausibility. He thought he discerned a certain cunning in Madrun: Perhaps her intent was to transform him into a ball of butter, so unattractive no woman would ever think to displace her in the vicarage.

"I don't recognise some of these people." Tom changed the sub-ject, looking over Màiri's shoulder. "Of course, I haven't been in Thornford long enough to know everyone. And not everyone comes to church."

"I think there's one or two who aren't here to appreciate the art."

"You mean—?"

"Takes all sorts," she murmured darkly.

Tom grunted. He was familiar with the voyeuristic response to crime. After Lisbeth's death, he had observed a few strangers in the sanctuary, gazing not at the stained glass or the memorial plaques, but at the stone tiles near the south porch that had once been stained with blood. And his first Sunday returned to the pulpit, though he had felt a tide of sympathy wash towards him from the crowded pews, he'd been sickened to note here and there as he preached eyes glittering not with sympathy but with remorseless curiosity.

"Pardon me," brayed a voice behind him, breaking into his thoughts. A whippet-thin man whose face had the pallor of London slush pushed past him, pulling a packet of cigarettes from his jacket pocket.

"And then there's the professionally morbid." Màiri gestured towards the figure departing through the hall doors into the early evening sunshine.

She didn't need to spell it out. The mien, mettle, and desperate need for a fag stamped the man as Press.

"Are there more of them?" Tom asked, glancing around. "Reporters, I mean."

"There's one over there." Màiri nodded towards a tall figure casting a gimlet eye over the assembled. He caught their assessing glances, realised he'd been rumbled, and turned, pretending to be fascinated with the quilt behind him—one that depicted the lantern procession at the wassailing evening in the Old Orchard.

"In search of local colour, I suppose," Tom mused, giving an unhappy thought to what might fill the Sunday papers.

"More likely looking for a chance to slip into the small hall to view the crime scene, the creep. But Liam Drewe's in there preparing nosh. I can't imagine him standing for any bother. Is that Enid Pattimore?" she continued, turning towards the quilt nearest them.

"Looks like it." Tom surveyed the photographic spread in the middle of Mitsuko's quilt. In it, Roger was standing behind the counter of the village shop, serving a customer whose Barbour'd back was to the camera. Roger's mother was peeking around the door to the back storage.

"Poor woman. She looks like she has a wee set of antlers growing out of her nose."

Tom looked closer. "Enid gets rather prodigious nosebleeds. Well, among other ailments. Alastair—Dr. Hennis—regularly fetches over to fix her up.

"It's a nose clip of sorts," he clarified, as Màiri leaned towards the quilt. "Staunches the flow. Sometimes she wears it to Sunday service."

"You could hang a Christmas ball from it." Màiri moved to the next quilt. "And this must be you."

"And that's Julia Hennis—my late wife's sister—with me."

". . . who teaches at Hamlyn Ferrers and started Twelve Drummers Drumming. Dr. Hennis's wife. Yes, I know her."

Tom snatched a glass of something red off a tray from a passing youth—Kerra Prowse, Jago's daughter, it looked like.

"How did you become a vicar, then?" Màiri turned from the quilt.

"Oh, the usual way. Spent some time at the vicar factory. Ordination. Curate for a bit."

This time Màiri laughed. "No, I meant what brought you to the Church? You were a professional magician, weren't you? So said the parish magazine some months back."

"The Great Krimboni of blessed memory, yes. Sleight of hand for all occasions. I had a great passion for magic when I was young. When I was about ten, I saw a magician at the carnival they have every year at Gravesend, where I grew up. I must have spent four hours that day watching him. He had these enormous silver hoops that he could link together, then unlink. But I examined them—he showed the hoops to me—and they were seamless. I couldn't understand how he could link them together. At any rate, I was utterly hooked. Kate—one of my mothers—"

"You have more than one mother?"

"Four, actually." Tom counted on his fingers. "There was my birth mother, who remains a mystery. My adoptive mother, who died in a plane crash—"

"I'm very sorry."

"I was barely two. I have no memory of her. My father's—my adoptive father's—sister then adopted me. My father died in the same plane crash, you see. And my aunt, as she was, lived with her partner. So that makes four mothers. But Dosh and Kate were the mothers major."

"I've no doubt they doted on you."

Tom regarded Màiri as she sipped her wine. Her interest in his background seemed genuine, but her eyes kept roving past his shoulders towards the nether parts of the room.

"I'm not looking for a better conversation prospect, if that's what's passing through your cerebellum," she said, which was exactly what he had been thinking.

"Of course. I just . . ." Tom was faltering over the word "dote." In truth, Dosh and Kate had doted on him, each in her own way— from indulgent Kate, it was more Eponymous prezzies than the neighbour kids and lots of holiday trips to America on her pass (she was a flight attendant); from exacting Dosh, it was extra tutoring in any subject he was deficient in, and permission for more than one dog, provided *provided!* he was responsible for their care (she was a veterinarian). By reckoning, as an only child, Tom should have been fairly spoiled. But maybe it was being knocked about as a kid for having two mothers in the first place, and maybe it was the steadying presence of the third anchor in his life, the daughterful but sonless Reverend Canon Christopher Holdsworth, rector of St. George's in Gravesend, Dosh's church, who came to his football matches, helped him build a doghouse, and taught him fly fishing in Scotland, that kept him on the straight and narrow. Still, even as a child, he had felt slightly at a remove from other children—marked out, as it were, by the unconventionality of his circumstances: twice orphaned, twice adopted, raised by two women. Being marked out stayed with him; it waned through adolescence, when being one of the crowd was the imperative, but it reasserted itself, and in a way wholly unexpected, on a cruise ship plying the Mediterranean, when he was twenty-six.

His thinking was racing ahead of his conversation, but he had this inexplicable urge to tell this attractive young woman, this police person—of all creatures; after being womanhandled by Bristol CID he wasn't awfully fond of the police—everything about himself. He looked at his glass of wine. He'd hardly had a sip.

"At any rate," he began again, "Kate went up to Davenport's in London and bought me a 'World of Illusion' magic kit, and that was that. By fifteen, I was a table magician at a hotel in Gravesend and while I was at university—the first time—I gigged in pubs and bars around Canterbury doing close-up magic for extra money."

"Did you ever figure out the ring trick?" They had moved on to a quilt depicting several pensioners at the bus stop near Thorn Cross. Màiri leaned in to read the haiku next to it.

"Oh, yes." Tom smiled. "I had a set of five golden rings—well, they weren't really gold, just gold-coloured—that I used to amuse and confuse. But by then I had got a bit more serious about magic as a career. I'd read religious studies at the University of Kent, which made me eligible to be a tea boy on British Rail, and had busked around Europe for a year or so working street cafés and local festivals. When I got back, I improved my skills with a master conjurer, developed The Great Krimboni persona, started doing large parties and corporate gigs, and even a few stints on a cruise—"

He stopped. He could see Màiri's attention had been drawn away. He was boring her!

"Shall I intervene, do you think?" she asked.

"What?" Tom turned. He followed her gaze towards the south end of the hall, opposite the stage, where a cleft had opened in the multitude and the din had fallen to a whisper. The pallid London reporter, who must have slipped back into the hall post-fag, was being escorted out again. Karla Skynner had his left ear pinched firmly in her right hand. "Such language will not be tolerated at a public event in this village, Mr. Macgreevy," she could be heard barking above his helpless cursing. Tom noted the other reporter in the room blanch.

"My question was rhetorical," Màiri said, as Karla pushed the outside door open with a swift kick. "She's remarkably forceful for such a wee thing."

"She's one of the more fiercesome churchwardens I've had in my career."

"I noted that from your meeting this afternoon." Màiri stepped to another quilt as the hubbub resumed in the room. "She wasn't keen on your verger's dereliction of duty. Did you get to the bottom of it? I noticed you had Sebastian stay behind."

"No, Sebastian prefers his privacy. But he told me something very interesting—" Tom was about to mention a curious concurrence of events the day the church architect arrived the previous year, but he was cut short by Madrun jabbing a tray at his elbow. "Oh, hello, Mrs. Prowse," he said, taking one of two tiny remaining pastries. "Has Mitsuko got you serving these creations as well as baking them?"

"I'm lending Kerra a hand. She had her first day at the Waterside today. She's feeling a little overwhelmed at the minute."

"Kerra is Mrs. Prowse's niece," Tom explained to Màiri, who murmured between bites, "These are absolutely brilliant. What's the filling?"

"Yew berries." Madrun frowned at Màiri before quickly turning back to Tom.

"Yew berries!" Màiri's eyes widened.

"Apparently Mrs. Prowse's yew berry tartlets are famous locally," Tom told her. "They're—"

"You really must circulate, Mr. Christmas," Madrun interrupted. "I believe Mitsuko wanted a word, for one."

"Of course," Tom said humbly as Madrun moved towards the doors to the corridor to the small hall, then made a face at Màiri. The policewoman was staring aghast at the remains of the pastry she was holding.

"She'll poison someone . . ." she began, hastily brushing a flake of pastry from the corner of her mouth with her other hand.

"You'd think, wouldn't you? But apparently Mrs. Prowse has

been serving them for more than a quarter century with no loss of life. She's extremely careful about removing the seeds."

"A health warning wouldn't go amiss!"

Tom glanced around the crowded room, noting Mitsuko kissing two men with short clipped beards who had just arrived. "Perhaps I should circulate, as my housekeeper has more or less commanded."

"But you haven't told me what brought you to the Church."

"Oh! Well . . ." Tom displayed the tiny pastry between his thumb and forefinger. He found himself loath to leave her company. "It was something very like this."

"I didn't know pastry cups could have such a profound effect."

"They can if there's thousands of them, along with tables groaning with other delicacies." He paused to pop the pastry into his mouth. "I was on a cruise ship, the *Star Odyssey,* in the Mediterranean. I had gigged on cruise ships a time or two before, but this time the ever-present still, small voice in my head—no, I'm not mad—it's the one that had been telling me all along that what I was doing in life wasn't quite the thing—anyway, the voice got louder." He watched Mitsuko weaving through the crowd and gave a passing thought to hailing her. "I had a bit of a Damascus moment at the buffet table," he confessed, watching her disappear through the doors to the small hall. "Have you ever been on a cruise?"

"Never."

"The buffets are grotesque, glory be's to dissipation—a medieval banquet barring roast swan and larks' tongues in aspic. Worse, you order off the menu, if you like; you can order eight dishes—or ten, or all of them!—and just have a nibble of each, because the price of food is included in the fare. And people do it.

"Once, late at night, after my last performance, I happened to be on deck and watched as the ship released an enormous tide of un-nibbled nosh into the sea. In the moonlight, the mess of it gleamed like an oil slick. The next morning, when I trotted down to the twenty-four-hour breakfast buffet, I came over all mad-keen to turn over the tables of eggs Florentine and bananas flambé and denounce the den of excess."

"Like Jesus with the moneylenders in the temple."

Tom raised an eyebrow.

"I have a vague affiliation with Presbyterianism," Màiri told him. "I'm a north-of-the-border lass, you realise."

"Well, it was a little like that. Only I'm not sure I wanted to turn the *Star Odyssey* into a house of prayer. Or would have had any success. At any rate, my appendix had been acting up and was fit to burst so I had to be taken off ship at Barcelona. While I was recuperating I had time to consider whether I wanted to spend life on a luxury barge doing little more than amusing people between bites of *tournedos au poivre* or whether I couldn't be of service in some other way. So when I returned to Southwark, I started going to the Cathedral, and before long—"

But Màiri was no longer listening. Her face had taken on an alert expression replicated by others in the room as the chatter, as though by an unseen hand fiddling a radio knob, fell to a hush. Tom noted Kerra, her tray empty by her side, hesitate before the door to the passageway connecting the large and small halls, then turn awkwardly to face the room, inadvertently becoming a centre of attention as people's heads swiveled towards the source of the furious voices—Liam's bass and Mitsuko's soprano. Listening to the Drewes arguing was becoming village sport. Tom motioned to Kerra to join him and Màiri.

"His bark is worse than his bite," he said of Liam, echoing Marg Farrant's comment, though he wasn't sure he believed it—then or now. "How's your first day on the job been?"

Kerra blinked back tears. "Awful," she said. "Aunt Madrun warned me."

"Liam has a sort of . . . artistic temperament." Tom groped for a soothing explanation.

"He was okay until two detectives arrived."

Again? Tom thought, glancing at Màiri.

"Then I couldn't seem to do anything right."

"If he's being bullying to you, you come and see me," Màiri told her.

Kerra smiled tentatively. "I'm taking kung fu classes at Totnes."

"Well, good for you then. Go take a look at that quilt nearest the stage, while you're waiting. I think you're in it. Have you had a chance to look at it?"

"No."

"Go on with you, then."

"Even hurricanes blow themselves out eventually," Tom called after her. Conversation was returning to its previous hum in the room. "I mean"—he turned back to Màiri—"an argument can't go on forever."

"True. It took a thousand years, but even England and France managed to patch it up." She ran a finger around the rim of her wineglass. "I assume DI Bliss and DS Blessing interviewed you, too."

"I couldn't be very helpful, I'm afraid. They spent more time being speculative in front of me. Wondered, for instance, if perhaps Sybella had been killed to somehow get at her father."

"An apparently motiveless crime is a bit wearing on a detective. They're digging through all sorts, not only here in the village but Sybella's London connections, her family connections . . ."

They stepped around one of the bearded fellows who had been talking with Mitsuko earlier. He and his compatriot were both studying the wall.

"Perhaps the intent is to amplify the complexity of the other works through the use of negative space," one could be heard saying.

"Mmm," the other demurred. "Or perhaps it's a statement about the vacuity of village life, that there is a profound absence of meaning at its very heart."

Màiri leaned towards Tom and whispered: "Whatever are they talking about?"

"I think they don't know a quilt has gone missing," he whispered back, taking in the aroma of the scent she was wearing. "Mitsuko reported the loss, yes?"

"And I've forwarded the report. It seems like more than chance a piece of art would disappear from the village hall where a young woman was murdered the very same night."

"Did Mitsuko tell you what the picture in the quilt depicted?"

"The churchyard. I understand she took a number of pictures from atop the church tower overlooking the village."

"She couldn't remember when she took the pictures when I spoke to her this morning," Tom said. Or claimed she couldn't, Tom considered, thinking back to his encounter with Mitsuko on almost this very spot earlier in the day. Her behaviour, her wariness, her impatience—in light of what Sebastian had revealed in the vicarage garden this very afternoon—now seemed to him peculiar. How could she not remember what day she had been atop the church tower? It had been the day *before* she had taken the photo of Julia and him exiting the Church House Inn, the afternoon of Ned Skynner's funeral.

The day before the funeral had been the day of the quinquennial church inspection, Tom thought. The day when Peter Kinsey was last seen. A funeral, an absent vicar, a once-in-five-years inspection—surely this conjunction of events would have resonated, even if months went by before you examined the photos you had downloaded into your computer. He wasn't prepared to express his qualms to Màiri, but he believed it served the greater good to name the day Mitsuko had taken her photographs from on high. But before he could do so, a conjunction of normally unremarkable events hushed his mouth. Mitsuko stepped into the large hall from the passageway. Her face was burning, her features fighting to regain composure. At the same time—and this was particularly odd—Madrun stepped into the large hall from the *outside* door, a full tray of pastries in hand. Each woman caught the other's eye. Each turned away in haste.

The Vicarage

Thornford Regis TC9 6QX

30 MAY

Dear Mum,

We are all girding our loins for the day ahead, what with poor Sybella's funeral, and I must get on with Mr. Christmas's breakfast shortly as I'm sure the day will be very taxing for him. Porridge, I think. It will stick to his ribs. I haven't made porridge in such a long time but I was at the v. hall last night for Mitsuko Drewe's ~~party~~ art show, helping Kerra serve, and Mr. Christmas was talking with PCSO White from over Pennycross way, who is Scottish (from Perth originally, I think), and I thought something homely like oatmeal would be just the thing for next day's breakfast. Funny how the mind works! Mr. Christmas spent too much time talking with PCSO White last night—Mairi, as she says you must call her. There's supposed to be a little accent over the "a" in her name, but I can't make this old typewriter do accents. Perhaps I should shift to a computer as Mr. Christmas suggests, but I am fond of this old thing. Mairi parted ways with Nick Stanhope around Easter, as I may have mentioned. He's in the security business now, and was seeing another woman in Totnes, so she's well rid of him, but she is rather striking looking and I could see Mr. C. was taken with her. He has been without a wife for some time, poor man, but Mairi wouldn't do as a vicar's wife as she's too blunt and apt to offend. I'm afraid I got a bit sharp with Mr. C. and told him he must circulate. I wouldn't want people talking about him the way they talked about Mr. Kinsey who was too attentive to the ladies, in such situations, as I've said many a time. I shouldn't wonder it wasn't one of the men in the village who put an end to Mr. Kinsey! I wonder if he will be buried in the churchyard? Buried again, I should add, as he was sort of buried there once, wasn't he? When I was in Pattimore's yesterday, Venice Daintrey was in the queue and she said Flo had been in Torquay to have lunch at the Imperial and spotted Oona Blanc getting out of a car, then slap a woman who was standing by the car door. Her assistant presumably. Up to her old ways I guess. I'll tell you tomorrow how she behaves at the funeral, although I expect you'll see tomorrow's papers before you get my letter and probably something on TV. I spotted two of those vans with towers in the road out my window already this morning. They're setting up a big TV screen in the churchyard because the church won't hold everyone and there's to be loudspeakers outside. It's a bit like Diana's funeral. Do you remember us all here in the vicarage watching it? I remember Mr. James-Douglas's nephew was so inconsolable, he ran through two boxes of tissues! Of course, Sybella's funeral won't be like that. Which reminds me, I was passing the church yesterday and what should I see but Mr. Christmas and Julia Hennis walking around the yew tree backwards, arm in arm. If Mrs. Hennis wants a child, she should be walking around the tree 7 times forwards. Perhaps they were confused. Of course, you know what it means when a man goes around backwards 7 times. We'll have to wait and see. That Penella Neels from Thorn Barton was at the v. hall last

*night, too, by the way, giving Mr. Christmas funny looks. I
managed to cut her off with my tray of nibbles. Useful things,
trays of nibbles. You can always interrupt people with them.
Which reminds me—I heard something astonishing at the v. hall
last night. I was in the kitchen in the small hall. I'd gone in to
get another tray of food, but there was no one there, so I picked
up the tray that was waiting. Just then both Liam and Mitsuko
came in, almost at the same time. I guess Liam had been in the
toilet. I'm not sure why Mitsuko had left her guests in the large
hall. But they began to argue. I know what it was—Liam must
have come out of the toilet and seen Mitsuko through the doors to
the large hall kissing someone, because that's what started it. I
think some smart friends of Mitsuko's had come to Thornford for
the opening, and she had probably given them one of those
greeting kisses people seem to do now, and that really set Liam
off. He's what you call insanely jealous, and I think it's getting
worse! Anyway, he accused her of all manner of things. But
Mitsuko, bless her, gave as good as she got—even accused him
of murdering Mr. Kinsey! Then burying him, all because he
thought she was having an affair with ~~him~~ the vicar, Mr.
Kinsey that was. The idea isn't all that outlandish, Mum, as I'd
often seen Mitsuko and Mr. Kinsey with their heads together,
and I don't think it was to talk about the flower rota. Anyway,
Mitsuko got* very *stroppy. She's such a tiny thing. You'd never
think she could be so forceful, at least not in that way. She is
rather good at getting her way with the flowers for the church
and such, but she's much more subtle at that. The thing is—she
said she had* proof *that Liam had been up to no good with Mr.
Kinsey and of course Liam said, what proof? And Mitsuko said,
as if I'm going to tell you. And it went on like that for a bit, while
here's me dreading that they're going to come into the kitchen and
find me. Liam backed down a bit and said he had been doing his
VAT returns that evening, which was more than a year ago, as
the Waterside was closed Mondays on the off season—which*

didn't seem to me much of an alibi, unless he does his VAT returns with some sort of VAT Returns Club which I'm sure doesn't exist and would be very dull in any case. Now I think of it, I don't know why Liam was defending his whereabouts for the evening of Mr. Kinsey's disappearance. But I suppose the whole village knows Jago was the last person to see him, in the early evening that Monday. So if Mr. Kinsey had any disappearing to do it would have to have been then. Or after then. On the other hand, Mr. Kinsey might have ~~disappeared~~ been murdered in the middle of the night, for all anyone knows. There's worse. Mitsuko then accused Liam of killing poor Sybella because he is jealous of her friendships with women, too. I thought that was the limit! I once thought that perhaps Mitsuko and Liam had rows because they liked rowing. Or at least I thought this after Celia Parry talked about the different ways couples communicate in one of her WI talks. But Mitsuko was quite over the top. As you might imagine, Mum, there I was in the kitchen rooted to the floor, feeling really very awkward. I thought about going over and knocking their two heads together, but they had said some very embarrassing things I didn't want them to know I knew. Anyway, when I peeked around the kitchen door, Mitsuko was about to leave through the door through to the large hall and Liam's back was to me, so I took the tray, which was getting rather warm on my fingers, and slipped out the fire exit, which is right by the kitchen. Of course, it was a bit peculiar being outside alone holding a tray with nibbles on it, so I was obliged to walk around the v. hall and come back in through the main doors. I didn't think anyone would notice, but Mr. Christmas happened to be standing inside the doors and he gave me a most peculiar look when I walked in. Of course he knows something odd happened as I'm sure everyone heard Mitsuko and Liam rowing but he hasn't asked. And I'm not sure whether to tell him what I overheard or not, as he does tend to frown on what he sometimes calls "talebearing." There was nothing Mr. James-Douglas liked more than a good old natter about village doings, but Mr. C. isn't very encouraging in that regard. I'm sure he'll eventually get used to the way we do things down here. I was going to tell you about Mitsuko's wonderful art quilts, but I must go and start that oatmeal! Cats are well. Love to Aunt Gwen. Hope your day goes well.

Much love,
Madrun

P.S. I am keeping my eye on Kerra as is Jago. She is quite safe working at the Waterside, so you mustn't worry. Jago went down with Kerra and let Liam know he'd better mind his manners. He also says he is going to drive Kerra to and from, especially after dark—although I don't think Kerra is too happy about her old dad treating her like a kiddie.

P.P.S. I am worried about your leg. I'm glad the doctor there is going to run you through some tests.

P.P.P.S. I did find an hour to see Colonel Northmore in hospital yesterday. He doesn't look well, I'm sorry to say. And he's quite keen for a visit from Mr. Christmas, but the vicar has so much on his plate right now. I said I'd see what I could do.

om pulled cassock and surplice from the vestry closet and readied himself for the next few hours. He was alone—or thought he was—and grateful for the silence, his mind skipping over the order of service as he eased himself into a prayerful attitude. Then he heard the scrape of a shoe along the stone floor of the short passage around the organ frame into the vestry. Expecting Dickie Horton, his verger at Pennycross St. Paul, he turned, to see a face of some little familiarity. The muscles along the mouth and cheeks were pressed into an attitude of supplication but the eyes were needle sharp. At first Tom thought it was the man from Thompson's, whom he had met at Ned Skynner's funeral. Then he realised the encounter had been much more recent.

"May I help you?"

"Possibly."

Tom frowned at the vague reply. "Didn't I see you at the village hall last night?"

"Yeah, I did drop in. Interesting work."

"I seem to recall you being shown the door."

"Occasionally I meet people who don't appreciate the free exchange of ideas that is the hallmark of a democratic society."

"Which paper are you with?"

"The Sun."

"I'm afraid I can't help you, Mr. . . . ?"

"Macgreevy. Andrew Macgreevy."

". . . The diocesan press office is handling all enquiries."

"So they are." The reporter's eyes roved the interior of the vestry.

"And I don't think you'll find anything interesting here," Tom insisted, wondering that the promised constabulary presence seemed a little lacking.

"I'm not sure that's true."

"It's simply a vestry—a small annex with much clutter."

"Yeah, it is a bit of tip," Macgreevy agreed cheerfully. "But, I ask myself, who are you likely to find in a vestry?"

"A priest, for one," Tom responded with rising asperity, trying to remember that newspapermen had souls, too.

"True. But I thought I might find the verger here."

"You might. But he's coming down from Pennycross and hasn't arrived."

"From Pennycross? I was sure your verger lived in this village. I thought I saw him come out of a cottage clearly marked 'Verger's Cottage.'"

"I have two churches, Mr. Macgreevy."

"Then you have two vergers."

"I can see your fine education has not been wasted on you."

Macgreevy scowled. "I was hoping to talk with the man who calls himself Sebastian John."

"Regrettably, Sebastian has been called away and won't be with us this morning. Perhaps I can take a message to him . . . ?"

Macgreevy's scowl began to curl into a smile.

"Mr. Macgreevy . . . ?"

The reporter raised a cautionary finger. Seconds later, Tom heard the sound of a key scraping the lock of the vestry's outside door. And then Sebastian was in the room, dressed in jeans, carrying a small rucksack. His hair was loosened from its band.

"Tom, I've had a call from Dickie's sister. He's . . . well, under the weather, I suppose you could say, and can't be here this morning. I'm very sorry that—"

Sebastian hesitated, as if sensing Tom wasn't wholly concentrated on him. He followed Tom's eyes.

"Hello, Sebastian." Macgreevy's smile grew wider.

"I didn't realise you had a visitor, Tom." A wariness had stolen into Sebastian's eyes.

Intruder, more like, but he let the thought pass as he introduced the reporter to Sebastian.

"I'm not commenting on this tragedy," Sebastian replied evenly, turning to leave.

"I'm not asking you to," Macgreevy said.

"Tom, I'm sorry about this complication with Dickie. I really must go—"

"Perhaps, Sebastian," Macgreevy interrupted, gripping the edge of the vestry door, "you might like to know that Lord Kinross has had a stroke."

Baffled, Tom watched as Sebastian stared hard at the reporter. Then the verger yanked the door from his hand and stumbled backwards over the step to the gravel path. He heard a pained exclamation in a female timbre, followed by a hasty apology in Sebastian's voice.

"Whatever's got into Sebastian?" Julia stepped into the vestry. "I thought Dickie was substituting . . . Oh, hello," she added, noting the stranger in the room.

Tom had been studying the look of satisfaction that lit Macgreevy's thin features during his brief exchange with Sebastian and felt a chill of foreboding. He, too, had experienced the sensation of a life—his own—made unrecognisable by journalists with inscrutable scripts. The Bristol *Evening Post* had callously exhumed an old quote of his supporting a safe-injection room for Bristol drug-users, juxtaposed it with police speculation that a thwarted drugs transaction lay behind Lisbeth's homicide, and implied that he shared in the blame for his wife's death. "Vicar Said 'Yes' to Drugs" had been the headline. He addressed Macgreevy:

"Do you think you could be persuaded to leave sleeping dogs— or at least sleepy villages—lie?"

"Not if there's a good story, mate."

"I see. But will your 'good story' serve some common good?"

"I leave philosophical speculation to my betters." Macgreevy rubbed his knuckles along the edge of the door. "Do you vet your vergers in this sleepy village?"

Tom flicked a glance at Julia and was rewarded with a mystified frown. Beyond the vestry, he could hear subdued voices echoing in the sanctuary. The choir was arriving. Reaching for his cassock, he told Macgreevy:

"I'm so sorry, but I'm afraid I'll have to ask you to leave. We have a funeral to prepare for."

The journalist's response was to flash him a tight smile and re-treat back into the nave. Tom noted the choir's chattering halt momentarily, and then resume.

"Do you know of a Lord Kinross?" he asked Julia.

She shook her head. "Scottish peer?"

"He seems to know something about Sebastian."

"Lord Kinross?"

"No, that reporter. Macgreevy. He writes for *The Sun*. If you'd been at Mitsuko's opening at the village hall yesterday you would have seen Karla give him the heave-ho."

Julia groaned. "Alastair decided he'd rather golf. I didn't feel like going alone."

"Oh, well. The quilts are up for the next ten days or so." He frowned. "What is it, Julia? Are you all right?"

"It's nothing. Really. It's . . . the thought of some Grub Street hack nosing into village affairs. Bad enough the police, though I know they have to do their job."

"Have they talked to you, the police? I meant to ask you earlier."

"Someone took a statement from me on Tuesday. A detective constable, a young woman. There wasn't much I could say, other than what I told you about finding the village hall unlocked Monday morning. I didn't know Sybella well enough to be of much use."

"I'm afraid we're all rather in for being poked and prodded, aren't we? By police or press. What with Sybella's cruel death and Fred finding Peter's body . . . although," Tom added, fastening his cassock, "I don't understand Mr. Macgreevy's particular interest in Sebastian, do you?"

He had asked it rhetorically, but when he looked up he was disconcerted to see Julia's face grown pale above the collar of her black suit.

"Julia? Do you know something about this?"

"No, I don't. I don't know why a reporter would have some particular interest in Sebastian. He's a bit of a mystery to us in the village, but . . ."

"But?"

Julia's face crumpled. Her beautiful eyes, ineffably sad, returned to his. "Oh, Tom! Surely the old rumour has reached your ears by now."

"What old rumour?" he asked, bewildered.

The question seemed to hang suspended in the air.

"The rumour," Julia replied at last, dropping her voice, "that Sebastian and I were having an affair."

Tom stared at her, shocked as much by a sudden wrenching of his heart as by the notion of his sister-in-law's faithlessness. Without thinking he mouthed the words: "And were . . . ?"

"No, Tom," Julia responded with some vehemence, pushing the door to the sanctuary closed. "Sebastian and I were *not* having an affair."

"Sorry, I really didn't mean to suggest . . ." Tom backtracked, ashamed that his mind found the coupling so believable, flustered by his sudden, unbidden jealousy.

"It's stopped now—the rumour, that is—but a couple of years ago, people would fall into a hush in the post office when I came in. Or there would be a titter behind my back if Sebastian and I happened to be in the pub at the same time. Finally, Belinda Swan took me aside."

"But what in heaven's name put the notion into people's heads in the first place?"

"Mrs. Prowse, that is what! She saw me come out of the verger's cottage one afternoon, and gave me what I can only describe as a 'look.'"

"I see," Tom responded, not quite seeing. Evidently, what might be a commonplace bit of social intercourse in the city could be fraught with import in a village. "And you think any reporter sniffing around Sebastian will dig this up."

Julia nodded. Tom found himself almost wanting to laugh with relief. Affairs and rumours of affairs were happening up and down the country. Surely they could be of little concern to any but the protagonists and their nearest and dearest. But Julia appeared worryingly on the verge of the sort of tears she had exhibited the day before, under the yew tree, and he wondered, not for the first time, if she was about to have a nervous collapse.

"But, Julia," he began softly, "I know it's unpleasant to be the subject of unfounded rumour, but I can't imagine *The Sun*—or any newspaper—being terribly interested, even if it were true you and Sebastian . . . Does Alastair know none of this?"

"No."

"Are you sure?"

"Tom, Alastair works, he golfs, he watches sport on TV. He's not the subtlest of men. He's not terribly good at detecting 'atmospheres.' But he doesn't like life to be untidy. If he had heard the rumour, I doubt very much he wouldn't have said something to Sebastian . . . or to me."

"Yes, I expect so." Tom reached absently for his surplice. "I'm assuming, however, that Sebastian wasn't oblivious to these rumours."

"No."

"Then why didn't he tell the rumourmongers to naff off? I'm surprised at him. I thought he had more integrity."

"Oh, Tom, you don't understand."

"Don't understand what?"

"I've said far too much." Her face now ashen, she turned to the door. "Look, I must get to the choir vestry."

"Julia!" Tom grabbed her arm. Touching the fabric, a part of his brain registered that it was the same suit she'd worn at Lisbeth's funeral. "You're clearly in some form of distress. The yew tree yesterday and now this. I'm worried about you. I'm your family. I can't say I'm your priest, but I wish you would tell me what's troubling you."

Ten minutes later, Tom positioned himself within the shadow of the lych-gate, clasped his hands in the folds of his surplice, and lifted his eyes, first towards Pennycross Road in the middle distance, down which the cortège would soon make its slow descent into the village, and then to the black-clad figures massed nearest him on the river cobbles of Church Walk. Framed by a burst of ivy tumbling over the short span of stone wall that turned into Poachers Passage, Colm's face was pale with strain, the skin around the eyes bruised and blue. He was staring sightlessly past the vicarage wall, beyond the tops of the apple trees in the Old Orchard towards the cottages that curled up Thorn Hill, one hand pressed onto the shoulder of his son, whose own face appeared to struggle for some composition suited to the moment, at once frowning, distracted, curious, bored, then—abruptly—pained. Tom noted Celia pluck her husband's hand from Declan's shoulder and give them both a tight, reproving smile before giving a sideways glance to a slender figure a cautious three yards distant squeezed into what looked curiously like Victorian bombazine embossed with a pattern of lace and scored with fasteners of no evident utility.

So this was Oona Blanc, Tom thought, trying not to stare. He allowed his eyes to pass over her as he looked down Church Walk to the silent mourners, those closest young and dressed either sharply chic or morbidly Victorian—London friends, presumably, who had arrived too late to find a place in the church—those farther, villagers of mixed age in unremarkable attire. Oona's face, under a black straw pillbox with a wisp of a veil, was alabaster, the skin taut over high cheekbones, her full lips silky with scarlet lipstick. Yet the face was unreadable. Giant sunglasses lent her the impassive faceted stare of an insect. Only her posture, her body bowed, her hand grasping the arm of an angular young man with a trimmed three-day growth of beard, suggested strong emotion.

Tom had been aware of her approach. From inside the church, as he was readying himself to exit through the north porch, he had heard a rustle of noise, as if a breeze had risen in the trees—the sigh of the common folk when tabloid celebrity is made flesh. Oona had arrived at almost the last minute—to be a sensation, he thought darkly—and he had witnessed her final steps as he had wound his way down the pea shingle path bordered with tombstones towards the lych-gate. How she had managed the cobbles in those shoes— the heels were torturously high—he had no idea, but he imagined they were as natural to her as a farrier's fabrications were to a horse. His eyes returned to Colm, who no more made a movement to acknowledge his ex-wife than she did him. Apparently shared grief had no dominion over pride and ancient belligerence.

Now, catching the first glimpse of the funeral car round the bend by the village hall, his mind went back to Julia. He thought he had not seen such a concentration of misery on her face—not when she had appeared at his door in Bristol in the hours after Lisbeth's death; not in her unguarded moments when he and Miranda had first visited Thornford; not when he tumbled at the base of the yew and mumbled some pagan wisdom. She was raw.

The cortège drew closer. Tom could see villagers straightening themselves mindfully, pressing against the stone walls, to let the flower-draped black Daimler pass unimpeded. One or two youths, he noted, stood or sat on the wall—a less respectful posture—but the village, he guessed, had not been witness to many such attention-garnering events and he could hardly blame them. There was genuine distress, but there was a dash of morbid relish, too. He could see the edge of a scaffold that some television network had erected next to the pub and another one, kitty-corner, where Pennycross Road intersected Poynton Shute—manifestations of indelicate attention, about which he could do nothing, and to which he contributed, oddly enough, in the form of the CCTV screen, tucked between the lych-gate and the north porch. Nearer, at the door of the Old School Room, DI Bliss and DS Blessing stood scrutinising the crowd. Behind him, the church was full, but for the chief mourners. They, like him, had turned their attention to the approaching hearse. He could hear, through the ancient stone of the church, the strains of Julia playing on the organ. And despite this admixture of solemnity and carnival, he couldn't help thinking like a foolish villager at the village pump, or like a jealous teenager:

What was *Julia doing in Sebastian's cottage?*

CHAPTER TWENTY-ONE

Oona's sunglasses remained as firmly affixed to her face as a fender to a car frame through the course of the service, which made her a distracting presence, particularly if one was facing the congregation, as Tom was. He glanced at her in the left front pew from time to time as he recited the familiar words of the rite. It was difficult not to be drawn to the famous visage, which he had first noted more than two decades before in the video for Colm's hit "Bank Holiday," lending her cool presence to a giddy scene in a Butlins holiday camp, later sighted on the covers of *Vogue* or *Marie Claire*, then more recently glimpsed in a somewhat less flattering form on the cover of one of the tabloids, accompanying a story that often involved noses—either stuffing substances up hers or hitting someone else's.

> *"May God our Father forgive us our sins*
> *and bring us to the eternal joy of His kingdom,*
> *where dust and ashes have no dominion."*

He intoned the words, then invited silent prayer as this was the moment before the Collect. In that pause, broken by intermittent sniffles, a squeak resounded, followed by a collective rustle, as if a multitude sought avoidance of mice. It was Enid Pattimore. Having sprung a leak once again, she leaned her head back while Roger, his bald pate bowed and glistening in the gentle light of the south window, rummaged in his mother's bag for her tissues and her nose clamp. Oddly, Oona alone had remained stock-still through this tiny eruption, as she had through the entire service. Was she slumbering behind those dark glasses? Tom wondered as he began the Collect. Her companion at least had flinched, which meant he couldn't be deaf, a thought which had crossed Tom's mind as he sensed the young man's intent focus not on the words he was speaking but on the movement of his lips. Possibly he was Italian or Spanish—he certainly *looked* Italian or Spanish—and in want of English lessons. The young man rose to his feet a little after everyone else for the hymns, cued by the commotion in the pews behind, lightly touching Oona's arm, signalling her to follow. Had Oona gone blind? Was this the reason for the eyewear? Perhaps the young man was a seeing-eye toy boy. But, no—if Oona had lost her sight, Madrun would have told him. She seemed to know these things.

He glanced at the coffin before beginning a reading from Saint John. *"Jesus said to his disciples: 'Do not let your hearts be troubled . . .'"*

He was returned by the soothing words to the gravity of the occasion, and obliged to face the truth that his heart was troubled indeed. And that his meandering thoughts had served more to avoid this single truth: that the funeral of someone young was a terrible, terrible thing. The last funeral he had presided over at St. Nicholas's—Ned Skynner's—had been untroubling because Ned, besides being a stranger to him, had lived well beyond his three score and ten. But Sybella had been a mere nineteen. Tom had attended to many bereaved people in the years of his ministry, watched eyes brim and heard speech falter, but he hadn't understood depth of grief until Lisbeth—a mere thirty-four—had been taken so brutally. He could never have guessed that he would find himself so plunged into sadness, so filled by a silent keening, that there would seem to be no surcease—though, slowly, he did glimpse an end to suffering: It had been vouchsafed to him on these very chancel steps, in this little church, in this pleasant village.

But now—at this moment—it was being reawakened by the presence of a coffin containing a young woman who, like Lisbeth, had been taken suddenly and for no apparent reason. He recalled the disquieting sensation in Bristol of having fallen out of love with God and, worse, the sensation that God had fallen out of love with him, and wanting desperately to rekindle the romance. He had learned since then in prayer and contemplation that faith is always only a reaching towards, an approximation.

"Have patience with everything unresolved in your heart." Canon Holdsworth had quoted Rilke in a letter to him sent in the days after Lisbeth's death. "Don't search for the answers, which could not be given to you now, because you would not be able to live them. And the point is, to live everything. Live the questions now. Perhaps then, someday far in the future, you will gradually, without even noticing it, live your way into the answer."

As he spoke the final words of the passage from John 14, he glanced at Colm Parry, who was—as he had been since Revelation Choir had sung the first hymn, "Be Still, My Soul," with such sweet gentleness—weeping profusely, swabbing his tears in a handkerchief as large as a dinner napkin. As Julia played the first notes of "I Surrender," Tom fought back his own tears.

At least, he thought, desperate to distract himself once again, the choir had been an inspired choice, and he let himself sway softly to its rhythms. How Lisbeth, a stalwart of the Cambridge Chorale, would have loved to hear these powerful, resonant voices. And how delicious she would have found this nontraditional music filling an old Norman church in the heart of the West Country. His congregation was captured by the spectacle. No one was fidgeting, though he suspected some were ruminating darkly on unorthodoxy. Only

Oona remained utterly impassive, even as the organ's final note faded. As he began the words to Psalm 23, he felt his throat catch, as a wave of empathy seemed to wash over the assembled and surge towards him. He steadied himself by glancing again at her and permitting himself a new thought: What we have here is the Madame Tussaud's version of Oona Blanc, waxen and surely imperfect.

"Surely goodness and loving mercy shall follow me all the days of my life, and I will dwell in the house of the Lord forever," he ended, and signalled to Mitsuko to come to the lectern to read another passage from the Gospels.

Though tribute to the deceased would normally be made after the opening prayer, Tom had decided to weave his remarks into the sermon. He had completed it only hours before, scribbling in a pad in bed, as Madrun was thrashing away at her typewriter with her daily letter to her mother, then transferring his notes to the computer downstairs in his study, as the rising sun cast new bars of light over the red Holbein carpet. If Sybella had been unknown to him, he would have woven a narrative based solely on the remarks of others, not always a satisfying exercise, as he felt at times like a mere synthesiser of information. But he had come to know Sybella a little. It saddened him profoundly that his first thoughts were not as kind as he wished they might be. She was a little cunning—was she not? She had a history of provocations, among them humiliating the naïve Charlie Pike, pestering the reclusive Sebastian John, and goading the incendiary Liam Drewe. Had there been others, here or in London? Her flirtation with Tom two months ago at the Waterside had been childish, and when he had seen her in the village afterwards, and more lately when she'd started coming to church, her response to his cheery hello was invariably a kind of smirk, as if exchanging greetings with the vicar was utterly uncool or too too ironic. She was a spikey little fish out of water, landed on Thornford's banks with tabloid headlines trailing after her, an object of curiosity that soon settled into indifference. But someone, for some reason, had harboured hostility—murderous hostility—towards her.

Or was her death, as the police reckoned with Lisbeth, the triteness of simply being in the wrong place at the wrong time?

Tom had paused here in his ruminations, stroking Powell, who had landed on his bed, mercifully without an offering of some dead rodent. It was the same unanswered question that plagued him about Lisbeth: Had someone harboured so deep a hostility towards her—or towards *both* of them—that he decided to take her life in the very place, the church, to which Tom dedicated long hours? Or was it, after all, as the trail grew cold and scraps of evidence proved elusive, a tragic conjunction of events: Lisbeth stumbling into a drug deal in progress; Lisbeth accosted by some crazed individual, desperate for what money she had in her purse, grabbing, too, the doll which was to be Miranda's birthday present. Would he ever know?

He had flicked a glance at the bedside clock next to the curate's egg when Madrun began her descent to the kitchen, and refocused on Sybella. Cunning she might have been, but at heart he knew she was really little more than a celebrity edition of that universal creature—the troubled teenager. How many wealthy households with warring, extravagant, narcissistic parents produced children of becoming modesty and fixed life-purpose? Few, he expected. Sybella was more casualty than cause. Her life had been mostly prologue. There was a first-chapter glimmer of the woman she might have become, and this is what he would present to the congregated mourners: that Sybella appeared to have—no, *had*—put much of her old life behind her, with the help of her father, who himself had banished his demons and found health and peace in Thornford. Tom had paused, imagining Sybella's mother's reaction to this. Oona, by all accounts, was quite attached to her demons, so praise for Colm's victory might need tempering. Yet it was Colm—who had battled first for custody; then, when Sybella had passed into legal adulthood, had fought to get her into treatment; then had beseeched her to live with him in the countryside—who had helped straighten out his daughter's zigzag path. In Thornford, she had met Mitsuko, who had helped her discover her talent as an artist.

What could he say about Oona's influence, especially when she would be there in a front pew?

Now, as Mitsuko reached the last verse of the Gospel, he looked over at Oona. Her companion held the funeral leaflet open for both of them, but Oona appeared oblivious, transfixed by some pattern in the rood screen, inasmuch as one could tell what she was looking at through black lenses. Though she had curled to her feet with the rest of the congregation at the appropriate moments, she made no movement—no calf stretch, no nose twitch. Well, of course! Her nerve endings were likely becalmed with some cocktail of the finer pharmacological distillations (which his own quack had dangled before him in Bristol) judiciously leavened with something amusing from the street. He asked himself, as he'd asked his doctor: What happens when the drugs wear off? In Oona's case, given her history, he had an inkling.

As he mounted the pulpit, aware of the delicacy of the duty before him, the words of his text, Psalm 46—*God is our refuge and our strength*—implanted in his mind, he recalled the anchors to his remarks: that courageous adults are sometimes born of reckless teenagers and that finer natures are sometimes revealed in small acts. Miranda's tale of Sybella taking Emily to Westways for Alastair to patch up her bee sting had been central to this. Of these things he would speak, but he would not praise Thornford's role in Sybella's healing, for he had to face the brutal truth that no matter how perfidious her mother's influence had been, if Sybella had stayed in bad old London, she'd be alive, wouldn't she?

The bells of St. Nicholas's began their dolorous peal as six young men carried Sybella's flower-draped casket through the cool shadow of the south porch into the blazing noon sun of the churchyard. Tom felt the light blast his eyes, and for a feverish moment the grass and

trees flared a sickly cellophane lime and the near-cloudless sky retreated into an inky blue. The feeling of discombobulation, of time
being out of joint, did not leave him as he preceded the coffin past
the ancient markers along the path and down the steps to the bottom terrace to the plot beside Ned Skynner's. He wondered if he
was coming down with something, perhaps a bug picked up in that
soup of infection, the hospital, during his visit to Colonel Northmore. Or perhaps it was having musical accompaniment at a committal that lent the scene a faintly surreal quality: Revelation Choir
followed behind the coffin, "Swing Low, Sweet Chariot" majestic
and mournful, drifting in and out of the tombstones and rising to
startle the rooks in the trees. Or perhaps it was the memory of having followed this path barely two days before, on the heels of Fred
Pike, to witness the horror of Peter Kinsey's hand, like a dead fish,
flopped out of the red soil. He noted with dismay as he took his
place at the foot of the grave that the police—or Fred—had left
things in less than pristine condition. Having been reopened then
resealed, Ned's grave looked like a lumpy misshapen loaf of earth.
Tom was surprised Fred hadn't shaped and smoothed it, and he
would have to have him do so before Karla caught sight. He glanced
about to see if she had inserted herself into the procession. She had.
Indeed, quite a number of the congregation followed, though family
and friends only was the custom at a committal. Villagers, visitors—
mourners many, curious some—dispersed themselves among the
gravestones, seeking purchase on thin strips of grass and along the
high stone wall that enclosed the churchyard. Most moved almost
reflexively to flank the Parrys on one side of the grave, leaving Oona
and her companion solitary figures on the other, their shadows fore-
shortened in the midday sun.

The pallbearers brought Sybella's coffin to the lip of the grave at
the moment the choir, as if by a miracle of timing, drew out the last
bittersweet note. The silence that followed seemed naked, raw. Only
a swan, beating its wings against the waters of the millpond, prepar-

ing to soar in short flight, broke the preternatural calm. Tom inhaled the pungent miasma of the damp earth. Then he began the familiar words:

"The Lord is full of compassion and mercy . . ." As he spoke he sensed a sudden motion to his left. Oona was removing her sunglasses, though if there was any time for eye protection, it was now, in the blazing sun. *"Slow to anger and of great goodness,"* he continued, lifting his eyes from his text to glance her way, momentarily stunned at the sight of her eyes. They were not, as he might have expected, red-rimmed with the effect of weeping, but empurpled like bruised fruit. More arresting than this were her pupils, needle sharp and dangerous. *"Slow to anger and of great goodness,"* he repeated, hastily seeking the comfort of the page, yet aware of his skin prickling, as if he could feel a storm rising on the edge of the moors. *"As a father is tender towards his children, so is the Lord tender to those—"*

But he was stopped by a sudden cry. Her spike heels had embedded themselves in the grass, and Oona pitched dangerously towards the grave. Her companion lunged to right her, and did so—to the collective gasp of the assembled—but she instead thrashed against his grip with a miraculous strength for one so thin, which sent him stumbling backwards towards the base of the beech tree. *"Cara!"* he shouted, as he tumbled over an exposed root. But his exit was nothing compared to the sight of Oona, shoeless, her imprisoning skirt hiked up to her hips, stalking the perimeter of the grave, scattering startled mourners, a blazing stare directed at Colm, whose face quickly went through a panoply of emotions—surprise, concern, denial, then anger—as he turned in a goalkeeper's stance to shield Celia and Declan.

"Father tender towards his children!" Oona spat as she advanced, and everyone waited with suspended breath for Colm to defend against the rain of blows made famous in Oona Blanc *vs.* various assistants tallied by tabloid press court reporters.

But Tom's attention was diverted from the impending brawl by another commotion. Some man, young, lithe, exceptionally tall, encumbered by a leather bag strapped to his shoulder, was cutting a swath through the mourners, camera at the ready, sending people spinning out of his way. One of the choir members snatched at the cameraman's bag, growling deeply, but without success. Unthinkingly, Tom snapped shut his prayer book and dashed towards Colm, unsure whether he intended to block the stranger from his intrusive mission or intercede with the flailing Oona. But it was too late. As the camera flashed in a staccato of mechanical shrieks and the crowd gasped in astonishment, Oona swung an open hand—a left hand—against her former husband, who had unwisely raised the wrong arm in defence. But in the melee that followed, it wasn't Oona or Colm, Celia or the nameless Italian, or even Declan, who was even more aggressive than he'd been in the village hall, that remained seared in Tom's memory. It was something glimpsed through an opening in the flailing limbs, and it was immediately teasing and troubling. Tom didn't believe in such things. In fact, he held out firmly against necromancy in all its forms. But, really, he couldn't help it: He felt as though he had seen a ghost.

CHAPTER TWENTY-TWO

"Dora is Thornford's funeral fairy," Venice Daintrey confided, sidling next to Tom, who was hesitating over a casserole dish of considerable proportions, the grey gelatinous surface of its offering punctuated by gobs of some darker material, possibly meat. "Although I can't think how *that* got on the table. I daresay someone's made a mistake in the kitchen."

Tom surveyed the expanse of white linen, down which he'd trundled, stopping at the stations of the nosh, adding cold ham, pasta salad, and the inevitable sausage rolls to his plate, mindful of restraint in his helpings (gusto being unseemly at a funeral reception), though he couldn't help noting that Venice had heaped her plate as if fuelling for battle. The food—hot and cold, savoury and sweet—was lavish and faultless. So, too, was the presentation. It was a pageant of white china, crystal, and silver, set on a three-pedestal dining table in an exquisitely proportioned room designed by Nash in the early nineteenth century and respectfully updated in the early twenty-first as a paean to harmony and serenity. Dora Speke's casserole dish, the green shade of mushy peas garlanded with a mimsy pattern of orange and yellow flowers, stood out like a blister.

"Be brave, Vicar," Florence Daintrey murmured throatily, leaning around her sister-in-law to address him.

Tom lifted a scalloped serving spoon and pierced the casserole's shiny skin, the first guest to do so, though he had hardly been the first at the queue. He was familiar with funeral fairies, women aroused to action by the news of death, no matter how remote the acquaintance. Their contribution usually arrived in the form of a casserole; their motive (he recognised this thought as uncharitable, if nonetheless true) often id-ridden eagerness to share the spotlight.

"Perhaps you should have Dr. Hennis look at that eye," Florence added.

"It's nothing." Tom dabbed at the tender flesh with his free hand, careful not to stick his fork into his eye, adding injury to insult. "It'll go away."

"She ought to be arrested."

"It really wasn't Oona's fault."

"Nonsense."

"I got in the way of her elbow."

Florence shot him a withering glance.

"I'm not making excuses. I was trying to stop Oona pitching into the grave when her elbow—"

"Oh." Venice cut him off with a disappointed frown. "Flo and I were rather speculating in the car coming up. None of us could see properly in the churchyard, being at the back."

Tom watched a forkful of salad pass Venice's lips. "I expect there'll be pictures in the papers—at least one of the papers."

"I suppose he was a paparazzi, then."

"A paparazzo, I think, Ven."

"There'll be a run on the newsagents tomorrow morning," Venice continued, ignoring her sister-in-law, her eyes scanning the room. "Perhaps I should get an order in with Karla. I wonder if she's thought to order extra copies. You wouldn't happen to know which paper he was with, would you, Vicar?"

"No, I would not," Tom replied dryly. One doesn't stop to question a freight train when it's barrelling towards you. The photographer had only a few seconds of weaving and bobbing around Colm and Oona as the latter released a farrago of post-slap invective against her ex-husband for dragging their daughter to this godforsaken village before the choir's basso profundo, as big as Lenny Henry, charged up and grabbed his camera arm with a meaty hand. This spun Oona towards the grave edge. Tom lunged to stop her fall, but as she struggled to right herself, flapping her arms like a startled pigeon, her right elbow smacked into Tom's left eye. Only the Italian, who had scrambled back to his feet, managed to catch Oona before she tumbled onto the coffin. She spun into his arms and released a howl of grief so unrestrained everyone scattered among the gravestones was stunned into embarrassed silence. It was between the duck and the lunge, before the poke in the eye, through the arabesque of twisting arms, that Tom's vision was gripped by a phantom presence. He could put a name to it now, but it was absolutely bloody ridiculous to do so. Sybella was in a coffin; she wasn't wandering spectrally about the churchyard witnessing her own undignified committal. If he'd had this hallucination *after* Oona's elbow met his eyeball, he'd have credited it to retinal shock. But as it happened *before* . . .

"Never mind." Venice interrupted his thoughts, waving a fork in the general direction of a knot of people visible in the next room gathered by a white grand piano. "I've spotted Karla. I shall go have a word with her."

Tom watched her waddle across the Aubusson and reflected on Colm's munificence in having the whole village—well, nearly—up to his home, to mingle among family—a number seemed to share Colm's sloped nose—and London friends. At the gate to Thornridge House, some minder Colm had hired had vetted the out-of-town crowd, and PCSO White and some constable Tom had never seen before vetted the locals, to ensure no unwelcome intrusions as there had been in the churchyard. He suspected many villagers had never been inside Thornridge House. They were deferential and doleful, as would be expected at a funeral reception at the Big House, but they were also avid with curiosity. He could see it in the roving eyes, sidelong glances, and fingers slinking out to stroke some bit of fabric. He spotted Julia, framed in the French windows, looking at him with some intensity over the rim of a glass of sherry. He had a prickly sensation that she had been doing so for some time. He excused himself to Florence and went over.

"Not eating?" he asked.

Julia shook her head. "It looks very good . . . well, except for that bit—"

"Apparently Dora Speke's casserole went walkabout."

"Ah."

Tom edged his fork into a sausage roll. "Revelation Choir was splendid, don't you think? And you were wonderful, too, of course."

"Mmm."

Tom glanced at her. She caught the glance and seemed to struggle with something to say.

"Your eye . . ."

"A bit of best British beef on it and I'll be right as rain."

"I think Alastair would tell you putting bacteria-laden meat on a mucous membrane would be a poor idea."

"Joke."

"Oh." Julia downed the rest of her sherry, then clutched the glass to her chest. An uncharacteristically awkward silence ensued. Behind him, Tom could hear people murmuring and greeting one another, their collective drone broken by the occasional titter or mutter. Over Julia's shoulder, through the French window, Thornridge's shimmering lawn beckoned in the middle distance, a haven from the polite and artificial society of the funeral tea.

"I think we're sinking into small talk," he said finally.

Julia deposited the sherry glass on a table by the window. "I've been thinking about what you said in the vestry earlier."

"Which bit?"

"Several bits, really. You're not my priest. But perhaps you can be my rabbi of a sort in this instance."

"Why don't I simply be—at the very least—your brother-in-law?"

"Priestly garb lends detachment." She traced a finger along his dog collar and looked into his eyes. Tom started. Lisbeth would make this same gesture from time to time, at odd moments, and her eyes would crinkle, as if marriage to a priest were both deliciously preposterous and utterly wonderful. Such was usually a prelude to a kiss. But there could be no such thing here. This was no flirtation. Julia, the more serious of the sisters, wore a wan expression which tugged at his heart.

"Do you think it would be rude if we went outside?" she asked. She didn't wait for an answer, pushing open the French doors and stepping out onto the partially glazed pergola that overlooked the pool garden. Tom set his plate down and followed. They walked in silence past the ornamental pool, then down a soft grassy path through a garden of shrub roses towards a bank of beech trees. Julia plucked a chaste white bloom from a heavy stem that blocked their way. A thorn grazed the flesh of her finger. She licked at it, then held the ring of petals to her nose and breathed deeply as they passed into green shadows.

"You know," she said at last, "about the child Alastair and I lost three years ago."

"Of course, yes." The news had come via Johanna, his mother-in-law. Deeply saddened, Lisbeth had phoned Julia, heralding a thaw in the sisterly glaciation, but the gesture had not been well received. Perhaps Julia was too addled by grief, Lisbeth had concluded when she set the phone back in its cradle. But she had behaved as though Lisbeth, the mother of a healthy child, had called to gloat.

"We did try again."

"I didn't know."

"No one did. It was too heartbreaking."

"Julia, I'm so sorry."

"In fact," Julia continued, head bent, "Alastair and I can't have children. Or, rather, we mustn't. We're genetically mismatched, you see. I'll miscarry any child we have together."

"You were tested, I presume."

"Alastair can be very thorough when he wants to be."

Tom released a moan. "I'm lost for words."

"Lisbeth chose wisely. If she had married Alastair, the same thing might have happened to her, the same genetic mismatch."

"Now there are no words."

"I'm not being bitter. I'm simply stating a fact—or at least a very strong possibility."

Julia turned away and moved through untrimmed grasses towards the crest of land over the river estuary. Here, the breeze was constant, filled with clouds of gulls coiling and twisting into the sky. But Tom paid scant attention to their noisy flight. His eyes were on Julia's slender figure, on her shoulders sagging in the black suitcoat, on the way the rose, held by the end of its stem, trailed along her leg.

"There's more," she said when they'd reached the cliff edge. High on the hill opposite, between the seams of hedgerows, defined against the skyline, a crop sprayer travelled a steady course. "I did become pregnant." She tossed the rose over the cliff's edge. Tom watched it absently as it floated in the air then tumbled against a hollow in the cliff, his mind racing ahead. There could only be sorrow here.

"And you had a termination," he intoned as he watched a gust of air lift the rose again and dispatch it further down.

"Yes. Of course."

"Well," he began gently, "I know it's a very sad thing, but I can't see you would have had any other choice, Julia, given the likely outcome."

She shot him a quick glance, then looked away. "It wasn't Alastair's," she said, her tone flat.

"Oh" was all he could think to say. He wasn't shocked; no novelty attended disclosure of adultery to a priest, but he was dismayed to his very bones that Julia was complicit in this most tawdry of human failings. One question burned in his mind, but he put it off. Gently, he asked instead, "Did this happen recently?"

"No, though it feels like yesterday. I had the termination shortly before your visit with Miranda last year."

"Julia, you should have put us off."

"And what excuse would I have given? What excuse would I have given to Alastair? He was actually looking forward to Miranda's arrival. He likes children, you know. He wants children. And . . ." Her voice dropped. "I can't give them to him."

"And he knows nothing of this?"

"No."

"You're sure?"

There was a heartbeat's hesitation. Tom turned to her. "You *are* sure."

"Yes . . . absolutely. Well, I had one worrying moment. I went to a private clinic in Exeter, just off Queen Street. The appointment was for Saturday morning, which seemed the best time, since Alastair would think I had gone up for synagogue. However, when I stepped out of the clinic afterwards, I crossed paths with Tamara Prowse—Jago's eldest—and Sybella."

"Sybella?"

"I taught Tamara at school. She's a lovely girl, and so we chatted for a bit. She'd gone up to look around the campus, since she was going to be attending the University of Exeter in the autumn. I guess Sybella had gone along for the ride, since her driving licence was still restricted then. I'm not sure the two were really friends. Anyway, Sybella didn't have anything to say, but I could see her peering at the clinic's sign and giving me one of those cunning looks of hers. But the clinic has a wide range of women's services and its name declares none of them, so . . ."

"She might have looked on the Internet."

"And found I may have been there for a Pap test. Anyway, nothing came of it. Sybella never said anything to me. And if she said anything to anyone else, it didn't get back to me."

"I can almost imagine her saying something to Alastair. I feel she fancied herself a bit of a slyboots."

"Then he would have said something to me. I know he can brood, but if he knew I had gone to some private medical clinic, he would have worried. He would have asked me about it."

"And what would you have told him?"

Julia fell silent. Tom glanced down at the sun glinting off the waters of the estuary and let the light dazzle his eyes for a moment. "I said something in the vestry to that reporter about letting sleeping dogs—or sleepy villages—lie. Perhaps I should suggest the same thing to you, Julia. Are you wanting to confess to Alastair? Is this why you're telling me this, now?"

"Good God, no! I don't want him to ever know. I am . . . fond of him, Tom."

"Only 'fond'?"

"I don't know. Our first years together were wonderful. I know Lisbeth always thought there was something insidious about our alliance. But there wasn't, really. I had just ended a relationship when I ran into Alastair. He had just finished with Lisbeth. I suppose it was misery loves company, but we fell in love. Our marriage only began to fall apart after the second miscarriage. He was very supportive and understanding after the first." Julia paused. "It's hard for Alastair, in a way. He's always had this perfect life mapped out for himself, and I've as much as thrown him a googly. He doesn't take to googlies. Cricket was never his game. I don't know why he sticks me really."

"Because, like your sister was, you're beautiful and full of life."

Julia smiled wanly. "He could find another woman to have a child with. We hardly seem to live together as man and wife anymore. I'm sure you noticed the sleeping arrangements when you were here last year. They haven't changed." She shrugged. "We go about our routines. If he isn't working, he's golfing. I busy myself with school routines. We have the occasional meal with his golfing mates and their wives. Earlier, we had talked about other solutions—adopting, egg donation . . ."

"Sperm donation?"

Julia demurred. "I rather think Alastair is certain he would want it to be *his* child. Anyway . . ." She trailed off, setting her eyes on the Totnes ferry, which had come into view on the water below. Someone on the top deck spotted them and raised a hand in greeting.

Tom waved back robotically, his heart constricted by anguish for his sister-in-law. "As commonplace as this sounds," he began, despairing of his inadequacy, "could I suggest professional counseling? *I* can't really counsel in this situation, if that's what you're thinking. You being family—"

"I know. That's why I'm talking to you in your 'rabbinical' role. Yes, I have a rabbi in Exeter, but I haven't been going to synagogue long and I don't know him very well. Besides, he's a little forbidding, and I need to talk to someone. I'd been able to keep a lid on things, but the events of this week . . . and then that reporter stirring things up. I'm frightened about what might happen."

"Julia . . ."

"Who can you talk to in this village without it being someone else's business within hours? Who is most likely to keep his counsel?" Her eyes beseeched him. Then she looked sharply away. "That's why I confided in Peter in the first place."

Tom started. "Peter?"

"I was wretched after the second miscarriage. He could see I was miserable when I came to choir practice. He was very sympathetic. One evening, after practice, we sat in a pew and talked . . . and it all came tumbling out." She glanced at him miserably. "You might imagine the rest."

Tom did. It was an old story. A marriage falters and a woman hears warm, affirming words from a priest. A hand squeeze or a genial hug follows. Sometimes the priest is unaware of the effect he is having. But from what Tom had gleaned, the late Reverend Peter Kinsey had not been marked by naïvety. He asked:

"Whose decision was the termination?"

"Mine, of course."

"Yes, Julia, I am aware of women's views on these matters, but what I meant was, how was the decision arrived at? Did you tell Peter you were having his child?"

"I was such a fool." Even in profile he could see the grim set to her mouth. "I so misread him. I thought he was in love with me. We talked about my divorcing Alastair—in my mind I rationalised that this would give him a chance to remarry and have a child—then, after a decent interval, Peter and I would marry. But I realised *I* was the one making all these silly plans. I was fantasising. He was being agreeable, simply to keep me sweet. When I told him I was pregnant, he was horrified. Clearly, I had to be either unstable or untrustworthy or manipulative. There was no question I was to get rid of it."

"And that was the end of the affair, I expect."

Julia nodded. "And I couldn't very well go through a charade of passing the child off as Alastair's. Since the second miscarriage, we had hardly been sleeping together. And since my chances of carrying his child to full term were so unlikely, he would be suspicious."

Tom watched the Dartmouth-bound ferry round the bend and fade from view. He brimmed with grief for Julia's losses, but just as much he abhorred Kinsey's cowardly default to self-preservation, an attitude reprehensible in a priest.

After a moment Julia continued: "I suppose one could ascribe irony to this. Me, falling for a priest—just like my older, smarter, stronger sister. It must be a family pathology. Celia would be able to run with this." She laughed mirthlessly. "I caught her talk at the WI on the psychology of sibling relationships. She said those second born often accept second place. They emulate their older siblings because it's comfortable. Someone else has already sort of carved out the path—haven't they?—and you simply follow along. Look at who I married. He was Lisbeth's first, wasn't he?"

"Sometimes," Tom responded, jolted by Julia's observation, for the sisterly parallel outside of their shared love of music had not crossed his mind, "a cigar is just a cigar. Birth order isn't fate."

"Perhaps." Julia looked up at him with wet shining eyes. He felt a terrible urge to take her in his arms, to comfort her, poor suffering creature—and sensed that she, too, sought comfort, for the air between them had become feverish. But what surged within him was another feeling, one on the unholy side of the ledger. Julia's vulnerability and her physical attraction—her resemblance to Lisbeth—were dangerously alluring. He half smiled and turned away, feigning an interest in the crop sprayer now vanishing over a rise in the field it had worked. After a moment, he said:

"I wonder how you could bear to be near Kinsey after . . ."

"If I abruptly resigned as assistant organist and choirmaster, it would have been a signal that something was amiss—"

"Something *was* amiss."

"—and Colm was taking his family to Mauritius for a week for a getaway. It was early April. And then a day or two before the Parrys returned home . . . Peter vanished, though we didn't know what had happened at the time, did we? You were there at the start of it all." Julia paused. "There was a moment, after some weeks had gone by and Peter hadn't reappeared, that I thought he'd run off because of me. I was torn what to tell the police who were investigating his disappearance. But it hardly seemed in character—Peter was so adept at *appearing* caring. He was an extremely good actor, really—and Sebastian suggested I keep it to myself."

"You talked to Sebastian?"

"He's the one person—layperson, I mean—in the village who can keep a secret."

"He has secrets of his own, I daresay. But why would you confide in Sebastian?"

"He knew Peter. They had some past association."

"Good heavens! Are you sure? What was it?"

She shrugged. "I did ask. But Sebastian wouldn't say. You know what he's like. And Peter was simply . . . smug about it, whatever it was. Simply wouldn't tell. I thought perhaps they'd been at the same school or something. Anyway, like most in the village—except your Mrs. P.—I long ago stopped being curious about Sebastian. In any case, I confided in Sebastian because . . . well, because he knew about Peter and me. You see, we would sometimes meet at the verger's cottage."

"Where Madrun happened to see you."

"And got the wrong end of the stick. Of course, if she had guessed correctly—that I was meeting Peter there—then it might have come out when the police were looking into his disappearance."

"I'm a little surprised Sebastian would permit his home to be . . ."

"Violated?"

"I didn't say that, Julia. But he guards his privacy so fiercely."

"Somehow Peter was able to sway him. The verger's cottage is ideal. There's a spare key tucked into the door frame. The door opens into Poachers Passage, not onto Church Walk. There's the churchyard wall across from the door. No window overlooks the passage—"

"—And if you think someone might be nearby, you can simply keep walking up the passage until you get to The Square."

"Precisely. The chances of anyone seeing you are negligible."

"Almost."

"Almost. But better Madrun's imaginings than the truth."

But, Tom thought, looking down the cliff face to where the rose, now a white dot, had fallen, with Peter's body unearthed, a pathologist's report indicating head trauma, and, no doubt, an inquest in the offing, truth will out. He turned back to Julia. Her face, pinched with misery, told him she was thinking the same thing.

The Vicarage

Thornford Regis TC9 6QX

Dear Mum,

I expect by the time you've got this letter, you'll have got through Saturday's papers. As of this writing, which is very *late in the morning for me, I haven't seen any yet! Daniel Swan is always behind with his deliveries at weekends. When I complained once he told me he had a right to a bit of a lie-in on Saturdays and Sundays. A right, mind you! And then he had the cheek to tell me I shouldn't get up so early. Those Swan children just seem to run wild. Anyway, I'm interested to see what pictures have been printed. Likely there won't be any in the Telegraph, but I'm sure one of the other papers will have it. The "it" I'm referring to is of Oona Blanc slapping Colm right by Sybella's grave when Mr. Christmas had started into the committal. A photographer pushed his way through to get a picture of it, and he got a picture of Mr. Christmas, too, as Oona jabbed him in the eye—Mr. Christmas, that is, which I don't think she intended. It was an accident of sorts, but Mr. C. looks a bit worse for wear, and*

maybe his picture will be in the papers, too. I hope it explains
how *he got the black eye. I wouldn't want the whole country to
think our priest ~~is a pugili~~ is a loutish sort of character. At least
Oona didn't get up to any mischief at the gathering in the
church. She came with this young man who might have thought
to shave before a church service, but he wore a very smart suit
and was very attentive to Oona. I thought he might be one of
those celebrity minders, though he wasn't big enough to be a
proper one, but Roger said he made his living modelling
underpants and did very well by it and was famous in his own
right. At least in certain circles, Roger added. I was sitting in the
seventh pew from the front, so I really couldn't see Oona very
well. You could hear Colm, though. He was quite overcome, and
that and the choir—Revelation Choir, from London, who
performed with Colm on one of his albums back when—was
really magnificent. There was hardly a dry eye, Mum. Which
was odd in a way because I'm not sure how well most folk knew
Sybella, but she was barely more than a child and so I'm sure
everyone was thinking about their own children and how awful
it would be to lose one. I couldn't help thinking about Tamara
and Kerra, for instance, or little Miranda, and, of course, how
it's been such a frightful week in the village and everybody
feeling strained and wondering what on earth could happen
next. I sat with Karla and Roger and his mother, and in the
same pew were the Drewes. Yes, both of them. I've never seen
Liam inside the church! His parents are apparently Pentecostals
of the most extreme sort up at Cheltenham so he had taken
against all religion and certainly never had a good word for Mr.
Kinsey, which I've probably mentioned before, but there he was
in church as ~~pretty~~ big as you please. He didn't join in the prayers
and responses but he was wearing a proper suit and was holding
Mitsuko's hand when they were seated—this after the great row
they'd had Thursday evening, which I told you about, with
Mitsuko all but accusing Liam of doing Sybella in, which I had*

thought about going to the police about, but perhaps it was just
words after all and I needn't worry. Anyway, I'd have thought
those two were headed to divorce, but they seem to have patched
it up. Mr. Christmas conducted himself well. He's getting on
decently at the job, I think, though Karla has her reservations—
but you know Karla's contrary nature! I think she just likes to
keep them on their toes. Mr. Christmas saved the day for her at
Ned's funeral, after all. And of course it was Mr. Christmas's
name she and Roger and the others put forward to the Bishop to
appoint anyway. At any rate, in his sermon, Mr. Christmas was
very good at ~~turning vice into virtue~~ presenting Sybella as a
spirited young woman, which I suppose she was in a way. It
made me think of when I was her age and went up to London to
study at Leiths School that year it opened. Do you remember? I
think that was fairly spirited of me, don't you think? Especially
as Dad thought catering college at Exeter would do. ~~He~~ Mr.
Christmas said Sybella was a daredevil and high-spirited and
how she was finding her way in life down here in the country
and that she was proving herself gifted in art. He talked about
her mischievous side with some story I didn't catch about when
she was a little girl, though I said to Karla later that Sybella
always looked like she was up to some sort of mischief in the
village, and she agreed and told me Mr. Christmas's story
reminded her that the Saturday of Bank Holiday weekend,
Sybella had been in the post office buying stamps for a quantity
of envelopes, and that she couldn't help noticing they were all
addressed to people at the papers and TV stations in London. She
said Sybella seemed to be quite keen to ensure Karla noted the
recipients, but then, after affixing the stamps, she didn't leave the
envelopes with Karla, and she didn't post them in the box
outside, either! Karla watched to make sure. I said what was
really odd was a young person using the post. I thought they only
texted these days. Karla said she had a mind to go to the police
about it, but I said surely if the papers had received a letter from

a murdered girl it would have been all over the news by now. Unless, of course, it's in today's papers, which as I mentioned before are very late. *During one of the Readings, it occurred to me that perhaps Sybella's murderer was among us—right in the sanctuary! There were a number of people I'd never seen before—relatives of the Parrys, I was able to gather later—but some others didn't look like they really belonged. Still, Mum, you mustn't worry about things you read in the papers. I'm sure the local constabulary has everything well in hand. Though they did rather let us down when it came to the churchyard, letting this photographer barge in and all. Which brings me back to Oona. Some phrase in the committal set her off, which I couldn't quite hear. But Oona herself could certainly be heard. Terrible language for a churchyard! And then she slapped Colm and nearly tipped into the grave. The underpants modeller fetched Oona off down the path towards the millpond and calmed her. Poor thing, she was shaking, and I felt quite sorry for her in the end. Colm set onto the photographer who hopped it smartly. I guess he's had experience in the past with these nuisancy people, and then we stood about in dead silence for a time waiting for Oona to recover. No one knew what to say and no one wanted to ~~spoil~~ further spoil the ~~solom~~ solemnity of the occasion. I couldn't help thinking what a splendid day it was and how it was sort of heartless of nature to be that way. Thornford is so lovely in late May, with everything so green and fresh. I think we stand a good chance of winning the Village in Bloom competition this year. Finally, Oona returned and the rest of the service went without incident, though I did think Mr. Christmas looked a bit peculiar. He stumbled over the "my own eyes have seen the salvation" part in the Dismissal, which isn't like him as he used to be a stage performer, after all. I could hear Karla make a disapproving grunt beside me. But then, Mum, we went up to Thornridge House! I remember going up there once with you. I must have been all of five, and it must have been just before old*

Mr. Northmore sold it, but I can't remember what we were doing there. You must remind me. It's not really my sort of place, not cosy the way the vicarage is, but it was marvellous to look at. Celia has had it done up all sort of modern and airy with creamy walls and these great swagging draperies mixed with lovely bits of old furniture and smart new things. There was a large painting in the drawing room of a mother and child in a ~~renee renaisen~~ *sixteenth-century style that so reminded me of those little paintings in the Lady chapel. Do you remember them? They were taken down a while back when the sanctuary was repainted and I'd quite forgotten them. I was rather fond of them, though I know Karla wasn't. I asked her where they'd gone and she said they'd been sent out for restoration and she wasn't sorry it was taking so long. Karla* is *funny—she can get sort of Bolshie, very much like her dad would, only in a different way, of course. At any rate, I must say everyone was rather thrilled to be at Thornridge, especially as many had never seen the inside, but of course it was a funeral tea and so everyone was on their best behaviour, though after a while folk did get a bit chirpy forgetting why they were there in the first place, especially after Colm disappeared upstairs to deal with Oona, who was too distraught or the like to come down and meet people. Celia looked put out, but I can't say I blame her, having her husband's troublesome ex-wife installed in the house. The oddest thing happened when we were leaving Thornridge H., though. Mr. Christmas was to drive us back to the vicarage—with Julia Hennis, I might add, with whom he had had a* very very *long conversation in Colm's garden—and we were walking down the line of cars outside the gate when we noticed Mairi White, who had been minding the gate with a few others from the local constabulary and some other very large men that Colm must have hired, tugging at something at the bottom of the hedgerow. She had thought the hawthorn was blooming oddly, but it turned out it was cotton batting, and the batting was from a*

*quilt, or at least part of one! There was cotton batting
everywhere as Mairi had pulled a little too hard. Apparently one
of Mitsuko's quilts from the v. hall that I was telling you about
yesterday had gone missing, and this was it—or at least it had to
be as finding a quilt in a hedgerow is like finding a tea tray in
the sky, isn't it? I forgot to tell you in yesterday's letter how each
quilt featured a big photograph of Thornford R in the centre
framed by squares of what looked like fields of corn and such.
Well, this one was missing most of the photograph. It had been
cut away, and quite neatly, too! It was very curious, everyone
thought, that the quilt was in the hedgerow along the lane going
up to Thornridge House. It's not a connecting road after all. The
only people who go up it regularly are the Parrys and Sebastian
and the postman, the Sainsbury's delivery van, cleaners, and
maybe BT, if the phone's out. Anyway, Mum, another mystery to
be solved! Now I must go down and mail this and if Daniel
Swan has managed to rouse himself perhaps I'll find the papers!
Cats are well. Love to Aunt Gwen. Make sure you stay well.*

*Much love,
Madrun*

P.S. Do let me know when the doctor schedules tests for your leg.

CHAPTER TWENTY-THREE

om's fingers performed a light tattoo on the keyboard of his computer, his thoughts a tangle. He looked up at the screen, at the beckoning nursery colours of Google's homepage, and hesitated. A theology of Google would be a fine thing, he considered, mentally filing the notion as future sermon-fodder. Perhaps an eleventh commandment: *Thou shalt not be a nosey parker.* On the other hand, no commandment would be more violated in today's cyberworld, especially with maidservant-coveting being much on the wane.

He depressed the third finger on his right hand. A lower-case *l* appeared in the window, and instantly resolved into the words "london magic circle." The infernal memory of these machines! For old times' sake, he occasionally looked at The Magic Circle's website. He was a club member, after all, and it was sometimes fun to see what some of his old mates were up to, but, really, he never lingered over its Web pages. Life held out too many other tasks.

He deleted all but the *l,* and once again diddled his fingers indecisively over the keys. In one respect, he didn't want to know: If someone in the village preferred privacy (a moribund notion in the twenty-first century) or preferred to fabulate about his life and was otherwise functioning without an evident need of psychiatric attention, then what business was it of his—Tom Christmas—to intrude? On the other hand, he thought, glancing at his other hand, the sinister one, the one always distractingly useful in a little sleight of hand, the murder—mur*ders*—in the village seemed to justify some form of information gathering. *Seek truth from facts,* said Mao's *Quotations.* He glanced over at the red plastic book, which he'd been idly flipping through while his computer warmed up. Old Mao was a bit of a homespun chappie, but he got to the point in short order. Did he know, as Jesus did, that the truth shall make you free?

His mind returned to the day before, to his exchange with Màiri White outside Thornridge House's gates. Rounding the stone pillars with Madrun and Julia, he espied Màiri bent into the hedgerow that divided the Big House from Thorn Barton, the former manor farm. She was in uniform, true, but she did present a fetching view as she bowed to her task. Only Madrun's waspish remark about some folk blithely picking blooms while other folk had lost loved ones saved him from slipping into an indecorous ogle. As they passed down the line of cars, though, he looked back and saw that flowers weren't the object of Màiri's attention. Driven—at least in part—by curiosity, he excused himself from Madrun and Julia. Màiri appeared to be pulling at something stuck fast in the hedge, nearly—oh, but only nearly!—stumbling backwards into his arms when that something gave way. It wasn't flowering hawthorn she'd dislodged, it was cotton batting spilling in a flurry of white from a patch of cloth that was clearly, even at a quick glance, part of the border of a Mitsuko Drewe art quilt.

"Ah!" Màiri murmured to herself. Then her eyebrows shot up. "Tom! I can see it's a man's life in the Church of England."

He put one hand over his bruised eye. "I was defending the notion of women bishops at a boxing match. The other bloke looks worse. I can still see, though, and I can see what *that* is." He gestured to the colourful fabric in her hands.

"There's more stuffed into the hedge. Strange place to hide it."

"Or not."

"A thief foolish and frenzied, do you think?"

"Or one cool and cunning."

"This isn't the most travelled road," Màiri observed.

"That it is not," Tom agreed as Madrun and Julia joined them and they began to pluck other scraps from between the hedge's thorns.

Now he revisited the thought: The road to Thornridge House was as good as private; it led nowhere beyond the gates of the Big House. He could think of few who travelled it besides the Parrys, but with a reluctance bordering on anguish, he found his ruminations settling on one individual who did, almost daily. More than wanting to know, he needed to know, if the truth was to set Thornford free—at least of anxiety.

His fingers dug into the keyboard and a fresh, new marshalling of letters appeared after the *l*. Then he clicked on the search tab and reviewed the results that leapt onto the screen.

Yes, by golly, there was a Lord Kinross. The lords Kinross had been earls in the peerage of Scotland since 1696, according to the top entry, which contained several paragraphs of dense type with an order of succession that reminded Tom of the numbing multiple begats in Chronicles. The ninth earl was a war hero, who had earned the undying respect of his men. The tenth, current, and living—presumably, unless the stroke mentioned by Mr. Macgreevy had proven fatal in the last day or so—earl was Gordon Allan, born 1940, succeeded to the peerage in 1981, a businessman who owned a few bits of Mayfair and Belgravia the Duke of Westminster hadn't gobbled up, as well as land in Scotland and Canada. He was variously a bloodstock breeder and a bank director, had been schooled at Shrewsbury and at the Royal Agricultural College at Cirencester, and was a patron of this and that charity and sat on the board of this or that institution. There were the usual honours and honorary military appointments—all in all the résumé of a sort of latter-day stalwart of the British Empire, if the sun hadn't gone and set on the bloody thing.

Tom ploughed through a few more sites. Lord Kinross had a wife, Hélène, a Canadian, as it happened; three sons, the eldest of whom was deceased; and one daughter. He reflected for a moment on the tragedy of a child predeceasing a parent—he could hardly imagine the horror of losing Miranda—and was set to scroll down to an entry subtitle, when the name of the youngest son caught his eye. He would have checked his pulse, but he found himself only mildly startled. The Earl of Kinross's third son was the Honourable John Sebastian Hamilton Allan.

A little transposition of names and Bob was your mother's brother or, in this case, Sebastian was your church's verger.

Oh, surely.

It had to be.

The birth date of the Hon. was nicely synchronous with the presumed age of the verger in question. And why would that shambolic reporter have otherwise mouthed the name Kinross with so much import if there wasn't some sort of vital link?

Of course, the question, Tom thought, as he half listened to Miranda's footfalls on the stair outside his study, was why Sebastian was at such pains to keep his identity a secret. And however, he thought again as he typed "Sebastian John" into Google, could he keep such a secret in a world where anonymity was becoming a passing fancy? Surely others in the village had typed the very name into their very own computers in a similar quest. But "Sebastian John" resulted only in thousands of websites about an American pop singer named Sebastian, John—John Sebastian—who was now well advanced in age. Likely others in the village had felt as daunted as Tom did at the prospect of panning through all these websites with slim hope of a nugget of a different sort.

Tom returned to the entry on the Earl of Kinross and scrolled further down. *Controversy,* said a subhead, followed by *See also: Vis-*

count Kirkbride murder scandal. The text was highlighted in blue, inviting him to click on it and bring up a new Web page. He frowned. Now, who was Viscount Kirkbride?

He read on; then clicked to the new Web page. In a moment, he knew, and this time he was more than mildly startled—so much so that he could barely keep his attention on polishing his sermon for tomorrow.

Stepping off the elevator onto the hospital's third floor, Tom was jolted from his worried thoughts by the sight of Detective Sergeant Blessing. The policeman was standing rather than sitting among the visitors in the cream-walled, hushed waiting room. He appeared to be studying the wall, and because he was absently worrying a welt on his neck—vivid even from ten feet—it crossed Tom's mind that a dermatology appointment was nigh. But it was a Saturday, and Blessing was wearing a sober suit and he was tapping something as black as the suit's fabric rhythmically against the side of his thigh, as if to some beat bouncing inside his head. Tom saw it was a notebook, its coiled cover glinting in the overhead light, and realised this was no private medical visit. He found himself suddenly rooted to the tile. In the car, driving up to hospital from Thornford, he had been possessed by warring thoughts. Should he pass along his gleanings to the police or should he question his gleanings before taking such a decisive step? Knowledge he had, but knowledge was not understanding. He thought to slip around the corner to the corridor to Colonel Northmore's room, but in that moment Blessing turned his head, cast him a vacant glance, then raised his eyebrows in recognition, noting either the dog collar or, possibly, the black eye. There was little choice but to greet him.

"I thought you usually travelled in twos," Tom said, trying for a light effect, stepping past a bank of empty waiting room seats. He saw that the detective had been studying a print of the millpond at

Thornford Regis, with St. Nicholas's tower in the background, one of a series of pretty south Devon scenes.

"Usually. But Detective Inspector Bliss has been momentarily detained."

"Oh?"

"May I count on your complete discretion, Vicar?"

"Er . . ." Tom hesitated, startled. "Yes. Of course."

"The inspector has an irritable bowel."

"Oh. That's . . . rather cheerless. I am sorry. Is that why . . ." he began, thinking to ask about Bliss's persistent kineticism when seated.

"Is there anything you'd care to tell me?"

"Well, I . . ." Mystified, sensing he was being mocked, Tom regarded the battered face. "I once had an ingrown toenail."

"Not really what I meant, sir. I was wondering—unofficially, of course—why you were here in Torbay Hospital on this very pleasant afternoon."

"I'm about to pay a pastoral visit."

"To Phillip Northmore? I think you'll find the old gentleman is very much under the weather."

"Oh, I'd heard—" Some instinct stopped Tom from further speech.

"Heard what?"

"Well, I expect there are ups and down when you're in Colonel Northmore's condition, that's all."

"Mmmm." Blessing's mouth formed a thin line.

"Was Colonel Northmore at all helpful to your investigation?"

"No, I can't say he was."

"I am sorry. I'm sure if he weren't dazed by medication, his intent wouldn't be to be uncooperative. He's ex-military, as you know."

"That's as may be, Vicar." To Tom's puzzled frown, he added: "Name, rank, and serial number seemed all Colonel Northmore cared to discuss. Or was able to discuss. In effect, sir."

"Might the reason lie in the subject of your enquiry?"

"Funny you should ask. We were thinking of paying you a visit on the very subject, Detective Inspector Bliss and I, but here you are. We seem to find our attention meandering to Mr. Sebastian John. Enigmatic fellow, don't you think?"

"Well . . ."

"Whereabouts at the time of Ms. Parry's death uncertain, for one."

"I shouldn't be surprised if he was having a meal with the colonel at Farthings Sunday evening. He often does."

"Time of death is well past the supper hour, Vicar. Mr. John told us he left the colonel's before nine." Blessing lifted his notebook as if he wished to check something in it. "I should wait for the detective inspector to finish his . . . ablutions, I suppose—"

"Well, then . . ." Tom made a move to turn, relieved. "I'm happy to meet you later at the vicarage."

"—But as you're here, perhaps *you* can tell me how Mr. John happened upon Thornford."

"Wouldn't it be best to ask him?"

"We can't seem to locate him at the minute. You wouldn't know his whereabouts?"

"No, I'm afraid I don't. And," Tom continued, praying God to forgive the falsehood, "I really know very little about him. I more or less inherited him when I came to Thornford, as I inherited the choir and the bell ringers and the members of the church council. Sebastian carries out his duties very capably so I've never had a reason to ask any more of him than that he carry on in the same manner."

"He was absent from Ms. Parry's funeral yesterday."

"Yes, well, he seemed to have some private reason for not attending."

"And you didn't find that . . . unusual?"

It was on the tip of Tom's tongue to say he was starting to find *everything* in Thornford unusual. Reluctantly, he replied, "Yes, I did, but there seemed little point in insisting, and as we can perform the funeral rites without a verger . . ."

Blessing pocketed the notebook. "And the two of you have never had a chat, over a drink, say, at the pub, about the good old days—yours and his?"

Of this Tom could be truthful. "No. But surely, Detective Sergeant," he added, "you of all people have the resources to look into someone's background."

"We do, Vicar, and we will."

"Colonel, you're looking well."

This time Tom's lie was white. He leaned over the hospital bed and laid his hand on the old man's. He realised in an instant it was the wrong thing to say, for the patient shot him such a withering glance from below a grey cliff of eyebrow that he might just as well have melted into the linoleum. Adding force to the lie was a new presence in the room—a cardiac monitor, tracking the rhythm of the colonel's heart with a slow steady beeping.

"Looking better, rather," Tom backtracked. This, at least, was the truth. A certain acuity had returned to the colonel's gaze, though the face over the coverlet was gaunt and the cheeks stubbly. Tom glanced at the tubing connecting his arm to the glistening ampoule dangling below an IV bag on a pole and wondered that the old man's body had adapted to the morphine, easing his pain, but not clouding his mind as it had on his earlier visit.

"I apologise for not coming sooner," he continued. "Mrs. Prowse told me on Thursday that you wanted to speak with me. But the week turned rather more . . . eventful than I would have expected."

Colonel Northmore held his eyes for a good long time, and Tom wondered if he would have to explain again, as he had to the young couple he had married only an hour before at St. Nicholas's, the black ring around his own.

"I hope the police haven't upset you," he rambled on, bereft of further conversation. "I understand they were here a little while ago."

But the colonel's intent look was one not of curiosity, but of rumination. Finally, he seemed to make up his mind. "Padre," he said, his voice thick with phlegm, "I want to tell you something . . ."

"Yes . . ."

"When I was in Omori—"

"The POW camp near Tokyo, yes?"

"—I killed a man."

Tom frowned, startled. "Oh, dear," he murmured, a feeble response he regretted instantly.

"Wrong thing to do."

"Yes, usually."

"Shouldn't have done it."

"It does tend to sort of bend one of God's commandments, Colonel."

"Didn't set my mind to do it."

"I'm sure you didn't. I'm sorry," he continued, noting an incipient glare forming in the colonel's eyes. "I don't mean to sound cavalier. You've rather caught me off guard with this." He pulled forwards one of the plastic chairs from the corner of the room and sat down. "Tell me the story, if you wish."

"Why I asked you here in the first place, padre." There was the ghost of a harrumph in his tone.

"And are you wanting to make a formal private confession of sin?"

The colonel's head turned against the pillow. He regarded Tom fretfully for a moment. "Hear me out, padre."

"Certainly." Tom was puzzled by the colonel's response.

"Japs were savages, I've told you."

"Yes, Colonel, you did."

"You can't imagine the hatred we felt for them. The NCO who ran the show was mad as a March hare. A brute. But so were the guards, the orderlies—all of them. Barbarous. Swore we would get our revenge when the time came."

Northmore stopped. His gaze seemed to turn inward.

"And did the time come, Colonel?" Tom prompted. He anticipated the details with a certain heavy heart.

"Eh? The time? Yes it did. Remember Takayama—one of the guards—ordering us to line up in the yard. 'War is over. No work today. War is over,' he said. Told us to paint 'POW' in large letters on the barrack's roof. The emperor had surrendered, you see, padre. But more than a fortnight passed before we were found. And when we were . . ." The colonel's face crumpled around the edges and his eyes filmed suddenly. His voice choked. ". . . I'll never forget the joy and relief."

Tom's heart went out to the old man. He could only imagine such release from long suffering.

"Didn't really want revenge, then," the colonel continued. "Flogging them for killing your friends or making your life an utter hell seemed senseless. We hated them with such hatred no act was fitting punishment. Simply wished to get home."

"I'm sure you did . . ."

"But I told you I killed a man. And I did. The day before the B-29 spotted us . . ." He stopped. "I've never been a brash fellow, padre. There are only two instances where I've behaved with utter foolishness. The other I will tell you in short order.

"NCO had fled," he continued. "He had grown more and more erratic after the emperor's surrender. But Takayama had been little better. An animal. Strutted about with a kendo stick. Do you know what they are, padre? Bamboo things. Longer than a cricket bat. He would beat us with it. During the lull, while we waited, when there was 'no work today, no work today,' I came upon Takayama inspecting something in one of the latrines. Don't know what, but I took no time to learn. His back was to me, his kendo stick was leaning against the wall. Didn't think. Snatched it up and lashed the back of his head." He paused, his breath was ragged. Tom noted the patterns in the cardiac monitor above grow more erratic. "I killed him. A wonder I had the strength. I was near nine stone by then."

He looked at Tom, his expression stark. "It was cowardly, shameful."

"Colonel, I can barely imagine the hell you went through," Tom responded in a calming tone, one eye fixed worriedly on the monitor.

"Tiny things, the Japanese," the colonel continued, oblivious. "Were back then, by comparison. Weak as I was . . ."

"Yes?"

". . . Weak as I was, I picked him up and . . . pushed him into the latrine. If anyone knew I'd been responsible, he didn't say. People looked the other way in those last days. And I was an officer, padre, a lieutenant then. I behaved disgracefully."

A young birdlike nurse flitted in at that moment and quickly triangulated the monitor, the patient, and the priest with her sharp little eyes.

"Try not to excite the patient, Father," she ordered, darting over to the bed. She peered at the colonel's face, then with swift motions tucked the coverlet, adjusted the pillows, and felt along the constraining tubes and wires emanating from the colonel's body to assure their efficacy.

"We were talking about old times." Tom watched her flying hands. "The war."

"Talk about peace, then, and see if it doesn't have an effect." She granted both of them a practised smile. "You must rest, Mr. Northmore. I don't want to come in here again."

She passed back through the door into the corridor. Tom got up from his seat and went over to the door to ensure it was sealed. "Colonel," he said, "I'm very sorry this episode has been weighing on your mind. You were under great duress in that prison camp in that long and terrible war, but I know you know that doesn't release you from responsibility for your action." He laid a hand against the bed's cold metal guardrail and looked down at the old face. "Shall we pray together? This would be a moment to ask for God's forgiveness and—"

"No." The tone was sharp.

"Colonel . . . ?"

"Not yet, not yet."

"I don't understand . . . ?"

"There's something else, padre. I must tell you about Peter Kinsey—"

"I presume Mrs. Prowse told you that he'd been found. Or at least his body."

"I killed him, too."

Tom blinked, then blinked again. Had he heard correctly? He rubbed his ear and stared at the colonel. "I'm sorry . . . did you say you . . . ?"

"I killed him."

Tom blinked a third time. He fought to keep his lips from curling into an indulgent smile. "Now, Colonel, you know that isn't true."

Phillip glowered at him. "I am telling you, padre," he said more forcefully, "that I killed Peter Kinsey."

Tom lifted his eyes from the colonel's and watched a prick of clear liquid, like a crystal, form at the top of the ampoule, swell into a tear, then slip from its mooring and dissolve into the tiny pool of liquid just as another drip cascaded down the length of plastic vein from the ampoule into the colonel's hand. He had been mistaken. The clouds may have vanished from the colonel's eyes, but not from his mind.

"Now, why would you have wanted to do that?" There seemed little recourse but to indulge the old man's delusions, though Tom recognised—too late—his own pandering tone, as if he were indulging a whim of Miranda's, for indignation sharpened Phillip's features. Tom rephrased the question, this time with the gravity of a high court judge.

Mollified somewhat, Phillip replied, "Wasn't my intention, padre. Lost control of myself."

"Rather as you had at Omori."

The colonel grunted assent. "I demanded that Kinsey meet me that evening."

"The evening of . . . ?"

"The evening before that fool Ned Skynner was buried. Been avoiding me."

"Kinsey, I presume."

"Didn't care for the fellow."

"Ned?"

"No. Kinsey. Spotted him as counterfeit right off. American teeth, don't you know. My daughter had some fitted for her. I ask you!"

"She *is* an actress, Colonel."

"Smile like a snake in Eden."

"Your daughter's?"

"No! That blaggard Kinsey. Pay attention, padre. Suppose Catherine can't help herself. Always such a hopelessly vain child."

"Is she aware you're in hospital?"

"No idea."

"I should like to call her, if no one has already."

"Waste of time."

"Nonetheless. Do you have a number?"

"In a book by the hall phone at my house. Sebastian has a key. He's been walking Bumble."

"On the subject of Sebastian—"

Phillip's unencumbered hand flapped dismissively. He glared up at Tom, his face reddening. "I have killed a man, Mr. Christmas."

Tom sighed inwardly. He rather hoped the colonel wouldn't make the claim again. He sank back down in the chair. "Yes, of course. Let's see. Peter had been avoiding you, I believe you said."

"Man was a thief."

"How so?"

"Fingers in the collection plate, for one."

Tom raised an eyebrow.

"In effect."

"You'd best explain, Colonel."

"Decline in St. Nicholas's income." Phillip shifted under the bedclothes, then winced. "Didn't notice at first. Not when Kinsey first arrived. Attendance grew—interest in the new vicar, don't you know. But revenues didn't match."

"There are swings and roundabouts, Colonel. Perhaps the jumble sales didn't do as well."

Phillip shook his head. "Figures lower in every case."

"Significantly?"

"Sufficiently. Fiddled the fees for weddings and funerals, too." The colonel interrupted his thoughts. "Removed the fee list from the board in the south porch and began charging more."

"But a church may add a surcharge, if need be."

"Never discussed at the PCC. And Kinsey asked people for banknotes. Pocketed the extra and didn't declare it to the diocese."

"How did you know this?"

"A fellow who works with me on the Campaign to Protect Rural England remarked the Christmas before last on the fee his son had paid for his granddaughter's marriage at St. Nicholas's. It was three hundred pounds more than the fixed sum. Knew it wasn't right."

"Did you ask Peter about it?"

"Said Richard was mistaken. Said he had no idea why the fee list wasn't displayed in church. Arrogant bastard. I asked around, you know. Discreetly. See if others had paid more. They had."

Tom calculated quickly. If one officiated at, say, twenty weddings a year, that, plus the intermittent funeral, would net you in excess of £6,000, with Inland Revenue none the wiser—a tidy addition to one's stipend.

"But, Colonel, why didn't you tell someone of your concerns at the time?"

"Wanted to catch him out."

"And did you?"

His face shuttered. "New broom," he said cryptically.

"What?"

"Kinsey. Wanted to sweep out the old. What he thought was old. He wanted to apply for a faculty to move our Victorian pews and replace them with chairs. I ask you! Fought him on that one. Roger and I. And won." A thin smile played along his lips, only to vanish. "Lost on the redecoration, though."

"I understand a number of artworks were taken down when the sanctuary was repainted. You wanted them back up?"

"I wanted them *returned*." The colonel spoke with sudden vehemence, his face flushing again. He winced in pain.

Tom looked anxiously at both the drip and the cardiac monitor. "Colonel, are you all right? Shall I call the nurse back?"

"No," Phillip gasped. "Let me have a minute."

As Tom watched the old man's features recompose themselves, he considered that though parishioners could get murderously exercised about changes to liturgy or decoration, they were rarely led to murder itself.

"There are a number of paintings and suchlike stored in the vestry," he pointed out.

"Two missing."

"Miss Skynner mentioned two had gone out for repair or restoration and still hadn't returned. I think she said they once belonged to your father."

"They did. Father sold them to Giles, who put them in the Lady chapel." He looked meaningfully at Tom. "They're Guercinos."

"Art isn't my strong suit, I'm afraid, Colonel."

"It was Kinsey's."

"Ah, yes, he read art at Oxford." Tom had a glimmer of the road the colonel was rambling. "He would have known who Guercino was, likely."

"He was Italian. Seventeenth-century. Baroque."

"And valuable, yes?"

"Father had an eye for beauty. Guercino was little regarded when he acquired the paintings. Not much more so when Giles bought them."

"But now?"

"One sold at Christie's last autumn for twenty-three thousand pounds."

Tom made a silent whistle. But it wasn't strange something so valuable could go so unnoticed in a little church tucked into the countryside. The eye soon grows oblivious to the familiar. A few churchgoers regret the loss of a thing or two for a moment after they're removed, but then they're quickly forgotten.

"Kinsey sold them."

"Then this must account for much of the ninety thousand pounds found in that safe-box at the NatWest in Exeter. Colonel, this is difficult to take in. Peter Kinsey was generally well regarded by—"

"Peter Kinsey was wicked."

Tom was silenced momentarily. He leaned forwards, elbows on his knees, cupped his face in his hands, and thought about what he had heard.

"But how do you know he sold the Guercinos?" he asked finally.

Phillip's nose flared as he took a deep breath. "He told me."

"He *admitted* it?"

"Yes. I told him to meet me in the vestry and no excuses."

"This was the evening before Ned Skynner's funeral last April, yes?"

"Knew he had no appointments Monday evenings. Day off, you know. He couldn't fob me off, saying he had a meeting or a home visit. Finally got him on the vicarage phone."

"Why the vestry?"

"So he couldn't claim the Guercinos were there, and I was some old duffer who couldn't see past my nose. Be in the vestry in half an hour, I told him."

"Did you tell him exactly why?"

"Told him the auditors had questions and I needed answers before we went to the PCC annual meeting later in April."

"So, half an hour later, you joined Peter in the vestry and . . . voiced all your suspicions? How did he react?"

"He . . . he laughed. 'Do your worst,' he said."

"No attempt to excuse himself?"

"None. He simply laughed at me."

"But he must have realised you could take your concerns to a higher authority or possibly the police. How could he think he would get away with it?"

"He was wicked. I said."

"Still, why didn't you have a word with the rural dean or the archdeacon?"

"Padre, how could I?" The old man regarded Tom truculently.

It took a moment for Tom to decipher. Of course. If you killed the vicar who was fiddling sums, you couldn't very well report the sum fiddling without dire personal consequence over the issue of motive. This would also explain the colonel's later unhelpfulness to the police over the mysterious sum in the Exeter safe-box. Nonetheless, Tom didn't believe for a moment Colonel Northmore had killed Peter Kinsey, and he said so.

"Well, I did," the colonel responded.

"In anger, I suppose? Without malice aforethought?"

"Yes."

Utterly unconvinced, Tom thought to test him: "What did you kill him with?"

"The verge—the verger's staff. It was lying on the vestry table."

"And how?"

"Hit him. Back of the head."

Tom bit his lip. The murder weapon was unspecified, and might remain so, but the colonel's last answer was correct. Eyewitness account or lucky guess? Had the colonel got wind somehow? Màiri White had told him, Tom, the postmortem results in confidence, but that didn't mean the knowledge mightn't seep out in other ways. Who had visited the colonel in hospital in the last few days? Madrun. Sebastian. Alastair. Perhaps others. He looked at the colonel and met defiant eyes.

"All right, Colonel, I'm willing to believe you killed Peter Kinsey, as you say," Tom white-lied again, "but I have trouble believing you . . . dragged his body or . . . carried his body through the churchyard and rearranged Ned Skynner's grave to accommodate him."

"Wasn't a large chap."

"So I understand. Nevertheless, not to make too fine a point, you're not in the flower of youth."

"I was in the grip of strong emotion, padre."

"Colonel, I haven't known you long, but this doesn't seem at all like you. Even if I allow that in the grip of strong emotion you did kill Peter, I can't believe you wouldn't do the decent thing."

"Didn't do the decent thing at Omori, did I."

"That was different."

"Oh? How?"

Tom could feel his patience growing thin. He didn't fancy a philosophical discussion. "Why are you telling me this at all?"

"On my conscience."

"But why now?"

"On my way out."

"Nonsense, you'll be right as a trivet once you're fixed up with a new hip."

Phillip made no response. He turned his head away. His lids sank over his eyes. Tom studied the figure under the hospital blankets, the bruised hand where the intravenous needle entered, the ancient visage with its bloodless lips, the thin, lank hair, at the tangle of monitoring wires disappearing into his chest. *Yes, old boy,* he thought, *you probably are not long for this world.* He felt a pang of sadness for that, and then, following like the sun upon the rain, the bliss of a tiny epiphany. He smiled as he said, "Colonel, you realise you've unburdened your conscience to me outside of the seal of confession. Colonel?"

Phillip opened one eye.

"I could go to the police with this information."

"Do what you must, padre." He closed his eye and crossed his hands over his stomach.

Tom lifted himself from the hard plastic seat. "By the way, Colonel, by any chance, did you serve in the war with—now let me think—the ninth Earl of Kinross?"

Phillip opened the other eye. "Yes."

Tom allowed his smile to widen. "I see."

"Bit off topic, isn't it?" The colonel opened both eyes and regarded him warily.

"Colonel, at the risk of being repetitive, I don't for a moment believe you hit Peter Kinsey over the head. Nor do I believe you put his body in an open grave. In fact, I'll wager you weren't anywhere near St. Nicholas's the evening in question."

"Was, too!" was the colonel's heated and uncharacteristically childish response.

"Was too what?" said a voice. "I trust you're not upsetting the patient, Tom."

Tom looked over his shoulder. The door to the room had opened on silent hinges and Alastair was slipping a clipboard off the edge of the bed. He frowned at it, then moved bedside, opposite Tom.

"I just thought I'd pop up to see how you were," he addressed the colonel.

"I'm surprised you're not golfing on this lovely Saturday afternoon," Tom remarked.

"I will be shortly," Alastair muttered. "I've just come off a shift at the health centre." He looked at Tom more fully. "Nice work on that eye. Should I ask what happened to the other guy?"

"Surely Julia told you."

"Actually, she did." Still smiling, he turned back to his patient. "How are you feeling, Colonel?"

"Dr. Hennis saw me." Phillip glowered at Tom.

"I saw you when?" Alastair responded, shifting to study the IV line.

"Colonel Northmore is fretting about Peter Kinsey's death."

"Mmm . . ."

"Doctor, you greeted me in the road. You had been up in the Pattimores' flat."

Alastair snapped his fingers against the ampoule. "What are we talking about here?"

"The period of Peter Kinsey's disappearance," Tom explained.

"You greeted me in the road," the colonel repeated to Alastair urgently. "It was a Monday evening, about seven. Remember?"

Alastair frowned. "Are you asking me to remember what I was doing on an evening . . . what? thirteen, fourteen months ago?"

"Well, even I remember, Alastair," Tom said. "It was the end of the first full day of my and Miranda's visit with you and Julia. You had a house call to make. I think your service paged you. I remember the news was just starting on ITV when you got it, about six-thirty."

Alastair's eyes roamed the room then landed on the two of them. "All right, yes. I do recall. I think." His frown grew deeper. "I'd been attending to Enid. I was just stepping out of their gate when you passed by, Colonel. You seemed to have something on your mind, now I think about it. I can't recall you returning the greeting. And then—this I do recall—Charlie Pike nearly knocked me over on one of those bloody skateboards." He paused and regarded Phillip. "Is this important?"

Tom looked to the patient, thinking that being seen on Poynton Shute that evening, around the corner from Church Walk, a few hundred feet from St. Nicholas's, hardly supported his contention that he had done away with the Reverend Peter Kinsey. Still, he expected an expression of complacency from the old man, but none came. Instead, the colonel's pupils dilated and a brooding, watchful intensity settled for a moment along the folds and creases of his face. And then he turned his head to the wall.

CHAPTER TWENTY-FOUR

"The usual?"

"Make it a pint."

Eric's eyebrows, red and thick as foxtails, twitched almost imperceptibly, but not so imperceptibly that Tom didn't know that Eric sussed that some planet was wobbling in its orbit. Publicans were sussers of information and keepers of secrets—not unlike priests, in their way—and therefore mindful to be open to soul-barers without sending out engraved invitations.

"Don't often see you in here of a Saturday afternoon." Eric closed the copy of the *Daily Mail* he'd been perusing and reached for the pump handle. "No weddings?"

"Only one. Strange—usually they're queued up four deep this time of year."

"It's been a strange week."

"That would be understatement."

"We haven't had a day like this since Thornford won the Cup final five years ago."

Tom frowned, not understanding. Eric placed a pint glass of

Vicar's Ruin in front of him and jerked his head in the direction of the saloon. Tom turned and glanced over the rim of his glass. He'd driven back from Torquay, parked the car at the vicarage, popped in to see if Miranda had returned from Exeter with Julia, had a brief and probably too candid conversation with Madrun, then hopped it to the Church House Inn, paying only half a mind to the crowded benches outside the pub, reasoning that it was a magnificent day in May at the end of half-term and why wouldn't people lounge about outdoors with a drink? He'd made a beeline to the bar and hadn't really noticed, as he did now, quite how sardine-tinnish the place seemed. Worse, a number of the punters had paused in noisy conversation and were looking at him. This he was accustomed to in church, and had welcomed on stage, when he'd been The Great Krimboni; still, it was rather disconcerting being gawped at in the pub, especially by strangers.

"You've seen the papers, yes?" Eric muttered, wiping the damp spot where Tom's glass had enjoyed brief congress with the polished surface.

"Glanced at them," Tom replied. And glance was all he had done. He'd been too distracted that morning with getting Miranda ready for Julia to take to synagogue in Exeter, Googling, and polishing his sermon to pay close attention to the coverage of Sybella's funeral. Madrun had raced from the post office to the vicarage weighed with every newspaper in the realm and plunked them on the kitchen table, but Tom's only interest had been in *The Sun*'s coverage—in Andrew Macgreevy's reportage, its omissions rather than its commissions. He'd quickly flipped past the picture of himself on page six, predictably of Oona's elbow growing out of his eye, under the sub-headline "Oona Funeral Fury," right through to the sports pages at the back, and was both startled and cheered to see no reference to his absent verger. If Macgreevy knew what he, Tom, now knew, why wasn't it in print?

" 'Ow's yer oi, Vicah?" A large man with a face red as a beetroot held his glass up in a toast.

"Never better," Tom replied, with a theatrical wink of the afflicted orb. "Have they driven down from London for *this*?" he murmured to Eric.

The publican shrugged. "I shouldn't like to see the state of your churchyard."

"This is terrible. Sybella's headstone isn't even in place."

"No fear. By Monday, they'll have moved on to something else." Eric folded the *Mail* and stuffed it under the bar. "At any rate, I hear Sebastian's got Fred doing crowd management down at the church."

So, Sebastian is back, Tom thought, gulping his ale while Eric shuffled down the bar to serve another customer. Wherever had his verger spent the night?

He, meanwhile, had taken Miranda and Emily Swan to the Apollo in Torquay Friday after the funeral reception to see some American film about high school students putting on a musical, a cinematic bonbon which thrilled the girls to bits, but which was so excruciatingly insipid Tom had ample opportunity to half-write his sermon in his head and ponder the week's harrowing events. After returning the girls to Thornford, he'd walked over to the verger's cottage, resolved to have a chat, but there'd been no response to his knock. He'd tried again an hour later, with no luck.

"Eric," he began, calling the publican over, "how would you assess your memory?"

"Depends on what you want me to remember."

"An early evening thirteen months ago."

"You want me to remember something thirteen months back—?"

"I've heard that once today."

"—then not bloody likely."

"What if I pegged it to an event?"

"'Where were you in the Great Storm of '87'—that sort of thing?"

"Something of less national significance. Where were you the evening before the day of Ned Skynner's funeral?"

Eric shrugged. He reached back to pull a packet of crisps off a nearby rack. "I was here. Where else?"

"Exactly."

"But it was a day like all days. Which is what I told the coppers when they were asking a year ago."

"Was it?"

Eric slid the packet down the bar to a young woman in a blazing pink sundress. "Ned was absent, of course, being dead and all, so we were still getting used to not having someone droning on about the inevitable fall of capitalism. It was a Monday. Early April. Just a few regulars." He paused in thought. "Jago Prowse came in for a quick one. Told the detectives that. Didn't usually see Jago at that time."

"What time?"

"About six-thirty? If the bugger had bothered to tell anyone he'd driven down from Thorn Cross and dropped the vicar off, then we wouldn't have spent three days wondering where the vicar's car—and the vicar with it—had got to. We could have got on to the local constabulary faster, not that any of this matters now. Is this why you're asking? About Peter's disappearance?"

"Yes. It's been on my mind."

"I see."

Tom smiled wanly. "You and I are similarly fixed, Eric. People tell us . . . things. The question is, what to do with what they tell us?"

"My policy is to keep *stumm*. It's all my job's worth."

"Mine as well—much of the time. But there are moments . . ." Tom drained his glass. "You didn't happen to see Colonel Northmore about that time?"

Eric's expression betrayed a flash of curiosity, swiftly suppressed. "Cops didn't ask me that one."

"Did you see him?"

"He didn't come in for a drink, if that's what you mean. I usually only see the colonel here after services on Sunday, when he comes in with you and some of the others from church. But I did see him that evening, now you mention it. Happens I glimpsed him out the window when I was clearing one of the tables. And I'm only remembering because it wasn't a time of day—it had to be after seven—when you saw the colonel out walking. Pretty regular he is—early morning and mid-afternoon. And he wasn't walking Bumble."

"Was he walking towards the church?"

Eric nodded. "Not what you wanted to hear?"

Tom tried wiping the glumness from his face. Two sightings of the colonel the presumed evening of Peter Kinsey's death, both of him church-bound, did not a murderer make.

"And," Eric continued, "now that you've set me off down memory lane, Sebastian came by earlier than usual."

"He comes in for a drink after closing the church, doesn't he?"

"The man's as regular as the Westminster chimes. When the sun sets, he goes and closes up. But in early April, the sun isn't fully set until about, oh, eight o'clock. Sebastian was here about"—Eric squinted into the middle distance—"about ten minutes or so after I'd sighted the colonel going by—say seven-ten or seven-fifteen."

Tom stared into the dregs of golden liquid in his glass. Did the anomaly mean anything? Sebastian's being in the pub outside his normal routine was surely unremarkable—people sometimes did deviate from their patterns—but it did call attention to itself, if anyone bothered to pay something so trivial any mind.

"Would you remember his demeanour?"

Eric did, actually. It wasn't what Tom wanted to hear.

"Pour you another, Vicar?"

Tom looked at the empty glass. "No, thanks," he replied, pushing away from the bar. "I need a clear head. I have a sort of pastoral visit to make."

Tom had called at the verger's cottage only once previously, when he'd first arrived in Thornford Regis, to ask Sebastian for the vestry door key, but then, as now, he felt he was a tolerated, but not wholly welcome, presence once he'd stepped inside. The terraced cottage, the last bordering the cobbled walk between the Church House Inn and the lych-gate, was small, a conventional two-up, two-down, its entranceway unadorned but for a pot of hostas facing Poachers Passage and the high stone wall that bordered the churchyard. On his visit in late March, the sitting room had been warmed by a low fire burning in the small iron grate, the elaborate Victorian hood of which was the single instance of decorative exuberance amid an almost punishing austerity. The walls were of the same distemper as the church's, and unembellished but for a wooden crucifix, complete with writhing corpus, over a plain round oak table near the door to the kitchen. Facing the fireplace were two armchairs separated by a short bookcase with a low table in front with tiny towers of books, neatly massed, and space carved out for a single cup or glass. There was no television, no computer. But for the concession to modern acquisitiveness in the form of a smart-looking, lightweight rucksack hung by the door—the only discordant note—it might have been a monk's cell. Or, perhaps, with no fire, and the sun absent on the far side of the sky, a prison cell.

Tom gave the latter a passing thought as Sebastian let him into the room. He now better understood his verger's tastes and bearing, but this gave him little cheer. There were no formalities. Sebastian motioned him to one of the armchairs and took the other himself. He made no offer of tea or coffee or a drink, as if sensing that the vicar's visit didn't bear fussing with kettles and bags and cups, glasses and ice.

"I was up at hospital seeing Colonel Northmore this afternoon," Tom said, aware of the thinness of the cushion as he lowered himself into it. He set his eyes on Sebastian's and got straight to the point. "He claims responsibility for Peter Kinsey's death."

If he expected a response, none came. Sebastian's eyes flickered momentarily, but he said nothing, and did nothing other than let his palms knead the oak surface of the chair's arm.

Tom continued, "He says that on the eve of Ned Skynner's funeral last year, he confronted Kinsey in the vestry over . . . various financial anomalies with St. Nicholas's, and was so infuriated at

Kinsey's blasé response that he struck him a blow with the verge, which happened to be sitting on the vestry table. The assault hadn't been intentional, the colonel says, but the effect was the same."

He paused, giving Sebastian a chance for response. Again, none came. "Naturally, I find all this troubling. The colonel was very keen that I should believe he ended Kinsey's life, but I don't. The colonel is—or has been until recently—a robust man, remarkable, considering his age. And I understand that he had to do terrible things in the war. I know he is impatient, that he can be imperious, stubborn, and quite intolerant. I can—almost—picture him striking Kinsey in a moment of rage. What I cannot picture is his skulking away from such a misdeed. Whatever his deficits, the colonel is forthright. And, furthermore, on a practical level, I cannot picture him somehow removing Kinsey's body from the vestry and managing to bury it in Ned's grave. Yes"—Tom held up his hand as if deflecting contradiction—"I understand that Kinsey was not a big man, but shifting a dead weight, even if it's only ten stone, is not a trifle. It would take the strength of a younger man."

Sebastian lowered his eyes to his lap, and let Tom continue:

"There's only one reason I can think of to explain the colonel's behaviour, other than the brain-scrambling side effects of painkillers."

He paused to take a cleansing breath, half waiting for even a monosyllabic reaction from Sebastian. Again, nothing.

"He believes," Tom persisted, "that he is shielding someone. Under normal circumstances, he would, I think, encourage anyone he thought had committed such a crime to own up to his responsibility and turn himself over to authorities. But . . ." Tom let the word hang in the air. "But," he repeated, "the circumstances aren't normal, are they?"

Sebastian looked up from his lap. His face was a mask.

"You're a sort of prodigal," Tom carried on with growing irritation. "Though not the prodigal son. More prodigal grandson, if you count Colonel Northmore as a kind of honorary grandfather."

"Then I can only assume you know about me." Sebastian spoke for the first time.

"Yes."

"That reporter?"

"He gave me the key. After that, it wasn't awfully difficult. Anyone given that key—a name, 'Kinross'—would have learned what I learned with a little diligence. Colonel Northmore, of course, knew. He fought with your grandfather in the war. He must have maintained contact with you throughout your . . . ordeal. He arranged for your sanctuary here in this village when it was over, yes? And Peter, of course, knew. You were at school together, at Shrewsbury, were you not? The sources say that's where you went, and Julia had a notion that the two of you went to the same school. Peter must have recognised you instantly.

"And," Tom continued, "there was one other in the village—who either knew or suspected—wasn't there?"

Tom thought back to what he had read online. More than a decade before, James Allan, the middle of three Allan brothers, married a Canadian woman named Jane Bee, at Crathie Kirk in the Scottish Highlands. Sebastian—or, as he was more properly named and titled, the Honourable John Sebastian Hamilton Allan—committed a heinous crime the day after they were wed. And the victim was none other than the eldest of the three brothers, the best man at the wedding, William, Viscount Kirkbride. The trial in Aberdeen was a sensation, in no small part because Sebastian refused to explain himself or speak in his own defence. He was sentenced to eleven years in prison. Two details in the entries had caught Tom's eye: the manner of Kirkbride's death—head trauma—and press and public speculation that nineteen-year-old Sebastian was protecting someone with his stubborn silence. The horror of fratricide—the sin of Cain—and Sebastian's reticence shattered the Allan family and divided its loyalties. His father and his sister shunned him, while his mother, his brother, and his new sister-in-law stood by.

"Sybella arranged to meet with you at the village hall last Sunday night, sometime after you'd closed the church, am I correct?"

Sebastian's jaw tightened. Then he nodded. "But I didn't go."

"So you say. But the afternoon of the fayre, after we found Sybella's body, the look on your face when you burst into the village hall suggested you knew something about her death the rest of us didn't."

"I knew nothing. Truly," he added as Tom's brows ascended his forehead. "It was . . . something . . . nothing . . . I was mistaken. It doesn't matter now. The point is, I was nowhere near the village hall Sunday night."

"Charlie Pike says he heard someone come in."

"And why was Charlie at the village hall Sunday night?"

Tom twisted his lips. "I think we both know Sybella liked to be provocative. Particularly with males."

"I wasn't about to let her provoke me. She was a child."

"But one with explosive information, possibly."

Sebastian looked away, towards the cold, empty grate. "I don't really know precisely what she knew, Tom. But she would drop hints. Had I ever met the Queen? for instance. My father's land is very near Balmoral. And 'aren't brothers awful creatures' and the like—all spoken with a certain tone."

Tom shifted in the uncomfortable chair. "Sebastian, in my ministry, I've met with others like you, men who have committed a crime and are trying to reintegrate themselves into society. One of the approaches—the preferred approach, I think—is truthfulness. People are generally forgiving, once they know you've paid your debt. But you've gone to some considerable length to hide your identity. I'm not sure why. And I suppose I have to say that I wonder how far you would go to keep your identity hidden."

Sebastian's expression had hardened. "Shall we take a walk?"

Startled, Tom replied, "Where? There's a lot of people about the village this afternoon."

"Along Knighton. Tourists don't know it, and Bumble wants walking. I left him at Phillip's for a few hours."

Tom hesitated. A few of the village's larger and better appointed homes clustered where Orchard Hill met Knighton Lane, but the homes soon gave way to hedgerowed meadows as the lane narrowed and then shrank to a trail invading thick stands of hazel, ash, and fir, before ending at a steep headland that dropped to a cove in the winding estuary. It was one of his own favourite walks because, at its farther reaches, it was so little used, so perfect for contemplation and prayer. He glanced at Sebastian, who was rising from his chair, at the torso stretched in a plain white T-shirt. The Sebastian he'd seen in pictures on the Internet had been a true toff—rail thin, lean faced, floppy haired, a boy really, with a vacant expression on his face. The Sebastian before him now was a solid presence, surely three stone heavier than the lad in the pictures, the product, he expected, of prison gyms and years spent outdoors, learning his gardening trade at open prison in the last years of his incarceration, then working daily for the Parrys and elsewhere in the village. Sebastian was fit, very fit, and he would forever bear the epithet "murderer." Unthinkingly, Tom pressed his forefinger into his own belly and found it bounced back all too readily, like a jelly. Pastoral work, endless meetings, and the responsibilities of a husband and father had devoured any private time he might have had for exercise. And then, more lately, there was Madrun stuffing him like an Eponymous goose. He was not fat—yet—but he was not fit. And he was being invited to consort between the hedgerows by a—

"Tom?"

The sound of his name snapped him from his reverie.

"Are you coming?"

Tom glanced up at his verger and met eyes cool with challenge. *"Valley"* and *"shadow"* invaded his mind, warning him away. But he paid no heed. The psalm contained promise of a strength greater than any man could have.

*I*n silence, Tom and Sebastian walked up Poachers Passage into The Square. There they glimpsed DS Blessing ushering his superior through the door of the Blackbird Gallery. The detectives didn't see them.

"Have you had any further conversation with either of them?" Tom asked Sebastian, glancing at a few of the other villagers window-shopping Mitsuko's display of local artists' paintings.

"No" was the curt reply.

"I happened to meet the detective sergeant in the hospital waiting room earlier this afternoon. He asked about you."

"What did you say?"

"I kept my counsel—"

"Thank you."

"—for the time being."

In renewed silence, they passed the post office and Pattimore's, then travelled up Orchard Hill, turning west through the shadows of lofty oaks demarcating the entrance to Knighton Lane, to Farthings, Colonel Northmore's home. As Sebastian opened the picket gate piercing the privet hedge and they passed under an arched trellis heavy with red climbing roses, Tom thought about his few parting words with the old gentleman. Alastair had absented himself, and the colonel seemed to sink into torpor, his face grey. Despite this, obliquely, before he himself left, Tom wished the colonel to know he understood the sacrifice he believed he was making.

"I understand Lord Kinross—the late Lord Kinross—was cited for his heroism in the war and for his sacrifices in the prison camp. His intercessions saved many Allied lives."

The colonel turned his face back from the wall to stare at Tom. He said nothing, but his rheumy eyes filled with incipient tears.

"And, Colonel," Tom added gently, "I believe I know one of his descendants."

The older man didn't respond immediately, but an intelligence passed between them. Tom could see a new worry disturb the colonel's features.

"What will you do?" he croaked.

Tom replied, "I don't know."

"Wrong," the colonel groaned, before the lids sank over his eyes and he made a feeble dismissive gesture at Tom, who said a quick and silent prayer and left.

Now, standing on the polished parquet floor of Farthings's hallway, watching Sebastian attach a leather lead to the excited Jack Russell's collar, he wondered—as he had on the drive back from hospital—what the colonel meant. If only the old man wasn't so parsimonious about starting a sentence with a subject. What was wrong? Who was wrong? He? I?

"As I see it," Tom told Sebastian, stepping first back into the lane and holding the gate open for Sebastian and Bumble to pass, "Colonel Northmore must have it in his head that you might be responsible for Peter Kinsey's death or he wouldn't go so far as to say that *he* was."

"Phillip has been more than kind to me."

"The question is: Why would he think—?"

"Because," Sebastian cut in, "according to a court of law, I've killed a man before. I suppose it's not unreasonable to think that having done it once, I might do it again."

Tom flicked a glance at him, at the strong hands holding the straining lead as Bumble snuffled deliriously along the hedgerows. "But the colonel has been your sponsor, your patron, your friend, the keeper of your secret. He must be one of those who believe you *didn't* kill your brother, despite the findings of the court."

"We've never discussed it."

"What?"

"We've never discussed the circumstances of my brother's death, Phillip and I."

Astounded, Tom could only grope for words. "But . . . ?"

"You think he's taken an awful chance . . ."

"Well . . . I . . ."

"He was devoted to my grandfather, and to my grandfather's memory. I believe Phillip feels he owes my grandfather a boon. In a way, helping me find sanctuary here is part of that payment, though, of course, he's never said."

"The colonel told me this afternoon he had killed a man— a Japanese—in prison camp. Do you know this story?"

Sebastian shook his head.

"I'm not sure I believe it," Tom continued. "I think the colonel's had time to ruminate while he's been in hospital. He may have concocted this tale to support the notion that he would be capable of killing someone again, namely Peter Kinsey."

Sebastian flashed him a look of doubt.

"I asked him if he wanted to make a formal confession, ask for God's forgiveness and take absolution. He more or less waved me off. Do you understand? The colonel may be prepared to lie to protect a man, but I don't think he would be prepared to offend God."

Sebastian received this without comment, looking upward momentarily as if seeking some answer from the sky, a warmer, deeper blue in the late afternoon. They walked on, past meadows that glinted through glimpses into gaps in the hedgerows, only their footfalls on the stony path and the occasional remonstration from unseen sheep breaching the silence.

"Why," Tom asked finally, pulling at one of the tall grasses poking through the soil, "are you pottered away down here in the Devon countryside anyway?"

"Why are you?" Sebastian responded mildly.

"You know perfectly well. A safe haven for my daughter—though perhaps I should rethink that notion after this week's events. But you haven't answered my question."

"Well, why not live here?"

"I think, Sebastian, if I wanted to create a new identity or live in anonymity, I'd slip into London's teeming masses. Or move to another country. I don't think I'd pick a gossipy little village, however out-of-the-way it is. Thornford has visitors. There are a number of holiday cottages for hire. We don't live in isolation. I know you look quite different than you did a dozen years ago, but you're still taking a chance."

"I'm up at Thornridge House with Colm most days. Few go there."

"There's the pub."

"I usually have my face in a magazine or newspaper."

"The church."

Sebastian smiled for the first time. "Tom, you know how meagre the attendance figures are for the Church of England."

Tom grunted, twisting the grass in his fingers. "You really haven't answered my question: Why are you living in Thornford under a false identity?"

"I'm sorry. I can't tell you."

"Why not?"

"I simply can't. That's all."

"I'm your priest."

"Leave it alone."

Tom watched Bumble tear after a sparrow that had flitted onto the path. The lead pulled taut. "That *Sun* reporter knows who you are, though he doesn't seem to have done anything with the knowledge—yet."

"I glanced at the papers in the post office."

"And what about your father? This stroke the reporter mentioned?"

Sebastian didn't respond; instead he said, "Did you know there is a ghost that walks this lane?"

"Have you seen it?"

"No."

"Mrs. P. knows all the lore. I shall have to ask her."

"Little to tell. It was a curate who murdered his vicar. Sometime in the seventeenth century. They would take contemplative walks this way, apparently."

Tom shot a glance at Sebastian. "And ought I to take a warning from this?"

"I merely mention it, as a point of interest. I did say 'curate.' Sorry."

Was he? Ahead Tom could see the path narrow, the trees grown closer to its edge, their black boughs knitting into a canopy. Soon he and Sebastian would be well away from the village, from its homes and cottages, and not far from the headland that tumbled down to the water below. He glanced at Sebastian's strong back—the straining dog had pulled the man slightly ahead—and felt for the first time a stab of anxiety, perhaps as some antediluvian might have felt if he had happened upon Cain who killed his brother Abel. He could turn back—his thoughts were for Miranda—but then his mind passed over a certain posture of Sebastian in the vicarage garden only two days before and he took a little heart. He tossed aside the grass stem he had been torturing.

"I'm told," he said, "that you weren't your usual self—or the usual self everyone's come to know—on the evening before Ned Skynner's funeral last year."

"Who told you that?"

"I think you can guess if I tell you that you went into the pub well before your usual time and that you appeared to be somewhat . . . agitated." Tom refrained from using Eric's exact phrasing—*"like he'd been handed a death sentence and National Lottery winnings at the same moment."*

Sebastian tugged at the lead to bring Bumble back from his inspection of some olfactory offering by a crumbled stone wall that marked the end of the civilising hedgerows. "I *was* agitated. I'd gone into the church to help Mitsuko back down from the tower. You recall that I told you the quinquennial inspection had been that Monday, the day before Ned's funeral, and that Mitsuko had asked if she might go up the tower? She wanted up around the supper hour— something about the quality of the light for photographs, with the sun low in the sky—and said she'd be half an hour or so, so I left her on the roof of the tower and went back to my cottage. I said I'd come and help her back down. Have you been up yourself?"

"No."

"There're some tricky bits climbing around the bells, for one thing. And I didn't want Mitsuko to injure herself. In a way, I shouldn't really have let her up. I doubt the church's insurance would cover an accident in such circumstances, but Peter wasn't around that day to ask, and Mitsuko can be quite persuasive. So at some point, I left my cottage and went back to the church."

"About what time?"

"I'm not sure. Shortly after seven?"

They passed under a leafy archway, into a twilight of long shadows and ribbons of pale sunshine. The path turned stonier, cruder, the ruts deeper where rainwater lay pooled long after vanishing in the pastures and meadows. Tom felt the spongy patches against his heels, the legacy of Tuesday evening's rain, and the cool air along his face. It was here, on his own walks, that he usually—usually, but not this instant—felt his spirit lift.

"When I went into the church sanctuary," Sebastian continued, "I could see past the rood screen. I noticed the vestry door was open and the light on. I thought that a little odd. Only a few people have keys to the vestry, and I wasn't expecting any one of them to be there at that time of evening, so I went to have a look." He paused, glanced at Tom, then looked off towards the shell of a derelict shed that had captured Bumble's interest. "I found Peter on the vestry floor."

Tom wished he could see Sebastian's eyes, as if the truth might be registered there, but his verger, having tugged at the lead, now crouched in the shadows and called the dog towards him.

Impatient, Tom asked, "And . . . ?"

Sebastian groped along Bumble's collar and unfastened the clip. "He was dead."

He rose from his haunches as the dog, released, bounded joyously down the lane.

"Were you sure?" Tom watched Bumble dart into a sprawling shrub and a bird flit out the top. "Perhaps—"

"I was quite sure, Tom." He flicked him a meaningful glance, and Tom understood in an instant: There was no novelty here. For Sebastian, this was déjà vu—one way or another. According to the archived news stories, he had been discovered in one of the bedrooms at Tullochbrae, the Allans' Highland home, over the body of his dead brother, clutching the murder weapon, a fireplace poker.

"I suppose the obvious question is why you didn't ring the police straight off. I think my first presumption would have been that there had been an accident, or that Kinsey had had a heart attack or the like, not—"

"He was lying prostrate," Sebastian interrupted with some exasperation as they continued down the path. "There was a trickle of blood at the back of his hair, the verge was on the floor, and—"

He let dangle the residual thought.

"And what?" Tom pressed.

"When I stepped out of my cottage earlier to fetch Mitsuko, I saw Phillip walking up Poachers Passage, turning towards The Square. I thought at the time it was odd to see him there, at that hour, and without Bumble. I was going to call out to him, but I was needing to get to Mitsuko, and he was walking away with"—he squinted as if in recollection—"with uncharacteristic haste."

"And then," Tom prompted, "two minutes later, when you saw Peter's body in the vestry, you thought perhaps . . ." He left the rest unsaid, thinking: *Three people now placed the colonel in the vicinity of the church at a crucial time.* He watched Sebastian's lean, strong fingers wind the dog lead into a coil and waited for a response. When none came, he continued, "Why would you think that? Why would you think the colonel might have killed Kinsey?"

Finally Sebastian spoke: "Phillip was troubled about something."

"About the paintings that used to hang in the Lady chapel?"

"Then you know."

"He told me this afternoon at hospital."

Sebastian flicked him an irritated glance. "I knew how angry and offended Phillip was, and so . . ." He bit along the edge of his lower lip. "I'm afraid Mitsuko flew right out of my head after seeing Peter lying there. I must have passed into a sort of daze, because next I knew I was in the pub, not quite sure how I got there. Walked, of course, but . . ."

In his mind's eye Tom imagined the flight out of the church and down Church Walk. But was Sebastian shocked at finding Peter Kinsey dead after seeing the colonel moving up Poachers Passage, or shocked at having rashly killed his old schoolmate before the colonel had even stepped into the church?

". . . Then, finally, I remembered Mitsuko up in the tower. I left the pub and went and helped her down. I don't think she noticed how late I was. She'd got caught up in the views and photographing everything. She was thrilled, talkative, oblivious to my mood. Then, when she'd gone, I went back into the church, to the vestry."

Sebastian stopped and turned to him. A crack of sunlight flashed across his face, setting his bronzed skin and fair hair aglow. "And when I got there . . ." He raised a shielding hand against the sun so that his eyes fell into shadow. "When I got there, the body was gone."

"What!"

"It had disappeared. Vanished. I remember simply staring at the floor. I wondered whether I was dreaming it all. It was like the women at the Tomb—"

"Only without the angels to supply an explanation." Tom regarded him sceptically, feeling an urge to push the man's hand away from his face so he could read his eyes. "No evidence of a body having been there? Blood . . . ?"

"Nothing. Though the verge was still on the floor where it had been. I left it. Left the vestry, locked up the church, and returned to my cottage."

"And didn't look around the churchyard?"

"I did, but as it was nearly dark . . ."

"But then, when the village grew concerned about the disappearance of its vicar, you did nothing."

Sebastian stepped away from the sun's punishing rays. "The colonel—"

"Did you discuss any of this with him?"

"No."

"Then he thinks he's been protecting you with his silence, and you indicate you've been protecting him with yours."

"'Indicate'?"

"Even if Colonel Northmore did murder Peter Kinsey, you can't seriously believe he was capable of burying him, for heaven's sake!"

Sebastian's eyes flashed with an anger Tom had not seen before in the man, and he turned abruptly back to the path. "Bumble!" he snapped, unravelling the lead. "Get back here!"

Tom followed in silence, his mind churning over the peculiar

mutual dependence between the two men, separated by two generations, each mutely thinking the other may have murdered a man.
Phillip kept Sebastian's secrets and suppressed his natural revulsion
at Kinsey's robbing St. Nicholas's, to protect the security of his old
friend's grandson, even if that grandson had killed again. *Greater
love hath no man than this . . .* flitted through Tom's mind. But were
Sebastian's motives as unsullied?

His verger turned suddenly to face him, snapping Tom out of his
reverie. The strong hands pulled along the lead. Chestnut brown, in
the woods' false dusk the leather strap appeared black, as minatory
as a horsewhip in the hands of a zealous groom. "Tom," he said, staring hard, "I cannot have attention drawn to me."

"And why not?"

"Because someone's life would be put in danger. Not to mention
my own."

Tom peered at him, trying to decipher his features in the crepus-
cular light. "I don't understand, Sebastian."

"I can't say more."

"Then, if that's the case," he said, stepping nearer the younger
man, "you've supplied a motive, haven't you? Peter knew your identity. He knew. He used that knowledge so you would be persuaded
to give up your cottage to his affair with Julia— Yes, I know all about
it. And he used it to silence the colonel as he pocketed money meant
for the church. He was, in effect, blackmailing both of you, wasn't
he? . . . and what a bloody disgrace he was," he added, pausing to
swallow his disgust. "But perhaps there was more—something else
he knew that was making life very difficult for you. Did Peter know
the identity of this someone whose life would be in danger?"

Tom realised they were now near the end of the level path. Beyond a ramshackle gate, unpainted for years, the path fell steeply
through coarse tangled shrubs to a rocky cove below. He looked
down towards the churning water. The tide was coming in; little
rivers from the estuary had begun to flow over the rocks. Bumble
had set a flock of gulls screeching into the air.

"And then there's Sybella," Tom said. "It seems she, too, knew your true identity—or at least knew enough to be a danger. Someone might observe that anyone—other than Colonel Northmore—who knows your story has ended up dead."

Sebastian pulled the leather strap taut; pectorals beneath his T-shirt strained visibly. "And now," he said to Tom, his eyes cold, "it would appear that you do, too."

The Vicarage

Thornford Regis TC9 6QX

1 JUNE

Dear Mum,

Mr. Christmas went up to hospital to visit Phillip yesterday and
I can hardly bring myself to tell you what Phillip told him. It
put Mr. Christmas in a right flap, and me too! Phillip told Mr.
C. he had taken Mr. Kinsey's life! Phillip, that is. Do you
remember last spring when I was with you when you had your
hip replaced and I couldn't get back for Karla's dad's funeral?
Well, the evening before the funeral, Phillip met with Mr.
Kinsey in the vestry and they had a set-to of sorts over those
paintings that used to hang in the Lady chapel that I wrote
about in yesterday's letter. It seems the paintings are worth quite
a bit of money and Mr. Kinsey went and sold them and pocketed
the money himself. I knew he was a devil. Anyone who doesn't
like my braised oxtail is up to no good, in my book. All that
smarm, too. Worked with some women, but not with me.
Anyway, I said to Mr. Christmas that I could not believe Phillip
would do such a terrible thing. He can be gruff—Phillip that

is—but I didn't think he would raise a hand like that, although I thought afterwards that maybe he did some awful things when he was in the War, but then that was war, wasn't it? Dad might have done some awful things, too, when he was in Malta and ~~Ceylon~~ Sri Lanka during the War, but then he never talked about it, did he. Well, maybe he talked about the War with you, but he never did with me or Jago. Anyway, I was quite shaken, and I could tell Mr. Christmas was, too. He usually keeps his thoughts to himself but he was quite talkative yesterday. I think he wanted to know what I thought. And I said I didn't think it was possible. I said I didn't even think Phillip would be out with Bumble, as it was about suppertime, and you know how Phillip likes his routine and always has his meal promptly at 7. But Mr. Christmas said both Dr. Hennis and Charlie Pike saw him— and without Bumble, too. But now, thinking about what men got up to in the War, I'm not sure about Phillip. I asked Mr. Christmas if he was going to say anything to those two CID who have taken over the Old School Room for an "incident room," and he gave me this look that told me his mind was much troubled. Anyway, he did say that what he told me was in the strictest confidence, and then he dashed off, but happened I needed a loaf from Pattimore's, so I stopped in at the post office first and told Karla what Mr. Christmas told me. Karla's very good, as you know, being a churchwarden and all—she's very ~~discreet discrete~~ discreet and wouldn't tell a ~~sole~~ soul. I thought no one was in the post office but lo and behold there was Roger's mother off in the corner looking at the knitting magazines which she dropped as soon as she heard me talking about Phillip. I told her it was all in the strictest confidence and she wasn't even to tell Roger, and she said okay, though she was quite insistent for some reason that Phillip couldn't have been out and about at the supper hour—something to do with the middle of Coronation Street, but as it's a programme I don't watch, I wasn't sure what she was on about and anyway Enid's apt to be a little confused

these days. "I feel rather like Jane Marple," she told me proudly.
Jane Marple with a touch of dementia, I thought. Anyway, I
was in Pattimore's a little later and who should I see through the
window but Mr. Christmas and Sebastian John going up
Orchard Hill together! Mr. Christmas was gone a very *long*
time. The veal I had made had turned to parchment and I was
quite cross, but Mr. Christmas looked very troubled and barely
said a word, though he did try to make an effort with little
Miranda who was still bubbling on about some film she'd seen in
Torquay the day before. And then he was in his study with the
door closed, though he does tend to retreat Saturday evenings,
rehearsing his sermon and such. But he left us with some low
spirits, so I had the bright idea of a board game before bedtime
for Miranda, only it took me a minute to dig through Mr.
James-Douglas's old games from his childhood that were
crammed at the back of the cupboard under the stairs. Of course
the die and the tokens had gone missing from Snakes + Ladders.
The cats had likely made off with them ages past. At any rate, I
found a die in the games table and I used my sewing thimble for
a token and Miranda pulled out her funny little "clue," which she
now tells me she found in the v. hall, from her jeans pocket,
which worked well enough. I wasn't sure if children play board
games anymore. Jago's two never seemed interested. Anyway,
Miranda took to Snakes + Ladders right off, though I think she
thought it a bit babyish in the end. She won, of course. She's such
a bright little girl. I think next time we'll have to try something
more challenging. I noted Cluedo in the cupboard, but you need
at least three to play properly, and "Reverend Green in the study
with the lead piping" probably wouldn't do after what's gone on
in the village this past week! I asked Miranda if her "clue" had
led her to any "solution" in whatever "investigation" she and her
detective Barbie were doing, but she said she needed more
"evidence." I wonder and worry at times how her mother's death
has affected her, but I don't know enough about the 9-year-old

mind, really, at least one like Miranda's. She's much more
thoughtful than that Swan lot who are always racing about
everywhere. And she rarely mentions her mother, at least in my
hearing. Maybe it's still too hard to bear, though I know she
misses that French au pair they had in Bristol. She often looks a
little vexed that her father and I respond poorly (me, not at all)
to her French speaking, though I thought I overheard Sebastian
speaking passable French with her the other day in the garden.
At any rate, I ended up getting Miranda off to bed at a decent
hour. School starts again tomorrow and it will be back to the old
routine. I can't remember Mr. Christmas not tucking Miranda
in before, if he was at home and not at some meeting, so me
doing it was a turnip for the books, as Dad used to say, although
I think Miranda was a bit let down. Your father has a lot on his
plate, I said to her, and I'm sure he will look in on you later,
which he did. He came out of his study when I was settled into
the news looking startled and asked if Miranda had gone to bed,
and I looked at my watch and said sternly as it's ten o'clock, Mr.
Christmas, yes she has, and he looked quite downcast, poor man.
Anyway, he went up and had a look in. I could hear talking, so
it seems she hadn't been asleep—waiting perhaps for her father.
I'm preparing roast beef for Sunday lunch, so I'd best get to it. I
can never get any breakfast into Mr. C. on Sundays, as I may
have mentioned before, since he has to run up to Pennycross for
services first thing, then back to Thornford R for the rest, and
seems to run on ~~adreniline~~ adrenaline. I shall try to take
Miranda to the service at 11, but I may have to send her on her
own. In a few years, she will have to go up to Exeter on Sunday
mornings to begin classes for her bat mitzva~~h~~h, but I don't know
how this shall happen as, of course, Mr. Christmas has his
obligations, and Mrs. Hennis, who takes her to synagogue on
Saturdays, is assistant choirmaster at St. Nick's and has to be
there at least when Colm Parry is not, as he isn't likely to be for a
while, I expect, given the great sadness that has befallen him.

Funny Miranda being Jewish while her father is a vicar, but we are all very modern in Thornford R!!! There were lots of visitors in the village yesterday. I reckon all the goings-on here were what drew them. So it shall be interesting to see if church attendance is higher. I know Mr. Christmas would like that, but I don't think he would be too pleased if it was simply because curiosity got the better of folk. I do hope the swelling in his eye has gone down. He will look a fright in the pulpit otherwise. I wonder if there will be anything in the Sundays on the doings here in the village? Of course, I won't know until Daniel Swan shifts his backside. Did you see the Saturday papers? At least the quality press had a respectful tone. The picture of Mr. Christmas in the Sun was awful. Must go. Cats are well. Love to Aunt Gwen. Hope you have a fine week ahead.

Much love,
Madrun

P.S. I looked in on Kerra at the Waterside yesterday afternoon. So far, so good. I think Liam Drewe is minding his p's and q's for the time being.

※

CHAPTER TWENTY-SIX

"I didn't take you for a reader of *The Sun*, Father," said Tiffany Snape, who minded the post office at weekends and didn't go to church. "More a *Guardian* man, I would have thought."

"I'm very fond of the Page Three girls," Tom responded, depositing all the flyers and rubbish that came with Sunday papers onto the counter.

"Ooh, you are a naughty vicar."

"None naughtier."

Tiffany giggled and counted change into his hand. "I wonder what Miss Skynner would think?"

"Let it be our little secret then." He winked broadly, though he felt fully cheerless, and slipped the coins into his trousers pocket. "It would be good to see you in church, Tiffany. You could bring little Jasmine. I'm hoping to get more Thornford families involved."

"You can see how I'm fixed." Tiffany gestured to indicate her responsibilities to the tidy shop and its contents.

"Then your partner . . ."

"Ryan."

"Ryan could bring Jasmine."

"Chance would be a fine thing," Tiffany hooted. "Do you not have Sky TV up at the vicarage?"

"Ah, football."

"Got it in one, Father."

"Tough competition."

"Perhaps if you did a bit of hocus-pocus at St. Nick's, I might be able to persuade Ryan to nip in with Jasmine. You were a magician, yes?"

"Once upon a time. I promise to pull a rabbit out of a mitre—if the bishop will lend me his—at the next harvest supper. You'll come to that, of course."

"Of course."

"By the way, Sebastian hasn't popped in this morning for one of these, has he?" Tom held up the newspaper.

Tiffany shook her head. "It's usually cricket mags for him."

Tom exited the shop and began turning the pages of *The Sun* as he dashed through The Square and down Poachers Passage, pausing for a nanosecond on page three, before snapping through the pages and pages of news and entertainment until he got to sports, which seemed an unlikely spot for the peer's son—shock—horror item he was looking for. When he'd returned from Pennycross earlier, he'd expected St. Nicholas's to be prepared for the morning service, the altar vested, the vestments laid out, the Communion vessels removed from the safe. But the church was locked, as it would have been, by Sebastian, the evening before. In the two months Tom had been in the parish, Sebastian had never been derelict in his duties. Concerned but not yet worried, he'd gone to the verger's cottage, visualising Sebastian having slept in, coming to the door disheveled and apologetic. But there'd been no response to his knuckles against the glass, no sound of feet thundering down the stairs. He'd looked up to the first-floor window and seen no shadow cross it, no curtain twitch. At that moment he'd felt the first tiny stab of anxiety.

Now, ten minutes later, he was again at the verger's cottage door, the useless *Sun* refolded untidily under his arm, his anxiety amplified. Yesterday, up Knighton Lane, where the canopy of trees ended abruptly as the path descended sharply to the water below, he had witnessed, for the first time, the intimation of a fissure in Sebastian's stoic bearing.

"But now that I know who you are and what you've done," Tom had said to him, his eyes fixed on the dog's lead, which Sebastian was pulling as if straining to snap it, "what shall I do with the knowledge?"

"Might I ask you to respect my privacy?"

"There are two people dead, Sebastian. The village is in an uproar."

"I'm not responsible."

"So you say. But you have had a conviction before."

Sebastian turned sharply. "If you think I'm a murderer, Tom, you were taking a chance coming to the end of this lane with me. There are no witnesses here."

Tom studied Sebastian's profile. He recalled sitting in the vicarage garden with him two days before. "It's something to do with you and a butterfly, I think. Of course," he went on as Sebastian continued to worry the dog lead, "I'm not the first idiot to mistake a gesture for character. I could be dead wrong about you. But I don't think you're a complete fool. There may be no witnesses to Kinsey's or Sybella's murders, but a few people noted us walking through The Square and up Orchard Hill."

"Will you talk to those detectives—Bliss and Blessing?"

"Much will depend on the questions posed—if they pose more questions to me. I didn't live in the village when Kinsey was murdered, so I can offer no illumination on that score. As for Sybella . . . I can only tell them what I know to be true, what I've experienced. It's not my job, I don't think," he added, bitter memories of the Bristol CID interrogation lingering, "to speculate *to* and *with* the police, but you must understand I don't want someone to get away with murder. Does that help?"

Sebastian was silent. He glanced at Bumble, who was scrambling back up the path.

"But," Tom pressed on, "all this is for naught if *The Sun* exposes you. Or if Detectives Bliss and Blessing put two and two together first."

"Then I will be gone."

"Is whatever you've mixed up in really this fraught?"

"Yes."

"There's a chance that reporter may do nothing." Saying it, Tom didn't believe it, but he continued, "If you leave Thornford suddenly, police attention will most certainly turn to you."

"And if I stay, and a story about me appears in the press, the same thing will happen. The only thing I can do, Tom, is stop in the village until something appears in *The Sun* or whatever newspaper, after which I must take my chances."

And they left it at that bargain. Now, at the brown lacquered door of Sebastian's cottage, Tom's mind roiled with fresh and worrying possibilities. Macgreevy had written no story. But maybe the journalist had spoken to someone, unwisely, unwittingly perhaps, and through an awful sequence of events some creature had slipped into the village, in the black of Thornford's night, down unilluminated lanes, and penetrated Sebastian's cottage. Tom was conscious he was letting his mind race towards some pitiless horror. But he also knew that this sensation held no novelty. In the seconds before he had stumbled across Lisbeth's body, a presentiment of tragedy had raced inexorably along his nerves—some animal instinct in play before his mind caught up to grasp its full meaning. His hand darted up over the door. Thornfordians, he knew, lived in cloud-cuckoo-land where—until recently—break-ins and home invasions were the unpleasantnesses only of England's great conurbations. Julia had said Sebastian kept a key tucked above the frame. But his groping fingers found none. Nor under the mat. He shifted the pot of hostas next to the door. Only a scurrying insect met his gaze. His hand went to the door handle, some notion of forcing the door with his shoulder playing along his mind. There was little time. The bell-ringers would be tripping along Church Walk shortly; Julia, too, to ready herself to play the organ in Colm's absence. His fingertips slipped along the cool metal of the doorknob. Miraculously, it turned. Tom pressed gently against the door, and it opened. It had been unlocked. And that in itself was unnerving.

And now, he was inside. He let his eyes grow accustomed to the gloom. No lamp was switched on; no fire flickered from the grate. "Sebastian?" he called out. He took a deep breath, as much to still his thrumming heart as to detect the pheromonal trace that had attended Lisbeth's lifeless body—and Sybella's, in that coffin-drum. Mercifully, the air was redolent only of dust, worn oak, and paper. And yet, he thought, as he passed through to the kitchen, past the low table, now limned in the feeble light, with its books and magazines of the day before, no morning aroma lingered in the air—no blend of toast and coffee, or of bacon or eggs. A few dishes occupied a rack next to the sink. He touched the dishcloth that lay over the rack, but it was stiff and dry. He retraced his steps back to the sitting room, then hesitated before the stairs leading into the shadows above. "Sebastian?" he called out again. He strained for some aural evidence of human occupation—a drunken snore? most unlikely—but was conscious only of the tapping of his shoes along the uncarpeted stairs as he passed upward.

The stairs led first to the unlit recesses of a book-lined room at the back with a single chair and a standing lamp. Drawn to the bright square of the window, Tom looked past a tiny garden towards the back courtyard of the Church House Inn, where he glimpsed Belinda Swan busy hanging laundry. He exited this private library and moved down the dark passageway, past the bathroom to the last remaining unexplored room. He hesitated by the door. Partially open, it emitted a thin wedge of light onto the floorboards. "Sebastian?" he said in a low voice, then taking another deep breath he pushed the door inward and prayed God for mercy. For a moment, the light dazzled his eyes. South facing, its window looking towards St. Nicholas's tower, the room glowed with new June light. And then he looked at the bed, pressed against the eastern wall, and felt a cleansing surge of release. It was empty, made up, like a hotel bed awaiting a guest. No horror lay in wait.

Now puzzled, he surveyed the room more carefully. As on the ground floor, the furniture was simple and anonymous, personal accoutrements nonexistent. There was a bureau, but nothing occupied its surface. Likewise, the bedside table, but for the lamp. On the bed, the blanket was pulled taut over the pillows. Then he glanced at the wardrobe, a plain affair, white melamine. One door had been left swung open on its hinge. He moved to close it and then released a little groan of dismay. The wardrobe was empty, but for a few hangers that rattled along the rail at his unbelieving touch. The bureau drawers, too, he quickly ascertained, were bare. He raced downstairs and saw what he hadn't noted before by the doorway. Backpack, jacket, hat, boots—all were missing. Sebastian had gone.

Tom felt a sudden spurt of anger. Sebastian had broken their pact and bolted, perhaps planning his escape even as they had walked Knighton Lane. He had no car. How far could he get? A walk to Pennycross? A taxi to Paignton? But the last train was at ten and stopped at Exeter overnight before proceeding to London. It was unlikely he had yet reached the capital, or Heathrow, if that was his destination. Or perhaps his intention was to slip into another small community and concoct a new identity. Tom reached into his trousers pocket for his mobile, then hesitated over the keypad. Perhaps Sebastian's flight had been motivated by the proximity of some unnamed menace, which had come in the night after all. If he shopped Sebastian to the police as a suspect in Kinsey's and Sybella's deaths, was he, Tom, putting an innocent man in some sort of peril? Some instinct—it was not reason—made him snap the phone shut. He turned to leave; then noted, his eyes now sharpened to the dimness, familiar outlines on a table near the door—final testimony to

Sebastian's flight. There was the ancient key to the north porch door, of which the verger was the keeper; copy keys to the vestry, to the church tower, to the verger's cottage itself; and a key that he'd seen Sebastian use the day before to enter Farthings. And there was a note. *"Tom,"* it said, *"please take care of Bumble."* He had signed it simply, *"S."*

He lingered over this for a moment, his heart troubled; then stepped out of Sebastian's cottage as Julia was rounding past the lych-gate and into Poachers Passage, her organists' surplice billowing.

"I was delegated to fetch Sebastian," she remarked to Tom, pushing her arm through her winged sleeve to tidy a loose strand of hair. "I've never known him to be . . . Is something the matter? You look like you've seen a ghost. Where's Sebastian?"

"Under the weather," Tom found himself explaining, closing the door behind him, averting his face. "I've got the keys."

"Oh," Julia responded. She glanced over his shoulder to the bedroom window above, then back to his face. Her expression was one of uncertainty. "Never mind, then. I expect we can carry on without him."

It was during Holy Communion, as he intoned the familiar words to those kneeling along the altar rail, that Tom again had the sense of presentiment, of something febrile burrowing at the edge of his consciousness, hinting of some small illumination. He had been delighted to see so many new faces, and for a split second wondered if he'd forgotten it was some special day in the liturgical calendar before realising the chaos and sensation of the last week were the forces more likely driving villagers to the church, as trouble and danger had done in the past. The choir had sung with extra fervour, he thought; Julia seemed to mine a new, rich vein in the old organ; and he sensed his sermon attended to with particular concentration, and not because the yellow crescent emerging from the bruise under his eye was a point of local interest.

"This is the time," he had concluded, taking in their alert faces, "to recall Jesus' words to Simon Peter: *'All who take the sword will perish by the sword.'* They are words of caution for those who may be tempted to take matters into their own hands. And for all of us, they are words of assurance that ultimately justice will be done." Gratified to hear several murmured *"amens,"* he had felt his uneasy spirit slowly lift, then soar—a little—through the Creed and the prayers and the giving of Communion—until the moment at the extreme end of the altar rail, as he was wiping the chalice with the purificator and happened to glance at the back of the last departing communicant as she made her way back down the aisle, stepping from the shadow of a pillar into a hazy shaft of light streaming through the south window. In that instant, his mind bloomed with a sensibility that had been nascent since that moment in the churchyard, before Oona blacked his eye.

Of course, he thought, and nearly tripped over the step in the chancel as he returned the chalice to the altar. But there was no pleasure in knowing; rather, this epiphany did little more than present a new horror. In the short silence after the Communion, he tossed permutations and combinations in his head, the way he had in his days as The Great Krimboni tossed five golden rings in his hands. Then he had amazed and amused; now the rings lay in a metaphorical heap about his feet. He wished he could end the service this moment and found himself growing impatient through the final hymn and almost rushing through the Dismissal. There was one parishioner he needed to speak with at once.

"Mitsuko," he called out a few moments later, having reached the church door, espying her and Liam moving down the path towards the lych-gate. "Would you mind staying a moment?"

He felt Tilly Springett grab his absently outstretched hand. Members of the congregation, murmuring decorously, milled about in the shadow of the north porch. "I talked with the police," Tilly whispered, leaning towards him. Tom could see little particles of dusting powder around her excited eyes. "They were *most* interested to hear about—"

"Splendid." Tom raised his voice to cut her off. "We'll talk later, shall we?"

Surprise replaced excitement in her eyes, then alarm as Liam, with Mitsuko, hove into her view. She released a muffled shriek and Tom's hand at the same time, and stumbled backwards into Florence Daintrey, who grabbed her arm and led her down the path.

"What's she on about?" he overheard Liam grouse to his wife as they waited for Tom to process the line of voluble parishioners. After a few moments in receipt of gratifying comments about the service, Tom was able to turn his attention to the pair.

"It's good to see you in church." He addressed Liam with a feint at good cheer, though the man seemed to be scowling over some interior rumination.

"She's the one who bloody grassed me up to the police, isn't she?" Liam suddenly snapped his head towards the lych-gate, which Tilly was well past. "It had to be her. Hers is the last cottage before you get to the village hall."

"Someone reported seeing my husband going up Pennycross Road last Sunday night," Mitsuko told Tom. She placed a calming hand along Liam's meaty, multicoloured forearm, exposed beneath the short sleeves of a red football jersey.

"And if she had waited half a minute, she would have seen me turn around and walk back up the lane. But, no, she closes her bloody curtains and only gets half the story."

"Then you didn't go into the hall."

"What do you know about it?"

"I'm afraid, Liam, I was the one who advised Tilly to talk to the police."

"Well, thanks a bloody lot. I should black your other eye."

"Liam!" Mitsuko's tone was sharp. Her arm dropped from his. At that moment Julia stepped from the church and flicked each of them a cautious glance as she passed. "Will we see you at the pub . . . Tom?"

"I'll catch you up," he called after her. "Give me a few moments."

"Sorry, Vicar." Liam's struggle for contrition led him to study his shoes—black trainers that looked like they'd seen better days.

"Tilly didn't intend malice, nor did I," Tom told them. "It's simply that people in the village don't feel safe with Sybella's death unresolved. Or Peter Kinsey's, for that matter."

"And everyone thinks because I was once sent down that I'm the one that did it."

Tom had no answer. If you offend once in such manner, others' knowledge of it will likely follow you the rest of your days. Instead he said:

"Tilly was surprised to see you in the lane at that time of night. I've been here long enough to observe that this village is a place of habits and conventions. Colonel Northmore walks Bumble the same route twice a day. Mrs. Prowse goes to the post office to post a letter at almost the same time every morning. The same schoolchildren walk the same lanes at the same time with their mothers every weekday. I could go on. Anything that breaks that pattern sets curtains to twitching and people's minds to speculating."

Liam's mouth twisted with annoyance. "Mitsuko had left her labels for me to put up in the hall next to her quilts—that's all."

"But why so late in the evening?"

Liam shrugged. "The game on telly was crap. Didn't feel like sleeping. I thought I might go up to Thorn Court for a drink. The village hall's on the way and I had Mitsuko's keys so—"

"But I found Mitsuko putting up the labels on Thursday before the Neighbourhood Watch meeting."

"Never did it, did I."

"Why not?"

"Because I saw Sybella hanging about outside the door. And I had had enough of her, so I thought fuck this, I'll do it another day."

Tom flicked a glance at Mitsuko, then addressed Liam. "You two had rowed earlier."

"You know, too?" Liam scowled.

"Half the village does, I expect."

"I'll tell it," Mitsuko interjected, flicking her hair impatiently over one ear.

"Leave it!" Liam said hotly.

"Liam, if you can bear the police hearing it, you can bear Tom hearing it. He's a priest. I'm sure he's heard worse examples of idiot human behaviour than yours. As I'm sure you know," she continued, casting Tom a wan smile, "my husband is unreasonably jealous and wants a refresher course in anger management."

Tom could see Liam stiffen, his face redden. "I am *fine,* once things are explained to me."

"Things *were* explained to you, but you chose to indulge yourself in some sick flight of fancy. Liam," she again addressed Tom, "happened to find Sybella and me in . . . an embrace of sorts in the kitchen on Sunday and in his fevered imagination thought we had been having some sort of . . . affair. There! That's what started the row. I can't believe I said anything so plainly silly, but I expect having had to say it once to the police has got me used to it."

"You were spending far too much time with her," Liam snapped.

"I was *mentoring* her. I've said!"

"You were practically eating her face."

"Sybella was having a little triumph," Mitsuko explained, flicking her hair back again. "Something to do with some man she fancied. I was excited for her, that's all. We were mates. It was a girly moment. Women aren't as emotionally constipated as you men, and a kiss—Liam!—does not mean a snog will follow in short order."

"Did Sybella say which man she was interested in?" Tom asked, though he was sure he knew.

Mitsuko shook her head. "The detectives asked me that, too. I don't know. She wouldn't say. She was strangely secretive about it. Some boy in Torquay was my thought."

Tom regarded the couple. They were an incongruous pair. Mitsuko barely came up to Liam's chest. With her hands now behind her back, her delicate frame clothed in black shirt and black trousers, and her black hair tumbling to her shoulders, she looked like an exclamation mark appended to Liam's blunt mass in loose jeans and jersey. Her face was oval and smooth; her eyes, fixed on Tom, beseeching, as if willing him to her side, though he found the idea of two women, two close friends, not sharing the name of some prospective lover faintly implausible. Liam had turned his bulldog-square head towards the lych-gate and Church Walk beyond, his expression sulky and impatient, his arms folded defensively over the Cheltenham Town lettering on his chest. Ill-paired they appeared, but each forceful in his or her own right, Mitsuko the more so, he thought. Together they were a unit despite the habitual quarreling. Was their account truthful? Had Liam turned back from the village hall that night? Had a misinterpreted kiss really fuelled a quarrel? Tom realised these questions would have been more troubling, but for the *frisson* he had experienced not fifteen minutes earlier at Holy Communion.

How to begin?

"I don't wish to alarm you—either of you," he began, running his hands down to smooth his surplice, gathering his thoughts, "but I seem to have become possessed quite suddenly by . . . a very unsettling notion."

Liam flicked him an irritated glance. "Is this why you asked us to stop?"

Tom nodded, but addressed Mitsuko. "You'll allow, as you said a moment ago, that Sybella began to see in you a kind of mentor, yes? You were helping nurture her artistic abilities—"

"So she could skive off working at the restaurant," Liam muttered.

"—and letting her see that life was more than clubbing and drugs and such. That perhaps she had a gift, a talent."

"Talent to annoy, more like."

"Liam, then why didn't you sack her?"

"You know perfectly well why." Liam's face reddened.

"Why?" Tom couldn't help asking.

"Because," Mitsuko flicked her husband an irritated glance. "As it happens, Colm was paying Liam the cost of Sybella's wages. Margins are so tight in the restaurant trade, Tom, that it made a difference."

"Did Sybella know about this arrangement?"

"That was part two of Sunday's row," Mitsuko replied. "I didn't know about it, but Sybella did, it turns out."

"And she accused me of hiding it from Inland Revenue!" Liam exploded.

"And were you?"

"That's my bloody business!"

"It was hardly 'accuse,' Liam," Mitsuko intervened. "Sybella was simply being her usual provocative self." She turned to Tom. "And, no, we didn't mention part two to the detectives. But perhaps—"

"It has nothing to do with anything!"

"Liam, please don't go on so."

Tom said: "Your husband may be right."

Liam cast him a startled glance.

"This is what I wanted to say to you," Tom continued. "The first time I met Sybella, at the Waterside, more than a year ago, she was got up a bit like a Goth—you know, the black-lacquered fingernails and heavily lined eyes, the dyed black hair, those odd, lacey skirts . . ."

"Yes . . ."

"But when I came to live here this spring, she was much toned down—still the black hair, of course, and the ear piercings—but more in emulation of . . . well, you. Simple, sort of." Tom frowned. "I'm afraid I'm not good at explaining women's clothes."

"I admired Audrey Hepburn when I was a teenager, you see. Simple, as you say. Clean lines. Classic. A style more enduring than Goth."

"From the front, you and Sybella look quite different. You, of course, have Japanese features. Sybella looked more like an English pixie. But from the back—"

"Save it, Vicar." Liam held up a hand. "We've already sussed this one. From the back, Mits and Sybella are almost dead ringers. Why do you think I'm at church? I'm not here for my spiritual health, if that's what you're thinking. I'm here to make sure no one gets any clever idea about doing my wife in—for whatever sick reason they might have."

"Oh." Tom felt strangely one-upped. "When . . . ?"

"Yesterday," Mitsuko said. "When those two CID were interviewing us at the gallery. Liam happened to remark on it."

"I noticed it before. Never seemed worth mentioning before, though."

"And, of course," Mitsuko murmured, "I can't see my back, can I? So . . ."

Tom's heart contracted with new horror and pity as his mind's eye travelled the village hall. He could see a shadowy form advance through the soft greying gloom as twilight gave way to black night, the slight figure of a young woman standing silvered by the last strands of the setting sun through the west windows, turned away, perhaps in smiling expectation of an encounter to come. A hand slides noiselessly along the smooth length of one of the wooden sticks arrayed along a table—a *bachi*, perhaps, or Eric's morris stick, or the colonel's forgotten walking stick—and swiftly, swiftly, before the woman's conscious mind can grasp the succession of footfall, rustle of clothing, and the sharp rending of the air and cry out, she succumbs to brutal force at the back of her skull. Despite the late morning's warmth, Tom felt his blood run cold. Did her killer not see his mistake then? When he pierced the skin of the great drum and bore her body into its pitch interior, did he not notice, in some last shred of evening light, when the strands of black hair fell back from her face, that this was not the face of a woman of East Asian ancestry?

He studied Mitsuko's grave expression. "You're worried someone wants to . . . correct a horrible mistake," he said.

"Too right I am." Liam answered for them, indignantly.

Tom kept his focus on Mitsuko. "You had an inkling of this Thursday morning, didn't you, when you discovered the quilt with the photo of the churchyard had gone missing. You couldn't remember when you took the picture—simply that it was the day of the last church inspection, more than a year ago."

A shadow of remorse passed over Mitsuko's features. She hesitated before replying. "It took me a few moments, but I did remember. I . . ." She glanced up at her husband. "I remembered the church inspection had been the day before Ned's funeral and that that was the day Sebastian let me up the church tower to take photographs. But . . ."

"But . . . ?"

"On Wednesday, Peter's body was discovered in Ned's grave."

"Yes, of course . . ."

"Well, when you and I were in the village hall on Thursday morning, I remembered a detail about the photograph. In it, at the very bottom of the frame, there's a figure—a tiny figure, really, from the perspective of the tower—of someone sort of leaning over a freshly dug grave—"

"Good Lord."

"I gave it little thought when I was running up the quilt. I mentioned to you before that months passed between taking the photographs, then downloading them, then choosing among them for the artworks—"

"Can you identify the figure?" Tom interjected, his excitement mounting.

"No." Mitsuko moaned. "I'm so sorry. The picture was taken when the sun was very low in the sky. There were deep shadows in the churchyard below. The figure is almost in silhouette, grey-scale, and leaning over, so I couldn't identify the back of a head when I was making the quilt. I didn't really pay it much attention at the time anyway. I knew it was a man, somehow, simply from the general shape, but . . . I took high-resolution photographs, and if I had my computer still, then the figure could be enlarged, and perhaps . . ."

"A guess?" Tom pressed.

"At the time, when I was sewing the quilt, I thought it was likely Fred Pike doing some last-minute chores. I even alluded to it in the haiku—'sexton digs' were three of the syllables."

"And you saw nothing else?"

"I was taking mostly panoramas of the whole village. And sometimes I was simply waiting for the light to shift and enjoying the view. At times I aimed my camera down for certain details, but . . ." She shrugged. "And I could hear very little. It's windy up there, and the flag hadn't come down from Easter and was making quite a loud snapping noise."

Tom frowned. "Why didn't you say something to me on Thursday?"

Mistuko glanced up at her husband, who responded with a sour look. "I thought . . ." she began, then sighed and rushed on. "And this is why I lied about that particular haiku label being missing. I thought that the figure in the photo might be Liam, who—"

"I was up to my fucking eyeballs in VAT returns that evening!"

"—who was not at all fond of Peter."

"I wouldn't trust him as far as—"

"We shared an interest in art, Peter and I. That's all. But my absurd husband thought otherwise."

"Clearly," Tom spoke quickly to quash further argument, "someone thinks you're a witness to Peter Kinsey's murder . . . or at least his burial—"

"But I'm not. Not really."

"—hence the theft of the quilt, and then the theft of your laptop and camera—"

"Mitsuko," Liam interjected, "there's still your memory, and there's only one way to steal your memory, isn't there?"

"But I have no idea who that little figure in the quilt might be."

"Well, whoever it is doesn't know that, right?"

Mitsuko's face sagged. "I can't bear to think Sybella died by mistake." She looked off towards the oldest of the churchyard gravestones that lined the path to the lych-gate. "Perhaps the thefts and her death are unrelated. Perhaps she *was* the intended victim, not that that makes *anything* better."

"Mits, we've been through this. *You* were the intended victim. I know it."

"Did Bliss and Blessing ask you if you thought anyone in the village would have any reason to take your life?" Tom asked her.

"They asked, yes."

"And what did you tell them?"

Mitsuko hesitated. The glance she flicked at Tom was furtive. "I said I had no idea."

"And were you being truthful?"

"Not completely."

CHAPTER TWENTY-SEVEN

"The Drewes not with you?" Julia removed one unshod foot from its resting place on the chair opposite.

"No." Tom set his half pint of Vicar's Ruin on the table and slipped into the emptied seat. He glanced past his sister-in-law's shoulder out the pub window and watched an attractive young couple walk by the old red phone box and continue up Church Walk hand in hand. He was conventionally dressed in light summer trousers and a dark blue shirt, but her top was eye-catching—wildly colourful, batiked, vaguely African. Tom felt a pang: he and Lisbeth in an earlier day.

"Fancy seeing Liam, of all people, in church for a Sunday service, football jersey and all," Julia remarked, wriggling her foot back into her shoe. Tom could feel the force of her curiosity. "You were gone a long time. I nearly gave up and set off for home."

"I'm glad you didn't."

"Bad morning? You look more troubled than when I found you outside Sebastian's."

"I think I can fairly say I'm very troubled."

The mention of Sebastian reawakened the quandary of the hour before the service: to go to the police with news of Sebastian's flight or not to go? Much depended on whether he believed Sebastian responsible for the murder of one, if not two, people in the village. Tom had put his face up to the window of the Old School Room when he'd passed from the church to the pub, but the space had been dark. The door when he tried it was locked. Perhaps like God (but unlike priests), the detectives rested on the seventh day. What, he wondered, would he have done if the lights had been on and the door open?

There was the phone. He might ring DI Bliss and DS Blessing, but simply sitting here in the pub over a half made him realise how resistant he was to the notion. On the other hand, if he delayed, he might rightly be accused of withholding vital information. Yet on still another hand—if, Shiva-like, one were permitted more than two—to shop Sebastian was to expose his identity and, if he were to be believed, expose him to some unspecified danger. Prayer would be the thing, but as Tom gave his mind over to this felt need, he could hear the cautioning voice of the woman who could maintain a medical practice, raise a child, chair committees, sing in a choir, and pull together dinner for six at a moment's notice—his wife: *Life is a practical task, Tom. Fine to ask God's advice, but never wait for the answer.* Sharing his dilemma with Julia would be another thing. She was like Lisbeth in many ways, but not in a vital one—she was perhaps less wise in judgement.

"Then what are you troubled about, Tom?" Julia affected a smile. "Other than perhaps me? Or everything that's happened this week ... or ..." The smile faded. "Please ... I don't think I can bear any more bad news."

Tom glanced around the pub. Fortunately, the corner that some members of the congregation normally commandeered after church had emptied. Sunday lunches beckoned. Still, he lowered his voice. This he could share with someone. It would be public knowledge before long. "I had a sort of revelation in church."

"Really? Are you on the brink of dementia?"

"Julia, I'm serious."

Julia looked faintly aghast.

"I don't mean I was visited by the Holy Ghost." Tom hastened to clarify. "I mean, I came to realise something—something devastating. But then so did Mitsuko and Liam, so I can't say it's a revelation unique to me."

He explained. As he did, he watched wonder and horror advance in Julia's dark eyes. When he had finished, her face crumpled. "Colm! He lost his child because . . ."

"Because of mistaken identity." Tom finished the thought, worrying his fingers around the edge of his glass. "Perhaps. It's only conjecture, but it's a conjecture shared. Oh, let it not be true. If it is true, it's beyond heartbreaking."

"And Liam comes to church acting as bodyguard because he thinks his wife is not safe."

"They're going again to the police, Mitsuko and Liam."

"Then the questioning will start all over again."

"Yes, I expect so," Tom responded miserably. He looked past Julia again, through the window, alerted to the earlier couple, now turning down Poynton Shute. He noted the woman's dark hair pulled into a ponytail with the same colourful material of her shirt. He said without thinking, and then with immediate regret: "Mitsuko is less bothered about her safety than Liam, though."

Julia plucked the sliver of lemon from her glass. "Really? Why?"

"Oh . . . no reason. It's just . . ."

"I have a feeling you're not telling me something."

Tom regarded his sister-in-law. *A talebearer reveals secrets*—the proverb flitted through his mind—*but he who is of a faithful spirit keeps a secret*. But was it a secret? Mitsuko had banished Liam, it was true. "You'd better get back to the Waterside," she'd urged him. "Kerra Prowse can't cope all by herself, not on her fourth day of work. I'm perfectly safe with Tom." When Liam objected in his demanding way—"What do you mean you're not being completely truthful?" he'd snapped at his wife. "Who in the village would want you dead?"—she'd snapped back, "It's *nothing*! I want to have a private conversation with my priest. Go! Begone, husband! For heaven's sake, Liam, no one is going to do me in in broad daylight."

Liam clamped his jaw shut and departed, his footfalls crunching furiously on the shingle. A certain gravity had settled along Mitsuko's fine features as she studied the back of her husband. Abruptly, leaflike, a tremble passed through her slight figure.

"You're shivering," Tom had said.

"At a memory," Mitsuko responded, "but some sun would feel good."

They took the path from the shadowed north porch around the east window to a bench near the south porch dedicated to Lydia Northmore, which the colonel had had placed many years before to afford a meditative view of the churchyard.

"It happened last Sunday," Mitsuko began, recoiling a little at the brass plaque before settling onto the curve of the wooden seat, "when I was installing the memory quilts. Colonel Northmore wandered in with Bumble. I expect he was drawn by the activity setting up for the fayre and all, and hadn't thought he would find me there. Not that he goes out of his way to avoid me, but I rarely get more than a polite, but strained, nod if we pass in the road. Will you sit?" She looked up at him, shading her eyes against the sun with her hand.

"Sorry, yes. I was just—" Tom felt the warmth seep through his surplice and cassock into his back as he sank onto the bench's sun-bleached wooden slats.

"—looking at Sybella's grave," Mitsuko finished for him. She turned her head towards the lowest terrace, where a mound of fresh earth proclaimed the recent burial. She shivered once again, despite the warm air. "It's so horribly unfair."

And then for the first time in Tom's presence, silent tears fell down Mitsuko's face. "I'm sorry," she whispered. "I managed to get through the whole week without this happening, but . . ."

"It's not your doing, Mitsuko."

"But I feel somehow as if I caused this . . ."

They sat in silence a moment. Then Tom prompted her gently: "About the colonel . . ."

Mitsuko wiped at her eyes. "He's never come into my gallery— at least when I've been there." She sniffed loudly. "And I don't recall Sybella ever mentioning him visiting. Of course, my very features offend him at every turn. I understand why, Tom, though I think it unjust. I'm not personally responsible for the horrible things that happened to him in the war."

"I expect the colonel has moments of Old Testament wrath. Sins of the father and all. Though that's not to excuse him."

"Have you guessed, then?"

"What do you mean?"

"Isn't the verse something about visiting the sins of the fathers on the children and the grandchildren and so forth?"

"Yes. Exodus. God does not leave the guilty unpunished. He visits *'the iniquity of the fathers upon the children, and upon the children's children, unto the third and to the fourth generation.'* Are you suggesting the colonel decided to assume God's agency?"

Mitsuko met his startled expression with utter seriousness. "I don't know." She wiped at her eyes again. "What I do know is this: He's never come into my gallery, so he's never seen my work. If he had, he would have noticed how I sign my paintings, or he might have picked up a card or brochure. Everyone in the village refers to me as Mitsuko Drewe. And so I am—I took my husband's name when I married. But I sign my work with my maiden name— Mitsuko Oku. Even though Liam and I have lived in Thornford for almost four years, the colonel has not been aware of this."

"How would you know?"

"Because when he came into the village hall last Sunday, I gave him a copy of the brochure I'd designed and printed for the exhibition. I happened to have one in my pocket. I was trying to build a friendly little bridge—the memory quilts feature Thornford. They aren't screens with Shinto temples and cherry blossoms! I thought it might appeal, but—"

"When I visited him in hospital Tuesday, he was hallucinating," Tom interrupted, certainty dawning on him. "He'd been given morphine for the pain from his damaged hip. But it was a word that sounded like *oku* that he kept banging on about. Do you mean to say, Mitsuko, that he was hallucinating about your name the whole time?"

She hesitated. "This is very difficult to talk about, Tom."

"I understand," Tom responded, though he didn't really.

"It's never been discussed within our family. My parents don't know that I know. I gather these things are simply not discussed in Japan, either."

"What things?"

"My brother, Hari, who I told you about—the ornithologist at the Smithsonian—looked into our family history. I think he was curious that it was so little discussed. There was always this . . . *atmosphere* when we were growing up in Bridgend if any of us asked our father about the Okus—"

"You mentioned an estrangement between your father and your grandfather earlier, but you didn't seem to know its nature."

Mitsuko flicked him a guilty glance. "Well, I do. Or at least I think I do. We do—Hari and I, though we haven't broached it to our little sister, and of course we've never confronted our father about it."

"*It* being . . . ?"

Mitsuko lowered her head, her black hair descending like a shuttering curtain. "It being," she replied in a near whisper, "that our grandfather Ichiro Oku was the notorious commandant of a prison camp outside Tokyo in the Second World War."

"Omori?"

"Yes." Mitsuko pulled back a length of her hair and regarded him with misery. "How did you know?"

"The colonel told me a little of his experiences when I visited him in hospital." Tom paused in thought. He glanced at a couple of noisy rooks settling along the branches of the beeches at the bottom of the churchyard. "Did you know the colonel had been in Omori?"

"No. I only knew that he had been in a camp somewhere in Japan or Singapore or some such place. There were many of them, I've learned. It never occurred to me that Colonel Northmore would have been at the very one that my grandfather—I can't even think of the word—ran? managed? administered? None of them are adequate. My grandfather was a beast. When Hari presented the evidence I felt so thoroughly ashamed."

"Mitsuko, none of it was your fault."

"Nevertheless . . ."

But Tom's thoughts were now racing ahead. He could feel a gnawing dread in the pit of his stomach. "So when you handed your brochure to the colonel in the village hall . . ."

Mitsuko regarded him with pinched eyes. "He said nothing at first. He stared at it for a moment, then he lifted his eyes and stared at me with . . . with *such* profound hatred that I was paralysed, unable to speak or move. I could feel this intense fury surge from him and sweep over me like a wave. I must have gone into shock. I couldn't understand at first—it was so much more than his usual vague disinterest in me—and then he said—in a sort of flat, controlled way—'Is Oku your maiden name?'

"And then I knew . . . knew that he had not been simply at *some* prisoner-of-war camp. He had been at *that* camp, my grandfather's."

Tom groaned. "Lord . . ."

"I must have nodded yes. I can't remember speaking. He said nothing more. He simply handed the brochure back like it was something nasty, turned and left. He left his walking stick behind. He'd put it on the stage when I handed him the brochure, but I didn't want to take it to him, you understand."

Unbidden, Tom's mind summoned up the colonel's face when the taiko drum had been found slashed—the fleeting, gratified smile. He had thought it a response merely to the violation to the

Japanese instrument, but had it been more? He put his hands up to his face. Oh, God, surely not. Justice for POWs, not revenge, had been the colonel's passion.

And then he thought of another person who had come into the village hall in the minutes after Sybella's body had been discovered. "Mitsuko—did the colonel speak to anyone on the way out?"

"Sebastian, for a moment. He was coming in with some of the doweling to hang the quilts and got tripped up a bit in Bumble's lead. They talked briefly, though I wasn't listening. I think I was still in a bit of shock." She canted her head at Tom. "Why do you ask?"

Tom shrugged. "No reason."

But, seated with Mitsuko in the churchyard, he had been dissembling, his mind again playing on the binary relationship link between the colonel and Sebastian—the man with no son, the son with the estranged father. If he were to give the faintest credence to the colonel's role in either Kinsey's or Sybella's death, it would be to envision it as a cooperative venture, the younger partner faithfully executing the heavy lifting: burying one body, entombing another. This is why he could not be candid with Julia. To offer up Colonel Northmore as perpetrator—a strange unlikelihood, Mitsuko said, which prevented her from raising it to Bliss and Blessing—was to compromise his pledge to Sebastian to keep his secret. Or was it a pledge worth honouring now? Had wool been pulled over his eyes?

"I'm sorry, Julia," he said, watching her nibble at the flesh of the lemon sliver. "I can't say more."

"I see. Your priestly garb may be hanging in the vestry, but you're still wearing it."

"In effect, yes. I'm still wearing my collar, am I not?"

The corners of Julia's mouth twitched. "You may become the single bulwark in the village against gossip." The twitch turned to a smile. She plopped the lemon rind into her empty glass and raised it in a toast. "Good luck to you, Father Christmas."

Tom smiled. "Thank you. Virtue becomes me, don't you think?"

"Try not to be too saintly."

"I'll do my best. Temptation abounds, but I shall keep to the straight and narrow."

Julia regarded him with a gimlet eye. "You're a single man—"

"I'm a widower with a nine-year-old child."

"Which may make you more attractive in some books."

"Lisbeth has been dead not even two years, Julia."

"I'm not sure you understand the effect you have on this village in certain ways."

"That's not true. I have some notion. I know that some women are attracted to priests. And I know there's temptation on the priestly side."

"Abstractly put."

Tom ignored her. "We do get schooling on this, you know." He frowned, giving a passing thought to the late Reverend Peter Kinsey. Had he been alive, he might well be accused of taking advantage of vulnerable women—the one sitting before him, empty glass in hand, for one. "Why are you bringing this up?"

"I've had two gins and I'm ready for a third."

"I see." Tom studied his sister-in-law. He only knew her to down one on Sundays after service. "Don't you have to get lunch on for Alastair?"

"No point in cooking a roast for one. Alastair's doing the nine-to-three shift at the health centre. A working weekend."

"Of course. He popped in to visit the colonel yesterday when I was there."

"Then I presume he'll be off golfing."

"So you're at a loose end. Come and have lunch at ours. Mrs. P. makes enough food to feed a regiment."

"I don't think Madrun approves of me."

"*I'm* the master of my household."

"Are you sure?"

"Well, not entirely. Mrs. Prowse is certainly a presence. Still, she's not going to bar the door." He took a long finishing gulp of his ale, glimpsing over the rim of the glass a red Astra squeeze into an available space outside the pub.

"We haven't even had you and Alastair over for a proper meal, it's been so busy since I arrived in Thornford."

"Mitsuko will be safe, won't she, Tom?" Julia pushed her glass to one side and moved to rise.

"She has Liam. And they're going to talk with the police. They've just arrived, I see."

"I'm not assured."

Tom grimaced. *Nor am I,* he thought as he watched DI Bliss and DS Blessing step towards the Church House Inn rather than the Old School Room.

"Working on the Lord's day?" Tom remarked to the two detectives as he and Julia crossed their path on the pub's stoop.

"No day of rest for us, Vicar," Blessing responded. "Although we had intended to come to your eleven o'clock service. We were, however . . . detained." He cleared his throat delicately.

Tom flicked a glance at Bliss, unable to quash the image of probable cause, the irritable bowel. "I would have been delighted to see you both in church."

"We thought we might catch Mr. John in his natural habitat— well, one of them, at any rate," Blessing continued.

"You weren't able to have a conversation with him yesterday?"

"No," Bliss barked, scowling deeply.

"Well, he was around." *When exactly* did *Sebastian up sticks and leave the village?* Suddenly he wondered how long poor Bumble may have been alone at Farthings.

"Sebastian's under the weather today," Julia supplied, echoing his own feeble untruth to her earlier.

"I imagine he very much is!" Bliss snapped. He pushed past them into the pub, Blessing in his wake.

"What was that about?" Then Julia frowned. "Tom . . . ?"

Tom sighed. His mind had conjured up antique weighing scales: in one dish, his loyalty, however frayed, to Sebastian; in the other, his duty to seek justice for those wronged. Sybella, for instance, and Colm. *A false balance is abomination to the Lord,* said the Proverb. *But a just weight is his delight.*

What, however, he asked himself, *would be a just weight?*

"Well, whatever it is," he responded to his sister-in-law, "it's not stopping them having a pint first." He took her arm gently. "Shall we put this past week out of our heads for a few hours? I'd very much like it if our goal could be to have an untroubled Sunday afternoon."

The front door of the vicarage opened so abruptly that Tom, his hand barely grasping the knob, nearly pitched over the umbrella urn in the vestibule.

"We have guests," Madrun announced in a marvellous tonal aggregation of delight, curiosity, and warning, vigorously working the back of her apron.

"Oh" was all Tom could think to say, as people showing up at the vicarage on some quest or other wasn't exactly novel.

"They've driven all the way from London." Her voice dropped to a hoarse whisper.

Fancy! Tom felt the urge to exclaim. "Mrs. Hennis is joining us for lunch," he told her.

But Madrun had already whipped off her apron and darted into the sitting room ahead of them, announcing him to some unseen presences. O where were the heralds and silver trumpets? What had got into the woman?

Rising from a seat opposite Miranda at the games board when Tom ushered Julia into the sitting room was a short, slim young woman wearing a shirt of many colours, joined from the couch by a tall, angular young man in plain garb. Both were oddly familiar. And then he realised he had seen them not twenty minutes earlier walking past the Church House Inn, their intimacy touching him with a certain wistfulness.

The woman spoke first. "I'm Jane Allan," she said in an accent vaguely American, though nothing like Kate's Virginia drawl. She offered her hand. "And this is my husband, Jamie."

"We're awfully sorry to barge in on you unannounced, Vicar." The man's handshake was firm, dry; the hand large. "But we thought you might help us on a matter of some urgency."

Tom supposed he could declare himself mildly intrigued, if anyone had bothered to ask, but something else was niggling at his brain as Jamie Allan spoke. What was it? And then he remembered too late—too late to warn husband and wife to wait until a private moment could be found. It was their last name, and his looks— a slighter, taller, and less-bronzed edition, but with the same bright blue eyes, the same strong, bony face.

"You see," Jamie was saying, "we've been looking for my brother, John, and we were told he was the verger at your church here in Thornford Regis. We were directed to the verger's cottage but . . ."

He stopped and glanced at the others in the room, who were staring at him with varying degrees of consternation. "Have I dropped a brick?"

"No," Tom replied, though he wanted to shout, yes, one large enough to shatter the cucumber frame in the back garden. "Your brother is known to us as Sebastian, that's all. Sebastian John—John being his surname."

"Ah. We were told something along those lines, I think. Jane . . . ?"

"Andrew said John had been using a different name. They're two of his Christian names, you see, Mr. Christmas. He's—"

"John Sebastian Hamilton Allan, I know."

"How do you know that?" Julia interrupted, regarding him with surprise.

"He told me yesterday. In confidence, I might add. But I expect that doesn't matter now." Tom frowned. "This is my sister-in-law,

Julia Hennis, who lives in the village, and, of course, you've met my daughter and Mrs. Prowse." He glanced at the latter. Madrun, eyes shining behind her spectacles, had the appearance of someone eager to sprint off on a news-breaking mission to the village pump.

"But how did you know your brother was here in Thornford?" Tom continued after the usual politenesses had been executed.

"Andrew Macgreevy told me," Jane replied for her husband. "The reporter for *The Sun*," she clarified. "I understand from the papers you've had a terrible week down here."

"I bought *The Sun* today in dread that he would expose Sebastian."

"Not yet he hasn't," Jane said with a bright, sweet smile that suggested a hidden reserve of steel.

"My wife dances with the devil."

"Andrew has moments of humanity. You see, Mr. Christmas—"

"Tom, please."

"You see, Tom, to put it plainly, Andrew Macgreevy owes me one. He knows he owes me one. And he knows what he owes me, should he ever stumble across something oweable, if you catch my drift. He found it here in Thornford Regis."

"I believe I have caught your drift," Tom said, full of admiration for a woman, especially one so petite, who had tabloid reporters on a short leash.

"My wife has been useful to Mr. Macgreevy in some instances in the past," Jamie explained, adding, "Jane is a bit of an amateur detective."

"*Comme* Alice Roy!" Miranda piped up. Tom had noted his daughter looking at their guest with increasing fascination.

"*Oui, un peu,*" Jane said with a laugh. "*Mais je ne suis pas aussi réussie qu'Alice. Tu a lu* Alice Roy? *Combien merveilleux! J'ai une fille a près de ton âge qui l'a lu, aussi.*"

"Daddy! Mrs. Allan has a daughter who reads Alice Roy, too!"

"Lady Kirkbride, I think, darling, not Mrs. Allan."

"Please, none of that. 'Jane' is fine. 'Kirkbride' belonged to

Jamie's brother at one time, so"—she shot Tom a meaningful glance—"so we prefer to keep things simple."

"Sebastian?" Miranda asked, confused, but eager as ever for clarification.

"No, Jamie's older brother, William." Jane crouched to the Persian carpet to address her. "William died many years ago. It was very sad."

"My mummy died," Miranda confided.

Jane put her arm around the child. "I'm very sorry to hear that." She glanced up at Tom apologetically. "You have a brilliant father, don't you? I can tell."

Miranda regarded Tom shyly, then took his hand, as Jane rose. *"Madame Allan est canadienne,"* she remarked. *"C'est pourquoi elle peut parler français."*

"Now my clever child can discern accents."

"Silly Daddy. Mrs. Allan told me."

"I made her guess. She was very good. Only two tries."

"'American' being first, I expect," Julia said.

"We're a forbearing people, we Canadians."

"Before my wife begins pouring maple syrup on troubled waters," Jamie Allan interrupted with some impatience, "I wonder if I might enquire further about my brother? As I said, we did ask someone in the village to point us to the verger's cottage, but he wasn't in. And we tried the church, but there was no one there—"

"I expect you just missed me."

"—and we asked at the village shop . . ." He regarded Tom expectantly, as a kind of curious silence settled on the room.

Tom realised they were all still standing, gathered about like guests at a cocktail party. Even Powell and Gloria, who had been trailing after Madrun, had stopped in their ablutions. The heavenly aroma of roasting beef wafting in from the kitchen suggested one way of clearing the room of certain people:

"I wonder if you would care to have lunch? Julia is joining us, and

Mrs. Prowse is a superb cook. I'm sure she'd be delighted if you'd stay, wouldn't you, Mrs. P.?"

"Of course!"

"Well . . ." Jamie began reluctantly, but Jane caught the nuance in Tom's invitation and put her hand gently on her husband's arm.

"We'd love to," she said.

"Good," Tom responded. "Miranda, why don't you lay three more places in the dining room, and I'm sure Mrs. Prowse has some final preparations in the kitchen."

"Well . . ."

Tom gave her a penetrating look.

"Of course, yes, I had better look in on the joint."

"I could help Mrs. Prowse," Julia ventured, uncertainty in her voice.

"No, stay," Tom said, knowing he couldn't hide the truth from everyone for long, assistant organist and choir director Julia Hennis included. "We'll have a drink. Please, do sit down—all of you," he added, gently closing the connecting door to the dining room and moving to the drinks table. "What will everyone have?"

"Whisky, please," Jamie Allan said, while the women begged off liquid refreshment. "We made rather a mad dash down here this morning. Jane almost wanted to come last night, after Macgreevy phoned, but with two children—"

"He took his time," Tom remarked, handing a glass of amber liquid to his guest. "He was here in the village on Friday."

"My guess is he was wrestling with his conscience," Jane replied, resuming her seat by the games table while her husband pushed his back against a nest of pillows at the end of the sofa. "His speech was a little slurred. I could hear pub noises in the background."

"At any rate, here we are," her husband added, looking almost with dismay at his whisky, which glinted in the light through the windows. "We're most anxious to find John. Does he go somewhere particular after Sunday service . . . ?"

Tom flicked a glance at Jane, who winced slightly and said to her husband, "I have a feeling, Jamie, that the vicar has some bad news for us."

"I'm so sorry," Tom began. "You have come all this way, I know, but I think you've missed him almost by a hair. Sebastian . . . your brother, that is, John, seems"—he could hardly believe it himself—"to have vanished."

Presiding over the dining room table, Tom thought his guests ably hid their disappointment and worry for the sake of the child in their midst. In the sitting room earlier, he had given the pair an abridged version of the eventful week in the village, careful to represent Sebastian as little more than a peripheral figure in the unfolding drama, compelled to abandon Thornford from fear of press attention. "He believes exposure is a threat to his life and to that of someone else," he told them. They received this news with a kind of grave acquiescence.

"He's been absolutely maddening," Jamie said at one point, pushing a lick of hair, a shade lighter than Sebastian's, back from his brow. "He refused to defend himself at his trial, or even speak. It was a feat of utter stoicism and folly, of course. In jail, he refused all visits, and when released, he disappeared. And now he's done it again."

"All along we've believed him to be protecting someone," Jane explained, glancing at her husband. She had big eyes in an oval face and looked the soul of innocence. "We're not entirely sure who. I think it's a woman—or one of the women that seemed to hang around William in those days."

"I'm afraid my elder brother was involved in a number of dodgy enterprises, Vicar. I'm sure any of a handful of people might have been his killer, but John was caught virtually red-handed, he put up no fight, and the authorities were quite happy to bring events swiftly to conclusion—despite my father's heroic efforts at throwing his weight about."

"And your father, I understand, is not well," Tom interjected.

"A stroke. I expect Mr. Macgreevy told you. It happened a few weeks ago. We don't know what the outcome will be, but Father is certainly weakened. That's why I was so pleased to get this news of John. Part of it is for selfish reasons. With William gone, I've been drawn more and more into managing the family business, but my passion is organic farming. With Father ill, I'm becoming even more involved. I was hoping John would help me—possibly take over, if he felt up to it."

"Of course, the real hardheaded business person in the Allan family is Caroline," Jane said.

"My sister," Jamie explained, "but Father's views on women in business are . . ."

"Out of the Ark?" Julia supplied.

"Very." Jamie smiled briefly, then grew serious again. "But what I really want is to effect some sort of reconciliation. We have worked on Father—Jane and I—for years to create, at the very least, doubt in his mind. He was black with grief and rage when William died, his heir, the apple of, and so forth—and then the shame of fratricide in the family. My mother was completely torn apart—her firstborn killed, and John, her favourite—"

"Oh, Jamie, I don't think your mother plays favourites." Jane reached behind her head to adjust her hair.

"But he was an angelic little boy—very sweet-natured. You couldn't help loving him, and my mother was besotted by him. You weren't there, Jane. Of course, his good nature just seemed to goad William, for some reason. They never got on." He turned to Tom and Julia. "I expect John's become hardened from his experiences. How is he? Is he well?"

Tom glanced at Julia and replied for the two of them. "I would describe him as very very self-contained. But not hard, I don't think.

And very well. He seems to live outdoors. He's a gardener. And as a verger, he's been most helpful."

"He was the only one of us who had a real interest in the church. Sorry, Vicar."

"No need to apologise."

"It's amazing no one rumbled him before Andrew did," Jane said.

"I think most people accepted him for what he was," Tom responded, though Sybella's dangerous machinations flitted through his thoughts.

He turned to Julia, who nodded confirmation and said, "People were naturally curious when Giles—a previous incumbent as vicar—brought Sebastian—John—on, but I think he satisfied them with a few cursory details. Giles ran through rather a few vergers in his time, so people became less invested in knowing about them."

"And why this village, I wonder?" Jamie sipped his drink thoughtfully.

"Do you know Phillip Northmore—Colonel Northmore?"

Both visitors' brows puckered. "I think he was at our wedding, Jamie. I seem to recall your mother putting him on the guest list."

"Yes, of course. Elderly gentleman. A friend of my grandfather's, I think, but my grandfather died when I was very young so—"

"He took an interest in your brother and more or less arranged a life for him here."

"How unusual." Jamie frowned. "And kind, I suppose."

"I think Colonel Northmore feels he owes a debt to your grandfather, but I'm not sure what exactly—something from the war. I understand your grandfather was greatly admired by his troops."

"We'd love to speak with him, wouldn't we, Jamie?"

"Unfortunately," Tom said, "the colonel took a nasty fall last week and is in hospital. He's not very well, I don't think."

Disappointment settled over the couple's faces. "So close," Jane murmured.

"This is the one . . . case, I suppose you could say, that has eluded my wife's deductive powers." Jamie smiled at her and reached for her hand.

"William was killed the day after our wedding," Jane explained, reaching to take his. "But we were already en route to South America for our honeymoon and didn't know what had happened for several days. We turned around and came right home—"

"But the trail was cold—is that how you say it, darling?"

"I think you can tell my husband doesn't watch a lot of television or read a lot of detective fiction."

Over a lunch of roast beef with wild mushroom sauce and gooseberries with mascarpone cream for pudding, Jane turned her attention to Miranda, amusing her with her tale of ending up in England, broke after a backpacking tour of Europe, and taking a job as a housemaid at Buckingham Palace. She met her husband at Windsor when, before her astonished gaze, he fell over a sandwich board outside a pub—a story Tom could match with his of Lisbeth's saving him from drowning in the Cam. Madrun's ears, Tom noted as she buzzed between kitchen and dining room, were on stalks.

Tom had proposed coffee in the sitting room and after some little persuading—*Oh, we mustn't keep you; we do have to get back to London; we've left the kids with Jamie's mother; they don't know the reason for the sudden trip*—they agreed.

"Half-term's nearly over," Jane remarked to Miranda, as they rose from the table. *"Seras-tu contente de retourner à l'école?"*

"Oui."

"I think Miranda's enjoying school, aren't you?" Tom trailed after his guests. "She had to switch schools from Bristol just before the end of spring term. That's always difficult, but I think she's adjusted. You've made some good mates, haven't you? She has a good friend in Emily Swan, whose father runs the local pub," he answered for her.

"You speak very good French." Jane addressed Miranda as they reentered the sitting room. "I've enrolled my Olivia in extra French lessons, but she is being stubborn about learning. Of course, her father speaks no French, and the English aren't much for learning foreign languages."

"I took German at Shrewsbury," Jamie said. "I have no idea why. Best I can do is order sausages in German. *Ich möchte einige Würste, bitte.*'"

"We had a wonderful French au pair in Bristol," Tom explained. "She stayed on after my wife died, which was very kind. She and Miranda chattered away *en français* the whole time."

"I miss Ghislaine," Miranda said, and turned her mouth down.

"Oh, look, Miranda, we didn't finish our Snakes and Ladders game. Shall we?" Miranda nodded vigorously and Jane settled into the chair. "I think it was your turn."

Miranda rolled a die as the adults gathered around. "Six!"

"Up the ladder with you then."

"*And* I get another turn."

"Miranda's well ahead," Jane remarked as Miranda rolled the die again. "As you can see." Miranda's token was near the top of the board. A lucky roll of the die and she would be on the ladder to the winning square. "There must be some sort of morality lesson behind this game."

"Ladders virtue, snakes vice, you mean," Tom said, watching Miranda shift her token a couple of squares over, one shy of the vital ladder.

"There's more snakes than ladders, though," Julia noted, counting under her breath.

"That's a cheerless summary of life," Jamie said.

"It's a wonderful old board." Jane took the die and rolled it. "I think my grandmother had the exact same one when we were kids. *Tch!* One! I'm not doing very well. I don't remember these tokens, though," she added, moving hers over one square.

"They've gone missing," Madrun said, entering the room laden with a tray of coffee things. "Miranda and I improvised when we played. Mine was the thimble."

"Yours looks like a sort of wizard's cap, Miranda," Jane remarked. "Like Harry Potter."

"Gnome's hat, I said." Madrun placed the tray on a large slipcovered ottoman near the couch. "Miranda says it's a 'clue' for something."

"For heaven's sake, you people." Julia reached over and lifted the yellow token. "Don't worry, Miranda, I'll put it back on the exact square." She turned the token over and held it up for everyone's inspection.

"Oh," Jamie exclaimed, "of course. It's a golf tee. A rather old-fashioned one at that."

"It's vintage, a wooden thing from the thirties, I think," Julia said, handing the token back. "My husband usually carries one around for luck. He's golf mad. Collects all sorts of golf memorabilia. You're a favoured girl. He's never given me anything like this." Then she started, stared at her niece. "Whatever's the matter?"

They all turned to look at Miranda, who had transformed from a cheerful intent little girl to a whey-faced waif. An unreadable emotion, something like fright or guilt, registered in wary eyes.

"Uncle Alastair didn't give it to me," she said in a small voice, clutching the token.

"Oh, darling." Julia flicked Tom a puzzled glance, bending down to the chair to cuddle Miranda. "I'm sure Uncle Alastair doesn't mind if you have it, however you came to have it. He has others."

And now Miranda, pallor turned crimson, released a heartrending sob that sent Powell and Gloria bolting. She struggled from Julia's arms and sprang up from the chair, set to run, but the forest of adult legs around the games table confounded her. Tom snatched her up in his arms, startled at the weight of his growing girl, and held her tight as she sobbed into his neck. "Miranda, it's all right," he crooned, bouncing her a little as though she were still a baby, looking at the other concerned faces with consternation. "Come, let's go to my study for a minute and leave these good people to their coffee."

He shouldered his office door open and placed Miranda gently on the old settee. Sunlight poured through the French windows and spread gold over the carpet, the oak desk, and the bookshelves, and glistened on Miranda's dark hair, which Tom smoothed back from her face, as he had so many times after Lisbeth died.

"Daddy," she sobbed, as he settled next to her, "I didn't steal Uncle Alastair's . . . thing."

"Tee. Sweetheart, no one is accusing you—"

"I found it."

"That's all right. You can give it back to Uncle Alastair the next time we see him—"

"You don't *understand*!"

"Darling, what don't I understand?" Tom reached over to his desk and pulled several tissues from a box.

"I found it at the fayre."

"Yes . . . ?" He dabbed at her cheeks.

"I found it in the village hall when we were looking at Mrs. Drewe's quilts. It was on the floor by the wall. Where the missing quilt was."

Tom stopped in his dabbing motions. He stared at Miranda, seeing himself again as he had been at the village hall, readying to push through the doors to the corridor between the large and small halls, impatient with his daughter's dawdling by the skirting board. A dawning realisation possessed him. It was as if the sunshine streaming into the room was penetrating his very skull, clarifying his mind with its searching light. So rooted was he in this moment of horror that he didn't even hear the telephone ringing beside him.

wo calls had come in rapid succession. Each time Tom had let the answerphone intervene. But the third ringing had stopped short, and he was unsurprised a few moments later to find Madrun at his study door, though dismayed at the change in her demeanour. Colonel Northmore sought Mr. Christmas's presence urgently, the sister on the hospital ward had relayed, with little apparent embellishment. The implication of the message was clear in Madrun's button eyes and pinched lips, and only Miranda's presence had kept her from stating it boldly: The colonel was failing.

More dismaying was tearing himself away from his daughter at this fragile moment. *Oh, my clever, brave, frightened, mysterious child,* he thought, as he silently forbore the traffic into Torquay and yearned for a time, more than a generation before he was hatched, when "rest" and "Lord's Day" had more than a passing acquaintance. Had she sensed, like some small creature, nose to the wind, some nascent change in the atmosphere that moment when she'd snatched the tee from its resting place by the skirting board? Or had it, at the very first, been only a lark—then only a "clue," as Mrs. P.

had said—maybe, perhaps—in some Alice Roy–type fantasy over the quilt she had cleverly discerned was missing? She had never exclaimed, "Look what I found, Daddy." Not then. And then, later, in some confused way, in the wake of Sybella's murder, had it taken on a greater significance? Was it a puzzling thing to be hoarded, to be contemplated in private, then turned out in plain sight, among people who wouldn't recognise it—that is, until Aunt Julia came to lunch? He had had no time to probe further. *He that loveth son or daughter more than me is not worthy of me* were Jesus' rather harsh words—childless man that He was—and so the needs of His church took sway. In these moments he ached for Lisbeth—not only would she have taken their child into her comforting arms, but she would understand instantly the insidious demands of vocation: She, too, had had to rush from the house to a patient's side, dropping the feeding spoon, the nappy changing, the bedtime story.

He had hastily said his good-byes to the Allans, and to Julia, who offered to stay with Miranda at the vicarage or take her to Westways. He had rebuffed the latter suggestion rather too sharply and modified it with grateful thanks if she would take the key to Farthings and give Bumble a feed and a walk. At that moment, he had begun to doubt the implications of Miranda's find, or perhaps he had wanted to, because he needed to look Julia in the eye unevasively before he snatched up his stole and his portable Communion set by its shoulder strap and made his way to the car. Alastair might have dropped the tee Sunday afternoon when he went to the village hall in search of Julia, not Sunday night. Or perhaps at some earlier time, though he was pressed to think of a recent occasion when Alastair would have been at the village hall. Too, he thought: Miranda was a child and there were no witnesses to her discovery. He turned the ignition, feeling no victory in the conjecture of the last minutes, and was about to back out into Poynton Shute when Mrs. Prowse darted from the vicarage, tea towel flung over her shoulder. At first, what she told him, as she leaned into his window, seemed silly and tangential—not to mention that it was the gleaning of gossip—and he had been about to give her short shrift. But then he understood the implication. He understood, too, why Madrun braved his certain disapproval for making public what he had asked her to keep private: She had seen Tom in his study take the tee from Miranda's hand. She had read the look of horror on his face.

Stepping off the lift onto the toneless corridor of the orthopaedic ward, Tom was assailed—not for the first time, nor, Lord knows, for the last—by the sickly sweet brew of hospital aromas, unvanquished by disinfectant, but his old notion to pipe in the fragrance of garden centres, clean laundry, and baking bread fell quickly from his mind, as he glanced in passing at the knot of sturdy pink women in loose blue uniforms at the nursing station, absorbed in private conversation. One of them, the ward sister, gestured to him.

"He had a difficult night," she said without preliminary. She was thickset and starchy in bearing. Tom recognised her from his Tuesday visit. "And he was quite agitated earlier, confused and incoherent in speech. We could just make out that he wished to see you."

"Japanese words mixed in?"

"Possibly. I only recognised 'Gladstone.'"

"The late prime minister?"

"I suspect he was referencing the bag. Quite fixated on it." The tilt of her eyebrows indicated that the ramblings of medicated patients were of little practical use to her. "You may not find him very responsive now. The doctor increased his sedative."

"He seemed so clear yesterday."

"Much can change at his age and in his condition. I can have Dr. Vikram speak to you. He's the attending physician on the ward this weekend, and should be along shortly."

"Will the hip operation be going ahead?"

"I'm afraid you'll have to speak with Dr. Vikram about that."

Colonel Northmore's room was at the tunnel end of the ward's long corridor, its door slightly ajar. Tom hesitated a moment outside, his attention diverted momentarily by a sharp, anguished cry—a woman's cry—from a nearby room which pierced his heart, but which stopped as abruptly as it had started, leaving only the distant squeak of wheels being pushed somewhere and the faint hum of hospital machinery leaching from the walls. No one raced to the woman's aid. He pushed the door on its silent hinges and stepped into the colonel's room, now rendered in twilight, blinds drawn, a single soft lamp high above the bed acting as pale moon. So concentrated was he on the still and craggy visage limned by its feeble light that he failed at first to notice the other figure in the room.

"Alastair."

The head turned sharply. Eyes flicked him a wary glance. "Tom. What are you doing here?"

"The colonel's asked to see me," Tom replied evenly, dropping his Communion set on a nearby chair and moving to the bedside, of necessity pushing his earlier disquiet about Alastair from his mind. The colonel's transformation shook him. *How frail he looks,* he thought, noting even in the shallow light the grey skin, the wrinkled liver-spotted hand above the white sheet pierced by the IV drip line. The colonel's septum was now clipped by an oxygen feed that hissed faintly. His mouth, with lips dry and cracked, was open, his breathing a barely audible wheeze.

"Colonel," Tom pushed the food trolley aside, leaned towards his ear, and spoke calmly. "It's Tom Christmas. Can you hear me?" His hand absently reached for the colonel's. He registered the loose papery skin, its limpness, its warmth.

"Tom, would you mind stepping from the room?" Alastair said. "I'm attending to the colonel."

Tom glanced at the beeping cardiac monitor, seeking some truth about the patient's condition in the glowing green lines, but the patterns appeared rhythmic and regular.

"Tom?" Alastair said impatiently. He was dressed casually, as if he was on his way to or from the golf course.

"But—"

"I won't be a minute."

Tom dropped the colonel's hand and retreated into the hallway. Again, a tortured cry assailed his ears; again, no one responded. He frowned. Precipitated by a troubling thought at the edge of his consciousness, he edged towards the narrow window set into the door to glimpse Alastair going about his business. Alastair's back, however, was to him, blocking the IV pole. Despite the room's low light, he could make out Alastair's movements: a hand reaching into a pocket, then disappearing in front of his chest, the motion repeated, upper arms shifting minutely. The top of the pole, a few inches above Alastair's head, stirred slightly. Alastair was engaged in some sort of adjustment to the colonel's medications, presumably, though what else it could be, besides the sedative Dr. Vikram had ordered, Tom couldn't imagine. Then, the troubling thought half slipped past the border of his conscious mind and his stomach lurched. Something was amiss. What could it be? It was as if his brain were unwilling to fully grasp what his eyes were seeing. And then, when it did, when the sound—faint, but perceptible—of the cardiac monitor kicking into frantic staccato bursts penetrated the thick door, his blood ran cold.

"Stop! Stop what you're doing!" He pushed through the door to see the lines on the screen bursting into wild patterns, then plummet. Tom reached the colonel's bedside in time to see the old man's lids suddenly fly open and his head jolt towards Tom, as if to take in his presence. His eyes stared, as if at some unseen marvel; his mouth rounded, as if in astonishment, and then the animating light in his eyes, once so fierce and vivid, vanished. The colonel now stared with empty eyes. The cardiac monitor emitted a single solid tone. Shocked, gasping for breath, Tom turned to Alastair, who had moved towards a container mounted on the wall.

"You are an unchristly monster."

"I'm a *what*?"

"You heard me. Doctors don't administer drugs into IV lines, which is what you were doing. *Nurses* administer drugs, on doctor's directives."

"You don't know what you're talking about."

"My wife was a doctor—"

"I'm aware of that."

"—and I've paid many hospital visits, Alastair. I know the protocol."

"What on earth makes you think I was putting anything into his drip?"

"I think if I examine what you've put into that . . . thing on the wall over there, I'll find a needle and a vial of something."

"I'm his doctor. The colonel's treatment is none of your business."

"You're *not* his doctor."

"I am bloody too his doctor."

"Not when he's in hospital for orthopaedic surgery. You're his GP, that's all! You have no *medical* reason for being here."

"I'm a doctor, I've been the colonel's GP for a number of years, and I have every right to look in on his well-being."

"You were *killing* him, Alastair!" Tom banged his fist on the food trolley. "Deliberately."

Alastair's eyes narrowed. His voice was sharp and indignant. "I'll have you for slander if you keep on with this."

"No! I'll have you for—"

But Tom found his words cut off as the door suddenly opened into the room and the ward sister bustled in. Wordlessly, she checked the colonel's pulse and breathing; grimly satisfied with what she found, she closed his eyelids and moved around the bed to switch off the cardiac monitor. The machine's insidious tone stopped.

"If you two gentlemen would care to leave . . ." She gestured towards the door. "I'll have Dr. Vikram make the declaration."

"Sister." Tom fought to calm his voice. "Dr. Hennis and I need to have a private conversation, so I wonder if you might leave us and come back in a moment or two."

The nurse bristled. "This is most inappropriate."

Alastair ran his hand through his hair. "Leave him with me, Sister. I think Father Christmas here"—he injected the honorific with a note of disdain—"wishes to say a few prayers for the departed. You see, Phillip Northmore was a great character in our village. By the time you find Dr. Vikram," he ushered her towards the door, "we'll have finished up here."

"Nurses—bloody cows, the lot of them," he remarked through his teeth when the door had barely closed behind the woman. "Now, what the fuck are you on about, Tom?"

"You've deliberately taken Colonel Northmore's life."

"This is an outrage. You simply happened to walk in at the moment of his death."

"You were administering something—"

"I was not!"

"—an *overdose* of something into his IV. Potassium, I'll wager. I learned a thing or two from Lisbeth."

"Again, you're outrageous. I was merely checking his IV out of professional habit. His death was merely coincidental."

"Bollocks! His death is the direct result of your actions."

"He's 'Do Not Resuscitate.'"

"I'm aware of that. It makes no difference. You're the agent of his death, and there's a test that can prove it. I know that from Lisbeth, too."

Alastair shrugged. "Well, I suppose electrolyte measurement might indicate high levels of potassium in the colonel's bloodstream, but such a test will never be ordered."

"Not if I don't go to the police, it won't."

"Tom, after all your years with Lisbeth, surely you've picked up that the medical profession is a club, and the club would quickly close around and resist any intrusion in this area. The dirty little secret of the health care system is that elderly and frail patients with numbered days are often eased painlessly into death. It's a great kindness to them and to their families. That you happened to arrive in the room when Colonel Northmore was—perhaps, maybe, who's to say?—being eased into his, is little more than—as I suggested earlier—interesting timing."

"Then you admit it."

Alastair shook his head, as if the misunderstanding of laypersons was unfathomable.

"Colonel Northmore may have been elderly, but he was *not that* frail." Tom gestured towards the corpse.

"He was very old. His hip was broken. The orthopaedic consultant would be telling him tomorrow that he was not a candidate for a hip replacement. I can say that for certain because I asked him about it. Phillip would have had to go into some form of care or assisted living. His wife has been dead for years. His daughter in America ignores him. Lacking opposable thumbs, Bumble would have been quite useless. Phillip would have had absolutely no quality of life. And," he paused to take a breath, "as it happens, we had a conversation yesterday—he and I—in which he signalled his wish not to carry on should he not be able to carry on, as usual, at Farthings, stiff upper lip and all."

"You left this room before I did yesterday."

"I came back."

"I don't believe you had this conversation with the colonel, Alastair. And I don't believe you *eased* him into death. You killed him to *silence him.*"

The air in the room seemed to condense and crackle with electricity. Tom could sense tiny shocks tripping along his skin; his heart raced. It was out. He had said it. Alastair reddened. He stared at Tom, nostrils flared. He snapped:

"Silence him over *what,* for fuck's sake?"

Tom pushed the trolley aside. "Over Peter Kinsey. The colonel and I were discussing his death yesterday. You trailed in at the end of it. I think he became conscious, when we were all talking, of something he hadn't put together before. I could see it in his face, though it didn't seem important at the time."

"How mystical."

Tom continued, "The colonel sought your corroboration yesterday about seeing him in the road the evening before Ned Skynner's funeral. You said you'd been up to see Enid Pattimore and you were on your way out of her and Roger's flat when you bumped into him."

"And so I was."

"You left Westways at around six-thirty—I remember that because Miranda and I were staying with you and Julia, and the news had just come on—"

"Yes," Alastair said impatiently.

"And the colonel said he met you in the road shortly after seven—"

"Yes, yes, what of it? There's not much to attend to with Enid Pattimore. The woman's neurotic. Give her a pill, stuff some cotton wool up her nose, pat her little hand, and she's happy as Larry."

"But there's nothing wrong with her brain. She told Mrs. Prowse, who told me barely an hour ago that you didn't arrive that evening until *Coronation Street* was more than half over, which would be about seven forty-five—an hour and a quarter after you left Westways. And I'm sure Roger was at home with his mother and could confirm. Just after seven o'clock, you weren't coming *out* of the Pattimores'. But you weren't going in either. What *were* you doing between six-thirty and seven forty-five other than loitering outside the Pattimores' for a few moments?"

"Christ!" Alastair exploded. "I was probably having a bloody drink in the bloody pub!"

"No, you weren't. I think you'll find Eric has a decent memory of that evening."

"Then I have no idea what I was doing on an evening more than a year ago."

"And yet yesterday you managed to recall meeting the colonel in the road when he prompted you."

"I was indulging him. I repeat: What are you on about? What does Kinsey's death have to do with *me*?"

Tom studied his sister-in-law's husband, the man who had once courted his wife, who had been thrown over for a mere theological student and all the promise of a parson's stipend . . . and who he now believed to be a murderer. But the anguish Julia had poured out on the lawn at Thornridge House—about her affair with Kinsey and the termination—was not his to reveal. Alastair, Julia had said, knew nothing of either.

She was wrong. He was sure of it.

"You couldn't," he said slowly, "go up to the Pattimores' flat that evening, the time you bumped into the colonel, because"—the truth now burst forth like a diamond in his mind's eye, unearthed by the colonel's ramblings—"because you didn't have your black bag with you. Your medical case. The one . . ." His eyes searched the room. ". . . you usually carry, at least when you're doing house calls. Your Gladstone bag, as the colonel would call it."

"You're insane."

"Of course!" Tom persisted, oblivious. "You had left it in the church somewhere, hadn't you? Probably in the vestry. It was only yesterday, when the colonel was fretting about that evening, that he realised what he had seen. As with any good magic trick, the eye doesn't see what it doesn't expect to see. The vestry is a tip, as everyone says. You wouldn't expect to see a Gladstone bag amid all the rubbish. And the colonel didn't. He was only there for a moment—long enough to witness Peter sprawled on the floor, but his unconscious mind took in the whole room.

"You said you were seeing a patient—Enid Pattimore—and yet you weren't carrying your bag. And then yesterday the colonel not only remembered that, he remembered where he *had* seen your bag that evening.

"Because," Tom's mind leapt ahead, "when the colonel saw you outside the Pattimores', you hadn't buried Peter yet, had you? It was only just seven when the colonel ran into you in the road. Your house call to Enid wasn't until some forty-five minutes later."

Alastair glared at him, his arms folded tightly across his chest. "I'm afraid," he said, jerking his head towards the colonel's body, "you've got no one to corroborate this nonsense now, do you?"

"I suppose Enid might also recall, if prompted by the police, the state of your clothing or your hands," Tom countered. "It can't be the tidiest work burying someone at twilight, even if the grave's largely been dug for you. At any rate, all this will give those detectives something they might work with."

Alastair's face was now flushed. In the half light, Tom could see the marvellous working of the jaw muscles in that heavy face. The door opened before either could speak again.

"I really must—" the ward sister began but Alastair cut her off. He thrust his arm towards the door.

"You haven't got Dr. Vikram, have you? Leave! We're not done here."

The nurse recoiled, as if slapped. She glanced with misplaced fury at Tom, who said, to mollify her, "If you wouldn't mind, Sister. Another moment or two."

"And that's all you'll get," she warned, departing. "I won't have this on my ward."

Alastair stared after her, then looked at Tom, warily this time.

"It's interesting," Tom added, "that when Julia called you to attend the colonel after his fall, you didn't bring your Gladstone bag. Have you spent the last year making sure the colonel didn't see it? You should have bought a new—and different-looking—one."

"It was a gift from my parents," Alastair murmured. He appeared lost in thought. His eyes roamed the room, falling last on the colonel's body. His mouth sagged a little. When he spoke again, it was in the tone of one brought to the brink of a new understanding.

"I should like to make a confession."

Startled, Tom asked: "A confession or an admission?"

"A confession."

"I see."

"A proper confession."

"A *formal* confession, you mean? Under the seal of the confessional?"

"Yes, that."

"I can't say I've seen you in church, Alastair."

"I did attend when Giles was priest."

Tom's heart and mind seethed. Private confession was a rare request, and he had taken none so burdened with corruption as this one. His impulse was to simply shop Alastair to the police and be done with him. He could now barely look the man in the face, a face now watchful with beseeching eyes.

But the ward sister's vouchsafed moment or two drew nigh. He decided. He was a priest. The office subsumed the man. He could do no other. But there was a caveat. He spoke quickly:

"Confession is part of contrition, Alastair. And contrition means facing up to the responsibility of what you've done. I cannot—I *will not* absolve you unless you agree to go to the police with me afterwards. Do you understand?"

Alastair folded his arms behind his back and bowed his head. His expression passed into shadow. "Of course."

CHAPTER TWENTY-NINE

"Are you locking me in?"

Tom turned the ancient key in the lock of the north door and then slipped it back into his trousers pocket. He had pulled the great bolt across the south door. The outside door to the vestry he knew was locked. He had made sure when he'd gone into the vestry to fetch a copy of the *Common Worship* text appropriate to private confession.

"No, Alastair, I'm locking everyone else out. Given the gravity of this . . . occasion, I don't want folk wandering in. I suggest the Lady chapel." He moved purposefully down the north aisle.

Inside the chapel, a single votive candle burned on a pricket stand. Tom pulled two straight-backed chairs forwards and beckoned Alastair to sit. Battling a visceral repugnance, he remained standing and regarded the man who had been his wife's lover, who might have been her husband, had not he, Tom, fallen into the Cam that day and thus changed the course of four lives. In the car, returning to Thornford, he had wondered again if he could bear this, bear hearing Alastair's confession, bear being an instrument of

God's clemency in this instance. He had heard not many formal private confessions during his years of ministry. A few divorced men and women had confessed past wrongdoings—their "manifold sins and wickedness"—seeking to wipe the slate clean before remarrying. He had had two instances of men confessing to abusing children, but each in sorting out his life had reached the end of a road and knew and accepted that police involvement was inevitable. The details had been grim, their remorse grievous and pitiable in expression, and Tom had absolved them. But he had never heard, nor had he expected to ever hear, a confession to murder. Reconciliation lay at the foundation of his vocation, but he felt his heart cold and barren as he faced Alastair. Summoning what fortitude he could he sat down and spoke.

"Before we begin, we must have a conversation. I need to know that your desire to unburden your conscience is sincere. Then we'll go to the Old School Room and meet with Bliss and Blessing. If they'll permit, we'll return here and perform the rite together at the font. If not, wherever the police designate will be fine."

Alastair's hands were folded in his lap. "And you will keep my confidence?"

"To the grave, Alastair, unless you permit me otherwise."

"Then it's true. I confess it. I did kill Peter Kinsey. I didn't intend to. I didn't plan it." His eyes darted towards the mullioned window over the altar and he affected a sorrowful little shrug. "It . . . simply happened."

"Are you suggesting you're not responsible?"

"No, Tom, I'm saying it wasn't done in cold blood . . . though I was bloody-minded, I don't mind saying. I didn't plan it—that's all."

"You'd better explain."

Alastair paused. "Your visit last year came at the very wrong moment. I had had some . . . shocking—I suppose you could say—information on the Friday before your arrival."

"Yes . . . ?"

Alastair's mouth twisted. "Julia, I learned, had had a termination." He glanced at Tom and raised an eyebrow. "You don't seem at all bothered. You know about it, I suppose. You two are thick as thieves now, aren't you? After all the years of indifference."

"Your wife is the assistant organist and choirmaster of this church, Alastair," Tom responded with some exasperation. "Of course I see more of her than I see of you."

"That doesn't answer my question."

"Your question being . . . ?"

"Did you know about Julia's termination?"

"If I should start telling you what people in the village have told me in confidence, then how could you trust me to keep your confidences?"

Alastair appeared hardly mollified. "Then you must excuse me if I'm being redundant, but as you may or may not know Julia and I cannot—or, rather, should not—have children. The child we conceived some years ago was miscarried—that you know—but what you don't know, or *probably* don't know—is that there was a second miscarriage. We are genetically mismatched, it turns out. We were tested. I'll spare you the details, but almost any pregnancy will result in miscarriage."

"I'm sorry."

"It was devastating. I know you may not believe me—I know Lisbeth never believed it—but I love Julia with all my heart. There's nothing I've wanted more than to have a child with her."

"There are other solutions."

"I don't want a divorce. I want Julia."

"I meant adoption or surrogacy or the like."

"Yes, well . . . I was coming around to that. But the disappointment after the second miscarriage was so enormous, we could barely speak of children. I think it must hurt Julia to go off and teach them each day." Alastair paused. "Lisbeth made the wise choice, didn't she?"

"I don't know what you mean."

"Lisbeth and Julia were sisters. The same thing might have happened had Lisbeth and I—"

Vexed at another reminder of this history, Tom interrupted, "Perhaps you should get on with your story."

Alastair's expression hardened. "I'm afraid a certain amount of meaning leached from our marriage after the miscarriages, after the test. I'm sure you've noticed—the sleeping arrangements when you were staying at ours, for instance. They haven't changed. It's as though sleeping together is simply a reminder of . . . well, never mind." He straightened in his chair, crossing his legs at the ankle. "At any rate, sometime early last year, Julia had an abortion. I think you can figure that she hadn't conceived the child with me.

"I stewed about it most of that weekend," Alastair continued, "but then you and Miranda arrived, so I had to put on a face for the guests." He paused. "You're very lucky to have Miranda."

If this was a bid for sympathy, it wasn't working well, Tom thought. He made a noncommittal noise and gestured at Alastair to get on with it.

"Anyway, on Monday evening, as you know, since you were there, Enid Pattimore called with one of her manufactured emergencies. The woman is a hypochondriac, but as she's one of my few remaining private patients I indulge her whims.

"When I'd walked as far as Church Lane I happened to look left and noted Kinsey going through the lych-gate towards the church. I suppose if I'd never turned my head, or if I'd left Westways five minutes later . . . anyway, I followed him into the church and found him in the vestry."

"Why would you turn your attention to Peter Kinsey?" Tom interrupted.

"You know perfectly well why by now." Alastair brought the chair forwards with a bang on the stone floor. "The little shit was having it off with my wife."

"But how did you know?"

"I *knew,* that's all. I was *told.*" Alastair's face flared. "At least about the termination."

"By Sybella?"

"*What?* No. What are you talking about? One of my colleagues, learning of the termination through his wife, a doctor who works at the clinic in Exeter, and assuming the termination was wrapped up in our genetic mismatch, happened to commiserate with me. Of course, I had no idea.

"Figuring it was Kinsey wasn't hard. I'd heard that stupid rumour about Sebastian, but I didn't believe it. Sebastian's too . . . pure. Not Kinsey, though. I could think of no other man in her orbit that would fit. Besides, Kinsey admitted it. I accused him, and he didn't deny it. In fact, he hardly seemed repentant. He had the cheek to blame Julia. He implied that it was *she* who made a play for him. He said priests get it all the time from lonely women with inattentive husbands. '*Husbands, love your wives, just as Christ loved the church,*' he had the gall to preach to me, as if it were now all my fault. The arrogance of the man!"

Alastair turned silent for a moment, stared off towards the pricket stand where the candle, now low, began to flicker garishly. Tom's eyes, too, went to the pricket stand and then travelled to a homely felt banner depicting the Virgin and Child in a scene with Thornford's millpond, the handiwork of some devoted parishioner. On the wall above the banner, he thought he could see in the fresh paint the ghosts of holes that must have supported the screws that had held the missing Guercinos. He had hoped the Lady chapel might be a comforting venue for this ghastly interview, but he was wrong. Pallid, cool light filtered through the plain faceted glass of the north and east windows, greying the colours of the banner and the altar cloth and weighting the air. He sensed damp seeping into his bones as he waited for Alastair to resume. And when Alastair did, it was in a voice of wonder, as if he were seeing his own actions for the first time on a screen:

"It was a blinding moment, Tom. I gave no thought to what I

was about to do. He simply dismissed me and showed me his back. The verger's staff was on the vestry table near the door. My hand reached for it and . . ."

Tom felt a shiver course down his spine as Alastair paused again. In his mind's eye, he could see the staff, with its crucifix atop a heavy brass ball, whipping the air, smashing downward to crush the bone at the back of the skull, then the body flopping raggedly, sinking to the cold stone floor.

"It was a killing blow," Alastair resumed, adding with some little surprise, "only a slight tear to the skin. Very little blood. Remarkable."

Tom looked at him aghast. "And you simply left him there?"

"I lost my nerve, I suppose you might say. It's not an unreasonable reaction. I don't think I knew what I was doing until I found myself by the gate next to Pattimore's shop and realised I'd left my bag in the vestry. That's when the colonel happened by. I affected that I was going through to the back on my way to see Enid."

Tom was suddenly possessed by the vision of Lisbeth lying in the south porch of St. Dunstan's, her life's blood draining. Someone had left her there, too. Some swine, some coward. Choking back his growing disgust, he was barely listening, as Alastair continued, voluble now, as if telling the tale to someone for the first time, as he was.

"When the colonel turned at Church Lane, I thought before long a cry would be raised, that the road would be crawling with police cars and ambulances, and I would soon be found out. The colonel wasn't walking Bumble. He's not often in the pub. One rarely sees him about at that time of the evening. He had some business either with Sebastian or with the vicar—and the vicar was in the church. I must admit I waited with some trepidation. But it wasn't five minutes before he reappeared, coming out of The Square into Orchard Hill, walking rather briskly back to Farthings. Whatever he had been up to, I presumed he had not come across Kinsey's body." He scowled at Tom. "Or at least I presumed it *then*."

Tom didn't respond to the provocation. Alastair's mouth settled into a hard, thin line for a moment; then he resumed:

"I managed to get back to the church without being seen. Thank God the English love their television. I went into The Square, through the little side gate into the churchyard—which was the way I had come. I suppose I was in a bit of a lather, but it's a marvel what the mind can come up with under pressure. I knew Ned's funeral was the next day. I could see the grave prepared at the bottom of the churchyard when I passed through. Kinsey wasn't a big man, and I'm fairly fit. It was a bit of a chore getting him off the floor, but I was able to put him over my shoulder, pick up my case, and get out of the church. No one was about. It was twilight. Everything was in shadow. I dropped him in the hole, near to one side of the grave—which wasn't wise in retrospect, given Fred's pulling a stone away later—lifted the synthetic grass over the mound of earth, shovelled in some dirt—Fred had conveniently left his tools leaning against the tree—and it was done and dusted."

An odd smile played at the corners of Alastair's lips. "And then the next day, you—as it happened—committed Ned to his grave."

Tom doubted calm and simplicity had reigned over this appalling exercise. He imagined Alastair panicked, sweating, frantically shovelling earth. He imagined Enid, later, perhaps wondering at his appearance, if she wasn't too absorbed in her health or in the television. If only, he thought, he'd paid more attention that evening. He remembered seeing Alastair leave after Enid's phone call, but remembered only hearing him come back—it must have been sometime after eight; they were well into the Disney DVD—and not joining them in the living room at Westways. They could hear Alastair in the kitchen; Julia had called out to him, but Alastair had replied that he was having an early night, and gone to the ground-floor bedroom suite.

"It's hardly amusing, Alastair," he responded.

"I'm sorry. Really. I was merely reflecting that it worked so well. I could hardly believe it. Kinsey seemed to have disappeared. People disappear all the time, don't they? There was no evidence anything had happened. The grave was soon filled, the vestry trampled by the likes of Karla, Roger, whoever . . . you. I did wipe prints from the verger's staff, but I hardly needed to. Other hands would hold it in the days ahead. All in all, really, a perfect . . ."

"Were you going to say 'crime'?"

"I was going to say 'solution.' I thought with Kinsey . . . gone, Julia and I would get back on track."

"You didn't think she might mourn Peter's loss? Or mourn having a termination?"

"I thought that in due course everything would right itself. Julia would invite me back into her bed."

"You're very forgiving for a man whose wife broke her wedding declaration to be faithful."

"I told you I love her. I forgave her."

Was it love or possessiveness that motivated him? Tom wondered. True love was terra firma; possessiveness was quicksand. People who seek to possess live in fear of loss, and those who fear can commit terrible acts. He took a head-clearing breath. He was dreading what he had to say next:

"It was a perfect . . . solution, perhaps, until you walked into the village hall last Sunday afternoon when Mitsuko was installing her memory quilts."

There was a beat of silence, in which Alastair turned to stare at him. "What are you on about?"

"You noted one of Mitsuko's quilts featured a picture of the churchyard taken from the tower and you noted the date stamp on it—the date of the very day Peter Kinsey was last seen. You also noted a lone figure near a freshly dug grave. It was you."

"I don't know what you're talking about."

"Alastair, who else would nick that particular quilt? Who else would have a reason to slip into Mitsuko's studio and take her computer and camera? You're the only one in the village that I can think of. Mitsuko had been taking hundreds of pictures with her digital.

Who knew that she had taken a sequence of pictures from the church tower that, if they were blown up or scrutinised in some way, would reveal a man burying something just about the time of Kinsey's disappearance? Maybe someone in the village would look at the quilt at the opening and think, 'That's odd. Isn't that Dr. Hennis?' There would be questions, curiosity. You know what this village is like.

"I expect you were desperate to get your hands on that quilt before anyone started to give it a close look," Tom continued, reaching into his jacket pocket. "What you didn't know was that, late in the evening, there would be someone in the village hall—Sybella Parry. In the dark, you thought it was Mitsuko—well, kill two birds with one stone, yes? Who knew what she might remember of that evening more than a year ago? Vanish the living memory along with the memory quilt."

"This is outrageous."

"Do you have *no* remorse for killing that young woman?"

"There's not a scrap of evidence that I had anything to do with her death."

Tom responded with an icy stare. He held his right hand palm upwards, tilted slightly forwards for Alastair's viewing. Balanced between his thumb and his forefinger was the wizard's cap, the gnome's hat—top side up, the golf tee.

Alastair's eyes narrowed. "Where did you get that?"

"It's your lucky tee, isn't it?"

"Yes," he responded tightly. "I've been wondering where it had got to."

"Miranda found it."

"Then give it back."

Tom brought his left hand over the top of the tee, as if to pick it up. "She found it in the village hall, near the skirting board of the large hall."

"I must have dropped it Sunday afternoon."

"Possibly." Tom's left hand closed over the tee. "But you know how diligent Joyce Pike is. I can't imagine she wouldn't have swept this up at the end of the day and put it in the bin with the sweepings. Miranda found your tee on Monday afternoon, almost exactly where the missing quilt should have been."

"Would you give me my tee!"

"She's a very clever girl, my daughter. She knew it was your golf tee and she knew in her heart it was somewhere it shouldn't be. She's known it all week. Poor thing," Tom continued with rising anger, "she simply didn't want to get anyone into trouble. She's lost her mother. She didn't want another family member out of the picture. She's fond of you."

"The tee, please."

Tom closed his left fist and held it out towards Alastair. "I'm sure if your golfing mates were questioned," he said, moving his right hand in a circular motion over his bunched left fist, "they would recall that you didn't have your lucky tee with you Bank Holiday Monday morning."

Alastair lunged at his fist, but Tom flipped it open, palm upward. The tee had vanished. Alastair's eyes darted to Tom's right hand, which he quickly turned over. Nothing. It was a sleight of hand older than the pharaohs, a double misdirection, one of the first tricks he'd mastered when Kate bought him his magic set.

"*Where is it?*" Alastair spat.

"Not such a lucky tee, really. Is it?"

Alastair's hand dived towards the pocket of Tom's jacket. Jerking back to avoid the intrusive fingers, Tom tipped off the chair, landing on the floor, his head cracking nastily on the cold stone. His eyes seemed to roll in his head and he watched, as if from a distance, in collapsed time, two Alastairs leap upon him, then swiftly resolve into one thrashing figure with a face in flame bordered by the ribs of the church's vaulted ceiling. One hand pushed hard against his neck, while another rummaged over the pockets of his jacket and trousers. Legs widespread pinned his arms on either side.

"Where the fuck is that tee?" Alastair snarled.

Struggling against the weight, gagging as the hand squeezed his windpipe, Tom managed to jerk one arm from its confinement. He felt a sharp pain shoot through his wrist as it hit the metal base of the pricket stand. The stand swayed and toppled towards them. Alastair released the hand pressing Tom's neck to shield himself, but hot wax from the single candle spattered against his face. He cried out and twisted his body away, sending the stand crashing against the altar, giving enough purchase for Tom to release his other arm. With all his force he pushed at Alastair with both free hands, sending him sprawling backwards onto the floor. Alastair scrambled to get up, but not before Tom leapt on him in turn and pinned his arms to the floor. He could feel the fierce beating of Alastair's heart along his knees.

"This is not how we hear confession, Alastair." Tom gasped for breath.

"Give me back my property."

"I'm sensing very little contrition. A young woman was killed a week ago and the evidence points to you."

"What evidence?"

"The tee, for one."

"It's spurious. Circumstantial. Found by a *child*."

"Then why are you so anxious to have the thing back?"

Alastair glared up at him. He bucked his midsection in an effort to throw Tom off, but Tom pushed down harder.

"Confession, Alastair, is supported by mutual trust. You trust that I will keep your confidences—and I shall, absolutely, without equivocation—and I trust that you will unburden your conscience so that you may receive the benefit of absolution. Do you want to reconcile your soul to God, Alastair? *Do you?*" he shouted, finding in himself a sudden fury that he hadn't felt since the hours after Lisbeth's death.

Alastair's face flinched as though hit by a fierce wind. The glare melted, and his eyes glistened with incipient tears. "Oh, Jesus. I'm sorry. *I'm sorry.* I was just trying to make everything right again."

Tom looked hard into Alastair's eyes and thought he detected in them a measure of defeat. He released the pressure on the man's arms, sat up, and scrambled to his feet. He extended a hand to Alastair, who took it.

"I didn't plan it." Alastair rose awkwardly and wiped at his eyes. "You have to believe me. It wasn't any more planned than it had been with Kinsey. I only knew I had to remove that quilt before the whole village saw it. I didn't expect there to be anyone in the village hall that late."

"Why take the trouble to deny your culpability?"

"Because it was bloody stupid of me, that's why." He peeled off a bit of wax that had cooled along his cheek. "It was as you say: In the dark I thought I was looking at the back of Mitsuko. It was only when I sliced open that drum, and lifted her to put her in, that I saw it was Sybella Parry. Bloody, bloody stupid."

Tom snatched at the pricket stand, righting it, anger simmering. Some of Lisbeth's student colleagues at Cambridge flashed through his mind—the male ones, almost exclusively, infected with an overweening hubris, Alastair not the least of them. Most of these peacocks sought glory as surgeons, which Alastair might have done, and pleased his surgeon parents in the bargain. But Alastair lacked imagination—he'd entertained no career besides Mummy and Daddy's—and, as Lisbeth had shared with Tom one evening at Cambridge over stir-fry at a nearby noodle bar, not long after that awkward weekend with the Roses in Golders Green, he was scholastically too indolent for the rigours of specialised medicine. Nonetheless, she'd continued, "rather like those buggery big cats in Africa lazing about the savannah who let the lionesses do all the running and yet are somehow admired by all the world," his narcissism remained vibrant. And so, taking Sybella's life was not a mortal sin; for someone like Alastair Hennis, who always thought life would go his way, murder was mere folly.

Tom asked: "You struck Sybella with one of the *bachi,* the taiko sticks?"

"No, actually. I thought the place was empty, though the door was unlocked—"

"Then how were you planning to get in?"

"Julia leaves her keys on a peg in the hall at Westways, so—"

"Ah."

"—so I went first to the large hall to get the quilt, but then I heard a noise coming from the small hall, so I went to investigate. I couldn't have a witness to my taking the quilt. There was just enough moonlight to pick out a walking stick—I think it was Northmore's—on the table in the lobby."

"Joyce must have moved it sweeping up when Mitsuko was done," Tom said absently.

"What?"

"It doesn't matter. So, you left the stick in the small kitchen when you were . . . done, went back to the large hall to remove the quilt, and then . . ." He frowned. "You must have had your bag with you."

"Of course. I'm a doctor making a late evening house call. My bag contains a set of scalpels, and it was a useful carrier bag to stuff the quilt in. Gladstone bags are surprisingly capacious."

"Then on Monday, you stuffed the quilt into the hedgerow near Thornridge . . . why there?"

"Secluded. And the whole village was at the fayre."

"Then later that day you broke into Mitsuko's studio."

"I didn't break in. I found keys on Sybella's body. I thought one of them might be to the Blackbird as she works there from time to time. Found letters addressed to *The Sun* and some of the other tabloids, too."

Tom's brow furrowed.

"Something about Sebastian. It made no sense and I burned them. Anyway, the alarm was switched off at Mitsuko's. That would have been the tricky bit, and I was prepared to take a chance—again the whole village was at the fayre—but I had a stroke of luck there."

"And what did you do with Mitsuko's computer and camera?"

"I think it best I tell the police."

Wearily, though he was certain he knew the answer, Tom asked finally:

"Why did you put Sybella in the drum?"

"I couldn't very well take her out onto the road, could I? The village is pitch at night, but someone might have come along with their beams on. I expected her body wouldn't be found for hours, by which time a roomful of kids would have trampled any evidence I'd been there. Not that anyone would suspect me. I'm a doctor, after all. And I was right." He extended his arm and wriggled his fingers. "But for one thing—that tee."

Tom looked past Alastair through the latticework of the rood screen towards the old stone font, which sat like a splendid toadstool at the rear of the church. This was nothing like any private confession he'd ever heard. He could not detect if Alastair's loathing of his sin was even half formed, much less complete. Perfect contrition seemed elusive.

"Are you sorry for this great suffering that you have caused?" he asked.

"Yes, of course I am."

"Are you prepared to take further spiritual counsel and advice?"

"Absolutely."

Tom paused, then folded his leg behind him and reached into his shoe. He plucked the tee from its resting place, jabbing into the soft tissue near his heel.

"Very clever," Alastair muttered as Tom dropped it into the outstretched palm before him.

"It matters little now," Tom responded, moving past Alastair and stepping down from the Lady chapel, the very air of which now seemed tainted. He could hear someone rattling the north door from the outside, likely some unhappy tourist.

"I'll unlock these doors, then I'll go with you to the Old School

Room," he added, glancing back at the figure following him down the north aisle.

"I don't need someone to hold my hand," Alastair said witheringly, and Tom thought he noted in his eyes a flicker of the old disdain.

CHAPTER THIRTY

The hatch felt resistant against the pressure of his palm, and at first Tom fretted that he had made his corkscrew journey for nothing, to be frustrated at the end by some impenetrable latch or absence of key that only Sebastian knew the whereabouts of. He had grazed the top of his head passing through the Lilliputian door in the choir vestry to climb the first set of steps up St. Nicholas's tower to the ringing-chamber. He nearly tripped over the stoop into the darkness of the second set of steps winding to the clock chamber (cutting his finger against a sharpish bit of stone while fumbling for a light switch), then found himself beading with anxious sweat as his feet sought purchase in the dark along the third set, a stone staircase with slender treads that narrowed as it coiled to the belfry above. Charging ahead, he had somehow missed the toggle to flick on the string of fairy lights, but his hand brushed each tiny glass globe as he climbed. He was grateful to come upon a thin slit in the stonework here, and then here, that admitted a stab of light and a draft of fresh air, a mercy against the aroma of dust and damp mortar. He was more grateful still when his questing hand groped a wooden trapdoor above his head. It opened easily enough with a push, and he emerged out of the atavistic blackness into the soft grey shadows of the bell chamber. Relieved, Tom hauled himself onto one of the heavy beams of the bell cage to catch his breath, shaken a little by his moments of claustrophobic panic. Licking his wounded finger, noting a slight ammonia pong in the air—bat urine? pigeon droppings?—he let his eyes roam the silhouettes of the great slumbering bells and the rims and spokes of the wheels. The chamber felt brooding, ominous, the mood relieved but barely by sunshine stripes cast from the slatted windows of the old Norman tower.

Climbing the church tower had been at first notional; then it became a craving. The couple that crossed Alastair's path as he left by the north door eagerly affixed themselves to Tom, noting his dog collar and assuming, despite his protestations, that he was the fount of knowledge of St. Nicholas's and Thornford Regis. Late-middle-aged and voluble, they were from Peterborough. Her great-grandparents, Chubb by name, had been farm labourers in the Thornford area and were buried somewhere in the churchyard. Tom led them to the gravesites register and map deposited on the shelf in the south porch. He unbolted the door, and slowly disentangled himself from their questions and company as he ushered them outside, citing a pressing obligation. He felt a crushing need of solitude. If he hung about the churchyard or the nave, or even deposited himself in the vestry, he could still be got at. As he turned back into the church, his eyes went to the west end of the nave, through the mullioned glass, to the bell-ringers' platform perched on the second story of the tower, where six bell ropes vanished into the ceiling above, and where he, too, might vanish.

But now the hatch door to the roof was proving resistant. It was only with force, clinging precariously with one hand on a wooden rung of a short set of steps, that he was able to push it back on its hinge and feel a blast of light and heat on his face. From darkness to gloom to sunshine, he thought as he stepped onto the leaded surface. A rook squawked and fluttered off one of the pinnacles as he gripped the empty flagpole in the centre to steady himself in the wind, which was startlingly constant and ever-present. He could bawl, shout, scream into this wind. He felt like doing so. He wouldn't be heard.

He advanced to the mossy parapet that overlooked the sprawling roof of the church, a grey massing like a ship's prow parting invisible waters. He gave a passing thought to the church architect's report, which he had finally found, and read. Roof repairs were among the action items ticked off, and he envisioned the intensification of jumble sales, car boot sales, bake sales, bring-and-buys, and raffles, to raise the necessary funds. If there had been one benison in this fateful day, it had been Jamie Allan's offer of help. He and nine other peers of the realm spent part of each summer parachuting from airplanes raising money for various charities. St. Nicholas's was not unworthy of their efforts, Jamie said, advising Tom to get in touch for the year following. Reflexively, Tom raised his head to the sky, as if expecting a parachutist to descend through the armada of clouds. Instead he glimpsed a jet, a silvery cross scoring a patch of blue at the highest reaches as if marking the line where the heavens were to be pulled apart.

A little earlier, he had opened the north door to the cheerfully inquisitive holidaymakers from Peterborough, who had burst in, as oblivious to his absence of vicarish bonhomie as they had been to the figure who had shouldered his way between them and stepped onto the path. Tom ignored the visitors, stared after Alastair, prayed for him as he passed through the lych-gate onto Church Walk, waited for him to turn to the door of the Old School Room and give himself over to those inside.

And then he had watched, with growing numbness, and yet somehow with little surprise, as Alastair continued down Church Walk, past the Old School Room without so much as a glance or hesitation, past the Church House Inn, and around the corner to where he had parked his car. A moment later Alastair's late-model

Mercedes shot across the opening to Church Walk, disappeared momentarily behind the stone wall bordering Poynton Shute, then reappeared, heading—there was no doubt—up Thorn Hill to West-ways, to home, to Julia, as if the last few hours had had no more con-sequence than a game of golf.

He had released a moan of despair then, standing in the shadow of the north porch where only that morning he had been sharing greetings with parishioners.

Alastair had martyred him to the seal of the confessional.

He knew all.

He could say nothing.

A bell struck from below, preternaturally loud, startling him. It struck again. It was the clock, chiming the hour. He counted six, then checked his watch to confirm, as if the Victorian clockworks were an unreliable instrument. *Miranda and Madrun will be wonder-ing where I've got to,* he thought, looking beyond the church roof towards the vicarage nestled in its frame of beeches. Madrun, inured to custom, would be starting to prepare a light supper. Of Miranda he was less certain. Watching TV? Reading? Was she troubled still? How had his daughter's afternoon proceeded in his absence?

He grieved for Julia, for surely Miranda's outburst in front of the Allans had afforded her the intimation that something was askew. Had Miranda told her aunt what she had told him about her dis-covery at the village hall? Or had Julia gently winkled it out of Miranda? And what of Madrun? Before he had driven off to the hospital, he had warned her of the need for circumspection. But had she heeded his warning? Had she been down to the post office with the news? Well, what did it matter? In a village, he was learning, gossip spreads like a stain. Soon, very soon, Alastair would find vil-lagers turning away from him in the road or avoiding him in the pub— the rituals of shunning. Perhaps he wouldn't care. But Julia would suffer. *How could she remain married to someone such as he?* they would whisper. *How could she show herself in the church and work with Colm*

Parry? Quickly, very quickly, suspicion would seep into the Old School Room, and the detectives there would sharpen their focus to a fine point.

But what hard evidence would they have to make a charge against Alastair? Tom walked around the parapet and lifted his eyes to the hills, to the counterpane of parcelled fields on the horizon, luminescent green in the buttery sunshine. His eyes travelled along the tidy border of beech trees, darker green, that bounded Thorn Creek's gentle entrance into the river Dart, down to the first of Thornford's cottages, to the quay where the boats docked, to the Waterside Café on its promontory by the weir, and to the millpond, placid and silvery, its surface broken by nothing more than the chevron wake of a swan, a white speck from this great height. Six days ago, at the May Fayre in Purton Farm, in a mood of willful romance, feeling for the first time fully settled into his new life, he had viewed this cultivated landscape, as tidy as the borders on Mitsuko's memory quilts, as impossibly inviolate. This day, this hour, he felt poor in wisdom.

No clue that he knew of survived fourteen months of Peter Kinsey's absence. If Alastair had left any evidence of his presence in the vestry that evening (and he most surely had; didn't murderers always take something away and leave something behind? He had heard that on television), then it had vanished in the day-by-day traffic in and out of the tiny room. Colonel Northmore had memory of one piece of evidence that Alastair had been in the vestry that evening, but the colonel was silenced forever now. Tom agonised, as he had agonised in the hospital room, hastily praying over the colonel's body as the nurse ushered Dr. Vikram into the room, whether to voice his alarm. Alastair had not spoken to him under the seal of the confessional in the colonel's room, but neither had he admitted to any wrongdoing. He knew, too, from Lisbeth's conversation, after a glass of wine or two—this before Miranda was born—when they discussed the home truths of church and medicine, that death was lent a hand in hospitals, quietly, surreptitiously, none the wiser. Alastair was correct: The local health authority would reject any allegation of euthanasia by the back door and erect a defensive wall around any doctor accused.

And what of Sybella? Granted, the Twelve Drummers Drumming, their teacher, Julia, and whoever else had traipsed through the village hall last Monday had contaminated any crime scene, but surely the scene-of-crime officers had pulled some sort of rabbit out of a hat—that is, some strand of hair or flake of skin or *some bloody thing* out of the drum that pointed indelibly to the culprit.

Tom leaned forwards and glanced down through an embrasure in the tower's crenellations at the crown of the yew tree below, looking for all the world like a great green unfurled umbrella. He was reminded not of Julia, with whom he had circled the very tree only the other day, but of Lisbeth, of kissing her under the yew tree in St. Oswald's churchyard, in Grasmere, in the Lakes, on their honeymoon. He felt a stab of intense yearning for her, if not for her shrewd counsel alone, for she could take a priestly Gordian knot and slice it with a bold stroke. While he could no more share the secrets of the confessional with her than she could share patients' medical confidences with him, he would have been able to sidle up to her with a discreet question or two. She would smile—she would know there was a subtext to his query—but she would not pry. If she were here today, he would ask her, "Why did you break it off with Alastair Hennis?" And she would answer lightheartedly, as it was a question he had asked, long ago, at that Cambridge noodle bar: "Because he was so very predictable, darling." Even when Alastair had continued to court Julia, Lisbeth had mocked it as only another example of his lack of imagination, as if the Rose sisters came as a sort of job lot, one as suitable as the other, though Tom believed, without Lisbeth confirming, that a modicum of spite had provoked Alastair's attention to the younger sister, a getting back, made more triumphant by a lavish wedding, which Lisbeth suffered through as maid of honour. "Why did you break it off with Alastair?" She had never said. But Tom thought he now understood why. Lisbeth had intuited a profound absence at the very heart of Alastair's being.

He shifted down the parapet to better view the churchyard to the south and west—Mitsuko's view, he presumed, the one in the missing quilt, which she had said looked out to the quay and the river beyond. It was the view he had taken in earlier, only this time he let his eyes travel down to the graves, the slightly irregular rows of grey, brown, and black lozenges bursting from the grass, most plain, some adorned with crosses, others fronting marble platforms so they looked like headboards on vacant beds. He watched the Peterborough couple, two tiny dolls, toddling between the rows, pausing now and again. He considered that they might have been exploring the wrong end of the graveyard, perhaps having read the map upside down, but eventually the woman settled on a marker and called her husband over, though Tom could hear no sound in the wind other than the cry of gulls hovering over the millpond. Both hunched to read the inscription. Tom realised this was not only very much the view Mitsuko had captured in her photograph, but the situation, too: bottoms up. Bottoms, nice, pear-shaped female ones, were quite fanciable—an intrusive thought on this grimmest of afternoons—but from a hundred feet in the air he could barely distinguish the male Peterborian's from the female's. Little wonder Mitsuko had spared no time to attach a name to an arse. Even faces, he recognised when the pair unbent and walked around the gravestone (as if there were something written on the other side), were only vaguely hominoid from a height.

But the mechanical eye of a digital camera was like the Eye of Providence. It saw all. And what it saw could be downloaded into a computer and all the fine details made magnificent on a radiant screen—the back of a shoe, a trouser cuff, a belt, a shirt pattern, a hand, a fingernail, a wedding ring, a Gladstone bag. Mitsuko had shot high-resolution pictures and she had shot many. Who knows what else she had captured of the graveyard that April twilight more than a year ago?

Tom cast his eyes towards the far reach of the graveyard, between the stone wall and the beech tree, where Sybella's grave lay still mounded with fresh red Devon soil. He had not known the Reverend Peter Kinsey; the colonel he did know—or, rather, *had* known—and respected, but the colonel's great age, his having lived, as they said at funeral teas, "a full life," tempered his sense of loss. It was Sybella's death that tore at Tom's heart. She was a young woman of nineteen—only ten years older than his beautiful Miranda—who by fits and starts had been emerging from the mucky chrysalis of adolescence into a promisingly sane adult. He tried to suppress his loathing for Alastair, remembering that he had been prepared to say the words of absolution:

> *Almighty God, our heavenly Father,*
> *who in His great mercy*
> *has promised forgiveness of sins*
> *to all those who with heartfelt repentance and true faith*
> *turn to Him:*
> *Have mercy on you;*
> *pardon and deliver you from all your sins;*
> *confirm and strengthen you in all goodness;*
> *and bring you to everlasting life;*
> *through Jesus Christ our Lord.*

But now he would prefer that justice, not mercy, rain down. He looked again at Sybella's grave, headstone and marble slab still to arrive, noting the Peterborians zigzagging in its direction, as aware as anyone, likely, if they took a newspaper or watched television, of the week's events in Thornford. He watched the couple stare at the mound, then the man draw the woman to him, as if the sight had triggered some private grief. They stood intertwined for a moment at the foot of Sybella's grave, then separated, the man moving up the slope, the woman pausing at Ned Skynner's grave, bending to read the inscription. Her elbow crooked. She appeared to be calling out to her husband, as if the Skynners bore some familial relationship, but he'd disappeared below the branches of a spreading chestnut, and soon she moved to catch him up. They would shortly reappear on the path along the terrace back towards the church, Tom was certain, but his attraction to their excursion had evaporated. It was Ned's grave, and Sybella's, that lingered in his imagination—and then, as imagination will, sent him tripping down neural pathways, synapses firing like Roman candles: the untidy state of Red Ned's grave despite Fred's reputation for sterling earthworks, the absence of a prominent Thornfordian at Mitsuko's exhibition opening, Lisbeth's remarks in that Cambridge noodle bar, the astonishing nature of hubris. All these thoughts scattered randomly as stars in a galaxy until, suddenly, by some nameless force, they began to turn and swirl and coalesce into one burning white-hot sun and he felt the searing heat of certainty. He didn't know how long he stood there on the parapet, his hands gripping a merlon, but when he reawakened to the wind and the sky, his palms had become pressed with the pattern of the rough stone. He would, he knew, have to move Heaven—at least its corporeal representatives—and earth—literally—to atone for his folly.

And there was almost no time left.

The Vicarage

Thornford Regis TC9 6QX

14 June

Dear Mum,

I'm sorry I had to leave you on ~~tentacles~~ ~~tenderhooks~~ tenterhooks
with yesterday's letter. As I wrote to you yesterday, I'd awoken
about four in the morning, which I don't usually do because, as
you know, I sleep like a stone, but there had been a light shining
in the west outside my window, which was quite the wrong
place for a light to be shining. I think I wrote yesterday that I
thought perhaps creatures from outer space had landed in the
churchyard, which was out of the ordinary since creatures from
outer space always seem to gravitate to New York, at least in
films, and wouldn't it be a fine thing if they landed in Thornford
R, and I was half wondering what I might serve them for a
meal, feeling as I do that creatures from outer space are most
likely not to be vegans, when I fell back asleep. Of course, I
thought I was dreaming at the time, as I think I said, which
makes me wonder perhaps if having my own computer would be
useful after all as I could keep copies of what I write to you so I

*wouldn't repeat myself, but never mind. I know I wrote
yesterday that I thought something strange was in the offing. For
the first time in nearly a fortnight Mr. Christmas looked like he
wasn't bearing the weight of the world. Thursday supper, before
bell-ringing practice he tucked into my lamb chops with lemon
and mint con gusto as they say in Tenerife and little Miranda
brightened up, too. Poor child—I know she still thinks it's her
fault that Dr. Hennis has moved out of Westways into a flat in
Torquay, but "Aunt Julia" had a long chat with her niece in the
back garden on Tuesday, which I don't think I mentioned, did I?
She came down to the vicarage after supper while Mr. Christmas
had bolted himself in his study as he has been doing much of this
last while, since that day Lord and Lady Kirkbride dropped in
on us, and I managed to catch a whiff of the conversation as I
nudged the kitchen window open a bit while I was making some
lemon squash for them and it was all about "sometimes adults
fall out of love" and that sort of thing, which is true of course
(think about Jago and his wife), but you and I know a little
more about Dr. Hennis now, don't we? Poor Mrs. Hennis. I feel
quite awful for her. She's looked very sad, and frightened, I
think. Of course, there's been much talk in the village, especially
since Dr. Hennis moved from Westways, about why they've split,
and did it have to do with Sebastian vanishing as each
happened on the other's heels, and I've had to hold my tongue,
although I've told Karla my suspicions about Dr. Hennis in
utter confidence and she's been very good, as she always is. She's
sort of a repository, while I'm more of a fountain, I suppose—at
least that's what Mr. Christmas said when he told me I was not
to speculate publicly about anything that happened the Sunday
afternoon when L & L Kirkbride were here. Mr. Christmas can
be quite ~~addamint admin~~ firm when he's of a mind, which is
preferred to Mr. Kinsey who was flippant with me much of the
time. I suppose this is all to the good. I remember Karla saying*

she thought he might be a bit soft when they were first reviewing candidates. Yesterday she told me in complete confidence, of course, that she had happened to be speaking with the archdeacon in Morrisons in Totnes earlier in the week and he had asked her if she thought Mr. Christmas was sound. Well, I'll tell you why, and this gets to the shocking bit—it seems Mr. Christmas had been wanting Sybella Parry's grave opened but the very odd thing is that he wouldn't give anyone a reason! I think this has explained all the frowning comings and goings lately that I've written about here in the vicarage of those two CID types and Colm Parry and the rural dean and even the bishop's chaplain and an environmental health officer, and why Mr. Christmas has been so distracted and down at the mouth and all the phone calls to the diocesan office which I happened to catch bits of if I dusted near Mr. Christmas's study. And it probably explains why on Wednesday, Mrs. Hennis had come out of a long conversation with him in his study looking absolutely like her world had caved in. When I went downstairs yesterday morning on my way to post your letter, I noticed the kitchen in an untidy state from Mr. Christmas and a few others having what looked like some breakfast, and when I got to the post office, Karla took me aside and told me that Sybella's grave had been opened. The decision had been made to do it in the small hours of the morning when everyone was asleep so as not to cause more upset in the village, so I wasn't dreaming about space creatures invading our churchyard! They had used big bright lights so they could see in the dark. That's why I thought the sun was rising in the west. But when I went round to the churchyard on my way back to the vicarage, everything looked very much the same, which seemed odd. The grave hardly looked disturbed, though I could see that the soil on top was fresh, and of course the headstone and slab still aren't in place. I dashed back to the vicarage, as Miranda would be rising and needing to get off to school, but Mr.

Christmas was nowhere to be seen for the longest time, though I did find a note in the kitchen addressed to Miranda and me saying he was sorry he couldn't be at breakfast and would be gone much of the morning. Finally, in the early afternoon, as I was setting my baking ingredients out, he returned home. He really did have the most peculiar look on his face. I suppose he was sort of relieved and sad all at once. Poor man, he comes to Thornford for a bit of peace after his wife's awful death, and then there's these frightful events in the village that end up going right to the heart of his family's life. Anyway, he told me to make tea for us both and come into the sitting room where he had something important to tell me. Well, Mum, I had an inkling, to be sure, but no details, particularly as to why Sybella's grave was opened. When I brought the tea things in I couldn't help look over at the games table where Miranda and I had played Snakes and Ladders, she with her "clue" that I told you about. Mr. Christmas caught my eye and frowned and paused in thought for a moment, and then he told me that as what he was about to tell me would soon be public knowledge and would likely end up in court and in the press and how we needed to be prepared for Miranda's sake and others', he would tell everything now. It happens opening Sybella's grave was not to exhume her body, which I thought was a great relief, but to get at something he was sure had been buried under the coffin. And he had been right. Hidden in the earth below was Mitsuko Drewe's computer and camera and some other computer thing, which I told you had been stolen a few weeks ago from Mrs. Drewe's studio back of their place in The Square. At first I thought to myself it was a bit much disturbing a grave just to get at some silly machine, and Mr. Christmas must have seen the look on my face, for he said it wasn't about recovering stolen property—it was about the information on the computer and the camera and the other thing, which he said were not awfully damaged by being in

*damp soil. He was very careful how he put it, but he said there
were pictures stored in the computer—or maybe it was in the
camera—that now focused police enquiries sharply on to Dr.
Hennis as the killer of Mr. Kinsey. Well, as I say, I had had an
inkling this might be so, but it was such a terrible shock to hear it
said out loud. I couldn't help thinking what a terrible thing this
was for the village. Is Sybella's death connected? I asked Mr. C.,
but he wouldn't say. They are, of course. I told you about the ~~tea~~
tee. Mum, I can only imagine how the next weeks or months
will unfold. There'll likely be more questions, an arrest, a trial,
goodness knows what else. Funny to say, but I feel the worst for
Miranda. I can't say I was fond of Dr. Hennis—there was
always something a bit stuck-up about him—but Miranda was
quite fond of him, I think—in that sort of ~~nonjugeme~~ easy way
children sometimes have. She only has her father. I expect Mrs.
Hennis won't be able to hold her head up much longer in the
village, and there are no other aunts and uncles or cousins about
that I know of. Still, Miranda's a smart little girl and she has a
loving father who dotes on her. Well, there you have it. I hope
this dreadful news doesn't worry you too much, Mum. It'll all
come out in the papers eventually, but at least life has returned to
something like normal here in dear old Thornford after some
terrible days. Even Mr. Christmas's spirits seem to have picked
up. He was saying to me only yesterday that life in Thornford R
really is like a curate's egg. It is a mixture of good and bad, but
that the good bits always outweigh the bad so you mustn't
grumble, and I thought, HOW TRUE! even though I didn't know
what a curate ate for breakfast had to do with it. The cats are
well, though they are still not happy to have Bumble in their
midst, but Mr. Christmas is quite pleased to have a dog. He said
having Bumble relieved him from feeling like a country vicar in
a novel, what with 2 cats, a bicycle, and a housekeeper (me!), but
I wasn't sure I got his point. I should be able to get down to*

Cornwall next month for a visit. Love to Aunt Gwen. Glorious day!

Much love,
Madrun

P.S. Both Karla and I have an appointment with a solicitor in Totnes next week! Perhaps Phillip left us something! Still no sign of his daughter, though. Imagine not attending your own father's funeral! Commitments in Hollywood indeed!

P.P.S. I'm so glad to know the tests show your heart is strong. You'll live to be as old as the Queen Mum!

P.P.P.S. Venice Daintrey told me yesterday she was sure she saw Sebastian—our vanished verger—up on Dartmoor. There's a mystery there, for sure!

Acknowledgements

It may take an individual to write a novel, but it takes a village to publish one. I'm very grateful to the residents of my village—to my astute agent, Dean Cooke, along with his colleague at the Cooke Agency, Sally Harding, for their early enthusiasm for this project, and to my wise editor at Random House, Kate Miciak, who makes the good better and the better best. I'm also grateful to Randall Klein, Loyale Coles, Margaret Benton, Maggie Hart, and Karin Batten at Random House for their finishing touches, and to Kristin Cochrane of Doubleday Canada for her attentions north of the forty-ninth parallel.

I am grateful to the people who read and criticised the early drafts of the manuscript of this book in its entirety—Rosie Chard, Annalee Greenberg, and Clark Saunders—and to those who read portions with a similarly critical eye—Sandra Vincent, Frances-Mary Brown, Perry Holmes, and Spencer Holmes. I am also grateful to those along the way who lent their expert advice: in Canada—Michael Phillips, Phoebe Man, Carrie Walker-Jones, Pierre Bédard, Neire Mercer, Bradley Curran, Ryan Schultz, Ross Taylor, and Amethya Weaver; and in England—Norman Betts, Paula Frain, Trish Lilly, and Jill Treby.

I am grateful, too, to the Manitoba Arts Council for its generous support during the writing of this book, and to the Winnipeg Public Library—notably to Tannis Gretzinger and Danielle Pilon—for helping to make my writer's residency at the library pleasurable and productive.

I am most grateful to the Reverend David Treby, vicar of St. Mary and St. Gabriel's Church in Stoke Gabriel, Devon, England, for his willingness, patience, and good humour in helping me navigate my way through the complexities of the Church of England and for lending a keen eye to the finished manuscript. Needless to say, all errors and peculiar interpretations are mine.

And to the author of the carol "The Twelve Days of Christmas"—thank you, whoever you are, wherever you are.

If you enjoyed *Twelve Drummers Drumming*,
you won't want to miss more of Father Tom Christmas and
the world of Thornford Regis.
Read on for a sneak peek at

Eleven Pipers Piping

Available from Delacorte Press

id they not feed you after the wedding, Mr. Christmas?"

"I dropped into the reception for only a minute," Tom replied, conscious of the passing figure of his housekeeper, as he continued his contemplation of the bounty in the vicarage refrigerator. "I didn't have a chance for a bite."

He barely knew the young couple he had married that afternoon—Todd and Gemma—other than to have a brief preparatory discussion with them the month before. He had never seen them in church, nor had he seen their families or friends, and didn't expect to see them again, unless the couple wished their baby baptised—which mightn't be far off, given that the bride, wearing a meringue with a train half a mile long, had fairly waddled up the aisle at St. Paul's, the second of the two churches in his charge. Her plump face, when she'd pushed back her embroidered veil, had looked much like a blazing beetroot, he recalled, staring at a jar of the pickled variety inside the door of the fridge. Sweat had sparkled in tiny beads along her exposed hairline—this despite the glacial damp of the nave in January—which some might have construed as the effect of energy expended getting up the aisle, but which Tom interpreted as a dew born of anticipation and triumph.

The groom, however, had been a figure of bemusement, his face a kind of Belisha beacon, one moment as blanched as that leftover rice pudding in its puddle of cream on the second shelf, the next as pink as the Virginia ham one shelf below. Tom shouldn't have fancied their chances at marital success—they were much too young; he was a farm labourer and she was a health-care aide of some sort and they were living with his parents—but for some reason he did, and could only chalk it up to a decade's experience splicing couples of varied sorts. He imagined them receiving their sixtieth-anniversary card from the Queen (or the King, as would most probably be then) where other couples, more advantaged, would fall by the wayside. "When betrothal is brief, the marriage lasts long," he recalled his father-in-law saying, quoting some bit of Jewish wisdom when he was trying to reconcile himself to his daughter's elopement. How wrong he had been, at least in Tom and Lisbeth's case.

"The reception was at The Pig's Barrel," Tom told his housekeeper.

"A January wedding and a pub reception. Sounds a hurried affair."

"A little, perhaps," Tom responded noncommittally. He rarely went to wedding receptions anyway, unless he knew the family well. Receptions could murder the best part of a Saturday afternoon, and it wasn't as though he didn't have anything else to do—polish his sermon, for instance. He'd dropped in at Todd and Gemma's only because he'd seen the very attractive village bobby, Màiri White, pass through the The Barrel's doors when he went for his car after the ceremony and couldn't resist the allure of a chance encounter. But, alas, when he arrived, Màiri was ensconced, back to him, at a table full of—damn!—*men*. Anyway, snow, ominously forecast to bung up northwestern Europe for the weekend and more, was beginning to fall in earnest and so getting home to Thornford seemed more imperative than being stood like a lemon at The Pig's Barrel.

He looked past the edge of the refrigerator door, wondering if Madrun was about to launch into a mini inquisition over the newly-weds. Customarily, she would have ushered them into the vicarage study when they came for their marriage interview, but the wedding had come together all in a rush during busy Christmas week, which Madrun had spent with her aging mother in Cornwall, thus depriving her of an opportunity to inspect and pass verdict on events at home.

But Madrun's back was to him. He could see one hand resting against one cheek as she contemplated the array of cookery books marshalled behind the glass of a ceiling-high barrister's bookcase. He guessed her preoccupation lay not with the hapless couple. The Sunday before, after her return from Cornwall to Thornford Regis early in the New Year, she had cooked a joint, accompanied with roast potatoes and parsnips, green beans with caramelised shallots, and, of course, Yorkshire pudding. Tom and Miranda had been in the sitting room with their guests, Will and Caroline Moir, their daughter, Ariel, their son, Adam, and his girlfriend, Tamara, when their conversation had been riven by a piercing cry—such as he had never heard before—from the kitchen. Heart racing, expecting to find Madrun horribly burned or cut, Tom dashed into the kitchen, the others at his heels. Instead, they found her, oven-gloved, staring aghast into a steaming dish, the door of the Aga behind her a yawning maw. Nestled inside the dish's black and aged sides was a vast and even expanse of tawny gold—quite lovely to look at and smelling heavenly. Despite his still-coursing adrenaline, he had felt his stomach growl.

And then Miranda, on tiptoe, glanced into the pan and declared: "Oh, it's a dropdead!"

A kind of moan slipped from Madrun's throat as she turned and placed the hot dish onto a trivet on her worktable, next to the roasted beef and several bowls of thawing berries, which a little later spilled around a heavenly pavlova.

"But I'm sure it will *taste* wonderfully," Caroline had interjected quickly, and the others had murmured concurrence. *Dropdead* was his daughter Miranda's coinage for a Yorkshire pudding that failed to rise. Her mother's often hadn't. Lisbeth had been a blasé sort of cook whose Sunday lunches were sometimes a fiesta of Waitrose ready meals. When Lisbeth died, their French au pair, Ghislaine, tried her hand at English fare but could never quite get the knack of certain dishes, Yorkshire pud among them. Tom, who had never made one in his life, couldn't understand how a simple concoction of eggs, milk, and flour could be so temperamental and cause so much distress. There had been much crestfallenness back in Bristol when the Yorkshire, pulled from the oven, looked more like Norfolk-in-a-pan than Staffordshire-in-a-pan—flat rather than hilly. Lisbeth would feign indifference, but Ghislaine wept at her first failure. But then they were all in shock in the wake of Lisbeth's sudden, violent death.

Madrun's, on the other hand, were always a tremendous success— puffy and light, glorious umber hillocks set against deep golden valleys, a sponge to sop the rich brown gravy she would produce from the organic beef acquired from the farm shop at Thorn Barton. But not last Sunday. The pud simply looked . . . sad. After her initial distress, she had pulled herself together and brought forth an otherwise fine Sunday lunch in the dining room, although she remained subdued throughout. Since then, she'd had Fred Pike, the village handyman, in to look at the Aga, which Fred had pronounced fit as feathers on a duck, scrutinised the sell-by dates of the flour and milk, and had a barney with Roger Pattimore down at Pattimore's, the village shop, over the freshness of his eggs. She had adjured Tom to check on his computer to see if there were any chat rooms or forums devoted to Yorkshire pudding—the word *failures* didn't pass Madrun's lips; *mysteries* was substituted—and there were a few, not unpredictably, in the Internet age, but he had white-lied and said there weren't because—and this he didn't say out loud—for heaven's sake, it was *too* silly. All this bother for a simple—and not wholly necessary—side dish.

"Sometimes, Mrs. Prowse, things happen for no reason," Tom said finally, trying to keep exasperation from his voice.

Madrun flicked him a disapproving glance, as if he were being theologically unsound, and said, "It's an omen. I feel it in my bones."

Tom, who at the time was struggling to put the lead on Bumble preparatory to a walk up Knighton Lane, had bit his tongue and said nothing, because, of course, there was nothing to say: He was disinclined towards omens, particularly if they came in the form of collapsed savoury puddings.

Now his housekeeper had pushed back one of the glass doors of the bookcase and pulled out a cookery tome. Opening the book to the index at the back, she studied him a moment over the rims of her spectacles. "You'll let all the cold out, if you keep the refrigerator door open like that."

"Yes, sorry."

"You may be pleasantly surprised this evening, you know, Mr. Christmas."

Tom made a demurring noise as he closed the door. "Perhaps if I lined my stomach with a glass of milk."

"Mr. James-Douglas used to love the Burns Supper."

"I expect from his name he had a bit of Scots in him."

"You don't have to be Scottish to enjoy the Burns Supper."

Oh, don't you? Tom thought. It might help. He didn't know who his natural parents were. He didn't *feel* somehow they could have been Scottish, if one were permitted to feel such things. He himself felt thoroughly English, and if he were about to give allegiance to another people, it would be the French or the Italians, who had wonderful food, not the Scots, who could only have been led by a ghastly climate and impoverished soil to think a celebratory dinner should consist of offal and oatmeal stuffed into a sheep's stomach then boiled, turnips—his least favourite vegetable—boiled, and potatoes—yes, boiled. Without reopening the refrigerator door, he could see in his mind's eye the ham, the leftover cheese-and-onion pie, the last of the turkey orzo soup Kate had made after Christmas—any of which would make a fine Saturday-evening meal.

"He was hardly fit for the pulpit the next morning," Madrun continued almost fondly, licking her thumb and turning a page.

Giles James-Douglas, who preceded Tom, but for one, as incumbent, had been vicar in the village for over twenty-five years before his death. A lifelong bachelor of considerable private means and epicurean tastes, he installed Madrun as his housekeeper when she was a young woman, turned her into a superb cook, and left both the large late-Georgian vicarage—which he bought outright from the Church—and its housekeeper to his successors. Tom, therefore, had more or less *inherited* Madrun Prowse, who, though a spinster, retained the honorific *Mrs.* He was grateful for the help, being a busy priest and a widowed father, but there were moments when she did get on his wick a bit, especially when the matchless Mr. James-Douglas slipped into the conversation. He felt, to keep up, he should get as much malt whisky as he could down his neck Saturday then spend Sunday morning conducting services at two churches with a throbbing headache and a dry mouth, and trying not to gag over the Communion wine. He didn't fancy it. In fact, he didn't fancy attending the Burns Supper at all, but he was chaplain to a regional pipe band and Roger Pattimore, the pipe sergeant, expected him to come and deliver the Selkirk Grace. It was churlish to say no. Having been in Thornford less than a year and still finding his way in the parish, Tom didn't want to offend for small reasons. What he wasn't keen on was the food—the tatties and the neeps (potatoes and turnips, so called) and that acme of culinary horrors, the haggis. When he had been a curate in Kennington, he'd had an old parishioner who told him that in Botswana, where he held some rank in the colonial administration, they had used haggises (or was it *haggi*?) to poison hyenas.

Really, Tom thought, he should have gone to that pub reception, after all, and at least had a couple of greasy pasties. With such bricks in his stomach he might have an excuse to only nibble at the forth-coming supper.

He glanced at a couple of trays on the counter and wondered what was under the linen cloths covering them. He was about to step over and lift one when, unexpectedly, tantalizingly, the aroma of roasting meat tickled his nostrils. He began to wonder if hunger was driving him to fantasy. His glance moved to the oven.

"Am I smelling beef? Are you back up on that horse, Mrs. Prowse?"

Madrun glanced up from the cookery book. "I don't know what you mean."

"I thought perhaps you might be cooking a roast with a view to making a Yorkshire pudding."

"Well, it's true I'm cooking beef, but it's beef Wellington . . . of a kind."

"Beef Wellington!" Tom gave a passing thought to his food budget. "You're serving the children beef Wellington?"

"It's . . . an adaptation of beef Wellington." Madrun frowned at something in her book. "Minced beef, which I shaped into a ball and roasted earlier. Now it's cooking enclosed in chopped mushrooms and puff pastry."

"It's *en croûte*, Daddy," a voice behind him said.

Miranda had pushed open the kitchen door, followed by the vic-arage cats, Powell and Gloria, who began a lewd and mewling pace in front of the Aga.

"Yes, *oncrew*," Madrun murmured. "That's the word."

"We're having our own Burns Supper," Miranda said brightly, moving to the counter to examine the contents of various bowls.

"I shaped the mince to look like a haggis," Madrun explained.

Tom frowned at his daughter. "I'm surprised that you and Ariel and . . . who else is coming to your sleepover?"

"Emily and Becca."

" . . . had the faintest interest in Robbie Burns."

"Oh, we don't. Or at least *they* don't," Miranda added obliquely.

"Then . . . ?"

"It's because of Zak Burns." Miranda shook her head so her pigtails slapped against her cheeks.

Tom turned to Madrun helplessly.

"I believe he was the last winner on *X Factor*." Madrun raised a censorious eyebrow.

"It's because of Emily." Miranda shrugged. "She thinks he's . . . "

Oh, blast, Tom thought: *The word to follow is probably* cute, hot, *or* cool. He sighed inwardly. There was something awfully cunning about Emily Swan. Perhaps having two older brothers and an older sister, and living over a pub, made her more worldly wise than the other two girls joining Miranda at the vicarage for her first sleepover: With a brother nearly a dozen years older moved away from home, Ariel Moir lived the life of an only child, like Miranda, while Becca Kaif had lost her only brother to suicide, in August—a terrible tragedy for the village, and it had—cruelly—made Becca into an only child, too.

" . . . nice," Miranda said at last. "Emily thinks he's nice."

Nice seemed a good noncommittal word to latch on to, and Tom did. He couldn't help not wanting Miranda to leave the sweet, dreamlike realm of early childhood, to be swallowed up in schoolgirl pop-star crushes, with bedroom walls covered in posters of boys with peculiar haircuts and ludicrous trousers, though, come to think of it, his bedroom, when he had been ten years old, had been covered with posters of *men* with peculiar haircuts and ludicrous trousers. But all of them were magicians and magic had been his passion in those days. It had led to a career in magic—for a time—so at least his bedroom walls had not proved a waste of space, so to speak. He glanced at Miranda's furrowed little brow and wondered what was passing through her furrowed little grey matter.

"And do you think this Zak Burns is nice?" Tom asked.

"Oh . . . he's okay, I suppose."

He watched her reach into a bowl by the sink, pull out a finger of raw potato, and bite into its end.

"Are you making chips?" he asked Madrun, trying to keep yearning from his voice. A plate of hot chips slathered in salt and malt vinegar would go down a treat at this very moment.

"Yes, chips for tatties," she muttered over her cookery book; then she looked up. "You really can't expect little girls to want boiled potatoes, can you, Mr. Christmas."

But Tom's attention had been drawn to Miranda, who had skipped to the kitchen door and was looking through the glass into the garden. *"Papa! Regarde la neige! N'est-elle pas merveilleuse?"* she said, falling into French, as she often did when she was excited. In the darkness of early evening in January, the farthest end of the sloping garden, where trees screened the millpond in summer, seemed a void, soft and black, but where light spilled from the vicarage windows, demarcating the base of the old pear tree and two wicker chairs, all blazed white, diamond bright.

"Yes, it is marvellous, isn't it," he responded, joining Miranda to witness the thin veil of snow shimmering in the air. He put his hands on Miranda's shoulders and felt the straps of her dungarees. He could sense her anticipation: This would be her first full experience of snow, though in the garden outside it was neither particularly deep (patches of stiff grass were visible) nor terribly crisp (wet, more like) nor very even (the terrace had less than the lawn). But it might be before long, if the weather folk read the signs and portents correctly. Shifting weather partly informed his unwillingness to tarry at the wedding reception at Pennycross. Temperatures had dropped through the afternoon; patchy ice had formed in the lanes between Pennycross and Thornford, and the landscape glimpsed between the hedgerows was bleached and undifferentiated in the watery winter light. Perhaps the snow wasn't so marvellous, after all. Perhaps Madrun had been right: A fallen Yorkshire doth herald tempests drear. Or suchlike.

His stomach growled in response to the thought of food.

"Lions and tigers, Daddy," said Miranda whose ears brushed his shirt below his chest.

"You could hear that?"

"I could hear it over here, Mr. Christmas. You could have a biscuit, I suppose . . . " Madrun began, making Tom feel not unlike Bumble, soon to be rewarded for being a good doggy.

He turned. Madrun was studying her watch.

" . . . or perhaps not. Best not to spoil your supper. Aren't you expected soon?"

Tom glanced at his own watch. "Oh, yes, I suppose." Then he glanced again, longingly, at the fridge—a huge double-door chrome American model, surely the largest fridge in the village outside the commercial ones at the Church House Inn, the Waterside Café, and the Thorn Court Country Hotel. "But isn't there much standing about first, drinking whisky and the like?"

"I wouldn't know. I've never been to a Burns Supper."

Startled, Tom was about to ask how she knew, more than he, what he was to expect from such an event, but Miranda interjected, "Are they no-girls-allowed?"

"They are," Madrun replied stoutly.

"That's not fair," Miranda said.

"But yours is no-boys-allowed," Tom protested.

"Really, Daddy!"

"Really, Mr. Christmas!"

Faced with remonstration to what he thought was reasoned observation, Tom backed down, supposing, in a split second of reflection, that most of human history was no-girls-allowed. Even Jesus, whom he thought a rather forward-thinking chap, hadn't put a woman among His disciples. He was a bit snippy with His mother, too.

PHOTO: © ROBERT BARROW

C. C. BENISON is the nom de plume for Arthur Ellis Award–winning author Doug Whiteway. He studied comparative religion at the University of Manitoba and journalism at Carleton University, in Ottawa, and has worked as a writer and editor for newspapers and magazines, as a book editor, and as a contributor to nonfiction books. He lives in Winnipeg, where he is at work on his next Father Christmas mystery, *Ten Lords A-Leaping*.

www.ccbenison.com

Printed in the United States
by Baker & Taylor Publisher Services